The Importance of Staying Earnest:

Writings from Inside the American Theatre, 1988-2013

By

Todd London

NoPassport Press

Dreaming the Americas Series

The Importance of Staying Earnest

Copyright 2013 by Todd London.

NoPassport Press: Dreaming the Americas Series,

First edition 2013 by NoPassport Press, PO Box 1786, South Gate, CA 90280 USA; NoPassportPress@aol.com, www.nopassport.org; ISBN: 978-1-300-65504-6

For Karen
First, second, last & always

TABLE OF CONTENTS

Introduction: What a Difference a Play Makes

These pages got started by accident. They compounded the way accidents do, one unintended consequence leading to another, nothing like a plan. I can't even say the accidents were happy ones. If there was a plan, it boiled down to this: escape the theatre. It's a heartbreaking endeavor, the making of theatre. You dream art (or at least I did a lifetime ago) that sails into the sky like a magic arrow shot from a mythic bow. Instead, the dream falls short and hangs there, a cork on a string, popped from a plastic gun. And so, after college and graduate school, after training to do the only thing I'd ever wanted to do—make wonderful things happen on stage with other expressive, enthusiastic souls—I decided to get out before I got deeper in. I would return to school and become an English professor.

My escape plan failed. Before I'd finished the doctoral program, I'd fallen back into the clutches of the heartbreaker theatre. Like so many others, I pieced my professional self together from an occupational motley: directing, literary management, jobs with service organizations and with theatres large and small; I became an associate artistic director then an artistic director. Almost all these jobs offered opportunities to write about the theatre from inside of it. This accidental path, as I've said, wasn't too happy. How could I be happy when the theatre I loved was so flawed, so puffed up, so false to what I saw as its truer ideals. At first I wrote because I got asked to. Then I wrote out of disillusionment. My first book, *The Artistic Home*, a report on the aspirations of American artistic directors, seemed to me to be filled with insincerities, if not outright lies. I set out to *un-write* it in the pages of *American Theatre*, also published by TCG (Theatre Communications Group). I wrote to find a way, if not out of the theatre altogether, then at least out of the mess of it, to agitate for any change or new awareness that might make it inspiring to me again, also healthier, more humane, more—ok—lovable.

And suddenly thirty years had passed. Suddenly the accidental had defined the path. Here, then, are twenty-five years of that inadvertent journey (I've spared you the first five). These essays range over territories that drew me: the creation of new work; the relations between artists and institutions ("The Shape of Plays To Come"), criticism and its abuses ("What We Talk About When We Talk About Good"), the power of place ("The Theatre of Place"), the power of plays and playwrights ("What a Difference a Play Makes"), and the celebration of individual talent and freedom.

The artist's job is to take life personally. Passionate response to the things of this world is item one in that job description. We bumble around, blinkered by these passions, magnetized by our attractions, well-wadded with subjectivity. We make everything we touch an extension of ourselves by means of a deeply personal, unerringly partial understanding. This is why I love Chekhov: he understands the overheated, ingrown subjectivity that makes characters of us all.

The artist's intense over-identification with just about everything sits in contrast to the outside perspective of the chronicler. Arts journalist, critic, or historian, the relative position is the same: engagement at a remove. These essays, conversely, pretend to no such distance. Their perspective, my perspective, is from close in, probably too close. This writer (me) is frankly over-identified with his subject. His perspective is anything but consistent. Charitably, it could be said to evolve. But then, when it comes to the lack of perspective, there is never any lack of it. You hold proof.

Time doesn't help. It just makes things look different than they used to. Few of these essays are what I originally thought they were. Among them are pieces I believed to be groundbreaking, gamechanging; now their naiveté makes me squirm. Others felt functional when I wrote them and now make me proud; I see their historical service. Earlier I wrote to change minds, which I now try to avoid (if you don't understand why, there's nothing I can say that will make a difference). Instead, I want to celebrate individuals—those creative, freer souls who expand my sense of possibility and seem to add life to life. That's the impulse behind the final section of this collection: "Catching Light."

* * *

Nothing has had a greater impact on the writings gathered here than my work with playwrights. I see so much through their eyes that my own vision has forever altered. I am not a playwright. For the past 17 years, though, I have made a sort of sucker's bet with the theatre, staking my ambition and professional happiness, my sense of fulfillment and accomplishment, on playwrights. I work alongside them, keep their company. I run with them, fight their fights, celebrate their triumphs, witness and pay tribute to their growing bodies of work. In 2011, I married a playwright. It sounds like the title of a 1960s sitcom, *I Married a Playwright*, or maybe a slightly noir-ish dime-store novel. I contribute a column to *howlround*, the online journal; it's called "A Lover's Guide to the American Playwright."

I want to tell you what it means to live and work as I do, surrounded by playwrights, an "out" playwright lover. I want to give you this lover's guide to American playwrights, to let you see some of what I see.

During the research phase of *Outrageous Fortune: The Life and Times of the New American Play* (Theatre Development Fund, 2009)—a study of new play production and the lives and livelihoods of American playwrights—Amy Freed, who makes a reckless habit of writing large-cast plays, confessed that she enjoyed the feeling of being an anachronism. "I feel like I'm making the last buggy whip in America," she said. We are, maybe, a field of anachronisms, our wagons hitched to an aching old horse, urging the poor beast on with the whips playwrights have made. We are, maybe, as blinkered as that old horse, in denial of the shiny hybrids and computer-driven rigs zipping around us, ignoring the fact that our lame clip-clop in real time and space may rely on outdated ideas of space and time, when studies show that audiences no longer value "live-ness" and when we experience time moving every which way all at once, unity overwhelmed by simultaneity.

At New Dramatists, where I've worked since 1996, our logo is still a fountain pen. There's a vintage Underwood manual typewriter on the top shelf of our new play library, as if that war horse were the eternal symbol of this profession. We have entered the tweens of a new century. But which century?

New Dramatist shelters a community of about 50 playwrights in an old Lutheran church in midtown Manhattan. The building used to house, in addition to the church proper, a thrift store and a soup kitchen, where hundreds of men, mostly, were fed throughout the immigrant days and Depression years of the early-to-mid-1900s, and where their families could find cheap, used clothes and, presumably, spiritual solace. It is now, only somewhat metaphorically, a mission church for playwrights.

The altar area is now a writing studio with wireless access. The sanctuary and thrift store have been turned into workshop theatres. The soup kitchen is now a library, lined with the unpublished manuscripts of many of the nearly 600 writers who have passed through since New Dramatists's founding in 1949. This library, as much as anything, tells the story of continuity, community, and legacy.

We have found, on these library shelves, such hidden gems as typescripts by James Baldwin and Robert Anderson with their penciled marginal notes and edits. I pulled the mimeo of a little-known Maria Irene Fornes play called, *The Red Burning Light (Of the American Way of Life)*. My favorite find was a stage manager's workshop draft of a full-length play by August Wilson. It had the unfamiliar title, *Mill Hands Lunch Bucket*. Checking out the cast list, I realized I was holding a first draft of *Joe Turner's Come and Gone*. Now the shelves are full of new plays, and forty years from now, someone will pick one up—an unknown or forgotten play by Nilo Cruz or Lynn Nottage or David

Lindsay-Abaire or a playwright you and I have never heard of—and she will break into a similar sweat, her heart will pound, and the link will be made again.

I got my title, "What a Difference a Play Makes," from playwright Marsha Norman when I asked if she knew a good song about playwriting. It was spring 2009. We were ten days from New Dramatists' major fundraiser, our annual luncheon, responsible for twenty percent of our budget. The gala takes place in the dazzle of the Broadway Ballroom of the Marriott Marquis in Times Square; it's attended by much of the Broadway community, eager to be seen at Tony time. New Dramatists turned sixty years old that year, so we decided to honor one of its first member playwrights, from the early fifties, Horton Foote. Sadly and frighteningly for us, Horton had died a few months before the gala, so we faced a double problem: 1) how to celebrate this most humble of writers in such a glitzy space; and 2) how to create an entertaining afternoon while still acknowledging that we had inadvertently staged a memorial service.

So I went looking for a song. Horton's grieving family would be with us. We didn't want to do anything to insult his memory or vulgarize our tribute. Maybe a Gospel song from one of his beautiful family plays? Too maudlin. Too Christian. Is there, somewhere out there a perfect song about being a playwright? Well, no.

Marsha emailed back excitedly, suggesting that we write new lyrics to Maria Grever and Stanley Adams' "What a Difference a Day Makes" and call it "What a Difference a Play Makes." As you may have already guessed, we didn't.

It's a catchy phrase, though, and it has stuck in my head. It worries me—in the same way I was worried when I first saw the title of the American Theatre Wing's recent book, *The Play That Changed My Life*. Of course plays make a difference. Of course, if you round up a couple dozen playwrights or actors they'll be able to single out plays that changed their lives. But do plays really make a difference, and, if so, what kind of difference? To whom? Do plays really change lives? Maybe they once did, but do they still? Aren't these notions a bit hyperbolic, a bit self-satisfied? Are they the clichés we live by, that allow us to do our fun artmaking with the sense of importance that comes from actually *valuable* work?

I don't know. I love my job. I think playwrights are awesome. I like reading the hundreds of plays I read a year. I like it OK, though not with anything like the intensity I felt in high school and college discovering plays by Edward Albee, John Guare, Sam Shepard, Maria Irene Fornes, Amiri Baraka, Lanford Wilson, Tina Howe, and, yes, Marsha Norman. I long, instead, for good movies, long quiet stretches of time with an absorbing novel. I'm hungry for new music for my ipod.

10

But I work in the theatre. I'm a rabbi in a church for playwrights and I constantly question my faith—not in the talent of the writers who amaze me day by day, but in the enterprise itself, this throwback profession, whose innate old-fashionedness pricks me every time I say I work for a company with the word "dramatist" in the name. New *Dramatists*. Underwoods. Buggy whips.

No, I didn't find a song for our gala. Instead we had playwrights read short scenes by other playwrights—alumni of New Dramatists who had, like Horton Foote, recently died. Our vibrant and very-much-alive writers would celebrate the dead senior writers—Horton, Robert Anderson, William Gibson—and also their peer-writers who had, in the previous couple of years, died painfully young—August Wilson, Lynne Alvarez, John Belluso, Oni Faida Lampley. Would we *feel* the difference a play makes? Does the difference a play makes pass like current from writer to writer, one era to another, and, so, electrify, if not one theatre or one decade, then a whole continuous lineage of human endeavor?

How appropriate that these questions bubbled up around Horton Foote. It's hard to imagine a playwright more out of step with our times than he is.

There is no body of work in the American theatre to compare with his. No one has written for so long about so few square miles--the concentrated plot of land in Wharton, Texas that is the land of his family. For nearly 70 years he tried to stop time by remembering. Like a tender, merciful God, he sought to possess an entire world by loving it ceaselessly. He dared to bring the dead back to life. "It is a vanishing world, the world of these plays," he writes. "No, not a vanishing world but a vanished world….I think sometimes that Randall Jarrell speaks for me in his poem 'Thinking of the Lost World': 'All of them are gone/Except for me; and for me nothing is gone.'"

Nothing is ever gone, Horton Foote proves, as long as there are people to remember, to write it down. Nothing can be lost, as long as there are artists brave enough and persistent enough, to try and capture the ephemeral grace of our lives.

But is it true that nothing is ever gone? Is it possible that plays themselves are disappearing, that dramatic literature itself will go the way of the satyr play or Burlesque or the Living Newspaper? And if we mean to keep on keeping on, what are we doing it for? What are we preserving?

Robert Anderson, author of *Tea and Sympathy* and *I Never Sang for My Father*, also died in 2009; throughout his five-decade writing life he kept a note taped to his typewriter that said, "Nobody asked you to be a playwright." How do you respond to that cold-water truth? The same way Bob Anderson did, and Horton, and hundreds of other playwrights have. You respond by becoming the most perfect version possible of the thing that nobody asked you to be. You respond by writing those plays nobody asked you to write—that no one may ever produce. You respond with the crazy, obsessive, beautiful bravery of the artist, cultivating a garden that no one asked to see and that no one may ever want to walk with you. You find faith where you can. And you hope the world will meet you where you live.

This is, by any stretch, a foolish hope. The world, in the most consistent and practical ways, has no intention of meeting playwrights where they live. It's no secret where the energy of our culture and the attentions of our young are directed. We have good cause to worry about the marginalization of theatre and playwriting.

Even the American theatre doesn't care to meet playwrights where they live. For the past forty years our theatres have spent considerable money, energy, and person-hours on the cultivation and production of new plays. They've hired large administrative staffs, built monumental buildings. For all their organizational energy, however, these theatres have proven unable to create sustainable structures for supporting writers over time, for what Arena Stage artistic director Molly Smith has called, "a dignified life for playwrights." Bodies of work like Horton Foote's are almost inconceivable today.

From 2005 to 2010, I led the Theatre Development Fund study that became *Outrageous Fortune*. Victoria Bailey (TDF's executive director), Ben Pesner, Zannie Giraud Voss, and I gathered data from 250 playwrights across the career spectrum, working professional playwrights who, by all industry indicators, were among the most successful writers at their stage of development. We extensively surveyed nearly 100 theatres about their work with new plays and that of the field in general. We then tested this hard data by traveling to cities across the country, holding meetings with playwrights, artistic directors, and leaders in the field of new play and playwright development, followed by interviews with agents, commercial producers, playwrights educators, others. We published our findings in the book Ben and I wrote and spent another six months travelling the country, presenting the conclusions, stimulating local conversations, brainstorming solutions. I want to briefly highlight some of the findings.

As playwrights describe it, the American nonprofit theatre, our "art theatre," is corporate, board driven, risk averse, and formally conservative. It lacks bold artistic leaders and is overly, even obsessively, concerned with pleasing a subscription audience that is much older and far more conservative than the theatre's artists, and that may not even be an audience. Audience may be the convenient term artistic directors use when they're really talking about a handful of large donors or key board members or, as one artistic administrator put it, their theatre's "assets."

And the bad news is that within this climate our research shows that the economics of playwriting are impossible. It is a profession without an economic base and all who practice within it must be prepared to be a) otherwise employed and/or b) poor.

The typical "successful" playwright earns between $25,000 and just under $40,000, when averaged over a five-year period, with nearly a third earning under $25,000. Slightly more than half of that income comes from sources unrelated to playwriting, the day job. Of the approximately forty-nine percent of a playwright's total income that comes from playwriting-related activities—including teaching, and TV and film writing—only fifteen percent of our study's playwrights' total income comes from production-related activities, i.e. licensing, publishing, grants, awards, commissions, royalties. In other words, an average working professional playwright whose resume you'd look at and say, "that's a successful early-career or emerging or mid-career or even established playwright," is making between about $3800 and $5800 a year as a playwright. Only about **three percent** of a playwright's meager income comes from royalties, the foundation of the playwright's compensation. That three percent means $750 to less than $1200 a year, on average. And lest you think that this is about young bohemians, our average study playwright is thirty-five to forty-four years old, and the sampling includes winners of Obies, Tonys, and Pulitzers.

All to say, despite the implicit promises of MFA recruitment brochures, there is no career track for playwrights, no lifelong path, hardly any career there.

Of course playwrights live this and know it. In 2011 Tony Kushner told *Time Out/New York* that he can't make a living as a playwright. If he can't, then probably no one can. You want a sustained middle-class income? You want to earn on par with senior staff at the theatres that produce you? You want health care? Playwriting is not the answer.

In short, the mechanism of the theatre has cast playwrights out of the inner workings of the theatres themselves. The economics of theatre has not just marginalized but impoverished them. Are the leaders of American theatres willing to meet playwrights where they live? No. For that we would have to give up our health insurance and head for the poverty line or, at least, the temp agency. We'd have to do the math in accordance with our so-called values, and we'd have to live by it. I include myself; even at the head of a small nonprofit, I earn more than most of the playwrights I serve.

And what about audiences? Are they willing to meet playwrights where they live? We know that the culture in general is abandoning the theatre as a form, but even the theatre-going population within that culture is, to beat a dead idiom, "staying away in droves."

According to a December 2008 study by the National Endowment for the Arts, the percentage of U.S. adults who attended a nonmusical play over a twelve-month period fell from 13.5 percent (25 million people) to 9.4 percent (21 million people). In other words, the play-going audience has been dwindling by slightly more than one percent a year for nearly twenty years. The figures for Broadway may be even more disheartening. The decline for attendance at plays on Broadway during the same twenty years is 41.6 percent.

What are we doing here? MFA programs are pumping out more playwrights than at anytime in America's history, saddling them with debt they will, as playwrights, never be able to repay. Our playwrights are condemned to an economic environment that is impossible within an ecosystem that is at least broken and at worst profoundly hostile to the artist and individual creativity, within which it is inconceivable to either build a body of work alone or as part of a theatre company. Experiment and sustained growth are, for playwrights, as much a thing of the past as, well, maybe, American drama.

Think about O'Neill for a moment, the restive, uneven brilliance of his early works, the way he tried everything—sea plays, mask plays, classical tragedy, expressionism—the great messy churning of his nascent theatrical genius. And think about how he could have played that out today, without a Provincetown Players or a Theatre Guild or a Broadway that produces new American work. How could he have wrestled with scale, with non-naturalistic techniques, with all the chaff you have to sort through to get to the wheat? How could he have bought the years of internal struggle and external quietude that separated his early productivity and his later masterworks? Or Odets. Where would he have come from, if not The Group Theatre? Or Albee. Without the sensational attention garnered by his earlier plays, how would he have survived his long time in the theatrical wilderness, the time that made his renaissance over the past twenty years possible. Or again, Horton Foote. How can you sustain a loving body of work in a field that won't sustain you, that won't, excuse me but I have to say it, love you.

So we find ourselves in a strange land. Playwrights make their lives in a world that is, if not leaving them in its dust, at least pushing them to the side, paying them on the cheap, and voting against their relevance with fleeing feet.

The name of the song I take my title from was originally "What a Difference a Day Made." Past tense. Singers changed the song, and so it comes to us in the present. Is it possible that the difference a play makes is also past tense. That plays *made* a difference—in the days of Miller and Williams, the early primes of Hansberry and Albee, and the first explosive years of Off Off Broadway—but that the present is too imperfect, that the present of playwriting is a thing of the past?

For me, personally, this is all a challenge, first and foremost, to idealism, to those idealistic impulses that got me into theatre in the first place. Yes, Shaw warns us against idealists. Yes, O'Neill shows us people nursing their pipe dreams like desperate drunks with only a few drops left in the bottle. Still, the ideals are there, desperate, delusional, or even destructive as they might be. The ideal of individual voice. The ideal of imagination. The ideal of creative freedom. The ideal of the artist as the soul in the machine of institutional capitalist culture. The ideal of theatrical communion, sacred exchange. The ideal of a world, if only onstage, where mind, heart, spirit, and body work together to get us through the confused drama or pathetic comedy that is life. The ideal—which pumps the blood of every writer I know—that insists we take the ways of the world personally, that we respond to it wholly, that the world we have inherited is ours to re-create, re-write, revise.

Happily, some of the findings of *Outrageous Fortune* are undergoing revision. We knew when we were working on it that we were part of a moment of change. David Dower was researching what he called "the new work sector" on a grant from the Mellon Foundation. Others were doing similar research. Funders were reevaluating priorities. Long-term efforts were starting to pay off. *It is now an explicit imperative in our field to improve conditions for playwrights.*

The Dramatists Guild's multi-year push for theatres to give up subsidiary rights participation (the practise of taking a percentage of a play's future royalties in exchange for producing its premiere) swayed the Center Theatre Group in L.A. and subsequently, NYC's Roundabout and the Public, breaking the ice on a previously frozen situation, what past guild president, John Weidman, describes as a "weird seismic shift." Leading the charge for gender parity on American stages, Julia Jordan, with Marsha Norman and Theresa Rebeck, created a new award, The Lillys, which has in three years honored dozens of women in the theatre. The Guild has agreed to permanently fund it. Arena Stage, one of our first regional theatres, briefly embraced its historical responsibility to lead, creating five playwright residencies for three years with salary, health benefits, housing, budgets of their own, and the commitment for at least one production. Signature Theatre Company in New York City saw and raised the bet on playwrights with a multi-tiered residency program of its own. Even small theatres, like New York's Playwrights Realm and Ensemble Studio Theatre, are offering other theatres money to incentivize second productions. Finally, the Andrew W. Mellon Foundation, leading the charge for many years, launched in late 2012 a series of fourteen, three-year, fully salaried playwright residencies across the country.

15

The ground on which playwrights stand is shifting. These are just a few of many signs.

The ground on which they stand. The phrase makes me think of the late August Wilson. The magnificent example of his purpose. The example of the seriousness with which he took his task, the playwright's task. How grandiose the young Wilson must have sounded. A fellow playwright asks, "What are you working on." Wilson responds: "I'm writing a 10-play cycle, one play for each decade of the 20th Century. It'll encompass slavery, the African Diaspora, the migration of five million blacks to the north, and the lives of Africans in America against the backdrop of our evolving culture. One character is as old as slavery; she'll die at 287. They're meant to be performed at every theatre in the country and then on Broadway." What do you say to that ambition? Who dares dismiss it? Will a troubled profession trample it? Will statistics of a dwindling audience keep it down? Attention must be paid? You bet your ass.

And so, ten plays later, we have something no American playwright has managed before: we have the sweep and magnitude of Wilson's epic Century Cycle. We have his panoramic collage of holocaust, horror and celebration, of strength, joy, and resilience, what Wilson calls "the highest possibility of human life."

Where do we look for inspiration? Where do we look to pump up our ideals? Because the fates marked me down a theatre geek, I look to playwrights. Because we know, as every child knows, that when you stare at a thing, it grows larger. A flower, a face, a play. I am one of those people who stare at plays.

And when we stare this way, the machine of the culture quiets, and the soul in the machine speaks. The institutions that were once the hope of the American theatre and that are now its well-intentioned, 800-pound gorillas, shrink in importance. Individual talent sizes up. The institutional theatre isn't evil; it's misguided. It created important new paths and then, inevitably, got lost on some of them. It too often treats the individual artist with a sort of proprietary neglect. I own your opportunities; I neglect you.

I live with playwrights for seven years, watch them grow bodies of work. It's my way of staring. And when I write about them, when I celebrate the living or eulogize the dead, I touch something, even if I can't completely understand it. This something is the difference their plays make.

This something has to do with freedom. It's the only word I have for it. It's the thing about which playwrights have taught me the most. I've learned about it from the size of August's people, the things they carry, the *selves* they carry, despite the constriction they labor under. I've learned about it from less well-known playwrights, from adventurers

16

like Carlyle Brown and Liz Duffy Adams, from the exuberant maximalist Glen Berger and the architectural minimalist Melissa James Gibson, from Octavio Solis, Diana Son, Erik Ehn, Stephen Guirgis, Marcus Gardley, Karen Hartman, Luis Alfaro, Lisa D'Amour, Daniel Alexander Jones, and Annie Baker, all exquisitely, adamantly themselves. Lynn Nottage's refusal to write in a single voice. David Grimm's refusal to tame sexuality. David Greenspan's refusal to be anyone but David Greenspan.

They are slippery, free-thinking beings, these playwrights, Houdinis in a corporate culture, escapists from the boxes critics put them in, keepers of ecstasy and empathy, speaking on voice and in tongues, simultaneously holding fast to their points of view and suspending them utterly, so that the characters of each play can have their own angles of vision. Playwrights are slippery because they strive after freedom, knowing that freedom is a practice. You can aspire to it but never attain it. Personally, artistically, politically, and historically, freedom is fleeting. We glimpse it in the holy material of our ordinary lives. Art makes us happy because it gives us a glance at our potential for freedom.

Playwrights are slippery and they teach me freedom, but not because they are free—they are not. Playwrights are, like all writers, plagued by bitterness, which is the real enemy and which threatens even the most talented and enthusiastic. The poet Robert Kelly put it perfectly: "Bitterness has killed more poets than neglect and poverty combined." I wish our playwrights release from bitterness. They aren't free because they're forced to spend so much time thinking about money. They aren't free because the double whammy of neglect and lack of resources breeds envy, and envy fuels that killing bitterness. I wish them release from envy. No one can feel free when she feels besieged, which is a kind of self-shrinking. No group of artists can be free who remains passive, blaming the faults of the theatre on everyone else, instead of asserting its natural leadership role in the field. Playwrights have historically been the leaders of theatres and capital T Theatre, and I pray they make it so again.

No, I don't pray it; I exhort it. The facts are out, the economic facts. Playwrights generally and genuinely share a critique of their own field.

They know which way the wind is blowing and what's getting lost in the wind. On the other hand, they have in front of them examples of playwright Do-It-Yourself-ism from Aeschylus to Young Jean Lee, Richard Maxwell, and a pair of Chicago twenty-somethings, Chelsea Marcantel and Laura Jacqmin. Examples of playwright leadership from Shakespeare and Moliere to Emily Mann, George Wolfe, and, now, at Chicago's Victory Gardens, Chay Yew. There are many examples of playwright generosity to other writers, from Edward Albee's

Foundation to the teaching devotions of playwrights like Paula Vogel, Mac Wellman, Charles Smith, Naomi Iizuka, and Marsha Norman. Many more examples of collective power from the Playwrights Company on Broadway in the thirties to 13P and the Workhaus Collective today. Examples of playwrights working in ensembles, like Kirk Lynn of the Rude Mechs, and playwrights who write within communities, like Alison Carey and the dozens of Cornerstone playwrights who followed her. Playwright bloggers shape the field's debates. Playwrights have idols, mentors, and goads. They have each other.

And playwrights have power. They just have to use it. Passivity and blame, defaults of creative life in a market economy, are irresponsible. They are a squandering of gifts, which is, to me, the unholiest of unholies in this world. New Dramatists was founded 64 years ago by a disgruntled playwright after a frustrating meeting at the Dramatists Guild. This unknown playwright rallied the Guild leadership—Howard Lindsay and Russel Crouse, Moss Hart, Rodgers and Hammerstein, Maxwell Anderson and others. Her name was Michaela O'Harra. Her plays remain unknown, but her founding vision has served more playwrights more lastingly than any theatre in our history.

One of my favorite playwright tributes was written from a living playwright to a dead one: from John Guare to the visionary Thornton Wilder. Guare goes in search of the essential Wilder and finds two of them. Guare writes:

> [Wilder] reminds me of not one but of two great American poets—William Carlos Williams and Ezra Pound[...]The problem that confronted them in their youth was where to go for experience to feed their art....Williams stayed in New Jersey as a doctor and found his source of experience there...Pound fled to Europe to leap into world culture.

Like a man who contains the spirit of his lost twin, Guare tells us, Wilder found, in his life and art, "a way to live in his bifurcated world, staying at home and roaming the world...."

Guare finds the distinction of Wilder, the doubleness of his way of seeing. Maybe this is the kind of difference *we* make, when we stare at plays, when we stare at bodies of work. Difference in the sense of differentiation. Difference, then, the assertion of individual voice and vison, becomes the leading edge of a life or death struggle against homogeneity, against institutionalization, against monoculture. Difference guides us to abundance and profusion, to the glorious diversity of all living things.

Here's the really beautiful part of Guare's tribute. Having located Thornton Wilder's distinction—his double distinction—Guare follows Wilder's own example and connects him to all the playwrights before and since. Guare again:

> Take the image of the parade of philosophers from *Pullman Car Hiawatha* and *The Skin of Our Teeth,* and imagine that parade not of philosophers but of playwrights from Aeschylus on down, through Plautus and Hroswitha and Calderon and Marlowe and Webster and Dryden and Behn and Strindberg and Shaw and Wilde and Pinero and O'Neill and Hellman and Orton and Albee and Hansberry and Shepard and Mamet and McNally and Wilson and Kushner, to every member of the Dramatists Guild, and to the next class of playwrights leaving Yale or NYU or Juilliard or whatever drama school or no drama school[….] Hear each generation saying, "Finish my work. Finish what I started. These are the questions I leave behind."

What a brilliant gesture—a playwright's gesture. We find difference, the distinction of voices and being, and then we join them in a grand parade, trumpeting connection and continuity, lineage and legacy, the unfinished work the dead bequeaths the living. All those playwrights, all those plays, those that will be forgotten, those that will be remembered, and those that lie in wait to be discovered. A great, tortuous, continuous, accidental odyssey.

Adapted from a keynote address to the Dramatists Guild of America playwrights conference, 2011.

The Shape of Plays to Come

The Art of Theatre

We are in a room together. We are in a room with black walls, or maybe in a warehouse room with sides of corrugated steel. It might be a beautiful, gilded hall from an earlier century, plush draperies and portraits, the light from chandeliers crystalling off plaster friezes running along the base of a vaulted ceiling. How about an actual living room, where the hostess rings a little bell for the performance to begin? Perhaps we are seated around a fire or on stone benches embedded in the side of a hill, a sacred place rife with our shared history; this isn't what you think of as a room, but the open world has rooms, too, and our presence here circumscribes one. Maybe we're arranged on folding chairs in a raw barn or even in front of a painting of a barn on canvas hung at the back of an old Masonic Lodge; a young man from town, dressed as a cowboy, steps out from the side of the painted barn and begins to sing, "Oh, what a beautiful mornin'."

What is the first place you imagine when you read the word "theatre"? Whatever you imagine, wherever we are, the important thing is this: we are in a room together.

Think about it: you read a book, this book, alone. The author speaks to you, through the medium of printed words, soundless speech, his private thoughts entering yours. Think about a movie or television. You can watch it alone or with others, but the people who created it and performed it have moved on. Their past endeavor is your present. Likewise a painting or sculpture: you can enjoy either in solitude. Creation has already occurred; your experience follows.

Every thing about the theatre, though, depends on its live-ness and presence: at least one person must perform and at least one must watch. Everything depends on a real moment in time, a real shared space. Why is the theatre transporting when it works, and excruciating when it fails? How can something so thrilling be so boring, something so rousing be so embarrassing? The answers lie in its very essence, this double nature: the immediate and the intimate.

What exactly happens in these rooms, these theatres, when we are together? Sometimes we witness, as has been said of the plays of Ibsen, "great reckonings in little rooms." Sometimes these reckonings play out against a vast expanse, and the entire world seems to be a stage, or a stage appears to hold the entire world. We might attend the recreation of a familiar ritual—a passion play, a retelling of the birth of our community, the annual production of *A Christmas Carol*. We may even participate, may clap along. By contrast, we might witness something entirely unfamiliar, an oddity from another world played out strangely. Or we could be ushered, one person at a time, into a tiny space of almost unbearable proximity, and in those confines another single soul will tell us a story.

These are lists: possible theatre spaces, possible happenings in those spaces. I make these lists because I believe that the art of theatre is an art of possibility and that every possible place or use for theatre suggests more. Each vision of the theatre adds to the art; each version alters the way we see ourselves, our community, our nation. The theatre is a town hall, in which citizens gather to debate issues of great moment. You might have seen how this works: in 1953, at the height of the House Committee on Un-American Activity hearings—the "witch hunt" for Communists in America, spearheaded by Senator Joseph McCarthy— Arthur Miller wrote *The Crucible*, a play that uses the allegory of that *ur* American witch hunt, the Salem witch trials of the 1690s, to explore issues of societal hysteria and individual responsibility. When called before the committee several years later, Miller would refuse to name names; in the meantime, he used the stage as a different kind of witness stand by dramatizing "the handing over of conscience to another, be it woman, the state or a terror, and the realization that with conscience goes the person, the soul immortal, and the 'name.'" Miller challenges audiences to place themselves in the action, to cross-examine and judge themselves. This challenge to (or even implication of) the spectator, still powerful today, was all the more unsettling when McCarthyism was at its height and "the gale from the Right was blowing at its fullest fury," in Miller's words.

From Ancient Greece to here and now, such theatre serves as a civic forum. Anna Deveare Smith's documentary epics—*Twilight: Los Angeles, 1992* and *Fires in the Mirror: Crown Heights, Brooklyn and Other Identities*, most famously—provide more recent and equally breathtaking illustrations. In them, the African American Smith uses monologues drawn verbatim from interviews to portray a range of characters from every walk of life in the community that is her subject: men, women, blacks, whites, Asians, religious leaders, activists, cops, politicians, social workers, and social outcasts—all in their own words. These one-woman shows, performed by the many-voiced Smith, play more like huge ensemble pieces than solo performances. Through the medium of her living presence, Smith serves up the knotty contradictions of racial and ethnic unrest, confronting us with a complex "we," a choral debate of ourselves right before our own eyes.

The theatre is a democratic meeting place, and it's much more too. It's also a place of extremity, madness, cruelty, and violence of image. There are poor theatres, holy theatres, dream theatres, bawdy theatres, boulevard theatres, activist theatres, story theatres, dance theatres, migrant farmer theatres, classical theatres of many traditions, epic puppet theatres, community theatres, laugh theatres and cry theatres. Some are classical, some avant-garde, others improvisational, comical-tragical-historical-pastoral. There are theatres that zero in on the visible—behavior, mannerism, affect—and those that grope toward the invisible: the animating spirit behind the everyday.

Whatever your definition, whatever your reason for making theatre part of your life, it's almost certainly reflective of a vision or need you share with others. A theatre is a house into which the spirit of its time, place, and people is invited to dwell. In this way, all theatre is local. What is that spirit for you and your colleagues? What is the genius of your theatre?

So many possibilities, audiences, communities. I think about the upper classes of England in 1660, after the restoration of the king. Women appear onstage for the first time, decked in costumes designed to display their legs and breasts, flirting with the crowd. People eat and talk, some sell oranges, some throw them. Sexual energy electrifies the house—a vibrant licentiousness unleashed after years of Puritan rule. And then I imagine villagers in Bali, watching a puppet play; young New Yorkers carrying their beers into a cramped store-front on the Lower East Side; tourists in Ashland, Oregon, who've traveled a day or more to take in *Richard II* or *Richard III*. How do Shakespeare's histories look to them? How did the same plays look to a Polish audience under Soviet rule or township blacks under South African apartheid? How does August Wilson play in the Pittsburgh he writes about, and how does he play in Nairobi? I have a friend whose play about Cambodian genocide premiered in West Virginia, after she'd created performances in Phnom Penh with survivors of the Khmer Rouge out of their own stories. How did each audience engage with the event unfolding before them? Did they see themselves or did they see "the other"?

I remember seeing a brilliant, searing version of Anton Chekhov's *Uncle Vanya* in the early 1990s, performed in New York by a Lithuanian theatre from Vilna. Two images from this production have stayed with me all this time, personal examples of the immediacy of theatre. The crisis in *Vanya* begins when an old, ailing professor returns to the rural estate of his deceased wife, accompanied by his new wife, the beautiful, indolent Yelena. The visit takes the most profound toll on the professor's daughter, Sonya, and on Sonya's uncle, Vanya, brother to her mother (the professor's dead wife). The house is turned upside down by the professor's demands and by Yelena's magnetism, the lure of her idleness. Everything goes to pot, as the static nature of their lives—the equilibrium Vanya and Sonya had long maintained, running the farm to fund the professor's big-city lifestyle—gets called into question. Their usual behavior begins to feel foolish as the professor himself appears foolish; their desires for something different, long denied—repressed by routine—begin to feel unbearable.

The Lithuanian production, coming soon after the fall of the Berlin Wall and the breakup of the Soviet empire, recast this tension between stasis and change in historical terms without ever losing sight of the intense personal anguish of Chekhov's characters. The most powerful instances of this involved another character, Dr. Astrov, the province's most cultured man—a thinker and environmentalist—who begins to spend more time at the estate, tending to the despotic professor and dallying with the enchanting Yelena. Astrov's life, too, is going to pot. He becomes lazy, drinks too much vodka, and loses his sense of purpose. In this rethinking of the play, Astrov's drunkenness—which escalated with astonishing extremity throughout the evening—came to stand in for the alcoholism of a devastated Eastern Europe, a hopeless wasteland left by years of totalitarianism and vodka. "Stop drinking," Sonya shouts at him as the stumbling doctor reaches again for the bottle. And in their struggle, a vodka bottle is knocked over on a high shelf and, for what seems like minutes, a waterfall of vodka cascades five feet to the floor. This simple image was terrifying in execution—one bottle, an almost bottomless gush of anguish. When, at the play's end, the professor (whom we've come to see as the U.S.S.R. itself) and his entourage depart, they leave the rest of the family wasted. Their faith in any kind of future happiness is gone, too. Astrov takes his leave as well, but by this time he's so drunk that he must literally crawl to his horse-drawn carriage. Coatless and hatless, he grabs the rug off the floor for warmth—a bear rug—and lumbers off under it, the human image of the Soviet bear, skulking drunkenly off, leaving a ravaged world behind.

Every play that is written, every event that is staged, has a different relationship to its moment, to its place. I flash back through the things I've seen: outdoor folk pageants in the woods of North Carolina; a toy-theatre play for an audience of twelve, written in childhood by a playwright who died at thirty-four; a sadomasochistic sex farce about Israelis and Palestinians, performed on the night we started bombing Iraq; a Long Island teen theatre production of *Damn Yankees*; Moliere's *Tartuffe*, directed by a Romanian auteur in our nation's capitol during the Reagan years; a piece created by an acting company from rural Pennsylvania, based on a hundred years of letters to the editors of local papers; an antiwar parade led by towering puppets and performers in masks; and three minstrel shows (one enacted by an all-white, twenty-five-year-old experimental ensemble; another written by an African American playwright, descended from a traveling minstrel; and a third performed by male Ghanaians, as part of a traditional comic performance inherited from British colonists).

What they have in common: they happen in a communal context, when everyone's together in a room. This communality is reflected in the very process of making theatre, which is collaborative to the root. The playwright may compose a play in the privacy of her own writing space, but the play won't be complete before her creative impetus is joined by the interpretive energies of actors, designers, a director, technicians, and even composers, choreographers, puppeteers, fight directors, and others. Plays are written by a writer with a "voice," but because that voice is dispersed—into the mouths and dialogue of many—it can't be heard until its music is captured by others. A play is a partial thing until it's brought into real time and space by a company of artists.

Every moment of this group journey invites discovery and dares disaster. An actor may read a line in a way that brings out meanings the author never understood, and he may interpret a scene in a way the author never intended. A design choice may look beautiful on paper and distracting in practice, or it may seem drab until inhabited by three-dimensional bodies on an actual stage. One director may understand the play's themes and structure brilliantly but fail to create living, breathing events in the rehearsal room. Another director may remain silent on the play as a work of ideas or literature and yet know how to catalyze actors and designers to ignite whatever explosions of life lie latent in the text. Every moment of rehearsal—from the initial conceptual discussions, drawings, models, readings around a table, to the final technical and dress rehearsals where lights are focused, sound is cued, and costumes are paraded and altered—is a moment of artistic choice (this way or that way?) and human interaction (your way or mine?).

The most interactive of arts, theatre is also the most integrative. Everything comes together in the theatre—music, movement and dance, visual and spatial design, text, politics, history. It's the art that leaves nothing out.

This rough motley points to another, more important integration: the theatre, to a greater extent than any art form I can think of, brings together body, mind, heart, and spirit—the mind of the playwright, the body of the actor, the heart of each of them and of the audience, and the spirit of all of us together. Alive together in a room. This is what I look for in the theatre and, speaking personally, it's what I want from my life. I can think of no better definition of living fully than this combination of the physical, mental, emotional, and spiritual. Nor can I think of any better place to find it.

This profound wholeness of the theatre, its essential connectivity, has an added urgency in the contemporary, technological world. Not only does the theatre aim to connect us to ourselves and to each other, but it does so in a uniquely unmediated way. Increasingly, we are capable of staying virtually connected and actually isolated. We can attend meetings by phone and video, hold lengthy instant conversations by email, and travel great mental and visual distances without leaving our homes. The theatre is the antithesis of the virtual, and it's the antidote. The theatre demands our physical presence and our communal proximity. It forces us to breathe the same air, face the same action, and process the same emotional information in a public space at the same time. It is, I repeat, the natural antidote to everything that keeps us apart, drives us to our corners, tells us where to focus and how to feel, mediates, manipulates and spins our experience of the real.

Even the most synthetic theatrical event can't hide the sweat, the dust motes in the lights, the smell of musty curtains or new carpet. The danger of the immediate is always with us in the theatre: a chair might break; an actor might flub his lines, fall into the orchestra pit or spit into the first row on his big soliloquy; the woman next to you might shout at the stage. And when it goes well, you can hold its liveness close to your heart: you were there, you saw it, there was no second take, no stunt double, no close-up shot through gauze for effect.

We are all keepers of the spirit of the theatre—from the artists who identify and articulate our core human impulses, to the administrators who make homes for art; from the trustees who secure those homes and create the bonds between artists and the larger community, to the audiences, without whom there can be nothing called theatre. Sometimes shouldering the responsibility for this most consistently endangered, ever-ephemeral endeavor can feel like carrying burning embers wrapped in leaves through a rainforest. If the necessary spark goes out, how will we light the fire around which we gather, night after night, place after place? That spark is what we have; it's the art of the theatre, your theatre, any theatre. And so we carry and protect it, fan it to flame, watch it die down to a faint glow, wrap it up and carry it again, always hopeful, always together.

This essay was originally published in *The Art of Governance: Boards in the Performing Arts*. Ed. Nancy Roche and Jaan Whitehead, New York: Theatre Communications Group, 2005. It is reprinted with permission from TCG Publications.

The Shape of Plays to Come

> It would take forever to recite
> All that's not new in where we find ourselves.
> —Robert Frost

How will the new come into our theatre? Will we recognize it? Will we welcome it? Is it already here? If not, what's the best way to make it happen?

There appears to be general agreement that the old ways aren't the best. Rumors of the death of new-play development may have been exaggerated, but the obituaries won't stop. Last spring, within a few weeks of each other, three pronouncements signaled a new era for the cultivation of work for the stage. First, Denver Center Theatre, one of America's wealthier nonprofits, and one with a long history of support for new plays, announced that due to losses sustained in the diving stock market, it would be suspending new-play development, closing its literary offices, eliminating the position of associate artistic director for new-play development, and canceling its new-play festival and the prestigious Francesca Primus Prize for women playwrights. Within a few days, Lincoln Center Theatre's Anne Cattaneo, one of our most respected dramaturgs, was quoted in the *New York Times*, saying, "New-play development is dead. It just became too expensive to do new work...Today, instead of 50 regional theatres developing 50 new plays, what you have is one new play by an established writer that gets done 50 times at 50 regional theatres."

Two months later, the *Times* ran another article announcing that Jesse Ventura, pro-wrestler-turned-Minnesota governor (the muscular butt of a nation's jokes) would help address his state's fiscal woes by withholding money promised to major arts institutions, including that flagship of flagships, the Guthrie Theatre, which had counted on $24 million to construct a new $125-million facility. Joe Dowling, the Guthrie's artistic director, responded to the governor's gambit with one of his own: "In terms of encouraging new writers, staging new plays and co-productions, and sending our plays out to other places, we won't be able to do what we hoped."

Dowling's statement was revealing in a couple of ways. While the Guthrie has never been a hotbed of new-play development, by holding out its potential demise as a counter-threat, Dowling was making his priorities clear, despite a mission devoted to "classical repertoire" and "the exploration of new works." (Do theatres ever hold Shakespeare hostage in this way—no bucks, no Bard?) Second, as with the Denver amputation, it made palpable an attitude that many have noted over the years, a shared sense among institutions that work on new plays is dispensable, in a last-hired, first-fired sort of way.

Of course, no one asks playwrights if it's dispensable. Decisions about what appears on the nation's stages are mostly handed down without reference to the artists who write, perform, design and (with more exceptions) direct it. Like so many corporate actions threatened or undertaken in these hardish times—layoffs, division and regional office closings, corporate restructuring—they are top-down decisions. The workers (who, in the theatre, are precisely the "creators") are an afterthought, if that—pawns in negotiations with, say, Wrestler-Governors.

In the midst of the death knells, Theatre Communications Group, showing a will to positivism and a desire to spur radical rethinking, held a two-day "convening" in Portland, Ore., with an unlikely cast of characters. Joining a handful of playwrights and a slightly larger cadre of institutional theatre producers (managers and artistic directors, including a large children's theatre contingent) were an assortment of multi-arts presenters, ensemble-based theatre artists, directors, performance artists, literary managers, and people who run small theatres and developmental labs. The gathering was a clear attempt to transcend the ingrown discourse of new-play development (the "developed to death" debate) that is nearly as old as the movement itself. With hope in their hearts, the folks at TCG skirted the debates (and once again showed their determination to break free of a past identification with the League of Resident Theatres) by bringing unusual suspects—people interested in the new anywhere, anyhow—and broadening the semantic umbrella. As if heralding an epoch in the making, they called it "New Works, New Ways." New-Play Development Is Dead! Long Live New Work Making!

*   *   *

The clashing point of two subjects, two disciplines, two cultures—of two galaxies, so far as that goes—ought to produce creative chances. In the history of mental activity that has been where some of the breakthroughs came. The chances are there now. But they are, as it were, in a vacuum, because those in the two cultures can't talk to each other.
—C.P. Snow

In the '30s, Harold Clurman, that great inspirer and co-founder of the Group Theatre, was introduced to André Gide, novelist and Nobel laureate. "The problem with the theatre," Gide remarked, "is to find good plays." "The problem with the theatre," Clurman rejoined, "is to create a Theatre."

This exchange adumbrates a great divide in visions for the future: those who feel the American theatre suffers from lack of great, or even worthy, plays, and those who lay blame for a failing art at the feet of artistically deficient theatres. On one side sit, mostly, artistic directors and producers; on the other, writers, as well as a constellation of other independent artists.

Those who take the no-good-plays line often define quality by both artistic measures and those of the marketplace; a "viable" work is one that plays well and sells well. I've been talking with other artistic directors about this for nearly 20 years and have a sense that their complaints (which aren't always shared by their literary managers, whose tastes are often considerably more adventurous than their bosses') boil down to three: (1) American playwrights write too small; they aren't engaged enough with the wide world; (2) these playwrights don't understand structure; and (3) they aren't writing plays that will connect with "my audience."

The counter argument holds that we live amid a profusion of playwriting talent—that, as a profession, playwriting hasn't been this vital in decades—but that the theatres, long on business savvy and short on artistic vision, haven't kept up. Moreover, those theatres, having helped create a multigenerational playwriting community, have now abandoned it. Erik Ehn, playwright and co-founder of the itinerant, anarchic RAT conference—a shape-shifting network of small, experimental, and alternative theatres—stood up for this view in a recent speech to the Literary Managers and Dramaturgs of the Americas. In "slightly doctored" notes from his talk, he contends, "There are plenty of plays out there, lots of excellence," adding, "To create a new theatre by developing plays first equals trying to build a new house by moving around the furniture." He compares mainstream new-play development, especially challenging or experimental texts, to Audubon twisting "the necks of exotic birds to help them fit the scale of his renderings." He calls for a change not only in theatre practice but also in theatre space and architecture, the expansion of time for creation, and an emphasis on "hospitality over intellectualism." *New*, in other words, means creating a new theatre.

How will the new come into the theatre? How can we make it happen? Should our efforts be focused on the writing or the structures of production, the independent artists or the institutions? The answer, as well as the problem, lies in the relationship between the two.

Is it possible that at the heart of the creativity stoppage known as new-play development are not bad plays (I'm told they exist); bad working models (though these prevail everywhere, such as dead-end reading series and criticism from numerous people with no understanding of process and no interest in producing the play); or bad faith (which, god knows, pervades every theatre where programmers mentally doodle while the writers they've encouraged wait weeks or months or, yes, years before the inevitable rejection trickles down to them)? Maybe the fault lines are deeper, as deep as identity, the story we tell ourselves about who we in the theatre are.

I have a confession. For as long as I can remember, I have believed that theatre is singular—*the* theatre, or, just as grandly, the theatre *community*. I no longer do. I used to think the nonprofit theatre movement had given birth to a profession of shared values. I no longer do. Forty years after its seeding, this field (note the singular), which we've celebrated for its variety *and* its underlying unity of purpose, has become two, with a mostly unacknowledged rift running through them. Or, to borrow C.P. Snow's famous phrase, with which he dissected humanistic culture into natural scientists and literary intellectuals, it's become "two cultures." Two theatres, two cultures, two galaxies: that of the institution and that of the individual artist.

This dawning awareness has had, for me, the quality of slow-motion heartbreak. Like many theatre people born in the '50s, I was raised on the all-together-now harmonies of musical theatre and came of age under the sway of the utopian communality of '70s experimental theatre. As a young professional, I carried a torch for artistic homes, community regionalism, and the company ethic implied by "resident." I've devoted much of my writing life since then to the "insider" *American Theatre* magazine, in the belief that the "we" I used as the principal pronoun of address was actual, descriptive of a community in fact.

Now, as artistic director of a six-decade-old institution that serves playwrights—those most independent of theatre artists—I straddle two realities. One reality features a building, a board, a staff, a company of playwrights, and a tight annual budget. It's driven by a clear mission and sense of institutional responsibility—for vitality, quality, stability, and legacy. The second reality is that of the writers themselves. I'm fed by their inspired idiosyncrasy, dogged artistic ambition, bravery, and skill. And I'm angry for them, because their stressful, unstructured, mood-swinging writing lives exist outside of the very world whose present and, even more, future depend on their articulated visions.

Where are the theatres that are worthy of these artists? I don't see them. Not because there aren't theatres with the talent to stage their plays impressively, but because there are so few theatres willing to incorporate artistic lives and bodies of work into the institution's way of being. At best, playwrights (and, I suspect, all unaffiliated artists) are guests—sometimes welcome, sometimes tolerated, sometimes ignored—in the ongoing life of theatre buildings. It's worse, I'd venture, for

32

playwrights of color, who bring even deeper cultural differences to bear on a divided situation—a double disenfranchisement. How will we welcome the new when we don't welcome the bringers of the new?

I don't mean to suggest that this disconnection is willful. The situation is no one's fault. It's an inevitable product of history, generational change, and institutionalization. It's the American way: the innovative becomes the established. Yesterday's geek-renegades become today's corporate titans (All hail Misters Gates and Jobs!). The institutional theatre in America still sees itself as the alternative theatre, though the pioneers are gone, replaced by second- and third-generation artistic and management leaders without the pioneering spirit. It has become our Broadway, that which the new theatre must rebel against to get free.

Both sides of the theatrical divide contribute to the climate. Theatre leaders all too often fail to collaborate honestly or take responsibility for the huge imbalance in power that exists between those who hire and choose and those who audition and wait. The myth of community intensifies their astonishment at (or denial of) the depth of artists' alienation. In December 2001, Michael Maso, managing director of the Huntington Theatre Company and then-president of LORT, decried the use of anonymous sources in an article written by three designers about the difficult economics of freelance theatre design. Maso condemned the practice on journalistic grounds but missed the point. He assumed that freelance designers were part of his artistic village, where everyone should feel free to speak his or her mind. They aren't and they don't. Truthfulness endangered their livelihoods. They were whistle-blowers—nobody's idea of a pleasant hire—or, to steal a phrase from John Patrick Shanley, "beggars in the house of plenty."

Unaffiliated artists, by contrast, can be shockingly naïve about what's at stake when a theatre makes artistic decisions, about the complexities of running an arts organization, about its relationship with its audience/community, about the process by which it functions and the real human cost of programming risks. Moreover, unaffiliated artists in America (of whom playwrights are only one species) are too often mired in passivity, unable to imagine actions other than hitting their heads against the same closed doors. Where is a new generation of writer-founders, playwright-managers? Where are the manifestos?

At root, though, this division stems from the thousand particulars of daily life that create habits and systems of belief. What is a day like for the head of an institutional theatre? What's that same day for a writer or any freelance artist? The tendencies of those lives read like lists of bipolar opposites:

Institutional	Individual
Regularity of schedule and place	Uncertainty—every day is different
Public	Private
Top-down decisions	Solitary decisions
Selecting collaborators	Awaiting the invitation/Knocking at the door
Planning/Knowing ahead	Flexibility/Finding out as you go
Problems of compromise	Problems of isolation
Tends toward the common denominator	Tends toward the esoteric
Attempts to un-structure the structured	Attempts to structure the unstructured
Organization	Improvisation
Calculating risk	At risk
Programmed diversity	*Sui generis* of every possible kind
Serves many masters, and is served	One's own master, served by no one
Holds authority	Disempowered, except in the privacy of the work
Defense against people outside	Suspicion of people inside
Unnecessary busyness	Necessary idleness
The constancy of production	The inconstancy of productivity
Thinking outside the box	Living outside the box
Manic	Depressive

Add to the list or make up your own. Your story goes here.

* * *

> One man cannot produce drama. True drama is born only of one feeling animating all the members of a clan—a spirit shared by all and expressed by the few for the all.
> —George (Jig) Cram Cook

As the multiculturation of the arts has shown, cultural differences make creative sparks fly. Moreover, there's a natural, generative tension between the solitary artist and the organization, between the private creator and the public producer. You can see this creative dissension up close and personal in that powerful first collaboration of the American art theatre—between Eugene O'Neill and the Provincetown Players.

In his lovingly detailed paean to Greenwich Village, *Republic of Dreams: Greenwich Village, The American Bohemia, 1910-1960*, the late Ross Wetzsteon retells the story of O'Neill's relationship with Provincetown's founding spirit Jig Cook. O'Neill, young, tortured, almost fatally alcoholic, is introduced to the idealistic company by a fellow drunk who knows that Eugene keeps some plays in a trunk. These wildly uneven, blatantly experimental plays—and several subsequent ones—are just what the Players have been looking for. They thrill the neighbors on the Cape and stand out in the purposefully amateur evenings of one-acts mounted in several New York seasons. The newspapers discover O'Neill, Broadway beckons, a couple of Pulitzers follow and the playwright and soon-shuttered theatre part company. It's the Ur-story and the same old one: kindred spirits making dramatic whoopee, the lure of Broadway, loyalty betrayed, a playwright's posthumous profession of gratitude for the dead producer's grace. More important, it's a story of mutual dependence: a theatre helping the writer find a voice, a voice defining a theatre.

How would the emerging O'Neill have fared in today's theatre? Whose commitment would now buy that brilliant beginner the years of explosive experimentation he spent with Provincetown? Where would he go to find the heat to temper the talent expressed in his late, great works? And where would he find a statement like this one, taken from the Players' constitution:

> The president shall cooperate with the author in producing the play under the author's direction. The resources of the theatre…shall be placed at the disposal of the author…The author shall produce the play without hindrance, according to his own ideas.

Is it the hothouse of Provincetown that grows an O'Neill, or the playwright's fervid imagination—Shakespeare's, Moliere's, Sheridan's, Chekhov's, Churchill's—that dreams life into the Globe, Palais-Royal, Drury Lane, Moscow Art Theatre, or Joint Stock? This year in New York, the Signature Theatre will dedicate its season to Lanford Wilson's work. What would the season look like if there'd never been a Circle Rep—an acting company, a director, and a shared, evolving aesthetic to grow Wilson's corpus, play by play? Where are the new Circle Reps? It's hard enough to find an acting company of any size or consistency today, let alone one that includes a writer or writers in its ongoing artistic evolution.

The founding spirits of the American art theatre—Cook, Clurman,

Hallie Flanagan, Zelda Fichandler, Hebert Blau, Judith Malina and Julian Beck, Douglas Turner Ward, Joseph Chaikin, Luis Valdez—knew at the start what we've forgotten. Unlike today, when the homogenous seasons of our national stages reveal a unanimity that feels like anonymity, these pragmatic inspirers shared a catalytic vision, one vision with a mess of names: company, collective, group, troupe, ensemble, and clan. Every theatre must find its voice, and every writer must find her theatre.

*   *   *

> People have asked me, "Why don't we have more good plays?" I said, "Why don't you ask why we don't have more bad plays, because if you have more bad plays you'll have more good plays, because that feeds the ground." That's the manure that makes things grow. It's very valuable manure, as manure is valuable to growth. We need activity, we need action, we need trial, we need error.
> —Harold Clurman

Two things I know: (1) for writers to understand a theatre's community they must be made part of it; and (2) the fusion of individual talent and collective energy fuels great theatre. Twenty-five hundred years of theatre history tells us this, but too few have been listening.

It's a sad irony that the very systems set up to nurture writers and involve them in the theatre have led to their disaffection. New-play development—reading series, literary offices, and the emphasis on premieres—was conceived to foster both writers and work. Instead it demoted playwrights to overnight visitors—the artistic home as Motel 6—and created schism where there should be continuity—from development to production, page to stage.

These processes also disrupted what may well have been the most important theatrical relationship prior to the regional theatre movement: the tempestuous, vibrant, mutually self-interested partnership between the producer and the playwright. Certainly, the success of mid-20th-century plays and musicals brings to mind not only their creators but their producers, benevolent—Kermit Bloomgarden, Robert Whitehead, Alexander Cohen—and maniacal—Jed Harris, David Merrick. When writers and producers share a process, they can share a sense of direction as well. It's here, *in relationship,* that the scope of a play can be addressed, that the producer can cheer the writer's efforts to move away from the "small," to turn toward the wide world.

Before we knew it, artistic producers had literary managers/

dramaturgs running blocking for them. Instead of being wooed, playwrights were customarily held at bay. The intimate producing partnership became a distant one, with the creator separated from the means of production. Moreover, the reading and discovery of plays has been delegated to such an extent that many artistic directors appear to have lost the patience, time and, consequently, the reading ability to wade through a play that may be different or difficult or in progress.

These systems and habits have altered the aesthetic landscape. The different, difficult, and new are just what so many writers grope toward. I've come to believe that a most common feature of contemporary American playwriting is the search for form. The process of discovery and innovation is integral to the play, built in. Structure isn't imposed; it's immanent. Tony Kushner's *Angels in America* is a case in point. His "fantasia" structure is a kind of nonbinding structure, allowing Kushner's imagination to go where it wants, to digress, to elaborate, to move forward and back, like progress itself, one of the play's main themes. The play dreams itself into being. And then the second part, *Perestroika*, dreams itself another way. How many of the playwrights you admire possess this "setting out to parts unknown" energy? Think of Edward Albee, Maria Irene Fornes, Suzan-Lori Parks, Paula Vogel, Mac Wellman, August Wilson, John Guare, for example. Each of their plays is its own animal; each teaches us anew how to follow its tracks. American playwrights don't understand structure? They understand it well enough to know you have to discover it.

If these important writers—all important teachers as well—have made it up as they've gone along, pursuing those forms-in-formation, what undiscovered territory can we hope to stumble into as their students and less-established colleagues break ground? The solo mind will always be more nimble than an institution. So, playwrights, whether or not they write ahead of their times, will nearly always write forward of the theatres. But how will we welcome the new into the theatre if the theatres stand apart from it, if they no longer have the will or the skill to recognize it?

A second confession: I don't want to believe what I've written. My mind keeps doubling back, accusing itself of dramatizing—the institutional Pentheus on one side, the artistic Dionysus on the other. Pentheus, king of Thebes, up in a tree, decked out in the Maenad's drag—peeking down at the Dionysian revels (the drunken, theatrical revels), all the time thinking he's in control, in command. And I accuse myself of taking the analogy too far. Theatres are great ships turning in tidal waters; they resist change. Everybody in them, even the pilots, have their hearts in the right places.

Then I remember the hundreds of writers I've spoken to in the past few years, and how few theatres contradict the portrait of disengagement they've drawn. And I ask myself—and I ask you the same question—which theatres are truly important to me, which ones do I expect to lead, to draw us nearer to the future, to the new? And I know it won't be many of the ones our funding community has designated as "leading theatres," despite their impressive production values and eloquent leaders.

No wonder our theatre community has suddenly gone gaga over all those ensemble folks (despite the fact that many of these ensembles have been around for decades). It's natural to get excited about the work happening in companies. Who would not want what they have, those community-based and experimental troupes from Appalachia to Blue Lake, Calif., from Wooster Street to Cornerstone's corner of L.A.? You gotta love them. Collective models only apply so far, though; 999 times out of 1,000, someone will write the new thing alone in a room. But even the mammoth Oregon Shakespeare Festival, which boasts the largest acting company in the country, has been jazzing writers these days. And obviously, not all institutions are created alike: some are born artist-centered (think Steppenwolf and South Coast Repertory) and remain so in their bones, even as they grow. And then there are the scrappy young theatres—gangs as much as theatres—with funny names, who are the real harbingers of the new, because they refuse to check their imaginings at the boardroom door.

Elsewhere, the century that invented directors also cursed the theatre with one dominant model, supported by theatre consultants and unwitting trustees: the director-led theatre. It's almost a given that the first choice to run most theatres is a director, and, having selected directors, most theatres define themselves as artist-centered. This unexamined practice, despite a few hundred years of counter-examples, has inflated the importance of the director and devalued the work of the writer and the centrality of the play. Director training, meanwhile, makes matters worse, by shortchanging new-play collaboration and overstressing classical interpretation. The coups of discovering the next fine writer or skillfully telling the new story have been supplanted by the interpretive thrill of tackling *The Winter's Tale* or *The Wild Duck* or mounting both parts of *Angels in America*. The system self-perpetuates, as board members (in the absence of ensembles and company playwrights) sustain contact with a single artist—a director. Real directors' theatres can be as compelling as any others—who can't wait to see what Robert Woodruff brews up at the American Repertory Theatre, in a season where he works side-by-side with Anne Bogart, Peter Sellars, János Szász, and Andrei Serban? Not many directors, though, have developed a production "voice" rich and unique enough to compensate for the lack of other consistent, defining voices.

The gulf is real, and crossing it, bridging it, eliminating it is the primary work of this moment, more important than getting nonprofits and commercial producers together, more important even, I'd venture, than the financial health of institutions. What was envisioned as a community of artists has evolved into a community of institutions so cut off from its artists that it keeps looking outside for ways to save itself. The institutions envy performance ensembles, experimental troupes, and community-based theatres for the vitality they know themselves to lack. They want the flexibility found only in playwright centers and labs. They look to corporate gurus from the business world to jar their thinking. Maybe it's time (to paraphrase the *New Yorker*'s Malcolm Gladwell) to stop trying to think outside the box and start trying, instead, to fix the box.

The archetype for creative progress in America pits the individual (often in concert with other individuals) against the institution. We're seeing the hypertext version this year, corridor after corridor: the abused take on the Catholic Church; middle managers and investors take on Enron, WorldCom and the FBI; Tony Soprano bada-bings the networks. House minority leader Richard Gephardt, citing a crisis of "faith in Institutions," suggests that our hope is in reform.

In the theatre—which, in spite of evidence to the contrary, sees itself as exempt from institutional abuse and corruption—the individual has remained mostly silent. Like an insular family—or people operating under a fragile *myth* of family—the unspoken agreement calls for silence. During 13 years of "culture wars," survival pragmatics demanded a unified front under attack. This summer, however, in the process of restoring a mere sliver of past cuts to the National Endowment for the Arts, some in Congress declared the "culture wars" over. Maybe we have a bit more freedom now, freedom to be divided, freedom for raucous in-fighting, freedom to fight for the future in loud, angry, impassioned voices.

My hope for the new rides in two directions at once—toward the playwrights who, on a daily basis, strike out into the unknown, and toward a new generation of theatres, a new generation of founders. And my wishes go to everyone who might want to pave the way for the new—individual artists, funders, trustees, future and present theatre leaders. The wish list includes the tentative, naïve, impractical, and already-tried, but here goes.

I wish for a funding and support structure for nothing less than the total integration of companies of artists, including writers, in established theatres and new ones—not a place at the table but the table itself. I wish for funders who will reserve major backing for the theatres—most of them with budgets under $2 million—that are breaking ground for the future. Let young artists be the mentors, for a while, rather than senior administrators.

Any ideas that reverse the structure of power between institutions and independents make my list: give artists money to choose which theatres they'll work with, rather than the other way around; let the writers of last season's hits—rampantly produced across the country—curate a second production by a contemporary playwright. (You do the 12th production of *Fuddy Meers* or *Dirty Blonde*? That's great. You should. Then David Lindsay-Abaire or Claudia Shear gets to choose another play for your season!) In fact, I can stand behind any idea that links the productions of premieres to those of second and third productions (all of which are necessary and lacking). How about making sure that every list of potential artistic directors contains a full complement of actors, playwrights, designers, nondirecting producers, literary managers, and anybody else with a proven sense of service to artists other than themselves? And let's have a congress, not of commercial and nonprofit producers, but of institutional leaders and unaffiliated artists with full immunity for anything they might say.

I wish, too, that all director- and actor-training programs would devote at least half their production opportunities to the cultivation of new work—training for the real world and stimulus for the future, all rolled up. I wish we could find ways to add flexibility and time to development by partnering producing theatres with theatre laboratories, workshops, non-performance spaces, and artist centers. I wish writers could drive and design their own process at theatres. And I wish producers would stop peeking at the schedules *in American Theatre* to pick their seasons.

One final wish: more new plays in every season, more plays, more plays.

This essay was originally published in *American Theatre* magazine, November, 2002.

The Importance of Staying Earnest

"The creation of a work of art, like an act of love," writes Gore Vidal, "is our one small 'yes' at the center of a vast 'no'." If he's right, and I believe he is, then the choice to become an artist is a small, powerful bravery. From the catalytic act of courage—performed, more often than not, in ignorance—follow, potentially, many others.

The choice, however, doesn't get made once—when we take off for school, for example—but every day. Should I stay or go? Do I take this job for a living wage or hash it out on next to nothing? Do I live in a city I hate or in a community that I love, even though it holds fewer opportunities? Can I face another audition today? Can I swallow another rejection ever again in my life? Sometimes the answers stand as (also small) acts of spiritual defiance on the part of the individual within an institutional culture. Sometimes they buck the materialist values of our national life. Often, they are mere rebellions against Mom and Dad.

Now we are at war, the cries from both sides of the congressional chamber tell us, and war makes this choosing and all that follows harder than ever, if only because it pumps up the volume on the usual "no" that greets the American artist. The unquantifiable casualties of such a "culture war"—its collateral damage—are spiritual ones. I don't mean some universal, communal spirit, but your spirit and mine, as we try, in our daily ways, to find the will to do a kind of work that is, if not disdained, then deeply undervalued by our families, neighbors, and elected representatives. This will must now fuel not only the work but an ongoing defense of it as well. Lawyers and bankers rarely get called upon to justify legal careers or the amassing of personal fortunes, but a life in the arts is open season. How will you live? Do you really think you're good enough? Who needs theatre, anyhow? In the public forum, moreover, artists regularly have to answer to the very Goliaths of negation at whom their David's stone "yesses" have been hurled.

For artists-in-training, justifying the desire to make art (especially when you haven't really done it yet) can be hard. Parents want security for their kids; they want them to choose sensible courses of study. If good sense seems too much to ask, then at least they can expect good reasons. But as anyone who has ever acted, danced, painted, or sung knows, art is—first—something you do for yourself. You want to do it, you have to do it, it makes you feel better than any other thing makes you feel, it gets you out of the house and away from your family, or all of the above. You do it, on some fundamental level, just because.

Later, maybe, audience enters into it. Later, maybe in post-adolescence, artists develop a sense of mission or cultural conscience, reasons for endeavoring that go beyond the cathartic joys of self-expression. This, partly, is what theatre training is about. Through contact with working artists and history, aspirants learn the rhetoric of artistic purpose: how theatre creates community, for example, or how art reflects the soul of a people or nudges a culture forward.

Philosophy is rhetoric that proves true over time, and these arguments have done so. They become especially handy when the second phase of justification begins. Having somehow slipped past the parents, the artist must now justify his or her existence to the world at large. This is the stage we're stuck in nationally. At the second level of justification we must defend work already created and protect the environment—including the economic one—necessary to create more in the future. At this stage we trot out the aesthetic philosophies we learned in school, because they are the only acceptable lines of defense against so-called enemies of art.

Still, such statements of belief are only half-truths. The other half, the half left unsaid, admits that art *is*, at least in part, for the artist's sake. This selfish, yes-I'm-doing-it-for-me rationale—while perfectly acceptable in corporate, open-market capitalism—makes a lousy case for, say, a national arts endowment. Witness how scrupulously it's avoided in the bow-and-scrape rituals of public justification performed to convince Congress that art (even that itsy-bitsy, teensy-weensy, we-don't-like-it-either portion that turns nasty) deserves continued federal funding. If artists would serve the public good, the prosecution snorts, they should be good to the public; if they would serve themselves, let them fend for themselves. This argument gets an assist from the artists themselves who, holding forth about the value of art without acknowledging its selfish source, look shifty, like they're trying to hide something.

Maybe, though, the selfish reasons for making lives in the arts are deeply responsible ones. Let me try to explain. The theatre community (or communities) is a village within institutional America. In direct contradiction to much of the rest of American life with its corporate culture and party lines, life in our village demands that we take things personally. In an increasingly media-filtered, mass-market society, theatre's defiant, humanist personalness becomes a reminder, a call from our most submerged selves. Taking things personally becomes a profound political act. It elevates the energy of art over the power of economics. The embarrassing, self-righteous earnestness so common to theatre people is, in fact, a necessary defense against bland life and institutional behavior, against correctness, against denial. It's our radical assault on what sociologist Erving Goffman frighteningly called "the bureaucratization of the spirit." Social life encourages the bureaucratization of the spirit by requiring its members, Goffman writes, to "give a perfectly homogenous performance at every appointed time." In other words, we have to act in life. In the masked art of our village, though, we, paradoxically, demand the right to be ourselves.

The passion of this demand intensifies with resistance. The parental pragmatics, the governmental attacks, the critical misreadings and public indifference—they make us grandiose, defensive, self-important. The fray turns us adolescent. Of course, there's a lot of value in adolescence, especially for artists or budding ones. It's the moment in life when everything comes into play at once: sexuality, desire, terror, anger, expectation, and uncertainty. Adolescence makes a great source for theatrical emotion. When you're in it, everything feels personal, serious, life-and-death—the essential conditions for drama and (when viewed from a toasty distance) comedy.

At its best, school teaches you to preserve these emotional coals, introduces you to techniques for fanning them into flames, and, on the intellectual side, for containing the fires or at least for guiding them under some kind of intelligent control. In other words, during training we bring our adolescent selves into collaboration with our adult ones. We learn to distinguish between real life-and-death struggle and imaginary ones. We learn about "as if."

The famous phrase applies to the leaps an artist makes, but it also draws limits on the art itself. From the inside of "as if," everything that can be at stake is; from the outside, it's just play. To put it another way: the work of the imagination is only "as if" a matter of life and death. It feels like a mortal struggle, but it rarely is. AIDS is life and death, poverty is, or war. Landing or playing a role Off Broadway is not. At least in America, making or not making art probably won't kill you. Nevertheless, all creative artists must do as actors do: invest fully in this "as if," believe fully in what poet Robert Frost calls "play for mortal stakes."

There are, though, ways in which creative acts are, precisely, matters of life and death. In contradiction to the deadening "bureaucratization" of the spirit, such acts, by virtue of creating something that didn't exist before, adds life to the world. Moreover, they increase, if only temporarily, the wills of other to live spiritedly. If you wanted a reason to get out of bed in the morning, chances are Judith Malina's diaries would provide more inspiration than, say, Bob Packwood's. Also, creative acts are matters of metaphorical death because passages are sloughing off, taking us beyond what we were. They change us. Sometimes, because artistic work calls up profound and intricate emotional responses (at least in the people doing the work, if not in those watching), they change us enormously. This, then, is the small, personal, courageous choice: to pursue the things that add life to life, and to wrestle death in a regular, if imaginary, way.

Good training makes this choice dimensional. It encourages us to take everything personally. It rehearses us for lifetimes of commitment to imaginative acts while, at the same time, helping us understand their limits. It requires that we take ourselves absolutely seriously, but not too.

The two worlds—of professional theatre and of training—need one another. Professionals can help students get smart and sensible about what they do. Students, on the other hand, can serve as reminders, spurs, raw proof of artistic necessity. Young artists are selfish, earnest, open, ignorant, goofy, grandiose, eager, angry, willful and willing. We need them. The "no's" of this world are too winning, the "yesses" too hard-won.

This essay was originally published in *American Theatre* magazine, January, 1996.

What's Past is Prologue:

On Change and Mourning in the American Theatre

> I tell the future. Keck. Nothing easier. Everybody's future is in
> their face. Nothing easier. But who can tell your past—eh?
> Nobody!
> —Thornton Wilder, *The Skin of Our Teeth,*

The Fortune Teller was right: the future's easy; it's the past that's tough. Futures are written on faces: "*Plus ça change*…More of the same." The future's made up of small adjustments, nuts-and-bolts realism, daily days. The past sweeps. Sometimes it's dark, uncertain; sometimes it moves with bacchanalian abandon and broad gesture. It's cast with grand figures of genius and inspiration, revolutionary philosophers, visionary leaders, larger-than-life actors on the world stage. The future? Keck.

The past's turbulence makes it more compelling than the future. Last year's coup is more promising than next year's election; the first millennium holds more mystery than the turn of this one; who we were in childhood provokes more longing than who we will be in our dotage. This disparity is strikingly evident in the contemporary American theatre, a universe whose enormous changes in the past serve paradoxically to underscore how resiliently it now intends to remain the same.

The danger of the compelling past is that we continue to live in it, whether we know it or not. We fight to preserve it, measure our progress by its yardsticks, and recycle old messages in up-to-date packages. If we don't remember it, as the saying goes, we repeat it; if we don't mourn it, it haunts us. As a culture, the American theatre stands as a strange crossroads: one way marked "more of same"; the other, seemingly, "Abandon all hope." The only thing clear about the present is that it's mourning time. Without taking the necessary time to mourn what and who the theatre has lost, the theatre community can only harden in place. By mourning, we calculate our losses, shed them, and grow past them. It's part of the process of change. Like anything else in this world, the theatre must embrace change or it will die.

Reading Hebert Blau's 1964 manifesto, *The Impossible Theatre,* in 1992 is like pumping speed directly into your heart. You feel the roaring impatience of that original impulse, the crashing idealism that pulled you into the theatre in the first place. "The purpose of this book," he begins, "is to talk up a revolution. Where there are rumblings already, I want to cheer them on. I intend to be incendiary and subversive, even un-American. I shall probably hurt some people unintentionally; there are some I want to hurt. I may as well confess right now the full extent of my animus: there are times when, confronted with the despicable behavior of people in the American theatre, I feel like the lunatic Lear on the heath, wanting to 'kill, kill, kill, kill, kill, kill!'"

This is the voice of the American theatre's artistic mothers and fathers, not when they were running multimillion-dollar institutions, but when they were kids with an attitude and a world to change. When Papp went toe-to-toe with Moses in the Park, when the Fichandlers demanded an audience in the Capitol, when Beck and Malina insisted on Paradise (Now!) and put their bodies on the line for it, when Ball tried to shake the earth in San Francisco. It's the cry of others, too, who dreamed, with Blau and his Actor's Workshop of San Francisco co-founder Jules Irving, of an "Impossible" theatre or an Ideal, Open, Living, Organic, Immediate, National, Holy, Public one.

Blau's siren call "to wish the world back to sanity, bringing to our desire for joy the intensity of Artaud's scream," marries Lear's lunacy to John Donne's spiritual longing: "Batter my heart, three person'd God.../breake, blowe, burn and make me new." It's the whoop of overripe, erudite youths, unafraid to do foolish things for the right reasons, to follow Yippie advice and cry "Theatre!" in a crowded fire. Only two or three decades later, it seems a bit unsavory to cry "Theatre!" at all, even in a room with a stage.

I miss this rant—the impulse to tear down that fueled the building-up. Here resounds the modernist belief that we can make ourselves anew, as if from scratch. Here flows the blood of the hard-headed American pioneer, the nervy bohemian, the self-righteous radical, the audacious *artiste*. Here beats the compulsion to change what *is*—simply because it is—that moves a culture forward.

In our theatre, circa the verge of the millennium, the very spirit of rebellion has evaporated. The impetus to break away, found, and pioneer has been replaced by the need to maintain, hold on, secure. The language of the visionary has been watered down into the corporate jargon of the successor, one, two, three, four generations young, generations that have foregone their adolescent rebellions and bypassed the stage Blau valued—that of gifted amateurism—for the polish of professionalism.

Who were the theatrical revolutionaries of the past decade? The '80s brought us entrepreneurial presenters—Harvey Lichtenstein and Peter Sellars, for example— who reached beyond national and generic boarders to electrify the idea of the theatre festival. But these presenters, as Sellar's own theatre experiments at the Kennedy Center showed, never made work as exciting as what they imported, be it from Chicago, Scandinavia, or Bali. The '80s also ushered new companies into the mainstream. I'm sure, though, that no one believed a group like Chicago's Steppenwolf would revolutionize anything. Its flash-in-the-pan ascendancy brought us rebellion as raucous behavior, occasional rudeness, and food fights in the kitchen—not as aesthetic or political overthrow.

Perhaps the spirit of revolution manifests itself in the newly legitimized Performance Art? Postmodern performance has pushed the boundaries of what and who makes theatrical art, by including outlaw performers (and techniques) from fine arts, dance, opera, video, and you-name-it. Performance art has proved the theatricality of the performed self (be it Spalding Gray, Holly Hughes, John O'Keefe, or Richard Elovich). On a more substantive level, it has also continued to counter the lie of a singular America with visions of many Americas: black ones, gay ones, Asian, Hispanic, and native ones. Ultimately, performance art has served up an alternative practice, rather than a revolutionizing one. Performance spaces have imitated the institutions in structure and administration, and alternative artists have readily joined the mainstream when asked.

Strangely, whatever rebels lurk in the heart of the American theatre have remained nearly silent on the subject of institutional theatre, although that theatre as a movement is almost as old as Broadway was when it started being attacked by the likes of the Group Theatre and, later, the pioneers of Off Broadway and regionalism. We have heard the cries of: "Broadway is dead! Long Live the American theatre!" but no equivalent shouting has been aimed at the ossifying Great White Way of the institutional theatre.

In place of outcries, we get press releases. For manifestoes, we get grant proposals. Theatre as a culture of radical change, discovery, and entrepreneurship has been replaced by a system of succession and hang-by-the nail persistence. Nails can't handle the weight, though, and as the past few years of national arts funding controversies have shown, there aren't many willing spotters around to hold the net.

And why should the institutional theatre be immune to attack? With the help of organizations like Theatre Communications Group, management-obsessed funders, and eighties-style pragmatists, the theatre establishment has preached and practiced its own well-intentioned brand of trickle-down Reaganomics that, simply stated, argues that the only way to sustain artists is through the institutions. Keep money and resources flowing to Daddy-Bear and he can hire and protect acting ensembles, resident directors, playwrights-of-the-house, and assorted other associate artists. In other words, sustain the institutional infrastructure and rely on the largesse of those running the mechanism to provide for the welfare of the individual. But it doesn't work in public America or in theatrical America. Hard times and continual crisis of survival forces the machinery to feed itself first, and even then, it stays hungry, and leaves even some of our most talented artists out on the breadline.

*   *   *

> Yet herein will I imitate the sun,
> Who doth permit the base contagious clouds
> To smother up his beauty from the world,
> That, when he please again to be himself,
> Being wanted, he may be more wond'red at
> By breaking through the foul and ugly mists
> Of vapors that did seem to strangle him.
> —Shakespeare, *Henry IV, Part 1*

National boundaries change daily. Countries split apart, take new names, old names, no names until they can settle their disputes. Today's labels are tomorrow's memorabilia: who is the enemy? What is the mother tongue? Union of what? Who could map such an oscillating landscape or fashion a globe from a swarming hive? The world's cartographers go mad.

On a smaller scale, those of us who chart the development of the American theatre come to sound like Bud Abbott frantically trying to figure out who's on third. Dillon's out at Milwaukee; Wojewodski's in at Yale; Lewis goes to Baltimore; Perloff to A.C.T.; Hamburger to Dallas and Bishop to Lincoln Center. Who's taking over at Williamstown, Portland, Virginia Stage, CSC Rep, Indiana, Studio Arena, Arizona, Trinity, Jersey Shakes? Where does someone go after forty years at Arena or thirty-five at the Oregon Shakespeare Festival? What's up with Adrian Hall or Charles Towers, Anne Bogart, Douglas Turner Ward, Pat Brown, David Frank, L. Kenneth Richardson, Gregory Mosher, Nagle Jackson? What ever happened to...?

Leadership isn't only a question for presidential politics; it's a big issue in the theatre. Who and where are the leaders we need? Again, we're faced with a world in which the past seems richer than the future, which is not to say that those running our nation's theatres lack vision, but that the sustenance of those theatres lacks the drama of their founding. No one has found a way to fuse the rebellious passion for change which started this movement with the business savvy that has kept it alive.

Some leaders—Joseph Papp, William Ball, Charles Ludlam, Nikos Psacharopoulos, John Hirsch—have recently died. Partly, that's a fact of life for a movement in mid-life, and partly it's a horrible reminder of plaguetime. Some—Zelda Fichandler, Jerry Turner, Adrian Hall, Lloyd

Richards, for example—have left homes they created or advanced, passing the torch on their way out. Some visions, like that of Ellen "La Mama" Stewart and Music Theatre Group's Lyn Austin, seem too particular for others to build on. Still others—new leaders of similar, national stature—have yet to emerge.

Where will they come from? Will new leaders rise up from the ranks of natural heirs, the artistic directors like Arena's Douglas Wager, Oregon Shakespeare's Henry Woronicz or Center Stage's Irene Lewis, who were part of a systematic or natural mechanism of succession? Will leaders come from newer arenas outside the mainstream, say San Francisco's Life on the Water, Alaska's Perseverance Theatre or New York's Cucaracha Theatre? Will they be directors at all, or producers, designers, writers? Are they already out there, ensconced in prominent theatres like the Goodman, the Guthrie or Hartford Stage? Are they moving from theatre to theatre, waiting for the right time and place to break through "the foul and ugly mists" that seem to strangle them?

The answer to all of the above is the same: they might come from anywhere, but only against all odds. The system is too bogged down. Looking at the options one at a time presents a most discouraging picture. First, we have the apparent heirs. The skills that make a fine associate artist or second-in-command—e.g., supporting someone else's vision and making ripples but never waves—may create capable directors and supportive, diplomatic producers. Working within a system, however, doesn't rehearse you for changing it or for pioneering a new one. What about those who are working brilliantly on the outskirts of the establishment theatre? Here, too, the odds are daunting, because in order for marginal artists to make an impact in an entrenched theatre, they usually have to give up what they've got and go on to bigger (i.e., boggier) ponds. The small theatre, the truly regional theatre, the quirky/kinky/rinky-dinky theatre pays the price for the visionary's upward mobility.

As to the possibility that different kinds of artists (not just director-producer types) will come to the fore: sure, any kind of artist could rise up as a leader; there's authentic talent in the theatre community. Interior talent, though, can't be expected to survive the outward-directed responsibilities of administration, fundraising, and politics. Molière had it easy; he only had one king to please. Today's artist-manager has to please us all. Maybe they are already out there, these leaders, piloting large theatres or moving from job to job. Nevertheless, the deck is stacked against them: proficiency at salesmanship, advocacy, development, board relations, and systems management is the stuff of bureaucrats and lobbyists, not revisionist thinkers. In one light, it's encouraging that so many artistic directors are leaving their institutions for the freedom and uncertainty of solo careers.

Ironically, though, the theatre's established leaders have thus far proven less adventurous than a handful of activist funders, who, forsaking mainstream establishments, are giving gobs of money to minority and community-based artists.

Certainly, the most moving succession story of last year was the appointment by then-living Papp of JoAnne Akalaitis to follow him as head of the New York Shakespeare Festival. First and foremost, it was a painful admission of mortality by a man who was never supposed to die. Even in death the monumental Papp managed to capture the contradictory spirit of his time, losing a son to AIDS in the same year that he, one of many theatrical fathers who've left us of late, passed over. His choice of Akalaitis also reflected poignant shifts of focus, representative of our time: from the most public of men to a most private artist; from a sometimes benevolent patriarchy to rule by a woman used to working collectively; from a stance of righteous surety to one of righteous uncertainty. Moreover, what this appointment—which was less succession than surprise dubbing, like the king who shocks his subjects by leaving everything to his secret bastard—so stirring was that it was a total leap into the unknown. No one has the foggiest idea whether it will work or not, but, as with the ill-fated appointment of Anne Bogart at Trinity several years ago, it makes change—something different from what we have—feel possible.

How appropriate that Akalaitis chose *Henry IV*, a play that questions the skills needed for leadership, to kick off her tenure (she had been named artistic director at this point, though was not yet heir apparent). Prince Hal—the director's selected metaphor for succession—lives a dark low-life, until he bursts forth at the helm of England, ablaze like the sun. From recalcitrant bad-boy aristocrat, the prince becomes the glorious King Henry. Time will tell how deep the metaphor goes, as well as how Papp's gamble will turn out. A lot is at stake. NYSF is a flagship theatre if ever there was one, and Akalaitis is unproven as a producer. Still, unlike more orderly transitions, this one felt more revolutionary than evolutionary. It offered old-fashioned change in place of new-fangled sameness. As such, it was momentous and frightening—like a tremor from the ever-fascinating past. But who knows which method makes Henry Vs and which produces spurious leaders like the play's counter-father, Falstaff?

*   *   *

"I am moved by the theatre...as one is always moved by odd, off center hope, by people hanging in there and the persistence of the obsolete."
— Stanley Elkin, *The Muses Are Heard*

Maybe the language of succession is all wrong. It suggests order, transition, calm. It's a term used to assure boards of trustees and skittish funders that, in spite of apparent change, everything will remain pretty much the way it's always been. Ultimately, it's an institutional term, not a theatrical one. Institutions exist to maintain and solidify what is; theatre happens to make us re-see, to alter our perception of what is. The big mistake of succession is that it encourages us to pick up where our parents left off, instead of starting over from the place where they went wrong.

By definition, succession is change from within, a way of working inside an established order to further that order. Theorists of change, though, have showed that trying to change from within often means no change at all for a failing system. What looks like change is often a sign of its opposite: persistence. In *Change: Principles of Problem Formation and Problem Resolution,* psychologists Paul Watzlawick, John Weakland, and Richard Fisch explore two types of change. "First-order change," or what might be described as change of change, happens when a system shifts from one state to another. Running or jumping off a cliff in a nightmare, for instance, is first-order change: a change of behavior that fails to terminate the nightmare. Getting out of a dream requires second-order change: waking up, a change from one state of being to another. First-order changes is a kind of adaptation to a problem, usually without altering the circumstances of the problem—such as hiding from danger in a dream, or changing personnel within a theatre. In effect, when we look for solutions within the status quo—putting on suits to lobby Congress to save the National Endowment for Arts, speaking in corporate tongues to present our work to funders, emphasizing the development of successors over the nurturing of pioneers—we put our energy into maintaining the very system that too often fails us.

Second-order change or what popular psychologists and a new-age thinkers call a "paradigm shift," emphasizes total transformation. This kind of change occurs when problems are reframed in such a way that information we take for granted comes together in a wholly new way. With second-order change we reperceive and reconfigure the known. The founding of regional theatres exemplifies second-order thinking. What used to be a closed, either-or system—Broadway or the Road—became first a series of community alternatives, then tributaries fed by Broadway, then, with a burst of revisionary thinking, a nation of communities, of which Broadway was only one. The map—which contained the same basic information—changed shape.

For today's theatre, second-order change may mean addressing not the problems themselves but how we're trying to solve them. Instead of focusing on the problems, theatre people should try to reframe their responses to the problem and their relationships to the world outside theatre. Blau had the idea when he ventured: "If the world won't give us a better world, we shall try to give it a better theatre...." Watzlawick, Weakland, and Fisch argue that spontaneous and lasting change often occurs when decisive action is applied to the attempted *solution*—to what is being done to deal with difficulty, and not to the difficulty itself. Real change comes from rejecting the idea that one has to choose among alternatives.

This kind of perceptual revision is no less than what theatre at its best attempts to stimulate in its audiences. What seems necessary now for the American theatre establishment to move past its chronic troubles—lack of funding, cultural marginalization, too-rigid working processes, a deficit of imagination—is for it to revise *itself* with the same chutzpah and abandon that infused its founding. People are doing just that, but too often the theatre establishment dismisses their attempts as marginal or paratheatrical. ACT UP, for example, the AIDS activist group, finds freedom in its marginal status and its refusal to seek governmental or corporate funds. It makes political theatre—on a large and small scale—as vital and timely as any in recent memory. Similarly, theatre companies from communities as far-reaching as Appalachia, Alaska, rural Pennsylvania, and the Bronx embrace the kind of regionalism (i.e., community/place-specificity) that larger institutions eschew, reinventing our ideas about professional theatre as they go. Perhaps the map needs to be reshaped again through more radical regionalism, the type of true community-orientation which theatres, in their search for legitimacy, have foregone.

The confusion that currently pervades the American theatre, the shared awareness of the crossroads we face, is a necessary step towards this more significant change. As any teacher knows, confusion readies us to break the frame we're in and grab onto a new way of looking.

*   *   *

When there are so many we shall have to mourn
When grief has been made so public, and exposed
     To the critique of a whole epoch
     The frailty of our conscience and anguish,

Of whom shall we speak? For every day they die.
Among us, those who were doing some good,
     And knew it was never enough but
     Hoped to improve a little by living.
          —W.H. Auden, *In Memory of Sigmund Freud*

The American Theatre is confused because, as everyone seems to agree, it is in transition, a transition exacerbated by grief. It's mourning in America, and it shows in our work (even the funny stuff). Plays dealing with terminal illnesses, especially AIDS, are fast becoming the contemporary theatre's most significant contribution. Think of a national season including Paula Vogel's *Baltimore Waltz,* Cheryl West's *Before It Hits Home,* Scott McPherson's *Marvin's Room,* William Finn's Falsetto plays, John Kelly's *Akin,* Tony Kushner's *Angels in America,* works by Karen Finley, Terrence McNally, Larry Kramer, and William Hoffman. Even the current musical nostalgia of Broadway's *Most Happy Fella, Guys and Dolls, Crazy for You* suggests a redirected grief about what we've lost. The bewilderment of mourning comes through in the theatre community's stunned responses to sustained attacks on the arts by the right-wing radicals. It plays in conversation—in the shared disappointment over the quality and lack of fire in the work itself. Causes for mourning are tallied in the lists we share with one another: who's sick, who's recently died, what will happen when _____ can't work anymore.

As painful as this process of mourning is, denying it would be worse. In some ways, this mourning seems natural, inevitable. As our community ages, founders die, others retire, children grow up to become parents whose own parents age and die. This is happening in the theatre.

Even more troubling, because it feels unnatural, is the sense of hastened mourning AIDS has brought, in which all the injustice one feels over the death of a loved one is intensified because the loved one was really too young to have died. We're in war with no idealism to hang our grief on, and the onslaught continues to ravage our little corner of the culture.

The American theatre is surrounded by its failures, and these must be mourned, too. ACT founder William Ball's recent suicide embodied one type of failure—that of an enormous, imaginative talent, brilliant and difficult, too self-destructive to sustain a career, especially in so decorous a theatre. As others have pointed out in these pages, it's a sad indictment of the theatre community, that such a pioneer would up working as a maitre d' before killing himself.

Some of our theatres are dying out as well, and these failures deserve our grief. Big and small theatres are folding: Los Angeles Theatre Center, Long Island Stage, New Jersey's Whole Theatre, New Playwrights in D.C., Minneapolis's Brass Tacks, New Theatre of Brooklyn, and a number of others. TCG puts the total dead among its own members at 25 in five years, though the actual number—including non-TCG institutions—must be far greater. Even the ones that don't seem worth saving feel like losses. Each takes with it, to paraphrase Donne again, a part of the continent, the main, and sets a bell tolling for all theatre.

Also, we mourn the condition of a world that attacks an art we know as soul-saving. Recent attempts to disembowel the Arts Endowment—and liberal culture in general—provoke grief as much as anger and action. They represent failures of broader kind, failure of leadership that goes far beyond the world of the stage.

We are in a period of mourning because we must be, because there is so much, are so many, to mourn. If recent psychological research teaches us anything, however, it is that the process of mourning our losses is vital to our survival. We can't change without letting go of the past, and we can't let go of something we haven't faced, dealt with, felt our way through.

From mourning we learn about our own humanity, the province of this art. As Elisabeth Kubler-Ross's work with the terminally ill has made so clear, the dying have everything to teach us. The most astounding of these lessons is that of the capacity of human beings to embrace the whole of life, from anger and despair to love and acceptance. Facing the deaths of others, we face our own. We ask the big questions of our lives: What is important? What must I do to die fulfilled? What do I want from my life? How much suffering can a heart take? What gives this suffering meaning?

Is there an analogy between a dying/changing human being and a changing/dying system? I think so. Surely change and death are versions of one another. The mourning process in survivors mirrors the process the process of grief experienced by the dying themselves. We're subject to the same denial, anger, depression and hope when confronted with inevitable change. By mourning its own painful changes, perhaps the theatre can help audiences face this difficult time and experience their own humanity at its most powerful. By embracing change, we might find the courage to transform, to leap into a future worthy of the past.

*   *   *

You are left alone with yourself and the truth, and can never ask Dad, who didn't know anyway and who is deader than mackerel.
—Robert Penn Warren, *All the King's Men*

There are few guides left to ask. The present is a sad mire, and the past a closed shop. We—as members of a most humane profession— must redefine our humanity at this moment. That's where history can help; in history we're not alone. Changes the size of the ones we face have come before at least four times in this fading century: at its birth, following its two world wars and again during the '60s. Each of these changes has been reflected in the theatre's shape and dramaturgy—its re-vision.

Now is such a time, too. Our culture and our art are changing in spite of us. The imperative of multiculturalism and the devastation of AIDS are rewriting our dramatic cannon. Maps change, identities change; loss of the old becomes a spring-board for the new.

Leadership demands not the sustenance of failed systems but the seizing of opportunities such as these to revise our sense of what is important. Our current leaders may feel at home before congressional panels; they may create four associate artist jobs where once there were three. But these accommodations aren't enough. We need leaders who *reframe the purpose of theatre,* who make us see what we're doing in a new light, who spur us to find the energy to change, even if it means risking our jobs and institutional survival. We need new ideas of the theatre, not merely new structures for failing institutions, because institutions root us where we are. Ideas move us forward.

Almost 30 years ago, Hebert Blau demanded that theatre serve as "the Public Art of Crisis." For him and his contemporaries, crisis meant the cold war and its potential for nuclear holocaust. They responded artistically to that crisis and, in so doing, altered the landscape of the theatre. The cold war may be over, but its chill still hangs in the air. Death, far from being a future threat, is a present reality. This paradox provides us with a new starting place.

Today's theatre is more public, reaches more people in more places than ever. For raw material we have grief, rage, confusion and hope. They are paint, clay pieces of wood to build with; they are seeds for something uncertain, as mysterious as the past—maybe even as important. An almanac in Elizabeth Bishop's "sestina" foretells the future this way: *"Time to plant tears."* Now is that kind of time. The soil is waiting.

This essay was originally published in *American Theatre* magazine, July/August 1992.

How Empty is the Vessel?

> Which is the real person, so far as the actor is concerned? Is he
> more real when performing on the stage, or when he is at home? I
> tend to think that for people who have these many, many masks,
> there is no home.
>
> —Robert Jay Lifton, *Boundaries:*
> *Psychological Man in Revolution*

An actor comes home to find his house burned down and his wife a
wreck. "Who did this?" he demands. "Never mind," says the wife to
calm him. "I want to know who's responsible!" he persists. "It doesn't
matter," she says. "What's done is done." "Tell me," he cries; "I'll kill
the person who did this." She hesitates. "It was your agent, John." Actor
pauses, then with rising hope: "My agent came by the *house*?"

A typical joke presents a typical portrait: the actor, blind to the
sufferings of those around him, histrionic, self-absorbed—fixated on his
own success. Add to this description monomaniacal, childish, vain,
helpless, slightly mystic, intense, vapid—in love with the animated face
in the makeup mirror—and you have the mythic actor: Narcissus on
parade. Of course, everyone in the theatre knows actors who fit a whole
different set of adjectives, including sensitive, passionate, compelling,
idealistic, admirable, tough, intelligent—even learned—and more. Still,
humor reveals our biases, sometimes reinforces them, and in spite of the
well-mixed reality, it's the joke version of the actor that survives when
he or she leaves the room.

For American actors the dream of a theatrical home went up in
smoke long ago. Once, the promise of a decentralized theatre, based in
art instead of commerce, held out the possibility of a "normal" life:
community, real homes, family. Moreover, the ideal of company—
which often meant "acting company"—upon which many theatres were
founded, conjured up visions of a consistent and supportive artistic
community. But somewhere in the high-powered development of
theatre companies over the past three decades, actors have deserted or
been elbowed out of the institutional theatre family. They became its
homeless.

Unlike the above caricature, most actors noticed the smoke and
did more than rant; they set out to rebuild—elsewhere. As homeless
people will do, actors have made their beds under other roofs when they
could, and in the shelters of television and film they are well provided
for. Training programs have, if not retooled, at least somewhat
reoriented accordingly, readying students for careers in many media,
instead of preparing them for lives on stage. Theatres, meanwhile,

which have failed to sufficiently care for their own, find themselves vying with the "major media"—against all odds—for the high level of talent they've grown to expect.

Now, as some of the people running our nation's theatres commit anew to reincorporating the actors into the body of the theatre—raising salaries, building companies, searching for what's been lost—it's important to understand the psychic consequences of institutional behavior on the artist, the institution, and the whole community, and to acknowledge the damage the bureaucratization of theatre can do to the spirit of the actor.

We've grown accustomed to identifying "modern man" with the actor. Sociologist Ervin Goffman crystallized this connection in his famous study, *The Presentation of Self in Everyday Life*. "As human beings," Goffman writes, "we are presumably creatures of variable impulse with moods and energies that change from one moment to the next. As characters put on for an audience, however, we must not be subject to ups and downs." More and more, Goffman explains, "a certain bureaucratization of the spirit," is needed to enable us to "give a perfectly homogeneous performance at every appointed time." Like actors, people living in the modern world are expected to *perform*, on cue and in sync however we're cast, regardless of the streams of actual feeling we experience that run counter to the scene we play.

This ongoing command performance called life requires players to subjugate their personal drives and desires to outside demands. (A simplified example: Being "on" at an audition or business meeting no matter how rudely you've been treated, how long you've been made to wait, or which of your close friends died this week.) Whether in modern life or in the theatre, the constant pressure to perform has brutal consequences for the human spirit. Unrelenting attention to the requirements of others drives a wedge between the individual and his or her own needs, a mortal blow for artists who must remain hypersensitive to their interior lives in order to reveal them on the stage.

The acting process is naturally a narcissistic journey. Actors at work share with young children a "boundarilessness"—the egoless condition of seeing themselves in everyone and everything, which enables them to project themselves into a wide range of characters. In this way the actor is trained to exist as a "possible" being and to resist emotional constraint and even self-definition. Actors cultivate empathy—fine-tuning their bodies to the play of emotion like a violinist sensitizes the ear to the harmonics of sound—and the belief that, as human beings, we are mutable, varied and interesting. The work breeds a kind of inner-directed voyeurism, a fascination with one's own emotions that, if the self were a pool, would make it easy to drown.

In the best of situations, this necessary narcissism is balanced by the actor's adult intelligence and the collaborative context of theatre, in which the demands of working together with equal artistic partners offset the constant pull inward. The largely democratic process of making plays, and the requirements of the day-to-day business of acting, demands the same sense of self (ego) that the actor's exploration can suspend. When this collaborative counterforce fails and the actor is cut adrift—either through lack of consistent work, absence of a safe home base or hospitable creative environment—his or her isolation within the community grows. With their position (and, therefore, self-esteem) devalued, actors either grow lonelier and less able to work freely and confidently or they get defensive, difficult, grandiose—what we misguidedly call "egotistical"—subjugating others' processes to the greedy needs of their own. In both cases a dangerous rift opens between that sensitive and empathetic interior life and the exterior behavior.

This chasm between the outer mask and the inner life, building up the former at the expense of the latter—what popular psychology calls narcissism—is perpetuated by families and cultures who exploit their members to their own ends, instead of facilitating individual development. The values of contemporary America, as social critic Christopher Lasch argued in his 1979 bestseller *The Culture of Narcissism*, reinforce narcissism in its citizens by undermining individualism and fostering dependence on "the state, the corporation and other bureaucracies." Narcissism, he contends, "represents the psychological dimension of this dependence…the narcissist depends on others to validate his self-esteem. He cannot live without an admiring audience. His apparent freedom from family ties and institutional constraints does not free him to stand alone or to glory in his individuality. On the contrary, it contributes to his insecurity, which he can overcome only by seeing his 'grandiose self' reflected in the attentions of others, or by attaching himself to those who radiate celebrity, power, and charisma."

While Lasch's trenchant analysis of America's narcissistic culture and the menace of bureaucratic dependence helps illustrate the conditions of modern life (a mirror for the conditions of artistic life), his prickly dismissal of therapeutic sensibilities, together with his yearning for the rugged individualism and work ethic of an earlier paternalistic time, smack of a cultural conservatism dangerous in these dark days. Nevertheless, his description captures the false romance of the "freelance" or "independent" theatre artist in America, neither free nor independent, glorying in an almost desperate grandiosity about the importance of the art, totally dependent on the largess of the institution.

Narcissism, then, is a response to powerlessness. Deprived of control over his or her own life, the narcissist constructs a grandiose self-image and scrambles to keep that image sturdy. The stronger the mask, the safer its creator is from the feelings of pain and fear and frustration the mask was made to hide. The mask, meanwhile, is designed to give the outside world what is wants ("You're such a pretty girl; you don't want to make yourself ugly by being angry.").

Years ago, when all that we call "resident theatre" was in its American infancy, many institutions supported the actor's sense of possibility by encouraging company casting and promoting versatility and range. By establishing homes that provided some security, encouraged long-term relationships, and created relatively "safe spaces" in which to explore, theatres cushioned actors against the dangers of their own boundarilessness. They could swing out on emotional limbs and trust that others would be there with them and that the ground would be steady and soft if they fell. The communal ethic of the company compensated for the self-centered nature of the process.

Time and a hopeless tangle of semi-related conditions have complicated the nonprofit arena's early intentions and added to the confused state of actors within the theatre community. The growth of theatres as institutions, a process meant to make the artist's home stable into the future, paradoxically made the economics of securing that long-term home unfeasible. Simultaneously, film and TV options opened up (and invited stage actors in), holding out fistfuls of dollars and a whole new level of celebrity. As a result, actors (and their agents) have grown reluctant to commit to ongoing theatre work. Meanwhile, the boom of new play production on regional stages, previously preempted by Broadway's stronghold over rights, increased pressures on non-profit producers to cast to type rather than settle for the compromises of company casting. All this—and the watering-down of theatre training to accommodate business and film and TV components—have diluted commitments all around.

Out of this jumble of cross-purposes has emerged a system of theatre which functions as a narcissistic culture, fostering dependence without supplying reciprocal respect for the individual. Actors are expected to launch themselves out, and land on their own two feet, no matter how jagged the surface below.

The real-world demands of the actor's life have also changed. The "safe spaces" of the theatrical home have once again (as in the days before the advent of nonprofit companies) given way to the grind of the marketplace. In addition to all the obvious horrors of the casting process and the competing demands of film and TV, actors face a psychic/artistic threat from their slalom past agents and managers and casting directors, directors and producers: that is, the danger of fixity.

In contrast to the empathetic state that actors nurture in themselves to move from life to life in role after role, the marketplace increasingly expects the actor to "be one thing." The toll of typecasting and the commoditization of actors tells in the art itself, as the nonprofit theatre business becomes more like the rest of "the business" and steers actors away from their empathetic impulses and their sense of the possible in art. Instead of such indefinables as emotional range, versatility, and depth, actors come to be measured by more concrete traits: physical type, looks, the image they project, how well they conform to someone's idea of a role. The ability to work well with a group takes a backseat to looking right with the group, as if the theatrical experience were dependent on packaging.

Moreover, the increasingly businesslike practices of the profession (including the nonprofit theatre) tend to reward narcissistic behavior. As Lasch points out, "The narcissist often enjoys considerable success. The management of personal impressions comes naturally to him and his mastery of its intricacies serves him well in political and business organizations where performance now counts for less than 'visibility,' 'momentum,' and a winning record." (Lasch anticipated recent politics where the image is more important than the content—and where "spin doctors" handle "damage control" and "impression management.") Likewise, the exigencies of the marketplace make actors with name recognition, media credits, and careers "on a roll" hot property, even in the alternative, nonprofit arena. The aggressive role of job hunter hardens the artist and endangers his or her natural receptivity. Attractive faces and amiable manners are encouraged by the casting process, and are then expected to melt away to reveal the requisite rage or grief in front of an audience. But when the pretty face refuses to "get ugly" on stage, the work suffers and everyone's disappointed.

Of course, the discrepancy between the interior life and the exterior product comes with the actor's territory and part of the work of acting has always been to tap the inner pool of feeling and sympathy while, at the same time, modulating the exterior, the mask. (In fact, we recognize this duality every time we argue about actors working "inside-out" or "outside-in.") Unfortunately, though, the more itinerant actors become, the more they're treated as interchangeable commodities—the more they *are* their resumes—the more the interior/exterior is disrupted.

Narcissism, cultural or psychological, is a painful state. It isolates the individual from others and creates a disturbing split between the real self and the false, face-to-the world self. W.H. Auden speaks the language of the theatre when he writes about this rift in his essay "Hic et Ille": "When I consider others I can easily believe that their bodies express their personalities and that the two are inseparable. But it is impossible for me not to feel that my body is other than I, that I inhabit it like a house, and that my face is a mask which, with or without my consent, conceals my real nature from others."

Auden's mask is an involuntary prison which, instead of revealing his essential character—as the theatrical mask is designed to do—conceals it. The loneliness or alienation or despair or whatever we call that pervasive condition of modern life bleeds into the crack between our performed selves and our inner ones. Both the process and the result of theatre have an obligation to explore, even heal this interior fracture. More than that, the theatre builds community in a way that offers up an alternative to isolation and "performed life." It offers an opportunity to work honestly with one's self, to share the discoveries of that honesty with fellow artists and to communicate the findings to a larger community. When the mask suffocates the individual, it weakens the possibility of joining with others.

By reinforcing the actor's mask at the expense of his or her emotional fluidity, the theatre community risks creating its own Frankenstein monster: the actor who is all mask. Coupled with the insecurities of short-term employment, the power of the institution—which adds to the sense actors have of being insignificant and interchangeable—has made it impossible for actors to complain, criticize, demand, or generally speak the truth to those in power over their livelihoods. We—the non-actors of the community—have asked for the mask of compliance and that's what we've gotten.

But added to the barrier between collaborators is the one between actors and their own better selves. Without laboratories in which to "act on" their profession's natural narcissism (by which I mean the self without limits), they more and more must "act it out." As history has shown, the actor, treated like property, begins to treat him or herself as such. Actors are pushed to objectify themselves and then to worry the surface of that object (themselves)—like a face with too much makeup—until it becomes opaque rather than, as the mask at its best is, revealing. Devalued, confused by the tug-of-war between human and business and cut off from the emotional source of their power by the constant call to meet the needs of others instead of following their own artistic impulses, they run the risk of becoming truly empty vessels, unable to fill themselves up, except on command.

*   *   *

Bertolt Brecht's *The Good Person of Setzuan* offers a parable of the actor's bind. When the Gods come to the "half-Westernized" gates of Setzuan in search of "good" people, they find only one—the prostitute Shen Te—willing to put them up for the night. (At first even she hesitates to help because she's expecting a client and rent is due.) The Gods, eager to believe goodness is a simple thing, beat a hasty retreat, admonishing Shen Te to "be good." She knows better, though. The economic realities of life in Setzuan make it impossible to live and stay good.

Their injunction tears her in two: "To be good to others/And myself at the same time/I could not do it." She is beset by greedy opportunists, must fight not to starve herself by feeding others. Since the Gods won't accept the complexities of Shen Te's world, she must split herself. She must play one role at a time: the good woman or the economic realist. For the latter, she transforms herself into the ruthless businessman, Shen Te's "cousin" Shui Ta. Shen Te does good; Shui Ta does what needs to be done to survive, even if it's criminal.

Actors suffer the same split: not just between economic pragmatism and the holy demands of their art, but the split from the complexities of the self that make us good and bad, angry and pretty, ambivalent and directed, all wrapped up. Like Brecht's hotfooted gods, the "industry" of art in America asks actors to pick and choose "just one thing" from among their many selves. The theatre sends out double messages: despairing the effects of screen habits and poor training on stage acting and commitment, while, at the same time, buying into many of the values of Hollywood—type-casting, single project packaging with "name" actors from film and TV, or elevating the appeal of "hot" talent from large cities over dedicated talent from local communities. Increasingly, the system requires actors to be the thing they play, to stick with the mask—until acting, instead of serving as a means of exploring a multifaceted humanity, becomes an impediment to it. Actors are asked to perform all the time, onstage and off, until you cannot tell the actor from the act, until the actor cannot tell.

It's no wonder that, in the actor's case, Goffman's "bureaucratization of the spirit" has run alongside the bureaucratization of the art. Potential collaborators (artistic equals) are kept apart by legions of intermediaries (and not a few parasites): casting directors, agents, personal managers, assistants, theatre administrators, union reps, and dramaturgs. The bureaucracies of casting and theatre production have polarized artists—already sundered from their own better selves and dreams of theatre—from each other.

Our systems have created an environment that's antithetical to the actor's *human* heart. These systems have dispirited the actor and promoted the idea of actor-as-joke, actor-as-victim, or actor-as-prima donna when actors most need to participate in the process of improving the American theatre. In place of institutional distance, we need personal concern, empathy, and even what might be called love—not for the talent because it's exploitable, but for the person of the actor, including that person's anger, fear, neediness, temperamental outbursts, vanity, brilliance, passion, humor—all of it. On the other hand, actors need to take more responsibility for their circumstances and their personal and artistic growth. They need to honor commitments and to demand responsibility and partnership. The best defense against treatment that reduces you to a partial person is to respond as a whole person, a vital artist, a dedicated member of the community.

Certainly there are programs that can address the problems: higher salaries, better housing, increased commitment to companies and positions of artistic power for actors, planning farther in advance, and more diligent and respectful notification procedures for auditioners, for example. But any procedures have to go hand in hand with greater sensitivity to the actor's struggle—trying to find a way to preserve a self and deepen a craft while colleagues and "friends" struggle to commodify her, avoid him, or shove them both into easily labeled little boxes. This sensitivity is demonstrable in little ways as well as big, in personal gestures even more than institutional ones. The nurturing of actors demands breaking down distance the bureaucracy of theatre has created; it calls for careful listening. Performing in the theatre is the most personal of acts; it requires *personal* care.

This essay was originally published in *American Theatre* magazine, October, 1990.

Theatre On The Couch

If, in the course of a performance, an actor or audience member fell ill, everyone present would know what to do: look for a doctor in the house. What would happen, though, if the house itself was ailing—not the building, but the institution? Who gets the call when a theatre is sick, fostering unhealthy behavior among its staff, or going through a painful transition? What kind of therapy is available for a theatre community in crisis?

In a culture increasingly obsessed with physical and emotional health, it's more than a little shocking that America's theatres have no forum or framework for addressing the health of its workers and the psychological consequences of its methods. Nationwide, theatre lags far behind private industry when it comes to dealing with mental health issues. Corporations have started pumping money into treatment of alcoholism, drug addiction, burnout, and psychological dysfunction, problems that theatres too often avoid. Moreover, even the largest businesses study and try to improve human dynamics on-the-job; theatres are usually too broke or too busy to do the same.

Only in the relative calm of theatre service organizations has the search for a kind of institutional therapy hesitantly begun. Theatre Bay Area, San Francisco's service organization for theatre, brought in a clinical psychologist to usher the staff through the terminal illness of one staff member and the imminent departure of the group's charismatic director. TBA's Midwest counterpart, Theatre Chicago, runs confidential meetings between theatre managers and medical doctors, psychiatrists, and substance abuse professionals at Northwestern Medical Center for the Performing Arts. In New York, New Dramatists has begun experimenting with a theatre-trained therapist who helps the workshop's member playwrights overcome writing blocks.

The introduction of therapeutic models into theatre art and management is part of an attempt to heal from within an acknowledged invalid: the institutional theatre. Of these models, perhaps the most pertinent describes theatre as an addictive system, diseased and in need of recovery. An addictive system is what it sounds like: a system that fosters addiction and shares symptoms with those addicted to it. In her book *When Society Becomes an Addict*, Anne Wilson Schaef compares an addictive system to a hologram, where "each piece of the hologram contains the entire structure of the entire hologram." That is, each piece of the system has the whole system in it, and whole addictive system shares characteristics of the addict. To treat the system, then, the best bet is to change the way the individual thinks and functions within it. What that means for the addictive system of theatre is clear: we can't make theatre a healthy part of the culture until we make ourselves—as artists and managers—healthy in the theatre.

It's no secret that many of us come to the theatre from dysfunctional and troubled families. An eight-year-old knows that art of any kind, especially this most social of arts, is the great escape, and sometimes the great healer. My own family history is full of alcoholism, debt, and gambling, so naturally I take to the model of theatre as an addictive system. The theatre provided for me what my own home couldn't, and so I was drawn to the family-feel of acting ensembles and collectively created work. Time after time, though, like some perverse magic, I reconstructed my own family relations in the theatre: mediating between narcissistic individuals, creating intimate relationships that broke up weeks later, living on the edge of debt in theatres in debt, and feeling most alive conquering 11th-hour crises. Looking—like any other addict—for a "hit," for the "rush" of opening night, for an easier way to "come down" after rehearsal or performance. The thrill of the theatre "high" was the only cure for feeling misunderstood, victimized, homeless at home.

If there's a playwright for the theatre of the '80s, one who understands the addictive home, it's Chekhov. His portrait of Madame Ranevskya's family in *The Cherry Orchard* captures the spirit of today's institutional theatre. The family is threatened with losing their beautiful home to pay off growing debts. In an increasingly pragmatic world (like ours), they party too much, spend money they don't have and can't get, thrive on crisis and pain, escape into romantic fantasies of the past and future, and run away from their problems by closing their eyes to changes all around them. These characters have an inflated sense of self-importance, assuming themselves to be invulnerable even as they feel victimized and powerless.

The only hope of saving the Ranevskayas' fortunes is held out by Lopakhin, a *nouveau riche* neighbor who operates as part investment broker, part real estate developer, and part marketing director. He suggests they chop up the family's useless cherry orchard—whose anachronistic splendor he misses altogether—and sell it off as summer condos. The family, lost in denial and a general narcissistic haze, fails to heed all too obvious warnings and loses its home to this provincial Donald Trump and its culture to the ax of hard economic facts.

In the theatre, we labor under this kind of pragmatism daily: the shrinking of government and corporate support, an aging and dwindling audience, and a loss of prestige in an increasingly corporate culture. To stay afloat in the post-Reagan '80s means being more like Lopakhin: financier, developer, marketing strategist. We have to keep our feet on solid ground, keep our minds moving forward, and keep our emotions in check. Even in this most personal of arts, we have to become impersonal, bureaucratic, objective. Theatre people learn and adapt quickly, so we've become good Lopakhins. We keep up with the new technology; we dress for success, we run in the red; and we inadvertently cut ourselves off from some of our deepest sympathies while defending our work. Moreover, by so diligently looking out for ourselves, we isolate from a huge and diverse population of others.

While most American theatres were founded on principals separating art from commerce and devoted to building companies or families of like-minded artists, the struggle to survive these times has forced theatres to ensure a future life by increased institutionalization, even at the risk of displacing the artists they exist to serve. The communal energy of 20 years ago is behind us. No one in the theatre—least of all recent college graduates—is young anymore.

The ax that's been swinging at the theatrical Cherry Orchard has done real damage. Probably the greatest loss is a sense of theatre as a home and family for artists. The greatest practical threat to our theatrical future isn't that the NEA will shrivel up and die; it's that artists—actors, writers, designers, and directors—will leave the profession for good, give it up for dead, go away to television or film, or to other lives altogether.

And who can blame them? Few freelance artists can make a living in the theatre. That's old news. The newer news is that they also can't make a life. People who aren't getting financial rewards need human ones. The hours alone are enough to do you in. The traveling beats you down. The creative process has been sucked of sufficient time and flexibility to make it rewarding. We don't even have the space and time to treat each other as people, instead of as cogs in some perpetual motion collaboration. The way we make theatre is not only often unfulfilling; it is unhealthy, fostering a lifestyle that encourages isolation, loneliness, crisis, personal debt, and psychic pain from, among other things, too many comings and goings.

Everyone I know who has quit the theatre is happier and healthier. An ex-stage manager now trains welfare mothers for work; the New York City government treats her better than theatres ever did. She spends weekends skiing and is in her first serious relationship in years. A founding managing director now teaches the illiterate in Washington, D.C.; after almost a decade of putting her own creative life second to her theatre's, she sings regularly in new operas and chorales. One former artistic director is finally concentrating on his writing, another on his painting, and a third on creating oral histories with Jewish communities. None of them has sold out and none of them is sorry to be out. They have weekends to think and live and read. They have time for families. They have renewed energy for love and a home life and personal growth. They are recovering their health.

Certainly, the problems we face aren't all internal. The horrors of the '80s affect us literally and figuratively. AIDS, addiction, and homelessness, the decade's triple threat, are our demons as well. Friends and lovers and colleagues and mentors and people we've never met but wish we had are dying in a horrible plague that we have no control over. The theatre community shares this daily pain, this new ritual—that we're all too young to have—of checking the obituaries first thing every morning. We barely have time to mourn or help each other though personal losses. We are all affected by a society whose life is more and more driven by addictions: to faster drugs, stronger denial, and deeper debt. And, in addition to being surrounded by the homeless, we are among them. Our artists and staffs are among the middle class without pension plans and insurance and protection from the kind of catastrophes that put people on the streets. Our theatres, too, are in danger: According to a report by the Alliance of Resident Theatres/New York, 50 percent of all Off and Off-Off Broadway theatres stand to lose their leases in the next three years.

We can't expect to tend to any of these problems effectively, however, if we can't take care of ourselves. If we can't break through our own denial about death—express and share our grief and outrage—how can we expect to break through the deeper denial of governors and policy makers? How can we demand the kind of living we deserve when we're addicted to the struggle of debt and thrill in the image of ourselves as starving artists fighting to overcome societal insensitivity?

What would it mean to make the theatre a healthier home? What does it mean to call theatre a home at all? These questions were addressed last year in *The Artistic Home*, a TCG report based on discussions between 120 or so artistic directors and dozens of independent artists. After writing the report, it occurred to me that this "home" artistic directors longed to create was in fact being created. It was, though, being made the way many of us learned to make homes—dysfunctionally. It was being built in the image of an addictive family whose emphasis is on maintenance and survival at all costs and not on the health of its members. Like alcoholic families, caught up in hiding and defending our secrets from the world, theatre people tend to be isolated, insular, and incestuous. We lose ourselves in our own hype. We waste precious energy trying to cover up our failings. We put survival of buildings ahead of the health of artists.

The future of theatre depends on improving the quality of these homes and our lives within them, because the way we make theatre is as important as what we make. The way we treat ourselves as artists and managers is as fundamental to our survival as where the dollars will come from or who will watch us play.

The aim of therapeutic thinking within the theatre is to separate the worker from the workplace, to distinguish between the theatre and the family. Again and again, artistic directors struggle to learn "I am not my theatre." None of us who work in the theatres are our theatre, just as we are not our families. We may be driven by them. We may be unable to change them, but we don't have to *be* them. We can change.

Once we've stopped acting like Chekov's Ranevskaya family and stopped pretending that this is the only way to live and that we'll never lose the orchard, we can start to recover some of what we've lost: that is, the creative, communal and spiritual impulses that are the best of what got us into this in the first place. Certainly, the ax is already at work on the trees, but like addicts or children of addicts or members of any dysfunctional community, we've gained a lot of strength navigating the dangerous and often uncaring world, strength we can build on.

What are these strengths? One thing we've learned is that we have to rely on ourselves. We've even learned to make our isolation work. Performance art, for example, has sprung from the need to be self-sufficient. Performance artists are the runaways of the contemporary theatre, forced to make it solo on the streets, learning survival from fine artists, clowns, or whoever can teach them about weathering isolation creatively. Now, after years of looking after themselves when theatres couldn't afford to shelter them, institutional theatres are finally taking them in, and in some cases, depending on those performers' success for the theatre's sustenance.

Second, we've learned that no matter how isolated we feel, we are a community made up of many communities, and we can provide enormous support for each other if we open up and talk and share our work and fears and struggles. In rooms across the country, organizations such as TBA, TCG, ART/NY and Theatre Chicago remind members of the profession that we're not alone, that we have common concerns and tremendous power as a community: economic power, political power, creative power, and spiritual power. Dysfunctional family systems isolate the individuals within them; all recovery programs (particularly the 12-step programs based on Alcoholics Anonymous) stress bringing the individual back into the experience of community. The theatre as a community can do a lot to sustain its members even in the worst of times.

We've also learned how to change. The theatre has remade itself several times in the past 25 years and it will do so again. We've had to be canny to survive; we've had to be adaptable. The troubled family resists change, just as the healthy family embraces it. Transformation is the basis of theatre. If we want to use what we do to transform the world around us, we have to be prepared to accept changes in ourselves.

Talking about health means thinking forward instead of waiting for crisis to hit. Theatres need catastrophic-illness plans and humane policies for supporting sick colleagues. We need to develop child-care programs for new mothers and fathers. We need to take stress and burnout and the term "theatre junkie" seriously. We need to stop defending ourselves and find ways to open our artistic homes to artists and audiences who don't share our privilege. And we need to shake the guilt that keeps us from asking for and demanding adequate financial support. We aren't unworthy and we don't have to apologize for trying to meet our needs.

Theatre people have begun looking ahead and acknowledging that the way we work isn't working. They're starting to take concrete steps, big and small, to improve the conditions in the homes we've built. The following are ways new artistic and managerial leaders are changing the structures by which we make theatre and looking for healthy ways to re-integrate the individual into the institutional home.

For example, large and mid-size theatres like the Goodman Theatre of Chicago and California's Berkeley Repertory Theatre are expanding their artistic staffs and weaving associates and resident artists more thoroughly into the fabric of their theatres. In fact, Baltimore's Center Stage recently received a huge NEA grant to expand a thriving associate artistic program that involves designers, directors, and playwrights in the theatre's daily workings. At the same time, the Guthrie of Minneapolis announced a $25 million endowment campaign—the first of its size—aimed at substantially increasing actor salaries.

Theatres are also expanding their visions by opening their planning to artists and managers from a wider range of cultural backgrounds. Oakland Ensemble Theatre in California, Seattle Group Theatre, Los Angeles Theatre Center, and Minneapolis's Mixed Blood Theatre are breaking through the traditional insularity of the theatre community by integrating their staffs and productions at every level.

Long-standing ensembles—California's San Francisco Mime Troupe, American Conservatory Theatre, Eureka Theatre, and Dell'Arte Players, the Bloomsburg Theatre Ensemble of Pennsylvania, Mabou Mines and the Wooster Group in New York, American Repertory Theatre in Cambridge, Mass., Washington, D.C.'s Arena Stage, The Road Company of Tennessee and Roadside Theatre in Kentucky—are still, against all odds, sustaining and celebrating the power of the acting company. At the same time, other ensembles like Steppenwolf in Chicago and New York's Pan Asian Repertory Theatre and Circle Repertory Company are experimenting with more flexible commitments that give artists the security of a home base, while allowing them the time and space to work elsewhere, including the more lucrative worlds of film and TV. Theatres are likewise exploring the options of sabbaticals, leave-time, and mental health days for overworked and over-isolated staff members.

Finally and significantly, service organizations are pioneering health programs to support their members through change. TBA has sponsored coping workshops and seminars, including those for cancer patients. TCG offered sessions on AIDS and catastrophic illness policy at its national theatre conference. Theatre Chicago has developed an extensive "wellness program" in response to illness and addiction in their community. Aimed at prevention, the program disseminates health information and holds stress prevention workshops; they assist mangers in planning compassionate policies for employees' mental health and catastrophic illness; and they make sure that AIDS is addressed at every league function.

This is a partial list of practical ideas, many of them only ideas. They may not make our personal, theatrical, or societal situation seem any less dire, but they prove that the wheels are in motion for change. We're not stuck and we don't have to despair.

When the Cherry Orchard is finally sold, the Ranevskaya family finds itself strangely relieved. They've lost something beautiful, but they've also given up an illusion that was, at its core, paternalistic, decadent, and unhealthy. The real struggle—the struggle to deny reality—is over. They can face their various futures with some hope and a greater realism than they're accustomed to. The theatre community of the late '80s is better prepared to face a difficult future than Chekhov's dramatic family. We're stronger, more self-aware, more creative, more flexible—and less alone.

This essay was originally published in *American Theatre* magazine, May, 1989.

The Theatre of Place

Off The Map: Charting an American Theatre of Place

The Stage Manager, you remember, welcomes us into Grover's Corners with exquisite specificity. He points out all the churches—each denomination—town hall, the post office and jail, a row of stores, schools, houses, down to the burdock in Mrs. Gibbs' garden and to the butternut tree "right here." "Polish Town's across the tracks," he tells us, as if it occurs to him that someone might someday write *Their Town* about the marginalized Poles. By the end of Act I, Thornton Wilder, the playwright behind this tour, connects this pinpoint locale with a universe beyond imagining. We hear tell of a letter addressed: "Jane Crofut; The Crofut Farm; Grover's Corners; Sutton County; New Hampshire; United States of America; Continent of North America; Western Hemisphere; the Earth; the Solar System; the Universe; the Mind of God." From a single soul on a tiny plot of land to the mind of god.

Works of theatre take aim like the address on Jane Crofut's letter: They begin with a small circle on a map—the one the characters and, possibly, the audience inhabit—and cross time and space, linking us as they go, guiding our awareness toward the connective mysteries of creation. Ideally, like the letter, they reach their destination.

All theatre is local. The Greeks knew it, as did the Elizabethans, the U.S. frontier troupers, the Dadaists, and artists of almost every epoch in theatrical history. Only twentieth-century America seems regularly to forget, in the hunger to mass market art, to move it, to reach the greatest numbers. As a result, we exist in a state of perpetual tension between the local and the national, the regional and the Center.

It would be nice to believe that this tension—specifically between Broadway and the theatre of America's other cities and towns—was a dead issue. It's not. Broadway forever doubles as artistic black hole and a radiating center of the English-speaking theatre. Less than a decade ago, an exhibit at The Museum of the City of New York, called "Broadway: The History of the American Theatre," defined out of existence all nonmusical, non-Broadway theatre with a single "the." Ethel Merman had a wall and Rodgers & Hammerstein had a corner; others, from Le Gallienne to Le Mamet, not a mention. Provincetown, San Francisco, and Kentucky—all blown off the face of the theatrical-historical map by a twenty-square-block piece of real estate.

Meanwhile, the influential movement to "decentralize" the theatre, now a half-century old, remains chronically schizoid: is it regional (referring to place), resident (because it provides homes for artists), or Broadway bound? Is our nation's theatre centrifugal—perpetually in flight from New York—or centripetal—constantly headed back? Argue the preeminence of non-New York theatre (even to educated theatregoers) without using the Great White Center as your reference point. It can't be done. "You see, *Angels in America* began there and there...Wendy Wasserstein premiered her Tony-winning plays over there...August Wilson? Connect the dots." In 2003, Nilo Cruz's *Anna In the Tropics* stunned insiders by winning a Pulitzer Prize when only Miami audiences had seen it. Almost immediately, skeptics began questioning its value by asking, "Yes, but, how will it do on Broadway?" It didn't do well. The Prize's prestige didn't carry any more weight than it had eleven years earlier when Robert Schenkkan's *The Kentucky Cycle* became the first non-New York play to be Pulitzered and then got pummeled by the big city press. Even today, New York, specifically Broadway, is the final validator.

From its beginnings, the regional theatre sought out, but out is where it never quite got. What will it take to cut the cord that keeps Chicago, New Haven, L.A. tied to the mythical middle of midtown Manhattan?

What it will take, what it has taken, is a different idea of theatre, one that's been crystallizing over the past ten or fifteen years away from traditional centers of the art. New breeds of artists, more far-flung and unassuming, have broken the centrifugal-centripetal deadlock, not by forcing it but by walking away. A coincidence of era, the will to diversity, and a hardening of American theatrical arteries has propelled numerous theatre artists to the most unlikely spots: rural byroads, urban housing projects, quiet towns, and communities in crisis. They've staked out Grover's Corners *and* Polish Town across the tracks. On their way they're creating something truly radical and more uniquely American than the European-modeled institutional theatres: a professional, activist, community theatre of place.

*   *   *

It's called Jewish Geography, but you don't have to be Jewish to play. I learned the game at college in Protestant Iowa, surrounded by other Jews from Long Island, New Jersey, and the north shore of Chicago. Elsewhere, though, it's played by African Americans, Mennonites, and French semioticians. The game consists of two questions: 1) "Where are you from?" followed by, 2) "Do you know _____?" The blank is filled in with the name of someone else the questioner knows from the town or community identified in the answer to number one. The point of the game is to create instant community. By establishing shared knowledge of a place, you can find people you have in common. By discovering common ties, you connect yourself to new people in a new, shared place.

Theatrical events follow the same course. They move from place, common ground, to the people inhabiting it. Performers and audiences occupy the same room in a particular place on the globe. From Illyria to the South Pacific, however exotic the setting, the actual location of the play is always *here*. Beginning in the mid-eighties, "site-specific" theatres, such as New York's En Garde Arts and the Hillsborough Moving Company of Tampa capitalized on this fact by commissioning theatrical work for nontheatrical—"found"—spaces: hotels, parks, docks, abandoned buildings in splendid decay. Watching these "pieces," we participate not in the conventions of the stage but in the fact of a singular place. Likewise, environmental theatres of the sixties, such as Richard Schechner's Performance Group, revised the performer-spectator relationship by reinventing, with each production, the architecture of the theatre.

Even classics, which survive by universal appeal, start place specific. When Wilder set out to boil the theatre down to its essentials, as a way of probing the painful, transitory beauty of everyday life, he hit upon a bare stage, actors as actors, and the details of place. Moliere's another kind of example, three centuries away. We can laugh with recognition at the type of miser, misanthrope, or religious hypocrite he sketches, but when he wrote the plays he often had actual people in mind, many of whom were sitting in the audience, vying for a seat near King Louis. Most everybody watching knew everybody else. Sometimes the guy who thought he was being lampooned gave himself away by writing a furious letter of protest to the King. Sometimes, if the joke's butt was another actor, he'd stage his own counterattack—a re*butt*al. It was local satire, interclaque attack.

America's current theatre of place is an often-activist, community-based art that dreams globally and acts locally. It belongs not to regions or centers but to specific, square-yard-by-square-yard pieces of turf. If "decentralization" was a battle cry for the regional theatre, "recentralization" might be a motto for the new pioneers: to re-center the American theatre in neighborhoods and communities, from fishing villages of the West to the Main Streets of Pennsylvania to the Flatbush section of Brooklyn. The lure or repulsion of Broadway doesn't enter into it; sometimes, what we usually think of as theatre doesn't either.

Because it builds on the singularity of a where, no two artists or groups are alike. This makes defining a "movement" slippery. The shapes change, the means vary, but the primary ends remain the same: to foster community within an established place.

Some troupes seem fairly conventional, except for a devotion to their hometowns unthinkable for urban institutional theatres. The Bloomsburg Theatre Ensemble in rural Pennsylvania, for example, offers up a standard nonprofit repertoire in an area that, with a population near 12,000, should never be able to sustain a professional company; moreover, ensemble members are as intimately involved with the town's governance and economic struggles (the sustenance of a viable downtown, for instance) as they are with its cultural life. "It's the regional theatre goal cubed," a company member explained when I visited BTE, "not just a theatre in every major city, but one in each community." The tiny outposts of Northern California have been home to no fewer than ten permanent theatre companies (including the improbably long-lived Dell 'Arte Players in Blue Lake), back-to-the-land radicals with a taste for political satire and a survivalist dependence on their neighbors.

The roots of these companies are deep, not just geographically but historically as well. It's arguable that the first art theatres in America were, in fact, theatres of place, from the Little Theatre of Chicago (1912), the Toy Theatre of Boston (1912), and the Wisconsin Dramatic Society (1911), to university-based companies like the North Dakota and Carolina Playmakers. Even further back, art theatres began as part of the process of American assimilation and immigrant community-building through settlement houses, like Chicago's Hull House and New York's Henry Street Settlement, home to the renowned Neighborhood Playhouse.

Other contemporary artists gather material from actual places without settling in them. At the height of the solo performance boom in the nineties, confessional storytelling co-existed with more journalistic work. *Some People*, for example, Danny Hoch's one-man cavalcade of Brooklyn characters, provoked audiences to listen to the distinct strains of language and dialect that make up the five-borough Babel. His linguistic mimicry was precisely geographical, an artistic map of his street corner of the world. One of America's most original and successful solo performers, Anna Deavere Smith, began by culling material from women she met on the road, before setting her sights on the citizens of racially divided neighborhoods like Crown Heights, Brooklyn and South Central, L.A. She interviewed and taped her subjects, and then incisively impersonated them on stage, in their own words. Both these soloists created, and continue to create, personal/political landscapes, mapping the American present as they went.

What further sets this late-twentieth-century avant-garde apart from the movement that brought art theatre to mainland America is its insistence that the *process* of theatre, as much as the product, is integral to the nation's daily life, wherever it's lived. Fighting a national drift towards unconnectedness, these artists dig their heels into the soil of established communities, either for extended stays or for good.   Professional artists work with, not just *for*, audiences and amateurs. When the Cornerstone Theatre Company revises classic plays with folks from Watts, the Santa Monica malls, or the Chinatown of L.A., where the company settled several years ago after its itinerant beginnings, a sense of shared place animates the final product. In its earliest work with the citizens of Marfa, Texas or Port

78

Gibson, Mississippi, the company helped transform the landscape as well, by leaving newly formed theatres behind.

Sometime the theatre of place begins with the lore of a spot on the map. In Colquitt, Georgia, insiders and outsiders, pros and locals, have set in motion an ongoing, evolving oral-history—pure place; I saw a similar shared history enacted in an old barn by descendants of a Mennonite colony in Newport News, Virginia. The polymorphous American Festival Project, which began in 1982 as a cultural exchange between the African-American Junebug Productions from New Orleans and Appalachia's Roadside Theatre, now includes more than a dozen dance and theatre companies, such as Urban Bush Women, El Teatro de la Esperanza, Robbie McCauley and Company, and A Traveling Jewish Theatre. All or some of the project's companies offer joint workshops, performances, and full-scale festivals during residencies ranging from weeks to years in communities as disparate as Maine, Miami, and Montana. Twenty-one such festivals in nineteen states have promoted exchanges between the culture of art and that of daily, rooted life.

Because so much of this theatre of place has evolved from the issue-oriented theatres of the sixties and seventies—The Free Southern Theatre and El Teatro Campesino, to name two—it often mingles aesthetics with activism. As a result, these troupes are sometimes accused of mistaking social work for art. They lead with their social consciences and draw on models of social outreach, civil rights demonstration, and grassroots organizing, and political theatre as they try to activate healing in tribe-torn America. The Living Stage Theatre at Washington, D.C.'s Arena Stage, for many years one of the nation's largest activist theatres, ran workshops in schools, prisons, community centers—wherever there were lives to save through art—and created heart-stoppingly vital theatre with actors and non-actors. John Malpede's Los Angeles Poverty Department began working with homeless people in 1985, cobbling together shows one critic called "bizarre, unpredictable, emotionally supercharged affairs that walk a fine line between stark raving madness and frightening clarity."

All this activity comprises what Gerry Givnish, director of Painted Bride Arts Center in Philadelphia, once called "a giving back" by building community locally. Clearly, the giving goes both ways. Theatre artists share dramatic techniques and expertise and so help communities theatricalize their stories and play out crises within. The communities give back a sense of purpose, connectedness, and, of course, the stories themselves. They give artists a place.

This spiritual dimension, sometimes obscured by the work's stark political content, runs deep and—democratic, populist, and good-neighbor-transcendental—feels deeply American. Its motto might be taken from Emerson, who, in his journal writes: *"The place which I have not sought,*

but in which my duty places me, is a sort of royal palace. If I am faithful to it, I
move in it with a pleasing awe at the immensity of the chain of which I hold the
last link in my hand and am led by it...."

*   *   *

The professional regional theatre and the professional community theatre of place were separated at birth. Like so many extraordinary ideas, they seem to have sprung full-blown from the visionary brain of Hallie Flanagan, director of the Works Progress Administration's Federal Theatre Project. Begun in 1935 as a relief—read "jobs"— program and killed by an Act of Congress four years later, Flanagan's project anticipated everything that came after (including ongoing trouble with the Feds). "Part of a tremendous re-thinking, re-building, and re-dreaming of America," as she called it, FTP would radiate over the vast geography of America by creating a "federation of theatres," subsidized nationally but administered locally. They'd spring up in all shapes and sizes: new play theatres, classical ones, circuses, puppet shows. Metropolitan resident companies would tour regional circuits of small theatres and work with local groups to develop regional playwrights.

Flanagan envisaged her experimental, pioneer, populist theatre interacting with—feeding into—the commercial, Broadway theatre, and so she enlisted the talents of Broadway artists like Elmer Rice, John Houseman, and the very young Orson Welles. She also saw it leaving Broadway behind. Local work by local artists—a true theatre of place— would become part of the fabric of American life. Oklahoma got a theatre for the blind in which students from the school for the blind worked as actors from scripts transcribed in Braille. A unit in Omaha played to homegrown audiences, ninety percent of which had never seen a live show. (Afterward, the story goes, Flanagan watched audiences wait to touch the actors to confirm that they were "real people.") On Oct. 27, 1936, Sinclair Lewis's *It Can't Happen Here* opened simultaneously in twenty-one American cities. With labor and construction funds from the WPA, America's longest lived and most imitated place-based theatre—Paul Green's local-historical drama, *The Lost Colony*, in North Carolina—began its perpetual, perennial life.

After FTP's demise, one branch of Flanagan's revolution sprouted at a time. First, a decade later, the regional theatre movement began, resembling her metropolitan resident companies. Soon after, professional activity took root in America's smaller communities—a theatre of place. Both branches struggle for validation: one against the idea of New York's centrifugal power; the other, against the notion that quality art and outreach don't mix. Flanagan fought these battles, too. That's partially why she forged connections with theatre luminaries where she could; she had to prove that her enterprise was real theatre, that talented artists did, in fact, wind up on relief rolls.

As Flanagan made clear, powerful art can and does happen anywhere, for all sorts of alchemical reasons. It succeeds when it effectively confirms or challenges a community's idea about itself. When it continues to do so over time, it lasts. (Ezra Pound put it best: "Literature is news that *stays* news.")

It's too early to know what the implications of this renewed activity are for the future. Will it forever change the way theatre fits into American life? Will it foster real community or false art? Will it fall out of the arts altogether, until it seems a subsystem of grassroots social service? Will it save the arts from universal defunding—by being non-elitist and a justifiable contributor to down-home America—or prove too subversive for faint hearts with money to spend? Will criticism—which in reaction to a true theatre of place means something more like cartography—learn a language that goes beyond "universal" quality to one of purpose and context and local value?

When the citizens of Grover's Corners plan their time capsule, they choose to include copies of both *The New York Times* ("Of course," the Stage Manager shrugs) and Mr. Webb's *Sentinel*, the town paper. As a final object for future interest, the Stage Manager decides to include a copy of the play itself, so "the people a thousand years from now will know a few simple facts about us...." However the American theatre of place looks to our critical eyes in ten years or in that distant moment when the Grover's Corners time capsule gets opened, it's here now. Right here.

This essay began as a lecture at the University of Nebraska, Lincoln, before being published, in a slightly different form, as "Your Place or Ours?" in *American Theatre*. A different version appeared as the Afterword of the Bloomsburg Theatre Ensemble's book, *Letters to the Editor* (Simon & Schuster/ Touchstone Books). Finally, the present version ran as part of NoPassport Press's *Popular Forms for a Radical Theatre*, edited by Caridad Svich and Sarah Ruhl, 2011.

Open Call, Part One:

A Year in the Lives of 15 Actors Starting Out in New York

> We're *actors*—we're the opposite of people!
> —Tom Stoppard, *Rosencrantz and Guildenstern Are Dead*

Prologue

Spring, 1995. Cambridge, Mass. I witness a rare convergence. In the studios of the American Repertory Theatre at Harvard, at the Institute for Advanced Theatre Training, I behold the formation of a true ensemble of actors. It's not something you see every day, not something you expect to find in school, but there it is: the second-year class—a company-in-the-making—about to graduate. I've been in and out of training programs as a student, then as a teacher since the mid-'70s, including at the ART. (I'm guest literary director and lecturer when I stumble on this class.) I'm not prone to romanticizing student talent. Suddenly, though, I'm romanticizing full blast. I'm at the birth of something extraordinary, I think, a new constellation in the theatre. Here are 15 actors—disciplined, talented, and singular—who combust on stage together, who, each in possession of a steady, unique flame, set each other on fire. Several times I catch them in the act—in a wacked-out *Titus Andronicus*, staged in an abandoned (dry) swimming pool, and in a showcase of scenes, that many-headed monster known among graduating classes as "industry night." When I watch them perform—no, *seize upon*—Charles L. Mee jr.'s beautiful/horrific riff on *The Trojan Women* and *Dido & Aeneas*, my fantasy crystallizes: something must be done to keep them together.

Someone should coin a word for the love of talent, this racing of the heart and mind I feel. It's a tender infatuation, nearly erotic, partly worshipful, and always—when you're in the audience—unrequited. Imagine my surprise, then—my lover's betrayal—when I discover that they (with only one or two exceptions) don't want to stay together. They know they're good together; people have been telling them so for two years; they feel it themselves. They've been sharing this intensity for long enough, though. Besides, they have other plans. They want to make their own ways.

And imagine my surprise, too, when, four decades into the alternative/regional theatre movement in America, I learn that for all 15 of them, the way begins in New York. Fifteen actors from the reaches of this continent, ranging in age from 23 to 33, finish graduate training and independently decide to assay Mount Manhattan, to make it there and to make it on their own. Some fantasies persist. New York is one.

Mine persists, too. If this young corps can't be persuaded to keep company—by starting a theatre, maybe, or through the championship of one of the directors graduating with them—at least I can keep them together in words. So I ask their permission to follow them around New York for a year, to write the story of this year, which is, for many, the start of their professional lives. They agree. (Actors must cultivate vulnerability and bravery, and a print documentary promises to be an exercise in both.) Their group portrait won't be a sampling, a representative cross-section of all the actors venturing into Gotham; as a whole, they enjoy material privileges and academic advantages far beyond the norm. My interest alone—which they sparked—chose them.

June, 1995 comes and with it graduation. I speak at the ceremony, a parting wave from the dock. They have converged; now, one by one they will disperse, careering their ways to New York City and, over the course of the next twelve-fifteen months, out into the rest of the country. Converge and disperse: two operative verbs for a life in the theatre.

The next time they come together (all but one) in the same room is Nov. 4, 1996, when the photos are taken for this series. In the months, days and minutes between, life happens.

*   *   *

Every exit [is] an entrance into somewhere else.
—Stoppard

Sherri Parker Lee and her roommate stand second in a line of approximately 50 people. This isn't an audition; it's an open house for a two-bedroom rent-stabilized apartment that has been advertised in the Village Voice. They've arrived 45 minutes early, armed with completed forms, letters of reference and a checkbook, a strategy out- lined in a no-nonsense guide called *The Intrepid New Yorker*. They have also brought with them Sherri's vision, inherited in part from a mother who designs furniture and interiors, of what a trashy, cramped, monochromatic hole-in-the-wall can become. They're prepared to write a check—a big one—here and now. They are prepared for anything.

For the next year Sherri will be second in line more than a dozen times, not for housing but for parts—in plays, movies, television series. As of Labor Day, she's been runner-up for two Shakespearean ingénues, one production of *The Importance of Being Earnest,* and a national Cheerios commercial. Her fourth callback for the Acting Company, which she's told is mere formality, gets cancelled when a woman who'd refused a contract in June changes her mind. Until the end of a year of auditioning almost every day, sometimes several times a day, getting called back, according to her own calculations, two out of three times, "Miss Second Choice" will land only one short-lived paying job: an appearance on *As the World Turns* as a spoiled rich girl biker, clad in skin-tight leather. But she gets the apartment.

So, for two unbearably hot weeks in July, 1995, during the worst New York summer anyone remembers, Sherri scrubs, hand-sands hardwood floors, tears out a built-in closet, mounts shelves and sponge-paints the walls with an Italian villa-like dappling of three colors. Friends come by to help, but mostly it's her fanatical will to make a home that transforms this West Village apartment into a jewel box. This mix of fanaticism and foresight applies to everything Sherri does. She's seen by her classmates as the one with the plan, the one to phone when you need career motivation or a kick in the pants. She's called "a force" and "a business animal." "I'm a hustler," she says of herself—the intrepid actress.

By contrast, Jessalyn Gilsig's Upper-West-Side sublet reveals almost nothing of her taste. The place, hardly bigger than a half-dozen diner booths wedged together, doesn't hold much. The furniture, like the lease, belongs to a woman on tour with *West Side Story*. Most of Jessalyn's belongings are in storage, anyway. Jessalyn trained as a painter before shifting her intense focus toward acting, and a few of her small, experimental paintings hang on the wall, evidence of the same arresting intelligence that informs her work with dramatic texts. There's a watercolor nude—an attempt to work without outline—and a black-and-white Durer-like drawing, both on sketchpad paper, both dense with movement, the pen-and-ink almost scrawly. Beyond these, you'd hardly know she lives here. This lack of the personal masks an irony: the tiny 87th Street one-bedroom is the first home she and her boyfriend have shared since they started seeing each other at McGill University in Montreal four years ago.

Jessalyn moved in after graduation in June, but by late summer she's already packing to go. With little more than a suitcase, she's heading back to Cambridge for six months in the professional company at the A.R.T., where, until June, she was a student. She's contracted to play Miranda in Shakespeare's *The Tempest* and Marianne in a new adaptation of Moliere's *Tartuffe*. The theatre has a policy not to hire its Institute alums for a year after graduation. This policy has just been broken for Jessalyn. Sherri is also up for a role at A.R.T., but she knows it's a long shot. The part she wants—Shelly in Sam Shepard's *Buried Child*—is slated to be filled by a current Institute student.

Salary, travel, and housing for an Equity actress haven't been figured in the production's budget. (Jessalyn's roles, on the other hand, were planned to be jobbed-in, on union contracts.) Sherri and her classmates gained membership in the actor's union, if they weren't already members, during their stint at A.R.T. Now, in the sort of wry quirk of fate reserved for struggling actors, her newfound professional status is working against her. For this reason or some other—does any actor ever know the whole story?—she doesn't get the part.

An actor's personal life is, usually, elsewhere. Sherri's boyfriend stayed back in Cambridge with his 10-year-old son when she moved here. Jessalyn's, currently working as assistant director on the Broadway revival of *The King and I*, will remain firmly planted in his Manhattan hometown when she heads back to Cambridge. It goes on that way, art and life mucking each other up. At year's end, Sherri will be considering 60 weeks of work in Houston only 20 days after her significant other relocates, son in tow, to New York to be near her. Jessalyn, a Canadian who begins the year with a 12-month visa, will, as the clock runs down, reluctantly contemplate marrying her boyfriend as a last ditch effort to stay—and act—in the U.S. (When the group photo for this story is taken, Jessalyn is back in Montreal, awaiting clearance to reenter the States. But that's a story for later.)

*   *   *

Still a magnetic center of opportunity, New York is rarely the center of the work itself. As a result, no actor here can avoid goodbyes for long. The ability to endure them and keep keeping on may be the most necessary skill of their trade. It's easy to think of these comings and goings romantically, youthful dramas stirred up by Juliet's decision to seek fame on the boards while Romeo pines at home, all part of the myth of a life in art. But the sacrifices are actual, profound, and ongoing. Sherri, Jessalyn, and their classmates —and probably many thousands like them with fewer advantages and prospects and less support—make daily, often irrevocable decisions affecting home, family, livelihood, friendship, security and even health on the off-chance that life can be meaningful and self-expressive. They don't live Mimi-on-the-couch-will-she-live-or-die nights; they aren't characters out of *La Boheme* or its East Village equivalent, *Rent*. The personal cost is large but seldom operatic. It's exacted minute-by-minute, as they inch toward the lives they imagine.

When James Farmer sets out for the city, he has to say goodbye to his new wife. Standing 6'1" and weighing in at 200 pounds, James rates adjectives like burly and strapping. He appears to (and literally does) come from Steinbeck country. It's there, at a theatre called the Western Stage, in a park between Salinas, Calif. and Monterrey, against a backdrop of mountains, that he kicks off the summer by getting married to Tracy Bryce. Their honeymoon—weeks of scuttling across America in an un-air-conditioned Subaru from the Sierras down to the Gulf of Mexico, up to

Savannah, Ga. and back to California—follows two school-years of separation and precedes one final one. While James stakes out Brooklyn, Tracy completes her Master's degree in acting at the University of Washington, Seattle. This third year apart won't kill them or send either of them spiraling into madness; it will, however, for at least as long as it lasts, define the terms of their relationship. James estimates that 80 to 90 percent of their conversation centers on how lonely and miserable they are.

Granville Hatcher has to say goodbye to his seven-year-old daughter, Gabrielle, who will stay in Boston with his ex-wife. Fatherhood had always made Granville an oddity in his class, as well as adding strain to his time at A.R.T. He began as the only married student and the only one with a child. By the end of his second year, he'd become the only divorced one. The intensity of training, coupled with the demands of student productions and the A.R.T. main stage roles that are part of the program, meant that he had to choose between work and Gabrielle. "I would see her most of the time in bed, asleep," he explains. On school snow days, not uncommon in New England, he would have to miss classes to stay home with her. He is still torn by choosing. When he leaves Boston mid-summer, his daughter's words ring in his ears: "I wish Dad would give up theatre for me."

The prospect of separation from Gabrielle is made more palatable by Granville's idea of creating a stable, second home for her in New York. He wants to expose her to his actor's life "to help her understand why things are the way they are." In June, though, before the ink has dried on his diploma, Granville signs for a featured role in a major Hollywood movie, an A-movie, action-style, starring Kurt Russell and Steven Seagal and, a dozen credits down, in the role of Ahmed, a Lebanese terrorist, Granville Hatcher.

The gods of theatre, when they deign to give, usually take with the other hand, so that even a first success as hysterically swift as Granville's comes with a price: he won't land in New York or see his daughter for two more months. By August he's on the road between San Francisco and Los Angeles, or, as he puts it to my answering machine, "lost in America."

From the West Coast the best he can do is call his daughter daily. That's when the reality of their distance hits him, and with it the awareness that he's working towards stability—for her—that she'll never see. "She just knows I'm not there." The severance reinforces his "fear that she won't know me, won't know that there's someone who loves her unconditionally." Acting relies on freedom, emotional/imaginative freedom, as well as the freedom to follow work wherever it crops up. For Granville, guilt about what he isn't doing makes it harder to feel free.

Meanwhile, his temporary lifestyle in Hollywood offers enough absurdity on its own. While his role earns him $2,500 a week and his personal trailer on the lot, his real-world life offers little luxury. He checks into a cheap motel and every morning drives his 1986 Buick Century—"the brown bomber"—up to the studio gates; from there a limousine takes him to his private quarters. Inside his trailer, he orders a full breakfast. "At the end of the day the limo takes me back to my beater car. I leave the gates of Oz and go back to the Motel Six."

Lifestyle aside, Granville has instantaneously attained what a number of the other 14 desire—a well-paying, validating piece of work. But Granville exudes ambivalence about it. He's eager to point out that he's not angling for stardom or for Hollywood; in fact, he really wants to do theatre, maybe "country doctor"-like, community-based theatre. Shooting this mid-air thriller has, unfortunately, precluded theatre auditions. His part is, well, "stereotypical," but "not crap," though anything he brings to it has to be worked out alone, since the scenes are rehearsed just once before they're shot. He prefers independent films from across the Atlantic, with "more gut, less formula," but the presence of the Royal Shakespeare Company's David Suchet, who plays the master terrorist and whose appearances in the *Playing Shakespeare* videos Granville studied and admired in school, "is part of my little justification."

Gaining entry to Oz is, moreover, no guarantee of gaining membership. Granville's break, his sense of hitting "the greasy shoot," promises nothing for the future. "I try to stay within reality: this is a job I have for a few months. This is the time that I'm working and when it's done, I'm not." When it is done, he's no closer to providing a home for Gabrielle than the short-term sublet he's lined up in Manhattan. He's no closer to making a consistent living—still needs to defer payment on his student loan—or to the life he desires as a stage actor. The movie job doesn't even help him line up auditions. In fact, between early summer, when he signs on to *Executive Decision*, and early October, when he comes to a semi-full stop in New York, he hasn't gone on a single one. The momentum that people told him would result from this initial break out of the blocks hasn't yet taken hold. His big movie debut, meanwhile, becomes a difficult fact of his daughter's life.

Siobhan Brown lands in the city in June, but she doesn't stop moving till February. In eight months she stays in roughly 14 places, some of them more than once, most within a few Manhattan miles of each other. My files on Siobhan's year are littered with scraps of paper, addresses and numbers hastily noted during phone calls: *East 9th Street, temporary sublet....Gramercy Park Hotel, suite with park view. Washington Square Park, illegal sublet, landlord "flexes his muscles," boots her out....Calls all classmates looking for a place, rooms with Ajay Naidu's girlfriend and a homeless NYU student for five days while Ajay's out of town ("It was like the refugee house")....Gives Chandler Vinton two cats (Chandler already has two)...House-sits for friend while he's in London...Returns to Aunt's beautiful 94th Street apartment, by Central Park*

reservoir....Back in Boston, crashes on Ajay's couch again, one night only.
Manhattan may be sheer rock, but the earth under Siobhan's feet won't
stop shifting. During her stay at the Macklowe Hotel in Times Square, it
changes its name to The Millennium. "We got T-shirts," she explains,
"'Same Great Service. New Name.'" When the newly named midtown
hotel needed room for a convention, she and her boyfriend got relocated to
a penthouse suite in the Southgate Tower near Penn Station.

Siobhan lives with her British boyfriend Carl, an original cast
member/dance captain/keeper of the flame for the percussive dance-
theatre-music troupe called *Stomp*. When he's in town, the couple has
access, via *Stomp*'s producers, to fine hotels and decent sublets; through for
many of his long stretches touring or fine-tuning *Stomp*'s road companies,
Siobhan fends for herself. With Carl she travels as far as the Acropolis in
Greece and, later, to the green room backstage at the Academy Awards.
When she returns, it's to a life of not much happening, few auditions, and
no permanent address. This continual dislocation, the lack of work to call
her own, and her awareness that "my personal life is a lot louder than my
professional life" often leaves Siobhan depressed. She spends whole days
in bed in front of the TV—"lots of room service, lots of Spectravision"—as
if the only way to cease the movement is to give over to inertia. I call her
one October day to schedule an interview; it's after noon and I waken her
from a sound sleep. I ask her how her days look the following week. "My
days," she replies with a twist, "look pretty empty." She tries not to worry
about the depression, tries to see it as a natural response to her sudden lack
of framework, discipline, home. Counter to the noise and dance of her
Stomp-driven social life, she's struggling to regain a center, a motivating
spirit from inside.

Spirituality and home are prime concerns for Siobhan. The youngest
of four children, she comes from a tight-knit, African-American family still
living in and around Dorchester, Mass. Her father, in addition to his career
as an offset pressman, works with his two brothers in the neighborhood
gas station they own. Her mother, a devout Christian Scientist, was equally
active and hardworking until she suffered heart and other physical
problems near the end of Siobhan's training at A.R.T., a medical crisis that
precipitated a religious one. She ultimately accepted medication, which
meant, among other things, forsaking her calling as a C.S. practitioner.
Siobhan is, and wants to be, an important emotional support for her
mother. At the same time, Siobhan, who before Harvard did her
undergraduate work at Boston's Emerson College, is eager to leave the
nest. "I'm trying to jump out into the world, finally, on my own two feet, to
pick my own way spiritually." Her spiritual path no longer includes
practicing Christian Science, another hard pill for her mother to swallow.

Ironically, Siobhan's three professional acting jobs this year come from colleagues in Boston. That means going home again.

Vontress Mitchell will also return home, something he's been avoiding since his baby brother's murder two years ago. Before he faces Witchita, Kansas again, though, he'll have to extricate himself from a mini-drama that will leave him homeless and earn him his first "New York Story."

Vontress, finishing a run of *The Three-Penny Opera* at A.R.T., can't leave for New York until late in the summer. As soon as he does, the drama begins. He plans to room with an acquaintance, a Chilean woman he met in Boston, Melinda [her name has been changed]. Because of his student debt and lack of a job, Vontess discovers, after failing a credit check, that no one will give him a lease. So Melinda takes charge. She lines up one apartment, but on lease-signing day, they discover the apartment has been rented to someone else. Next, she and her boyfriend pose as a married couple from the Dominican Republic in order to help her rent an apartment in a mostly Dominican section of Washington Height's, Manhattan's northernmost neighborhood. The realtor coaches them to lie and create false employment documents. Vontress's roommate-to-be, fearing that he'll back out if he knows, keeps him in the dark about this. On the truck ride to NYC, "it unfolds." It also unfolds that Melinda's boyfriend has another woman and two children somewhere in Vermont. The truth dawns on him: "Trouble follows this girl."

It's hard to imagine Vontress getting dragged down by all this. He's a lively spirit, changeable and spontaneous. A singing teacher once told him that who he is is in his laugh. It's a fun laugh, wild, erupting from the goofy edge of anarchy. It's the laugh of someone being tickled, someone with too much sugar in his blood. Not surprisingly, Vontress is drawn to children, and they're drawn to him. Before New York he made his living as an *au pair* and babysitter, forming deep attachments to the families he worked for. Some deeply responsible impulse to give care clicks in with his compelling roommate. Melinda's *Sturm und Drang* makes it impossible for him to be selfish in the way an actor must, to carve the space he needs to prepare for auditions or concentrate on his career. On the night before a second *New York Undercover* audition, for example, Vontress plans to watch the show and learn his lines. Melinda, though, in a panic of boyfriend-trauma, cries on his shoulder until one a.m. He misses the show and has to study his part during the morning subway ride. When, in anticipation of another audition, he leaves town to prepare, she calls him insistently. It will take him nearly six months to get disentangled from her melodrama. Another six months after that, he'll still be house-sitting for touring friends and sleeping on sofas.

For Vontress, whom classmates describe as "the ideal houseguest" and "so loving," finding home has never come easy. As a black man in the still-white world of Harvard, he was visibly out of place. In Washington Heights, he's sometimes mistaken for Hispanic. Nor is his the conforming image of Kansas. "That's why I left," he says. Interestingly, despite strongly mixed emotions about New York, including a persistent desire to pack and run, there are moments of fit. Walking to meet me at a Starbucks Coffee on the Upper West Side, Vontress, moving gracefully through the integrated, international crowds, notices something new: he feels like an American for the first time. Then the moment passes.

*   *   *

A few numbers:

- Twelve start the summer on exclusive contracts with legitimate (theatrical) agents who saw their A.R.T. group audition.
- One of the three unsigned—Kevin Waldron—gets signed as soon as he returns from his first regional theatre job.
- Six find work in the food and beverage industry.
- Four temp in offices (one also waitresses).
- One cleans offices at night (also caters).
- One writes Mormon history books and CD-Roms for young people.
- Four make it through this year by acting work alone, some with a little help from their families.
- Five (approx.) end school debt free.
- Ten (approx.) face school loan and credit card debts of $30,000-$100,000 each.

*   *   *

Survival jobs, then, are required. Kevin Waldron, a trig parochial school graduate who comes from one of America's most affluent corners, Orange County, Calif., and who has nothing of the bohemian about him, works a regular graveyard shift as an office cleaner with a company of performers called "Feather Busters." He takes catering assignments, too, when he can. The formality of cater-waitering means suiting up butler-style and, on occasion, serving the very country club crowd he grew up as part of. The role-reversal feels like "comic retribution," but it beats the alternative: asking his family for hand-outs. "I have to do this now as an adult, thirty-three-year-old man on my own," he asserts in his kind, solid way. On his own sometimes means (openly) pilfering his roommate's laundry money for carfare or food (and, of course, replenishing it later), or cleaning out a friend's fridge while house-sitting. It means macaroni and cheese, rice and beans. Kevin just might be the most universally respected—loved—member of his now-graduated class. Love, however, can't buy him money.

Caroline Hall's mother wouldn't let her take typing classes. "It was a feminist statement," she shrugs. "Thanks a lot. Now I can't type." As a consequence, she relies on temp jobs that don't require this particular skill. Temping gives her a much needed sense of control during this "out of control time." "It's a good feeling to get up, shower, and go to work." Because she's broke, she won't turn down a temp job for a commercial audition. Meanwhile, her wealthy friends from Groton keep inviting her to parties at restaurants "where you spend forty dollars for dinner." She claims to worry about money all the time. You'd never know it, though. She's always so upbeat, so delightful, so damn chipper and friendly funny—the humor of the helpful. She forks out $550 to illegally sublet a railroad flat with "tons of bugs, water that doesn't work until the afternoon," and a landlord she can't call to complain, since she's not supposed to be there. The guy she rents from is in Vienna, conducting *Porgy and Bess*, but he won't let her put her voice on the answering machine. "It's okay, though, it's okay," she assures me, with a bright bob of the head.

The most un-actorly survival jobs probably belong to Tom Hughes. Tom is a devout Mormon whose commitment to God, his new wife Kristen, and the church takes absolute precedence over theatrical concerns. He considers potential conflicts between the two, but for now his religious/home life coexists peacefully with the theatre, not unlike the slice of upper Broadway that balances, on one side of the street, the Mormon congregation Tom and Kristen belong to and, on the other, Lincoln Center. Tom embarks on the year—after a week's delayed honeymoon in Maui—anxious about money. He spent the better part of twelve months in New York between his undergraduate years (also at Harvard) and the Institute; he knows what things cost. Education and living expenses have left the Hugheses almost $50,000 in debt. They want to start a family, though Tom doesn't yet know how they'll support it. Kristen isn't looking forward to the retail job she's lined up. The bulk of their money comes from royalties on *We'll Bring the World His Truth*, a collection for young readers of great missionary stories from Mormon history. Tom wrote the book after hours at A.R.T. He pitches a couple more book ideas—a children's novel and a book about Knights—before he sells a CD-Rom concept, a role-playing game also based on Mormon history. He begins to develop the script.

To supplement his advances and royalties, Tom locates, through friends at his church (a network that was also the source for their first Washington Heights apartment), what surely qualifies as the most interesting boring job of the year. He's hired to transcribe medical records from the Civil War for a Massachusetts Institute of Technology professor. Stationed in the rare books room of the public library, he feeds information from tables and nineteenth-century governmental forms into a laptop computer. He stocks a database with the measurements of soldiers' bodies, their eye and hair color, and more, sometimes the vital stats of an all-black regiment or a cadre of young people, information originally collected to determine the type of person or region best designed to produce an effective soldier. (I know of no such study on effective actors.) While he's working, he's projecting himself into another role, a dream part, and one that will, in the near future, become his: stay-at-home dad.

*   *   *

Since immigrating to New York in 1985, I've met dozens and dozens of people who came here to act, write, dance, paint, or direct, and got derailed, rerouted into a different life altogether. It can happen gradually or all at once. Usually it starts with the survival job. The bosses find out you're presentable, efficient ambitious, creative. They throw added responsibilities your way. You rise to the occasion. Then you simply rise, from temp to permanent, from hourly to annual, from self-employed to covered, insured, and pensioned. How do you leave? How do you go back? Frank Sinatra can sing it: "If I can't make it here, I'll find something else...."

Sometimes the decisions to break with the security of a paycheck or the thrill of a pocketful of cash tips can jumpstart a fearful artist. That's the way it worked for Mark Boyett, to hear him tell it. He had lived in New York for a couple years in the early '90s, taking classes and waiting tables at the Boathouse restaurant in Central Park.

When he moves back after Harvard, into the suffocating heat of an un-air-conditioned sublet in Queens, for "the worst summer of my life," he returns to the Boathouse for a job. He trains and begins working but hates it. It's a giant step backward, sapping not only his time but his energy. The manager rides him for little things, like wearing white socks. The thought of being the kind of New York actor who is always and only a New York waiter "just screwed me up. I needed to know mentally that I was an actor now—very hard to do because of my relationship to money." When he finds himself relieved at having missed an audition, "I realized how scared I was of the business. I realized I had to totally commit to this thing of being an actor."

Two weeks later, he rides the subway down to Circle Repertory Company for an open call. He arrives at 6:30 a.m., receives an audition number and heads home to nap. Mark climbs the stairs to the expansive

72nd Street studio he sublets from a friend. On his way up, he passes the door to "Bells Are Ringing," the prototypical answering service for actors, with long wooden counters and walls of pigeon holes waiting for messages and, presumably, out-of-work actors in white plastic chairs manning the phones. It is a constant reminder of the life he's in. He hops back on the train in plenty of time. The train stalls underground for an hour-and-a-half before spitting him out in Chinatown. "My gut had told me to quit my job; now my gut told me to go by Circle Rep and leave a note. Now I know I have to do as much as I can. The main thing is making it my top commitment, regardless of the money worries." Circle calls him in for another audition. It doesn't lead to a job, but it goes well. Leaving the note—going that extra step—becomes a second turning point. Mark Boyett has embraced his ambition.

*   *   *

Like Mark, Suzanne Pirret has been here before. She has already tackled New York City in what now seems like another life. For six years prior to her entry into the Institute, she took classes here, tended bar and waited tables, pounded pavements, slept in sleeping bags, and lived hand-to-mouth, often on a diet of cheap hotdogs. It was the classic struggling artist existence, right down to the tumultuous relationship at its heart, made desperate by the lack of family support.

Suzanne's father had wanted her, the "smart" daughter, to study something business-related at Smith College; she enrolled at Syracuse, instead, determined to act. When she moved to Manhattan, he cut her off. The typicality of this scenario didn't make it any less painful, especially when, three months before she began applying to graduate schools, her boyfriend killed himself.

His suicide and her acceptance to Harvard changed everything. Now she not only lives here with her family's blessing, she lives with her family. In this way, too, she's been here before: New York or, rather, neighboring New Jersey, is home. Her parents' two-story, French Colonial-style house occupies several acres of land surrounded by deer country and horses. Suzanne's room measures about as big as apartments she sees in Manhattan. It's cozy, this second time around, maybe too cozy. "You get very comfortable," she worries, "which is a danger."

This comfort doesn't make drumming up acting work any easier. I imagine it's even harder for Suzanne than for some of her classmates, because her suitability—her type (a word I use reluctantly)—is unclear. As a person, she offers her own succinct description: "persistent and oversensitive." In conversation, she displays an active confidence in her talent and intelligence. She flips quickly from fragile to tough and direct, and works hard to stay positive. How to describe her appearance, though? Olive-skinned, dark eyed and thin—suburban maybe, advantaged probably, high-strung, almost brittle. Here's where I grope for known comparisons: Julia Louis-Dreyfus, but different pretty, or Gilda Radner, but different cute.

"That's my problem," she admits. "One agent said that I was an agent's nightmare because there's no one else working who's like me. They can never figure out who my prototype is." (I'm not even sure what her age is; she's the only person in her class who plays coy on the subject.) She gropes too, casting about for a persona that's identifiable enough to market and expansive enough to contain the variety she feels within: "The problem is I have a pretty wide range. I know every actor thinks this. I don't see myself doing Sam Shepard, Mid-western. I'd get cast as a funny, quirky New Yorker or else a sophisticate, upper-class, dancer-looking." At one point she attempted to capitalize on traits inherited from her mother's heritage, Puerto Rican and Spanish-Majorcan (her father brings French and Scottish to the mix). "I tried to do the Hispanic thing."

The ridiculous, painful division between who we feel ourselves to be and how we're perceived, summed up, by others is exaggerated for actors, who live and die by their images, their persona, their packages. The best training opens actors to the range of possible selves within; the "industry" regularly subjects actors to a boiling down, a game of pick-one-now.

For actors like Suzanne, uncategorizable looks can be a drawback; for others, like Granville, they can be an asset. His swarthy, handsome features, neither exceptional nor particularly idiosyncratic, suggest a vague ethnicity that impresses casting directors as appropriate for a range of nationalities, including his first role as a Lebanese terrorist. His father's Filipino/Irish traits and his mother's Portuguese/French ones will make his face a cultural Rorschach. This lack of specificity, he believes, makes him unthreatening to middle-America—just what the media doctors ordered. Almost every audition he's granted requires a different dialect.

Sometimes a single physical fact defines an actor. Sherri is a blonde. She gets called on auditions because she's blonde. She loses parts to brunettes (or so she's come to believe) because she's blonde. "I don't want to be what they see," she declares. "I want to be taken as serious. Intelligent and competent and serious. Not because I'm blonde." Siobhan, contrarily, comes to understand that she won't be seen as an ingénue, but as "a medium height, woolly-headed, culturally mixed woman" She struggles to accept this cultural limitation and, still, "hold a good thought about the world."

Caroline Hall gets consistently pegged as garden-variety ingénue—Moscow's Irina or Illyria's Viola. Petite and blonde, she looks younger than she is, especially with her short, sporty haircut. The bad news is there's a character actress fighting to get out. Last spring she told a potential agent, at her third meeting with his prestigious agency, that she wants to do comedy, that "I'm more like a character actress, to be honest'. He said, 'No, you're not. You're a leading lady.'" But her timing works, even over coffee.

As she rattles off anecdotes from the roughly sixty commercial auditions (five for Tampax) she's booked by October, she can't stop the mockery. "Isn't that great," she seems to say, never caustic or histrionic, but buoyant and (to use a word that comes up a lot with her) "perky." Like the one where she was a waitress in a bowling alley reacting to a strike. They told her, "Be natural." "I looked," she says, "and went 'Damn.' Like they'd have somebody on a Quaker Oats commercial say 'Damn?" At a commercial for a mall, she met a director who "thought he was Artaud." 'Don't be perky," he coached her, going through a lengthy rap about subtext, in which he urged her to think of the mall as addiction. When, in her reading, she pursued this path to the dark side of suburbia, he disapproved, demanding to know why she was treating the mall as if it were death. So, the next try, "I was perky," she concludes, "and he said it was much better, we've really gotten somewhere."

Chandler Vinton, the youngest of the six women, could pass as the oldest. At school she played Irma, the brothel Madame in Genet's *The Balcony* and Hecuba, the last standing matriarch in the rubble of Troy, in *The Trojan Women: A Love Story*. Robert Woodruff, who directed the workshop production, warned her that she might go years without working in this country, 15 or 20 until she ripens into the roles she's meant for. The context has shifted more severely for her than for the others: at school she played mostly big, strong women, but now she's up for twenty-something parts in a pool of other 24-year-olds. She can't help but compare herself with her close friends, like Sherri and Caroline, who audition constantly. "Petite and blonde is in." When her agent sends her for "fragile people," she knows it's futile, wrong.

She tries to alter her appearance. Between June and October, she cuts her hair four times. "Image change. Image change. I don't know who I am." Is a woman her age, right out of school, supposed to know? Chandler's dilemma isn't about beauty. She resembles Glenn Close, as she's been told ad nauseum, but warmer, less crispy. When I walk past Kraft's Restaurant on 42nd and 10th, I'm startled by the face in the window. I don't recognize Chandler at first, but I recognize the face. It's that face, the one from the archetypal forties diner, from the New York myth—gazing out the window, waiting to be discovered. How long can she be expected to wait?

* * *

Todd Thomas Peters won't come out of hiding. He works through the nights, eleven p.m. to seven a.m., in the computer center of a midtown bank. He's part of a squad of three, "locked in a room where people have to call to get in." Within this room, next door to the Chrysler Building, he helps bank computers talk to each other. He tells his bosses he's a writer, a playwright. "You can't tell business people you're an actor," he explains. "Actors have messed people around too much." After a month of temping, he parlays his operations experience into a $40,000 annual salary. The money matters, since he's planning to get married and buy a co-op in West New York, on the New Jersey banks of the Hudson River. Sleep is the problem. "I essentially have jet lag all the time, since I try to spend the weekends with [his fiancée] Margo." He discovers melatonin, and that helps adjusts his body clock. What he can't find a cure for, though, is his deep-seated desire—the acting career-killing desire—to hide out.

Now he's pacing floors, riddled with doubt. He doesn't have an agent for theatre, hasn't signed yet with the commercial agent who's shown interest. Exactly half of him wants "to be onstage all the time" and the other half ducks. "Why would I subject anyone to having to see me?" he asks, almost robotic in his earnestness. Then he grins and these TV characters swarm around the image of his boyish face: Dobie Gillis, Eddie Haskell, everybody on *Happy Days*. He offers a detail, a concise scene: "Before making a phone call I have to sit for a minute and breathe and write down what I'm gonna say." I can picture him by the phone, upright on a kitchen chair in almost military stiffness. 1 recognize the posture, the full-body effort it takes to expose your insufficiencies to the world, to force yourself to sell a product that no one wants to buy: you.

He hatches a brilliant idea, a way to turn the tables on his auditors. "I'm going to audition one hundred times. By June, 1996 I want to have been rejected by one hundred people and twenty agents." If he aims at rejection and gets it, he succeeds. If he doesn't get rejected, he succeeds. It's win-win.

*   *   *

By the time his classmates begin lining up work, Randall Jaynes has been fully employed for weeks. He never really stopped working; he never does. From school he, Todd, Caroline, and Suzanne flew to a festival in Venezuela, where they performed a scaled-down version of Lorca's *Blood Wedding*. The production, staged by a director who graduated with them, was, by most of their accounts, troubled; Randall and Todd's two-man experimental *The Birdcatchers*, on the other hand, made a wee-hours sensation at the international event. Back in New York, Randall lived out of one suitcase, contemplating a slew of future self-generated projects and observing the art/music/performance trio Blue Man Group, while waiting to hear about a job in their long-running hit *Tubes*.

Instead of savoring this transitional downtime, he continued planning work, prowling the city for props and ideas for his unique blend of puppetry, psycho-physical mime and storytelling. (A.R.T. artistic director Robert Brustein once described him to me as a contemporary Buster Keaton.) Work defines Randall's life, even to his personal detriment. "The work is me and I am the work," he explains in a conversational tone that alternates between captivating insight and slow-motion identity crisis. This workaholism doesn't always make him happy; more, it sometimes isolates him, even from his closest friends. For much of the year, he'll obsess over a retelling of *Pinocchio*, whose wooden hero seems a metaphor for Randall himself, wildly imaginative and full of longing to be real. A transplant from "hick, cow, nothingville" in Sonoma Valley, Calif, he is down to his last seventy dollars, living with a former Institute student, when Blue Man calls him. Beginning in the group's training workshop, earning four hundred dollars a week, he graduates to the company, at well over double that salary. The troupe even owns the apartment he'll share with Kevin Waldron. Randall trades the bubble of his own art-is-life existence for the bubble of Blue Man Group's.

Elsewhere in Manhattan, phones start ringing. Randall and five other actors are summoned back to Cambridge to recreate *Winter Project*, a dance-theatre piece they developed in class the year before. (Blue Man Group's flexibility allows him to return for the short stint in A.R.T.'s fall festival.) Then Denver calls. Ajay Naidu, one of the original *Winter Project* troupe, is wanted by Denver Center Theatre for *Romeo and Juliet*. He auditions with a Tybalt scene, the same one he did at age seven when he acted for the first time. Ajay, visiting his parents in Georgia, has to miss the callback, but he gets cast anyway, as Paris. Ajay's family moved to America from India in the early sixties, but his Paris will be a Spanish immigrant, a matador come to mission-period California in the mid-nineteenth century. Instead of remounting his solo Winter Project dance, this agile, polished performer spends several weeks learning flamenco moves.

Louisville calls James. Then Denver beckons Mark. Other cities follow suit. Suddenly, Mark, James, Jessalyn, Siobhan, Ajay and Kevin are all working out of town. Several others get hired for smaller-cast projects here. At one point thirteen or fourteen of them are rehearsing or performing simultaneously, only a few without pay. New York is motion after all, not waiting by the phone. Converge, disperse.

In Denver, Ajay's phone rings again. It's Frank Galati calling from the Steppenwolf Theatre Company in Chicago. Galati, a renowned director/writer, wants Ajay for a new production of *Everyman*, in which he will alternate with other ensemble members in the title role. As a teenager,

Ajay played leads in several feature films, but Galati gave him his earliest theatre jobs, at the Goodman Theatre shortly before A.R.T. The only hitch with this current offer: Ajay will have to break his contract with Denver to go; he'll have to leave in the middle of *Romeo*'s run. The Steppenwolf job represents a cut in pay, but it makes up for that in prestige and in the happy prospect of working with Galati again. Denver is one of the poshest theatres in the country, and Ajay is revved up about the project. Steppenwolf, though, is an ensemble and launching pad of mythic proportion. Moreover, Ajay grew up in Chicago; it's his stomping ground. An embarrassment of riches becomes an ethical dilemma; to honor a satisfying commitment or break it to pursue a potentially bigger career boost and greater artistic thrill.

Another call comes, from Ajay's parents. His father's ill health is deteriorating. They're planning to leave Georgia and move back to the Chicago area. Coming one after another, the calls from Steppenwolf and his family seem to Ajay to represent the best and worst a year can bring, but they are not. By the following summer, he'll receive offers even more exciting and news even more dire.

This article was originally published in *American Theatre*, January, 1997.

Open Call, Part Two: The Great (And Not So Great) Work Begins

> No one can have made a seriously artistic attempt without becoming
> conscious of an immense increase—a kind of revelation—of freedom.
> —Henry James

Fall/Winter, 1995: Vontress Mitchell looks around the table in wonder. He's sitting at the Odeon, a quintessentially hip 1980s restaurant in the Tribeca section of downtown New York. It's a place you expect to spot artist-celebs after hours—Robert DeNiro or Jay McInerney, Deborah Harry or Mary Boone—but you don't expect to see them sitting at your table. There they are, though, Vontress's own kind of dream team: playwright Suzan-Lori Parks and actor/writer Wallace Shawn, Richard Price, the novelist and screenwriter who has just finished the movie *Clockers*, and theatre director Liz Diamond. He thinks to himself: "I'm here. This is going to take a while, but I'm here."

The "here" in that thought is Manhattan, the city, capital "C" city, to which Vontress and the other 14 actors in his graduating class made tracks when they left the American Repertory Theatre's Institute for Advanced Theatre Training at Harvard last summer. The transition into New York has been bumpy for him, and he's still embroiled in roommate dramas that sap his energy and thwart his concentration. For today, however, life feels hopeful. Today he clocked 10 hours rehearsing a benefit reading of Parks' *The America Play*. Vontress has the playwright to thank for this energizing day. He met her when they worked on *The America Play* in Cambridge two years ago and, more recently, she recommended him to Diamond, who is directing the reading. As a student at A.R.T., Vontress was cast in a nameless supporting role, but this time he reads the young lead, Brazil, a man digging in the "Great Hole of History" left to him by his father.

The audience, which represents to Vontress the "cream of the avant-garde," gathers in Richard Price's beautiful brownstone home. The event raises money for a smart arts-and-artists magazine called *Bomb*. It also puts $200 and a four-year subscription into Vontress's pocket. He needs the money, but even more he needs creative work and creative company, fuel for what has turned out to be a difficult journey. He isn't certain he wants to stay in New York, but for the moment he's rejuvenated, re-committed. He's having a glimpse.

He's witnessing something larger than public recognition or the lifestyles-of-the-rich-and/or-famous. Surrounding him are artists whose success allows them to live in their creativity. Their work, unlike that of so much of the laboring world, seems to set them free. What is this freedom? Henry James described it as the revelation that "the province of art is all life, all feeling, all observation, all vision." If the whole of experience falls within the artist's compass, if there's no off limits, then everything becomes a subject for wonder. Maybe, too, creative acts beget more creative acts, and artistic freedom increases with each exercise of that freedom.

For actors, unlike artists of many other disciplines, no serious artistic attempt can happen in isolation. Writers can write, painters paint, and musicians play without being hired to do so. But for actors, freedom requires a job.

It also requires risk, whether it's the colossal risk of moving one's life to Manhattan and committing years to a potentially disappointing endeavor or the small personal risk of making an ass of yourself for two minutes in front of a casting director. Having quit his day job as a waiter in order to more fully commit to acting, Mark Boyett is already flying without a net. In his callback for *Beethoven and Pierrot* at the Denver Center Theatre Company, Mark, improvising the role of Mephistopheles, gets asked to seduce Beethoven into selling his soul. The piece's co-directors, Pavel Dobrusky and Per-Olav Sorensen, looking for physically daring actors, push him toward a sense of physical danger. His Mephistopheles becomes a sex-charged southern belle with a demon inside. In the improvised audition, he/she throws the deaf composer to the ceiling and dominates him sexually. Mark is offered the part and asked, "Would you be willing to shave your head?"

The fear of appearing foolish doesn't end with his audition. He's contracted to make outlandish comic choices in a production whose text will be developed in rehearsal. "Improv has never been my forte," Mark admits less than a week before heading to Denver, "and now that's what I've been hired to do." His strategy involves meeting fear with fearlessness. "I'm going to have to put myself out in rehearsals right away. In this business the way to make a fool of yourself is to try not to make a fool of yourself."

It works. He faces down his fear, and has "hands down the best experience I've ever had in the theatre." In this "unbearably satisfying" collaboration, he improvises from sketches of scenes, listens to tapes of rehearsals, and writes lines and jokes and whole scenes of his own until his character has the strongest possible arc. Beginning as Beethoven's therapist in a simple suit and horns—intent on wresting Beethoven's soul—he weakens as Beethoven resists. As his relative power decreases, this devil goes to sillier and sillier lengths. He grows a moustache and goatee, wears a skimpy bikini (the belle from the audition finds her way into performance), and sports larger and more grotesque devil parts—huge horns and hooves—before giving up on Beethoven's soul and settling for a mere dedication. Mark is thrilled by what he learns about comedy. He also gets cast in the next two DCT projects, Brecht's *Galileo* and Tony Kushner's adaptation of The *Dybbuk*. Although neither of these productions sets him on fire the way *Beethoven* did, the consistency of work—nearly seven months of back-to-back acting assignments—allows him to test what he learns, to hone his comic skills and fortify his confidence and ambition. The no-holds-barred lunacy of Mark's wild ride offers a rare, explosive kind of freedom.

Randall Jaynes, hired in August as part of the replacement squad for Blue Man Group, must find his freedom within the most exacting restraints. His face, neck and prosthetically bald head are coated in vivid blue. His hands are sheathed in blue latex gloves. His face maintains an almost dehumanized deadpan. His body, at times, is outfitted with helmets, coveralls and tubing that forces creamy crud to spew from his chest. He never speaks. All the while, in what must be the most astonishing set of contraries on any stage today, he and his two cohorts engage in feverish athletic anarchy, an imaginative, futuristic rampaging that weds child's play with conceptual art, science fiction with primitive ritual, and fierce Taiko drumming with game show. They leap balconies, flick endless supplies of candy and marshmallows into each other's mouths across hefty distances, and beat out "White Rabbit" on PVC pipes. They slip seamlessly from clown silliness into bottomless postmodern irony, from Chaplinesque sweetness to angry battering against the soul-killing technology of the information age. All this without cracking a smile. Still, despite their automata exteriors and the mechanistic clip of their bodies, three distinct, compelling spirits shine through. When Robert Frost characterized freedom as moving "easy in harness," he might have been describing Blue Man Group.

For Randall, whose courtship with the company began before graduation, the job blends joy and discipline. It also gives him a security that, coming from an economically precarious family, he's never known. His Blue Man-owned apartment in the East Village comes cheaply, and the company pays for the physical therapy necessitated by 10-minute stretches of full-bodied drumming. Nevertheless, the job "doesn't ease 99 percent of what I go through." Even in weeks where he performs eight shows of an hour-and-a-half each, arriving at the theatre two hours before curtain for makeup and an elaborate sound-check, he struggles with having more down time than he's allowed himself since childhood. He's unable to read, unable to fall asleep or to get himself out of bed before afternoon. He spends too much time alone, watching videos, shell-shocked or obsessing over solo performance projects, missing "normal life—other people, a lover." He makes a list of all the people he's tried to have relationships or even dates with and tries to "figure out what the fuck's wrong with me."

Randall's personal discontent, standing in contrast to his professional success, combines the pain of leaving home and of carrying it with him. He describes his family life as an aquarium, suggesting a strange, sealed life underwater. His father died in the spring of Randall's first year at A.R.T. from a lifetime of deterioration, alcoholism, and what Randall calls "sensitivity." Unable to maintain a work life, despite intelligence and humor, Mr. Jaynes lived for some years as a virtual shut-in. Randall's mother, a relentlessly hard worker, became the family bastion. Randall sees himself as a blend of the two, and his current life, alternating as it does between enervating solitude and driven workaholism, gives supporting evidence. Blue Man's members meet on off days to brainstorm new ideas and to collaborate on each other's outside projects. This extra frisson makes Randall even happier to have entered the group's ranks. Nevertheless, he's more preoccupied by his inner landscape and his self-generated work— specifically *The Birdcatchers* and what will become *Pinocchi 2035*—because they connect so deeply to his personal concerns. Clearly, though, Blue Man has returned him to the aquarium life. With its multi-colored tubing projecting from the walls and spinning plankton-like from the Astor Place Theatre's grid, the environmental setting even evokes a world submerged.

This circling back must be one of the motifs of an actor's life. The necessary introspection of their work keeps memory stirred up. The dysfunctional processes of theatre recreate those of many original homes while the actor's nomadic life adds the feel of continual recurrence. Furthermore, by some strange almost supernatural set of convergences, certain plays and people keep meeting up again. Vontress's one-night reunion with *The America Play* is an example. It's a play that comes double-loaded with memories of professional satisfaction and personal trauma.

One day, during the rehearsal period for the A.R.T. production, the Institute administrator sought out Vontress at home. She came to tell him that his brother Corky (Cortez), the youngest of seven sons and closest to Vontress in age, had been shot and killed by the Wichita police. Vontress flew to Kansas, where the questionable circumstances of Corky's death had created a cause célèbre, catalyzing law suits and a vigil march in his memory.

According to Vontress, Corky had a current harassment suit pending against the police and had won a previous case. The white officers claim to have stopped the young black man on a traffic violation and to have shot him only after he fired on them. Vontress numbers the bullets in his kid brother's body as nearly 20. Corky was driving a "wonderful bright red jeep" when he was pulled over and, apparently, the police thought he was a drug dealer. He wasn't, though, Vontress says; his baby brother was just spoiled. "My mother bought him the jeep."

Their mother, a devout Baptist, went into a deep depression. (Their father, whom Vontress has only seen once, lives in California.) Vontress's trauma is evident from the painful contradictions in his telling: "I came out of it really well. I'm an adaptable person. I took it the hardest." After the funeral, he had to return to A.R.T. and *The America Play*, in which he enacted a ritualized assassination of a faux President Lincoln, shooting him repeatedly and at close range. He doesn't return home for two years. Now as he reads the part of a man poking around in his ancestral dirt and coming up empty-handed—a gaping absence of history that extends to African-American culture at large—Vontress is simultaneously set free from the difficulties New York has strewn in his path and routed back to the hole in his own history. When another brother's wedding draws him home to Kansas in early spring for the first time since Corky's slaying, he intends to gather information, to interview his family, and to begin filling in the missing pieces by making art, a one-man show about the incident. But, at least for now, something about being there deflects him from probing further.

*   *   *

Digging is one metaphor for acting. Actors must tunnel down deep into their own emotions and histories and hoist up the most striking, relevant finds. (This is the part of acting that's been emphasized by the American method.) Filling up is another metaphor. Actors fill up with energy and character, as though they're vessels, into which a character's spirit is invited. They also fill external forms, roles or physical scores or styles. To do so they must become larger, radiate out, like genies released from bottles. Actors, I think, must maintain these contrary energies, digging down and filling up, inward and out, listening to themselves and attuning themselves to others, planting their feet on the ground while their majestic skulls float atop their long, ready spines. Maybe this counter pull is what attracted me to this particular group of actors. Unlike those maddeningly imbalanced actors who seem too self-focused or too outward-projected and showy, these 15 seemed evenly attentive to themselves and alive to the world.

Jessalyn Gilsig navigates these contrary extremes with an almost electric conviction. More than her striking looks or distinctive voice, Jessalyn's indelibility as an actor springs from the density of her engagement with character and text. As Lavinia in a student-directed production of *Titus Andronicus*, for instance, she translated her character's rape and mutilation (her hands and tongue are cut off) into a savage expressiveness. Her Andromache in *The Trojan Women: A Love Story* workshop was a ferocious-funny portrait of someone both imprisoned by and rebelling against the protocol of upper-class womanhood. The wit and fury that infused this performance were literally splashed across the back wall of the stage every night in a sprawling mural she painted from scratch during the first act of each show. Attacking an expanse of brown paper in hysterical response to the trauma of Trojan ruin, Jessalyn became actress as action painter, digging in and flinging the colors of her soul onto a larger-than-life canvas. Scraps of these murals now hang in several of her ex-classmates' New York apartments.

For all the complexity of her portraiture and her feminist perspective, when Jessalyn circles back to A.R.T.'s professional company, she goes as a pure ingénue. Both Miranda in *The Tempest* and Marianne in *Tartuffe* are sheltered young women at the threshold of awareness, neither having faced hardship, much less the horrors endured by the Greek and Roman heroines Jessalyn played during her final student semester. (This will also be true of the two potentially career-igniting roles she lands after moving back to New York later in the season.) Still, her identification with these roles is intense. At the end of performances as Miranda, "I thought I should just disappear like Miranda disappeared." Part of this specific intensity comes from being the only woman in the cast, a position that adds unnecessarily to her already overwrought sense of responsibility, as if she needs to come across as an Everywoman because she's the Only woman. This self-imposed burden is relieved in *Tartuffe* because the four women's roles cover so many aspects of a woman's many experience; Jessalyn feels free to focus on the story. By now, she's stopped worrying about proving worthy of her new non-trainee status. "I was really worried, I thought, 'all these first-year students probably think they can play Miranda.' Then I thought, 'They will play Miranda.' "

Not surprisingly, then, back at the theatre where she trained, her experience is defined in large part by her shifting relationship to her former teachers. She's worked with both of her directors before. Ron Daniels, who oversees the Shakespeare production, ran the Institute during her tenure, and she's almost romantically drawn to his conviction about ideas and to his perceptions about texts. Francois Rochaix, guiding the Moliere, is more formal; there's little personal connection. Rochaix tries to shake up her preconceptions about period style and about being an ingénue. She has a hard time letting them go. Some days she'll feel herself beginning to cry as he speaks to her; he just keeps on talking. She's developing a real respect for the other actors she knows who bounce from job to job, now that she sees how lonely it can be. She takes solace in the company of the other women. Although she'll leave A.R.T. feeling that, because she went to school here, this doesn't count as a real first job, she knows how fortunate she is. Each night during bows for *Tartuffe*, she stands with Tommy Derrah, a former acting teacher of hers who's playing her father. She takes his hand and thinks, "I'm so damned lucky."

Not every job offers personal enlightenment or freedom. When James

Farmer first reads *Olympia*, by the Hungarian playwright Ferenc Molnar, he doesn't get it. It seems thin, emotionally superficial. He's grateful to be working at Actors Theatre of Louisville; it helps justify the painful year of enforced separation from his new wife, Tracy. Nevertheless, even once rehearsals begin, once the play comes into focus—its mean streak, rigid caste system, and emotional subversion—he's still groping, just finding his feet as an actor. He leans on the director too much. Even in performance before appreciative audiences, he can't seem to "make it mine," except in moments. Right now, he's still suffering from the student's self-consciousness; he hasn't yet recovered "the joy of playing." *A Christmas Carol*, in which he plays Young Scrooge, among other things, holds out no hope of deep fulfillment either. The Dickens chestnut simply demands "being cheerful about Christmas for an hour and a half." In his first winter of work, everything feels middling. He lives (without Tracy) in the Mayflower, apartments converted from an old hotel in downtown Louisville. Initially, he thought it would provide a funky pleasure, "like Camino Real. But now it feels more like the Betty Ford Clinic."

Kevin Waldron finds his work on *Room Service* at Denver Center Theatre no more transcendent. Mark Boyett is still there, living on the floor below him, and that's a salve for the loneliness of itinerancy. The leap into broad comedy, though, is unsettling. He's playing Harry Binion, the play's second banana, "the real cynical one who has all the funny one-liners, all the zingers." He thinks Groucho Marx played the role in the movie, but, since the director discourages the cast from watching the film, he's never seen it.

Instead, Kevin rents *His Girl Friday* and other screwball comedies to get a sense of the genre's rhythm and style. By the fourth day of rehearsal, the play has been fully staged. By the end of the same week, the cast is off book. For the remainder of rehearsals, the actors run through the show once each morning and once each afternoon. Kevin is used to a different kind of scene analysis and breakdown, but senses that there are professional boundaries in place that he should respect. Over the course of the daily double run-throughs, he finds comic bits getting stale from constant use. These he discards for new ones, which, similarly, lose freshness. His character is dictated, to a certain extent, by the exaggerated, black-and-white costume: black riding boots, jodhpurs, beret and riding crop. "I played him big, primarily because my costume was so big." He's directed, for instance, to enter at one point, take center stage and say "The rehearsal was terrific!" while slapping (and, of course, hurting) himself with the crop. Sometimes, the play works and is fun. And other times "it hurts to be onstage. It's like having egg on your face." Gnawing at his consciousness is the job he backed out of to take this one.

*   *   *

Options, which are luxuries that few actors enjoy, create anxiety. They can also create ethical dilemmas, situations in which personal freedom and responsibility collide. These dilemmas can be as straightforward as the escape clause in a contract or as knotty as friendship. The choices actors make resonate through the theatre at large, whose dictum sometimes seems to be: "You can't trust actors to commit. They're always on the make for something better."

During our first interview, in Cambridge a year ago June, Ajay Naidu said something that scared and shocked me. I mentioned that his classmates seemed suddenly ambivalent about leaving each other's company, fearful of the imminent future, even confused about what to hope for. 'Bullshit," he said, without malice, "They all know exactly what they want." Was he right? Are their aims so solitary? In the '60s and '70s, when professional nonprofit theatre was taking root in America, the idea of art theatre was practically synonymous with "acting company." Is the myth of young actors making history in a church basement now history?

Ajay is not usually this harsh. He's very sweet. The first time I saw him he was massaging a friend's shoulders so tenderly I assumed (wrongly) that they were lovers. As a performer, he is polished, athletic, and direct; he smacks of confidence and drive. He arrives at our first New York interview with flowers for my family. It's a characteristic gesture, combining genuine affection with flattery—a pitch for approval so transparent it's endearing. He knows I will ask him about Denver, where he was rehearsing Paris in *Romeo and Juliet* before he left, and about Steppenwolf, where he will soon begin work on *Everyman*.

Ajay has accepted a job in Chicago as an ensemble member rotating into the lead in the famous medieval morality play, directed by his friend and earliest theatres advocate Frank Galati. The timetable as he tells it: when Ajay is two weeks into rehearsals for *Romeo and Juliet*, Galati, who "ups the ante on my career regularly," calls him and offers him a job without an audition. While he's considering the offer, his mother phones with the news that his father, an emergency room doctor with a history of diabetes and two open heart surgeries, is ill; they'll be moving back to Chicago soon. Then she says "the magic words: if you can find work in Chicago. . . ." "I wasn't going to leave," he says, "until I found out my parents would be there." He remembers his sister's mental illness and blames himself for not being with her enough before her suicide.

He calls his agent and authorizes him to say yes to Steppenwolf. He asks the agent when he should give notice. With a four-week out in his contract, it makes sense to give notice four days before the first preview. He will then leave three-and-a-half weeks into the play's run, one-and-a-half weeks before it closes. By disclosing at this time, he hopes to earn both credits for his resume and spare Denver some hassle. The agent sends a fax giving his father's health as the reason for departure and the Steppenwolf gig as incidental, but in retrospect Ajay thinks this too equivocal. "They should have said it was my dad. Period. Or *Everyman*. Period."

The DCT administration replaces him immediately, before the show's director leaves town. They put the sub in at first preview, Ajay believes, "to make an example of me." Ajay helps train his replacement but can't claim the role in his credits. He watches the initial preview and flies out the next morning. "I don't think I'll ever do it again for anything, except perhaps a major movie role," he admits, somewhat concerned that his classmates will think he made a bad political decision. It's not worth the guilt, he explains. Moreover, he likes to finish what he starts.

I find myself pushing him for a more complete mea culpa: Did your father's health really decide it? How guilty do you truly feel? What would happen if everyone broke commitments like this?

When he hits Chicago, Ajay is home. *Everyman* serves up the kind of aesthetic fulfillment you dream about. He's ecstatically happy. He stays with his girlfriend's parents; works on a one-man show about Indians living in America, turns on to a new music called "Jungle," and even starts to design his own line of dance clothes. His parents haven't moved here yet, but they've bought a house in nearby Gray's Lake.

Kevin Waldron's choice takes him in the opposite direction—to Denver. He is scheduled to play the lead in Phyllis Nagy's *Weldon Rising*, directed by a colleague from A.R.T., at the small Coyote Theatre in Boston. He has a verbal agreement that includes a little pay; he also has a burgeoning friendship with the director, with whom he's been discussing the play for months. There's little chance of a conflict, since he hasn't been auditioning much. Anyway, he's vowed not to back out. Kevin notifies the agent he freelances with, gives the show's dates and tells him to expect a contract. When a *Room Service* audition he's sent on goes well, Kevin phones Mark in Denver to find out more about the theatre. (Mark, incidentally, would have overlapped with Ajay, if Ajay had stayed.) Mark tells him the show's dates; they conflict with *Weldon*, the director of which is out of the country. There's still no contract in hand for the Boston production (a common non-occurrence in the world of small theatres) when DCT offers him a part. Having left several messages—never responded to—for his friend in Boston, Kevin accepts the Denver offer. They haven't spoken since, though it's trickled back to Kevin how angry and disappointed he is. The director has only 11 days to recast and reconceive the play's major character.

Both decisions raise ethical questions, and neither actor takes these lightly. Kevin lacks a contract when he jumps ship; Ajay bails out midstream. Is either one more or less "wrong"? Is Kevin's choice more acceptable because he trades up in pay (he'll make approximately five times as much at Denver)? On the other hand, Ajay plays a secondary character in Romeo, while Kevin is the key player in the Boston project. What does a director do when s/he loses the Hamlet 11 days before rehearsal? How far in advance would Kevin's reversal have been okay? Ajay, as it turns out, does the right thing for him; his Steppenwolf experience is joyful. After the fact, Kevin harbors little doubt that he chose the less challenging work, but upon returning to NYC, his agent signs him, a move that leads to additional work. What are the boundaries of commitment: money, friendship, contracts?

Siobhan Brown, Kevin's classmate and friend, is also cast in *Weldon Rising*. She stays with the show, returning to her hometown for the second time since graduation to play a "lipstick lesbian," a less central role than his. For her *Weldon* is a positive experience—good work well received. It also leads to an even better one: playing Titania in an exciting, outdoor *A Midsummer Night's Dream* in Boston's Copley Square, produced and directed by the same man. Loyalty and talent are, in her case, rewarded. But what assurance do actors ever have of such rewards?

*   *   *

One of the long-lived mantras of American theatre training programs is, "Create your own opportunities." The stacked odds against steady employment for actors make this valuable advice for every decade, advice this group of actors heeds with a vengeance. Chandler Vinton enlists an actor she and her mates admire to start an acting class. It fizzles after a few meetings, through no fault of Chandler's. Different combinations of actors surface in a series of projects, many involving other A.R.T. alums. These include 15-minute "Monarch Notes" Shakespeare plays, directors' laboratory projects, student and small independent films, and even student-directed plays at other New York City grad schools.

Todd Thomas Peters and Caroline Hall are cast in a production of Odon Von Horvath's *Don Juan Comes Back from the War* at Columbia University, directed by a Masters student who saw them at A.R.T. You have to keep acting, Caroline explains. "You get creaky. You have to do it. I'd rather be in a bad production than in nothing." When a postcard for *Don Juan* arrives at my house in early spring, though, Caroline's name has disappeared and Chandler's has been added. Todd claims to be doing better than he thought he'd do to reach his goal of 100 rejections by year's end. He's logged about six failures so far, he says. He also continues to develop *The Birdcatchers* with Randall, after their successful performance in Venezuela. He and Caroline talk about starting a business "to sell something to somebody."

Caroline joins Tom Hughes with the Lark Theatre Company, an educational outreach group that mounts a 50-minute, 4-actor version of *Romeo and Juliet* to tour city schools. Tom teaches for the Lark besides. Vontress begins meeting with a theatre-in-formation he finds in the trade paper *Backstage* under "membership." Almost by accident, he's a founding member of what wants to be called Lone Wolf.

Sherri Parker Lee hooks up with a devoted, enthusiastic band of actors she meets through a regular customer at the restaurant where she waits tables. "Coach," as he's called, is one of four customers in the place during the record-breaking blizzard of '95—'96. "My son has a theatre company," he tells Sherri. "You should call him." Sherri, scouring Manhattan for a theatrical home base, is constitutionally incapable of ignoring a lead. She calls. Coach's son casts her as Lydia Languish in the Habitual Theatre Company production of *The Rivals*. They enjoy a "fun" run in a supportive atmosphere. When the steam pipe at their theatre breaks before their closing day photo shoot, four or five members of the nascent company empty the building and call everyone on the sold-out list for the afternoon's performance. They nudge the show from 3 to 5 o'clock, get down on their hands and knees and clean the theatre, salvaging everything they can, after which they assume the manners of the 18th century before a grateful audience.

Suzanne Pirret is beginning research on a one-woman play about the life of Edie Sedgwick. Mostly, though, she's thinking about L.A. "Everyone of my friends that is out there is working and seems happy," she says. "Here in New York everyone is complaining—just like me. Everyone here is self-deprecating and discouraged. Everyone's on Prozac." She visits Los Angeles in mid-January, meets an agent and a guy from ABC, all through friends. Ideally, she'd like to move there, she explains, "make a name for myself, come back and do theatre—good theatre." It's hard, though, especially having been around this same block before, to keep her confidence up.

*   *   *

While they work, look for work, and make work happen while they search for that revelation of freedom, life keeps going. Kevin, who began dating an HIV-positive man in November, something he has avoided in the past, waits for his own test results to come back from the lab. Jessalyn, home from A.R.T., watches the clock run down on her Canadian visa. Caroline, whose name has dropped off the cast list for *Don Juan* at Columbia, stops returning my calls, weeks then months of calls. I hear she's very sick. I hear she's left town, then I hear she's back. Still no contact.

Granville Hatcher lands his second job as an onscreen terrorist, a Jordanian this time, and shuttles between Manhattan and his daughter in Boston. Tom Hughes becomes the Elder's Quorum President for his new Mormon congregation close by his Washington Heights home. Also, after many months of orthodontia, he gets his braces removed, a necessary step towards commercial work. Todd Peters's marriage plans—made almost entirely without his input—roll along their juggernaut way. At 4:30 on March 11, Ajay phones. He's edgy, waiting to hear about something "very big. Major," but he can't tell me what. At 6:45 he calls back, "feeling stoned with excitement." He just booked a lead role in the movie of Eric Bogosian's *SubUrbia*, directed by *Slacker* whiz Richard Linklater. A few days later, Tom's biggest dream begins to come true: "We're having a baby," he announces. "We just decided to start and boom!"

This article was originally published in *American Theatre*, February, 1997.

Open Call, Part Three: The Spirit is Willing

Spring/Summer, 1996: Chandler Vinton has just finished reading Milton's *Paradise Lost* and *Paradise Regained*. She has a lot of time on her hands. Although she worries that she's not hungry enough to succeed, that she's "hiding out from the fact that this is a business," she also has a voice inside that says, "Make sure you're happy." For now, she's happiest in her new apartment "My definition of making it is not, 'I'm going to L.A. to be a big star," she explains. "I keep trying to tell myself that that's okay, that mine's not less or worse than someone else's ambition. But I'd rather sit home and read about God."

Making a home for herself has been Chandler's response to the feeling that hit her within months of her move to New York: "It's like I'm waiting here at the world's disposal." Chandler knows that it may take years before she grows into the parts she suits; she hasn't known what to do while waiting. The answers come to her gradually, over the course of the year. Her first apartment, a minuscule Upper West Side studio which rents for $1,050 a month, barely has room for her and her two cats, so she locates a floor of an actual home in Carroll Gardens, Brooklyn, a family neighborhood, and moves there. She retrieves from storage the furniture she got when her mother died, and cozies up the place. She reads. Early in the year, she takes two jobs—she's never had to work before—and derives from her own competence a dose of confidence. First she replaces an executive secretary on sick leave from a major advertising agency, a job that brings in $16 an hour and sets her crowing on the phone, "I'm making money!" Then she books a couple nights a week as a cocktail waitress at a place called "Jake's Dilemma." She is maid of honor for her mother's sister's wedding and, as a gift her aunt pays for her to start psychotherapy, another important beginning. For a time she works out.

In a year that offers little hope of high achievement or major reward, these small steps are saving graces. "I'm feeling very good about reading, good about working out. I feel proud of the fact that I'm a good cocktail waitress." While nothing completes itself for her this year, she becomes aware that "all my processes are probably 10-year processes, not yearly ones. What's most important to me now is meeting people who share my interests and aesthetics."

Not everyone can afford the luxury of patience. Chandler, though, belongs to that illustrious heritage of haute bourgeois theatre people with the means to bankroll their own dreams. She can pay for an audition class, join an organization that helps actors write resumes, organize mailings and network, and explore alternative careers in the arts by interning, unpaid, at New York theatres. She can punctuate the unspectacular year with revitalizing family trips to Grenada or Georgia's Sea Island or visits to her father's home in England. Thanks to her banker dad and a small inheritance from a distant relative, she can buy more time. This privilege is a blessing, one that Chandler is only beginning to register. "I've had a pretty easy life. Shitty things have happened, but it's been easy."

Is anyone's life really easy? Chandler lived with her mother's paranoid schizophrenia and survived, at 16 years of age, her suicide. Her classmates, some wealthy, some not, have suffered other traumas and tragedies. Is it the ease that makes an artist or the difficulty? Is acting a way for a woman of privilege to forge a personality outside the comfort of home or is it an opportunity for healing the wounds those same comforts mask? With Chandler it's hard to tell: she's so solid, and so adrift. As she talks, she wanders throughout her apartment. Sometimes she picks something up, a knapsack or book, as if on purpose, only to set it down randomly, wherever she winds up.

*   *   *

This middle territory, in-progress state is hard to describe. When, by way of contrast, Ajay Naidu snares the part of Nazeer, the Indian convenience store owner, in Richard Linklater's film of Eric Bogosian's *SubUrbia*, he has names to relate and details—of rehearsing in LA's Chateau Marmont for example, a swanky old hotel where John Belushi died. This big break is followed by another—an episode of HBO's *Subway Stories*, produced by Jonathan Demme and Rosie Perez and costarring (with Ajay) Danny Hoch and Sarita Choudhury. The single dramatic event of landing a movie gives way to a story of momentum, a young career on a roll. Days later, that story gains power when an Italian director hires Ajay for the leading role in a third movie, *Once We Were Strangers*, about a young Indian man who, having emigrated to America at the age of eight, faces an arranged marriage with a woman from his homeland.

But consider Chandler's story. Without defining events, like Ajay's string of jobs, a year that may turn out to be pivotal can look positively uneventful. The defining peculiarity of the actor's life arises from this disjunction: between the randomly reinforced rhythms of theatre employment—auditions, no auditions, callbacks, offers, contracts, dry spells, got-its and lost-its—and the slower, steadier pulse of ordinary days.

After a pleasant, horizon-expanding few months at the Actors Theatre of Louisville, James Farmer returns to half-a-year of daily life. He makes ends barely meet by waiting tables at the roof top restaurant in Bryant Park and tending bar in Brooklyn Heights at the Montague Street Saloon. He does some showcase acting and a couple of readings with friends. He obsesses over little details from auditions or things his agent says to him on the phone. He starts to feel "kinda crazy," just hanging on to himself. Then, for the first time in several years, Tracy—his wife of nearly a year, finished with her own graduate program—comes to town to stay. Now they have to learn to be together.

All this takes time, and it unspools in a distinctly undramatic fashion. "I'm trying to be happy with what I have," James explains. "Things are going okay, however slowly." He's starting to feel comfortable in New York and to accept more constant rejection—especially now that he's being sent on more auditions—than he's ever faced. He makes a Red Lobster commercial on Long Island and Fire Island. You know the kind, handsome folks walking around on docks carrying bushels of lobster on ice, "people having far too much fun." When it goes national, he finally has some money in the bank, but nothing compared to the $100,000 he and Tracey owe on their school loans.

With the exception of his pared-down Shakespeare performances in city schools and at the Museum of Natural History, Tom Hughes accomplishes a lot more this year as a writer of books for young people and as a future father than as an actor. He goes on a sprinkling of auditions, many for Shakespeare plays, mostly for Horatio-types—supporting players with integrity. "I'm not the kind of guy who gets cast as Macbeth or Hamlet. I'm too even-keeled." And he's in it for the long haul, despite a lifestyle that contradicts almost every actor stereotype—homebody, husband, and devoted churchgoer. (His wife Kristen has already shelved the idea of acting and found a less flashy career, one she loves, as a teaching assistant at an Episcopal preschool.) When his agent signs him for two more years he's told, "If you can be patient with us, we can be patient with you." He considers each part of himself in light of the whole: personally happy and professionally dissatisfied, ready to do more to take charge of his work, to be the "agent" of his own career. Worries about money—income, debt and insurance—wear him out.

Every concern is swept aside, though, by one. And before long he'll modem a message to my e-mail box. "Two days early, and not a moment too soon, Steven Thomas Hughes, with some assistance from his mother, a vacuum, a pair of forceps and a platoon of medical personnel, emerged from a murky world of moist darkness into one of bright lights, cold air and non-self-cleaning diapers....Date/Time of Birth: Friday, November 8, 1996; 7:26 a.m."

*   *   *

If the Institute of Advanced Theatre Training at Harvard's class of 1995 had taken a poll, Kevin Waldron just might have been voted most likely to enter the clergy. Now, with neither pomp nor circumstance, he's done it. His was a mail-order ordination, sent away for and bought with the sole purpose of performing Todd Peters' wedding ceremony. Kevin's holy orders came in an envelope from the Universal Life Church in California, which has been anointing people by mail, the story goes, since the Vietnam era. At the time these postal priesthoods were especially popular among draft-eligible Hollywood actors looking to authenticate their conscientious objections to the war. If this subterfuge was a tactical hypocrisy, it was also an actorly one, since priests and actors are related at their roots. Performance springs from worship, and the rituals of worship emulate theatre. Like the clergy, many actors express a fundamental spiritualism that jars with our secular age. Kevin's blessings will be on display on Saturday, the 26th of October, 1996 at 4:00 in the afternoon in San Diego, Calif., reception to follow.

How Todd has come to win the part of Margo Porras's bridegroom is another story. On Oregon's Cannon Beach a couple weeks after graduation last summer, he scrawled a proposal in the sand. (Years before Margo's father had written a similar proposal with a stick in the dirt.) In "one fluid moment," he slipped an engagement ring on her finger and they began strolling, as the sun set, amid the massive coastal rocks. Little did Todd know when he found the courage and grace to pledge his sandy troth that this moment of flow would be about the only time all year that he'd feel in command. He's thrilled about the wedding, but he complains all the time because, as with everything else in his life, it feels like it's out of his hands. His notion of waiting two years to get married gets whittled down to "next October." His family-by-marriage-to-be arranges the purchase of a New Jersey co-op for the couple. Meanwhile, Todd looks on, suddenly aware that trying to stop this juggernaut of energy and will "is like trying to hold the ocean back with a broom." Todd might grumble, but he does so winningly, ironically acknowledging his commitment and readiness to play the part of married man. The passing year shows him, though, that he is nowhere near as ready to assume the role of New York actor.

* * *

By dint of some unique charm, Todd is able to depict himself as the active agent of his own inactivity, a character whose lack of chutzpah approaches the heroic. Moreover, he transforms even the most uneventful detail of his actor's existence into a dramatic event.

He has quit his mole-like existence as a graveyard shift computer operator and is in high spirits, as if the year has agreed with him. He seems taller, brighter, more redheaded than ever. Todd usually has a story to tell—often an upbeat tale of personal failure. He recounts the life-changing

116

experience of playing the title character in Odon von Horvath's *Don Juan Comes Back from the War* in a Masters thesis production at Columbia University. Everything was going miserably and then his worst nightmare came true. His best friend Randall Jaynes came to a preview and told him the show was so bad there was nothing he could do to screw it up more.

Something opened up in him. He began to have fun, to concentrate on just telling the story. The performance grew 100 percent on opening night, he claims, and 100 percent each night after that. The experience changed him. "Suddenly I just realized, I can do this. That made me feel like an actor." Now that he's tapped this confidence in his acting, he's energized to "start acting like an actor." "I want that life more than anything. It's been so long waiting, so long being afraid. Not doing it has become more painful than doing it. I want to look like an actor. I want to have a bag like an actor. I want people to think about me what they think about [classmate] Sherri Lee. I want them to say, 'He's an animal.'" I assume this new energy has accelerated his attempt to pile up 100 rejections before year's end. (When I inquired a few months earlier, he'd only gotten the thumbs down half-a-dozen times.) So, I ask for a tally.

He stops a minute and mumbles something about, "Should I or shouldn't I tell you?" Then he confesses. "The closest thing I got to doing an audition was being a reader." He admits to lying last time we spoke. He hasn't had a single audition since hitting New York 13 months ago (Don Juan was simply offered to him). Now, though, he's rearing to go, and he's got this incredible network of school friends—his "mafia"—to back him up. Sherri has even offered to escort him to auditions. He tells Kevin he's "ready to be an actor" and Kevin says, 'Well, it's about time."

Sherri Parker Lee, it appears, was born ready to be an actor, but only now is her readiness paying off. After a full year of rapid-fire auditioning, constant callbacks, and numerous near misses, she lands a paying soap opera job and then a play and finally, following months of herky-jerky negotiation, a six-month repertory contract. "I've always been a person who says 'I want that; I'm going to get that,' and I've gotten that. Somewhere subconsciously I project myself into the future." When the future first rises up to greet her, however, it's not a pretty sight.

Sherri screen tests for a character on *As The World Turns* and is given every indication of having it in the bag. Ultimately, though, her agent tells her, "they went for type over talent," deciding they didn't want a blonde. A week later the show calls to offer a small part they've created with Sherri in mind, a spoiled rich-girl biker, who drives into town with a new male lead, a Calvin Klein model who's never acted before but has secured a three-year contract. Sherri's treated very well, and members of the cast compliment her on her earlier test. Her first scene on camera, which, due to the new guy's inexperience takes seven takes, consists almost entirely of kissing, with him cramming his tongue in her mouth. (After each kiss a female union representative comes over and asks if she is okay.) She's given notes like "flip your hair" and "pull your bikini down." Sherri cries when she sees the debacle on TV, but her grandmother, a big fan of the show, calls its 800 number 25 times to say how much she likes Sherri. Things get better.

After a previous New York audition for the Alley Theatre of Houston's production of Nicky Silver's *The Food Chain*, she'd written a thank you note to Gregory Boyd, the company's artistic director. When she's called in for Brecht's *In The Jungle of Cities*, he thanks her for the letter. She goes for broke with her singing audition, preferring "strong but wrong" to unnoticeable. Afterward, he requests that she stick around. When he finishes auditions, he invites her to walk with him. As they move along 43rd Street, he asks her if she's interested in joining the company on a season contract. A firm offer is made over the phone later only for a part in *Jungle*. Sherri accepts, goes to the Alley until October, returns, negotiates some more and finally, this past January, flies down for a six-month stay, which includes playing Electra in a three-part cycle of Greek tragedies. The groundwork she's laid fastidiously each and every day of this year is paying off. Her boyfriend Dan, has only days ago moved to New York with his 12-year-old son, despite some initial ambivalence on Sherri's part. Once he arrives, she's happy to be reunited and committed to being committed. Her anxiety over the right course of their relationship departs, but then so does she.

* * *

There's a classroom exercise in which actors bring onstage with them something from their lives—something that jumpstarts their belief in the given circumstances of a scene. The performer works with this object—a photograph, maybe, or an article of clothing or childhood toy—as a way of navigating between now and another time, one ripe with associations and feelings. This object becomes a real key to an imaginary world. The exercise is also emblematic of the actor's ongoing struggle. Faced with empty space, spirit-numbing obstacles and a life of creative expression that exists only in the imagination, actors must surround themselves with people and things that create—within them—faith.

"One of the most important things is surrounding yourself with really supportive, positive people," insists Suzanne Pirret. Building a community of loving others becomes the bulwark of her faith in herself. Everyone who doesn't fit that description, she literally whites out of her address book. She chooses her influences carefully, accentuating the positive. She looks for a teacher and an agent who believe in her, and ultimately finds both. Her new acting teacher, Wynn Handman, creates for her an intense and supportive, free-to-fail environment. He helps her find herself by finding comedy and by encouraging her to stick to character roles. Similarly, she signs with a new commercial agent who is consistent and excited about her. They speak on the phone several times a week and are, in Suzanne's words, "like family." Her blood family is, likewise, there for her, with love, support and, until she locates a place in the city, a home. She's also part of an ongoing comedy group, all alliances that help dispel the "black cloud" that threatens when acting work isn't there. History is repeating itself for Suzanne this year. Having returned to New York, she's taking classes again, pounding pavements again and, in her second autumn back, bartending in a new version of the same restaurant she worked in a few years ago. This sense of recurrence conceals an energizing difference: this time around she's not alone.

The reverend Kevin Waldron may be no evangelical, but he is a good listener and a deeply spiritual soul. So when the New York he's fantasized about taking by storm knocks him, instead, for a loop, he turns to meditation—"a lot of meditation"—as a pacifier. He reads Deepak Chopra's *The Seven Spiritual Laws of Success* four times, drawing connections between laws of the spirit and the practice of acting. In daily life, for example, you can never know ahead of time what will happen. The same is true on stage: actors must avoid thinking ahead or trying to recreate successful scenes by doing exactly what they've done in the past. As a person and an actor, Kevin has come to believe, "You need to embrace uncertainty."

Spiritual laws come into his relations with others, too. Kevin shares an apartment with close friend and fellow-alum Randall Jaynes. It's a funky little East Village cove, owned by Randall's employer, Blue Man Group, and renovated by Kevin and Randall (with Blue Man money) from a state of stripped, utility-less, maggot-infested wreckage. As part of their continuous bolstering of each other, they entertain the "law of giving." They describe their ideal apartments, and Randall suggests, "When one of us really makes it, let him give the other the ideal apartment." The class of 1995 may not have stayed together as a company, but in their various moves to New York, they stay together as a support network, sometimes one on one, sometimes in cells, groups splintered from the whole. Their telephones ring back and forth. They crash on each other's couches, collaborate on projects and offer advice as well as figurative kicks in the pants.

By quirk of fate, Ajay Naidu lives in the adjoining building on the other side of Kevin and Randall's nonworking fireplace. There he makes his way through a workbook of his own, melding art, psychological healing and spiritual aspiration: Julia Cameron's *The Artist's Way*. He calls it "creative I.V." Like Kevin, Ajay has shifted from early religious teachings to a more individualized system of belief. He emphasizes that his career choices have always been his own, that instead of being pushed, in a way typical to Indian families, he's created his own path. This includes the spiritual. Once a "heavy Hindu kid," he's a "heavy Buddhist now."

Both Kevin and Ajay's guidebooks offer practical steps to spiritual ends, a worldly and otherworldly mix that seems at home in the motley East Village. A quarter-century ago, theatre critic Kenneth Tynan dubbed Greenwich Village "the internment camp of Manhattan nonconformity," a label now more suited to the low-rent chic of St. Mark's Place, where, within shouting distance of a new upscale Kmart, junkies hang out in front of Japanese-inflected health food restaurants and a fetishist boutique called "Religious Sex" sells leather and lace up the street from the Gap. The bohemia of the early '80s is this decade's designer mall. Smack in the middle of the block—visible from the actors' windows—a community center for recovering addicts shelters a regular round of 12-step meetings, offering the support of human fellowship and a self-defined "higher power."

When Siobhan Brown tackles the first six weeks of *The Artist's Way*, she's "reminded of everything I'd been taught in Christian Science that I liked and wanted to take away with me." While she started the year feeling the strain she's put on her intimacy with her mother by not following her mother's religion, by year's end intimacy and distance have settled into an easier balance. Her spiritual direction seems more a modification of than a break with her Christian Scientist upbringing, which she learns is "nothing I can ever leave behind." Prayer and spiritual definition become daily, self-sustaining practices in a difficult year.

The pursuit of spiritual ends has an intellectual cast for Mark Boyett, though his personal history suggests much more. Mark's strict religious rearing included four years boarding at Ben Lippen—Mountain of Trust — a fundamentalist Christian high school in Asheville, N.C. If it hadn't been for a friend who was applying to A.R.T. and who encouraged him to do the same, he might have begun graduate study in religion. His "drift from a faith of sorts" occurred gradually, assisted in small measure by a dawning homosexuality that started him entertaining "the notion that the Bible as it was taught to me is not true." Now Mark's bookshelves show a continued interest in matters of devotion. The theological abuts the thespian, as Shakespeare and Stanislavsky lean against contemporary religious studies, such as *The Gnostic Gospels* and *The History of God*. I wonder what his 12th-grade tutors would have thought of his profession and of the infidel acts he's hired to perform this season: cavorting as the devil in *Beethoven and Pierrot* at Denver Center Theatre; defending the Talmud as a Hassidic yeshiva boy in *The Dybbuk*; impersonating, in Brecht's *Galileo*, a failing Old

Cardinal who insists the world is flat and still; and, for *Old Wicked Songs* Off Broadway, understudying the role of a 25-year-old piano prodigy, who keeps his Judaism in the closet.

Vontress Mitchell, reared a Baptist, "was in the ministry at 15." In college he detoured to Boston for conservatory training as a singer. His mother and five surviving brothers have all experienced comforting visitations from his younger brother Corky, since he was shot and killed by the Wichita police two years ago. Vontress has not. "Corky knew I'm the most fearful person when it comes to this spiritual stuff," he explains, as though his brother's spirit has purposely avoided him. They used to joke about it, and Vontress told Corky that if anything ever happened, he should stay away. "I said, 'Don't visit me; I will rebuke you.'" At one point, during his return home in early spring, he finds the house his brother lived in so eerie that he asks his mother to keep the bathroom light on.

New York weighs on Vontress. It appears to him that "everybody needs something; everybody has an agenda, and if you're not there for them, you're in the way. I have a deeper need for why I'm in it. I'm unhappy here because I'm constantly having to protect that need." Sometimes the effort isn't worth it. In August, Vontress leaves New York for San Francisco to play one of the five sages of Chelm in *Shlemiel the First*; he originated the role at A.R.T., where the musical, based on stories by Isaac Bashevis Singer, was developed. He'll join most of the original cast at the American Conservatory Theatre—still the only African-American Jewish wise man onstage. (This is after playing Roderigo in an all-black cast of *Othello* with a company of ex-Juilliard students in Manhattan.) He's not sure, though, whether he'll come back to New York or even continue acting. While rooming with family in Oakland, he stays in a lot, watching TV and listening to music. He reads *The Care of the Soul* by Thomas Moore. (If the self-appointed moralists of American life assault the theatre as a godless place, let these young artists stand as proof that it is anything but.)

For Tom Hughes, the deeper needs have outlets other than theatre, and spirituality goes hand in hand with doctrine. An active Mormon, he is part of a lay priesthood that firmly believes in modern revelation and an ongoing heritage of prophets. His family in Utah also belongs to the Church of Jesus Christ of Latter-day Saints. His father, head of his congregation in Provo, holds the five-to-seven-year unpaid post of bishop and the designation of high priest. Nevertheless, Tom describes Mormonism as something you choose, the result of personal, spiritual conversion. "All worthy male members of the church from 12 on up are priesthood holders, so it's just part of your life." Now he is an Elder Quorum President for his congregation, a largely administrative post that involves overseeing "home teaching" visits to each family in the congregation to make sure they're okay. He's gratified to be on call like this and to be of service.

Unlike his classmates, however, he doesn't see theatre as particularly continuous with religion. "I wouldn't say I put any religious value in it. I find my meaning for life in my religion and my life. I see theatre as a place that shows us life, explains it." He tries to articulate the conscience his beliefs set up in him—the constant search for worthiness—by quoting the Mormon character Joe Pitt from Tony Kushner's *Angels in America*: "The failure to measure up hits people very hard. From such a strong desire to be good they feel very far from goodness when they fail." God is not a way out of the consequences of personal action or, as the case might be, inaction. Rather, the will to be good, and the attendant self-judgment, underscores a principle of faith Tom takes to heart: personal responsibility, or what he calls "agency."

* * *

Agency. It's an unavoidable pun. Actors hope for agents who will share responsibility—agency—for their careers. They look for the right match of support and savvy. They find all sorts of things. Some agents strive to keep their clients in town; some send them out only for regional work. James's agent loans him the money for new head shots, and others do no more than warn, "You need new pictures," and then don't submit them for auditions until the expensive eight-by-tens have been delivered. Randall's representatives, who receive no percentage for Randall's Blue Man Group performances and his solo appearances at international festivals, get a big bonus from him at Christmas. Some offer the clout of well-known agencies and some the intimacies of a small, new staff. Still others seem to forget their clients exist.

In the end, though, the power is mostly on the other side of the casting table. Jessalyn Gilsig's agents may be able to line up major league auditions, but they can't guarantee her roles. When she lands the part of Sunny in the world premiere production of *Driving Miss Daisy* author Alfred Uhry's new play, *The Last Night of Ballyhoo*, scheduled to open at the Olympics in Atlanta, they can negotiate her contract, but they can't ensure she'll reprise the role on Broadway. In fact, after working with Jessalyn in Atlanta for four months (including a two-month sold-out run at the Alliance Theatre), Uhry and his producers and director keep her on a string for several months before deciding on someone else for the Broadway cast.

Some things no one controls. Jessalyn is in Atlanta watching television when the bomb goes off.[1] Later, the theatre has bomb scares of its own. One

---

[1] At Centennial Olympic Park in Atlanta, July 27, 1996, during the Olympics. The bomb, later found to be one of several acts of domestic terrorism by Eric Robert Rudolph, killed two people and injured one hundred and eleven others.

night the actors get word that there's an abandoned package upstairs but that they are expected to keep performing until the house lights go on— then they should head for the exit. Before another show the cast wanders into the green room to find five volunteer security people staring at a bag in the corner, as though they don't want to see it because it means they have to deal with it. Nor can Jessalyn, a Canadian citizen, control whether or not she'll have her visa renewed, though her agent and new lawyer are helping gather letters that make the case that she's an asset to the U.S. She rules out marriage; she and her boyfriend aren't ready. From June until late October she waits to hear, "sort of freaking" the whole time. When she does hear, her visa is denied. She is supposed to leave the country immediately.

She then learns that this is a mistake. An essential letter, written and sent, has never found her file. Still, the glitch means more waiting and, finally, reentering the country with her new papers in order. She leaves for her sister's in Montreal and bides time until her entry visa arrives.

*   *   *

For all the good fortune in this thrilling career year, Ajay can't control his father's decline. In early August Dr. Naidu enters the hospital with a mild heart attack. With a history of coronary trouble and diabetes, surgeons won't operate on him. Ajay speaks to him the day before he checks into the hospital. The next day, when he arrives in Chicago for a week-and-a-half vacation, his father is in a coma, apparently after suffering a stroke. The doctors shunt the blood from his cranium and for a while he's responsive. Then he slips into another coma. He never regains consciousness.

The family decides to pull him off the respirator and only give him food, knowing that he wouldn't want to live on life support. On Aug. 11, he dies in Ajay's arms. "I was holding him and my mom was there, across from me." Two of Ajay's uncles and one of his aunts are also in the room as 65-year-old Dr. Naidu gradually stops breathing. Ajay speaks for the family at the funeral. His father is cremated; half his ashes get strewn in Lake Michigan, after it is consecrated by an Indian priest. The other half will be spread in the Ganges.

Ajay returns to New York, where over the next few weeks, he shoots three films. He is on his own in ways he can only begin to imagine.

*   *   *

Granville Hatcher also learns a bit about the illusion of control. He sees his character work edited out of his first Hollywood movie until, as a principal Lebanese terrorist, he's "basically a face with a gun." He stands by while his second movie, a fact-based black comedy about the World Trade Center bombing, in which he plays a Jordanian chemical engineer, is held from release until the Ramzi Yousef (one of the indicted bombers) case concludes in New York City, so as not to taint a fair trial. He loses the chance to flesh out his third and smallest role, as an Americanized Hispanic lawyer in a TV show starring Stockard Channing, since the pilot doesn't get picked up by the networks. The possibility of this continuing role is reduced to a single day of work, one line in one scene, played naked from the waist up, in bed. "Our job," he determines, "is to wait."

He entertains notions of moving to Chicago or Minneapolis and devoting himself to a theatre company, but for the moment he's held in place. "It's like sitting at a blackjack table. To get up and walk away when the next hand could be blackjack." He tries to put his energy into developing his personal life, including settling in a large one-bedroom, river-view apartment on 175th Street with his girlfriend Blair, who has just graduated from A.R.T. this spring. He's in limbo, though, "waiting by the phone and putting so many other parts of your life on hold." Suddenly his ideas about creating a second home for his daughter Gabrielle feel naive to him. He knows that wherever he is, he may have to leave the next day or may have an audition or need to prepare for one. Moreover, everyday he "wakes up in a question of livelihood, income and where I'm going to be."

Nothing he sees holds out a pot of gold. Meanwhile, his eight-year-old may know something he doesn't. At the end of a summer in California, during which she tapped her own love of acting in a summer program where she appeared as the Polynesian girl in *South Pacific*, she is asked if she wants to play the main, title character in *Alice in Wonderland*. She'd rather be a ladybug, she explains, or a butterfly.

*   *   *

There was only one scenario of illness I'd ever considered possible among this healthy bunch: one of the gay male actors contracting HIV. Fortunately, it never came to pass. I knew that Kevin had tested negative for the virus but, being in a relationship with a positive man, his zero-status was a continual worry. He attended lectures, talked to counselors, and did reading but, in the end, he couldn't accept the fear. "There's a gray area you can't clear. I just couldn't take that leap." When they broke up, Kevin was—and still is—healthy.

Caroline Hall's sudden illness was all the more shocking for being unexpected. Caroline isn't the youngest of her graduating class, but, as long as I've known her, she has struck me as the most youthful spirit, funny without hostility and unambivalently kind. She's also the most consistently private of the group, despite her friendliness. From the first, exposing this year to any but her closest friends went against the grain. So, it becomes doubly incapacitating when she is diagnosed with cancer and told that both her life and her reproductive system could be in danger. Both these early prognoses prove wrong, but her physical problems continue, taking a chunk out of the year. She spends four of the next six months in bed, before and after major surgery, recovers and suffers complications from the operation, all before pulling through, active again, nearly well, and on the mend.

Basically, what happens is this: during rehearsals for the Lark Theatre's truncated *Romeo and Juliet* (in which she performs with Tom Hughes) she suffers severe pain and high fever. It continues into the first week of *Don Juan* rehearsals at Columbia. She goes to a doctor who tells her she has cancer. She has to quit the play and stop walking around. She moves in with her mother in Boston. When a new series of doctors find problems but no cancer, she's confined to bed rest, followed by surgery to remove ovarian cysts, and a month's recovery. She reads compulsively during her convalescence—Margaret Atwood, Kaye Gibbons, Ann Beattie, Joan Didion—a book every day or two.

When Caroline returns to New York, she starts temping again and gets cast as Posthumous in an all-woman production of *Cymbeline* that she's spotted in *Backstage*, a trade paper for actors. She starts feeling poorly again and the doctor tells her to quit either day work or the play. Since she's been borrowing money from her parents this whole time (while luckily covered by her father's business's insurance), she chooses the $13-an-hour temp job and drops Shakespeare, with regret. Her surgery has caused infections, it turns out, so the temping stops, too. She's confined to bed for another month.

By fall, with the end in sight, she's eager to put it all behind her. After nearly five months of silence, she returns my phone calls apologetically and agrees to meet. When I see her I'm stunned by a change in appearance and energy, as if in these missing months, she's been tempered into maturity. Her hair is longer now and, recuperating, she's a bit tired. But everything about her—even her humor—seems richer, more complex and interesting. She's hoping to regain some control of her life, she explains, not that she's had any since moving here. "I've never experienced this before," she says, "never encountered this open space, this lack of control, this inability to create my own action."

She continues with a vignette about small rewards and their oversized impact on the spirit: "The other day I was going to lunch, but only had $3. I didn't want a tuna sandwich. I really wanted a turkey sandwich. That day at Blimpies, the special was a Turkey sandwich for $2.99. I was so happy I told everyone. I called my mother. That was as good as it gets."

*   *   *

A hundred years ago, Anton Chekhov wrote what may still be the single best dramatic portrait of the actor as a young woman. Nina in *The Seagull* is Chekhov's anti-romantic antidote to the romanticization of the actor's life. She suffers the trials of a melodrama heroine. She runs away from a tyrannical father, locks into a romantic obsession and has her heart broken in love and work, before emerging as neither a star nor a corpse but as a dedicated, if ravaged, survivor willing to perform wherever she can and able to keep focused on the small inner voice, "my calling." Her lesson—that life is more about endurance or sheer stamina than about glory—is an often paraphrased sentiment among this class of 1995 in their year of transition. Many of the women attest to wanting to play Nina, anywhere, anytime. This year, they are, in fact, women and men, all Ninas.

Siobhan Brown's transformation dazzles me, though I can't immediately say what's different. She meets me in the audition room of Theatre Communications Group. Her hair is frizzy and full, as she's given up on relaxer. She jokes that it's the end of assimilation. Are her glasses different? Her hair color? Is she taller? Thinner? Certainly she's more self-possessed.

Little things have marked the change. She has a permanent part-time job now, at a decent wage. She's paying her own rent, now that her boyfriend Carl is out of town with *Stomp*. In fact, she's using the time apart to evaluate this rocky relationship, to build up herself. She's bought a dresser for her apartment and is staining it. For the first time in New York, she won't be living out of a suitcase. She's also just returned from Boston, where she played Titania and Hippolyta in *A Midsummer Night's Dream*, the first outdoor Shakespeare in Copley Plaza. While there she insisted on her own housing, rather than agreeing to commute from her mother's house. She started out playing the fairie queen straight but then got freer with the role, in a way that incorporated more movement. The director kept telling her they'd have 1,000 people in the audience, but the number seemed unreal. "The first night I looked out and there were 1,000 people there." The last night, as the actors moved across the stage constructed atop the drained Copley fountain, the audience barricades reached back as far as the street. She followed this fulfilling production with a family vacation on the Cape, where she spent time alone on the beach, running. "In my first year in New York I just wasn't able to do those things for myself," she explains.

She is beautifully present in a way I haven't seen her before. And she's looking forward. "I can't wait until I'm 30," she insists "That's why I stopped processing my hair. Oprah says you come into your womanness in your thirties. I feel like I'm coming into something that's been pounding down my door for a long time."

I ask her about the year as a whole, its highs and lows. Suddenly, she is weeping. A moment ago, she was joking and confident, in full flower, like her newly natural hair. Now, in this corporate room without windows or character, the year catches up with her. Her crying springs from memory, release, and sheer exhaustion. "As a girl I dreamt about coming to New York, and when I finally do, I'm hopping around with a suitcase and no place to be. It's just been kind of hard. My sense of home was destroyed." She cries for a while, one hand shielding her eyes, the back of the other wiping tears away. Siobhan is counting her losses, experiencing the weight of her unique, representative life. Then she looks up again. Her face is sad, radiant, and strong.

Epilogue

> Destiny stands with our dramatis personae folded in her hand.
> —George Eliot, *Middlemarch*

November 4, 1996. The year (year-and-a-half, to be precise) in the lives of these actors ends today. I have fallen in and out of love with each of them dozens of times since leaving Cambridge. I have been struck by their seriousness, talent, and smarts and been driven crazy by the opposite traits: self-seriousness, vanity, and smart-assedness. I have been jealous of their youth and beauty and irked by their careerism, their me-ism. On occasion, I've wished that they were many things they're not. In other words, after betraying me once by not wanting what I wanted for them—that is, to stay together as an ensemble—they have betrayed me regularly, simply by being themselves. Now it is my turn to betray them. I will do what any journalist must do—boil them down, sum them up. By putting these young artists into a few paragraphs each, I'll have to contradict their deepest, actorly conviction that they are infinite, possible—that they can be anything. Moreover, by making them into stories and examples, I'll be making their lives into mini-romances at the very moment that they're struggling out from under the mythology of "making it" as an actor and trying to take life as an actual, daily thing.

Today they come together for the first time since graduation. They're easy and nervous, familiar and uncomfortable with each other and with me, as if on the verge of some cosmic opening night. The photographer arrays them onstage at a Soho performance space called HERE, amid all the clichés of backstage life—black rehearsal clothes, a ladder, unhung lights. Their power as a group grabs me again, and my pulse begins to race. I didn't know them as individuals when we started this project. I knew them as a class, a company, and it was this all-togetherness that elevated each of them and moved me most deeply. Fourteen people in a room, pushing each other to their most creative extremes, under light, in full view. Lean slightly forward, the photographer tells them; it will make you more vivid, as if you are straining to come off the cover, out of the picture. Maybe it's the future they're leaning into. Tom doesn't know it, but in four days his son will be born. Randall will be spending the immediate future with his new girlfriend, Ela, breaking out of his workaholic solitude. He'll also be traveling to festivals throughout the world—he's just returned from one in Moscow—with his one-man *Pinocchio 2035*. Within hours Kevin will head to Norfolk, Va., on a three-play contract with Virginia Stage Company. Jessalyn is the only one absent. She's waiting in Montreal for her entry papers. She's about to land the lead voice in a new animated movie called *The Quest for Camelot*, opposite Cary Elwes, Gary Oldman, and Jane Seymour. Since the merchandise for the movie was designed before the screenplay was written, she'll also become a doll—of a young girl who aspires to be a knight of the Round Table. Each of them has someone to become.

When I say goodbye, they're still shooting. I slip out of the theatre, looking back at them. At the lobby door I turn around again and sneak back to where I can peer in without being seen. They will almost certainly never share a stage again. One last time I notice the way their bodies, having trained together, remember each other, the ways they give and take and seem to gain in stature by some alchemical mix. They are being photographed not as private people or as characters in a play but as actors, distinct and merged the way you are in any community. The flash pops, and I move away again. I exit the building and enter into a sparkling fall day in New York, a place, H. L. Mencken wrote, "where all the aspirations of the Western World meet to form one vast master aspiration." Within a couple of hours, they'll all straggle out too, to make their own ways.

This article was originally published in *American Theatre*, March, 1997.

Gentle Revolutionaries: Bloomsburg Theatre Ensemble

> A theatre with democratic commitments could operate very
> differently. It would maintain close contacts with members of it
> community, cultivating an awareness of people's interests and cares,
> participating in an ongoing dialogue with its neighbors.... It would
> build partnerships, not merely buyer-seller relationships.
> — Don Adams and Arlene Goldbard, *Crossroads:*
> *Reflections on the Politics of Culture*

The sign welcoming westward travelers to Pennsylvania reads: "America
Starts Here." This boast has a ring of truth, even if it ignores the obvious:
there are so many Americas; they can't all begin on the sundown shore of
the Delaware Water Gap. Mayflower/Yankee-stock American originates in
New England (Plymouth to be exact), just this side of the Atlantic. Melting
Pot America, with its multicolored masses of huddled tired and poor, steps
off at Ellis Island—all a memory this far west. Industrial America—the
sweaty, small cities of New Jersey, the Newarks and Patersons—is likewise
at your back by the time the wooded Poconos rise up around you.

If any America begins here, it's the one in quotations marks: "Middle
America" Go west, America. Purple mountain America. If any America
begins here—and it's easy to believe that one does—it's the wartime,
nightly news America: the land of yellow ribbons.

But under the decorative reminders of today's events, you can feel
the currents of another, older Americas, too. The Mystic Belt runs through
this part of Pennsylvania, the progressive, northern equivalent of the Bible
Belt, where Quakers, Shakers, Mennonites, Amish, and other pietistic
religious orders first settled. Here, in a little village named Catawissa,
American Indians held regular conferences of nations.

Nearby, just across the Susquehannah from Catawissa, about 75 miles
west of New Jersey, a quiet theatrical revolution—an experiment in
cultural democracy—takes place daily, just off Main Street, in Bloomsburg,
Pa., population 12,439.

By a quirk of history, one which divided the Keystone state into
cities, boroughs, and municipalities, Bloomsburg became Pennsylvania's
only legally defined *town*. Its unique status—the single town in the fourth
most populous state in the country—could possibly be Bloomsburg's most
distinctive trait. Beyond that, it is "heartland" central casting-style: the
county seat; the serene valley; the 10-plus blocks of Main Street shopping;
the sweep of surrounding farms, where vegetables grow and sulky horses
breed; the nearby creek that draws fly-fishermen from across the country;
the church suppers; the annual pet and toy parade through downtown; and

every September the Bloomsburg Fair—attended by more than 738,000—so tied to the life of the place that schools close for a week after being open for only three.

Bloomsburg feels like a small town grafted onto a college town, a coupling that keeps it from being too tiny, too old, or too staid. The streets are quiet but not dead; the Victorian wood-frame homes are well kept but not whitewashed, boutiqued, or Disney-pristine. The downtown economy, bolstered by a state university with 6,000 students, is altered but not broken by recent mall-sprawl.

For all its virtues, Bloomsburg remains an unlikely mecca. Nevertheless, in the summer of our country's bicentennial pilgrims began making their way here from suburban Chicago's Northwestern University in search of an 80-something-year-old acting teacher named Alvina Krause.

Some of the students who sought Miss Krause (she is always "Miss" Krause) had never met her. They had heard about her from their teachers at N.U., many of whom she'd taught in the '50s and early '60s. Some had participated in a clown workshop she'd run at the school. A handful of the men had just returned from a *wanderjahr* five months long in Europe, their heads crowded with images from a vital theatre scene: Grotowski's company, Mnouchkine's, Brook's. The idea of collective theatre had sparked their imaginations. They wrote letters to their retired master teacher. And when she accepted them, they packed their bags and showed up in the tiny town of Bloomsburg on the trail of an ideal of theatre.

Bloomsburg Theatre Ensemble, as it has evolved since its official opening in 1978, defines its ideal in concrete and unusual terms. This fully professional theatre is based in a rural community, where it aims to be as central to that community as schools, libraries, hospitals, and churches. This ideal demands "positive and demonstrable" impact on its region. The theatre's workers join that community at every level (including governance), as any other professionals would, no more or less important (or odd) than doctors, farmers, restaurant managers, or factory hands. BTE runs itself like an experimental theatre collective and fits into its community like a medieval craft guild. Actors take responsibility for all aspects of their art and business. And the company ideal values teaching; its members are constant, committed educators.

What you have here is a dyed-in-the-wool oxymoron: a professional community theatre collective.

*   *   *

The late Miss Krause oversaw the founding of BTE and instilled her young followers with this vision. She was the company's Thomas Paine, its Washington and its Jefferson, functioning as master-teacher, artistic director, articulator, guru, mom, and two-fisted goad, daring her students to start a theatre in a world where theatre was "dead," to make it work in this impossible small town, and to take their destinies into their own hands. According to Gerard Stropnicky, who arrived that first summer, when BTE was no more than a 10-week class on Chekhov held in Miss Krause' basement, "She set in motion all the prime directives that made this company." Her vision of "a theatre in every corner of the country is," Stropnicky explains, "the regional theatre goal cubed—not just a theatre in every major city, but one in each community."

To understand what makes BTE unique, it's necessary to understand its infeasibility. Peter Carnahan, the director of the theatre and literature programs for the Pennsylvania Council on the Arts for the past 18 years, is fond of saying: "Every theatre is an impossible theatre, but BTE is the most impossible theatre of all." When Stropnicky and fellow company member Laurie McCants first showed up on Carnahan's doorstep in Harrisburg and announced their intention to set up a professional theatre in this almost uninhabited rural area, he marveled at their naïveté. "You simply *can't have* a theatre in a town of 12,000, 45 miles from the nearest city," he thought.

Now, 13 years later, the company performs a varied repertoire for nearly 50,000 people a year, and operates a 369-seat theatre as well as its own rehearsal and production facility, on a budget of almost a half-million dollars. BTE maintains a subscription base of more than 1,000 (which greatly exceeds national averages in proportion to population), employs a mostly full-time administrative staff of ten and sustains an ensemble of eight (plus two paid year-round interns and numerous guest artists) for 52 weeks a year. Elizabeth Fuller, who with her husband Conrad Bishop runs the Independent Eye theatre in Lancaster, PA., a couple hours away, calls it "a true miracle in this area."

The hybrid BTE produces seasons like those of model regional theatres—world classics and recent plays new to their audience. It keeps a company of classically based actors as stage worthy, versatile, and literate as those found at major urban theatres. In addition to extraordinary discipline and facility with heightened language, says Bishop, who directed BTE actors in the recent Bloomsburg/Independent Eye co-production of Tennessee William's darkly expressionistic *Out Cry*, these actors "are capable of making radical adaptations."

Miss Krause preached, according to Stropnicky, "that the actor should be the first artists of the theatre." Heralded as a "teacher of stars" for the notables she inspired during 34 years at Northwestern (including Charlton Heston, Patricia Neal, Richard Benjamin, Tony Roberts, Cloris Leachman, and many others), Miss Krause abhorred the star system. She suffered personally when her former students abandoned the theatre for

131

movies and "stardom." Everything was ensemble to her. The only thing more powerful than a single actor, then, was a pack of them.

Forging a collective out of a mob of young actors was a long, gut-wrenching process. Laurie McCants refers to the company's early days as "the bloody beginning," when the group tried to create "a democratically run ensemble with an autocrat [Krause] at the helm." As actors staked out personal territory within the group and vied for the dynamic matriarch's attention, Miss Krause swung from letting them go to pushing them on. "She was so demanding of us and of herself that she almost had a split personality," McCants explains. "When she was our acting teacher, she was like a guardian angel. She could stand behind us and put her hands on our shoulders and phenomenal *things* would come out of us. When she directed or when any of us did or when we put something on for the public, all of a sudden she became this other person. We had two names for her: 'Miss Krause, our teacher' and 'Mrs. Withers,' the woman who runs the orphanage and locked Miss Krause in a closet upstairs."

Miss Krause's prodding intensified, grew more urgent with time. "The closer she got to death," remembers A. Elizabeth Dowd, "the more of a task-master she became. She had a lifetime of knowledge that she wanted us to get *now*." Dowd, who joined the company in '78, during its transformation from classroom to theatre, describes the 88-year-old Miss Krause, on her literal deathbed, fending off questions about her health in order to grill Rand Whipple (Dowd's husband and former ensemble member) on his performance as Scrooge in *A Christmas Carol*. She tried to asses a performance she couldn't see and give him notes based on her assessment. Later, the company—unable to visit her—gathered outside her door, singing carols. Miss Krause's hand, waving from the bed, was the last they saw of her.

Their mentor's death on New Year's Eve, 1981, became a turning point for the company. Prior to the opening of *You Can't Take It With You* in 1982, BTE had mounted its work in the "cafetorium" of a local school. Now—having made a pact never to say, "Miss Krause would have wanted..."—they were ready to move into their own theatre, a former movie house that has since been made over into the Alvina Krause Theatre. On opening night, though, the place had been jerry-rigged with a temporary stage and a fake proscenium. With a corps of volunteers the actors had scraped the gum off the old seats. A half-hour before the audience was to arrive, the minster of the Presbyterian church was still on hands and knees laying carpet in the aisles.

"That was a great passage," McCants recalls. "We all started to get our own wings—I mean that almost literally. And when we stepped out on that stage to warm up, I could see a burden being lifted off our shoulders and there was something that happened in everybody's spine that said,

'Now we're off!' And we took flight that night." Dowd corroborates: "Miss Krause was gone. And it was a good show. For three of our members it was the last show. I was getting married at the end of the run. And I remember taking that bow and feeling so proud that we had done it, that we were going to stay. And you could feel the community say, 'They're gonna be here.' "

* * *

The town that witnessed the troupe's collective sigh of relief, this first solo flight, has been as important to the theatre's survival as Miss Krause herself. To an observer entering Bloomsburg from the highway, everything feels a bit retro, even clichéd. On my first Saturday as a reporter in Bloomsburg, I walk to the fairgrounds, happen upon an old man in a winter cap running a horse and sulky around a track. Behind the stadium sit industrial office buildings—Magee Carpet Co. and Bloomsburg Mills— looking like they might have looked when they opened 101 years ago.

The whole town is American flagged, festooned with ribbons: yellow bows and red-white-and-blue pom-poms. It could be fair time, could be Fourth of July, if it weren't a bitter February morning, hours before the ground war is to begin in Kuwait.

Shortly after the decisive Gulf battle starts its quick, painful roll, more than 300 people crowd the Alvina Krause for the penultimate performance of Shaw's *Candida*, breaking audience projections for the night and the run. A progressive cultural conscience has often shown through Bloomsburg's Norman Rockwell veneer. The first mandatory recycling law in the east was instituted here. This community boasts one of the country's only day-care centers funded exclusively with municipal monies. Its downtown revitalization program has become a national model. And Bloomsburg provided the fledgling BTE with an incubator: an entire floor of Town Hall that served as office space, rent-free (utilities included) for six years. And though the actors' eyes start to water with gratitude when they talk of the freedom and space to grow that the Bloomsburg community has given them, what hatched three flights up in Town Hall has paid the town back handsomely.

"We've always said it was BTE that kept us alive for the first several years that we were open," explains Maria Lewis, who with her husband Russell, owns and operates Russell's restaurant on Main Street. "They were very supportive. When we first opened it wasn't unusual for the actors to be the only people in our building. Especially at night. We used to make them sweep up before closing." The ten-year-old steak-and-seafood restaurant draws as much as eighty percent of its weekend dinner crowd from the theatre, before and after shows, a benefit other local restaurants likewise enjoy. "You couldn't get a meal in this town after eight o'clock when I moved here," Stropnicky recalls. Now, at Russell's, before or after a Friday night show, it's not easy to get a table.

Russell's has reciprocated the support it received from the BTE actors as the two establishments grew up together. Many of the company members financed their early work by moonlighting at the restaurant. Early on, the restaurateurs threw a surprise party for the theatre in the part of Russell's dubbed "guppy corner," so named because once a couple of actors show up, they're joined by audience members and friends, and seem to multiply like small fish. At the bash, the Lewises unveiled a wall of photos—all shots of the ensemble members—a celebration of their local Sinatras, Streeps, and Newmans. Currently, the menu lists a BTE sandwich: bacon, tomato, Swiss, and—no insult intended, according to Lewis—ham.

Russell's (or Sardi's West, as it has come to be nicknamed) is not the theatre's only haunt. BTE members are equally esteemed familiars at Hurr's Dairy Store, Allen's Subs, Harry's Grille, and the Texas Lunch, where Stropnicky breakfasts daily with trucker friends: "They know what I do, and I know what they do."

For people who relocate to Bloomsburg—especially those who come from cities—the theatre offers them a cultural life raft, a place to meet people, and a gentle front line to nudge against the town's conservative impulses. Bob and Constance Miller, for example, arrived here six years ago from New Jersey, where he served as a senior vice president for Prudential and she, a dancer and choreographer, commuted to New York City, where her dance company was based. After buying the farm of their dreams—they grow Christmas trees and operate an herb shop on a rolling expanse of land called Green Horizons—the couple set about forming a circle of friends. This process took them to Friday night "talk-backs" at the theatre (free-ranging post-show discussions between the audience and cast) and to the local Quaker meetings. The former became a resource for meeting people whose ideas stretched beyond Columbia County. "They've broadened the intellectual horizons of the people in this community who attend theatre, maybe without the audience even knowing it," Bob points out. Constance concurs, citing BTE's Theatre in the Classroom program, its cross-cultural programming and its introduction of black artists to the mostly white community as important to the town's future. "Educationally they're making big waves," she insists. "They're bringing things to people here that they don't see, to people who've never left the state of Pennsylvania."

Everyone in town seems to know the actors personally, to have their favorite performances, the show they'll never forget. At the talkback following *Candida*, I interviewed the couple dozen people who stayed. Everyone had a story. From the medical chaplain whose work had been greatly influenced by a production of Michael Cristofer's *The Shadow Box* to the woman whose child had grown from classes with the company's school to a part in a main stage play, from the philosophy professor who told me that the university uses BTE as a draw in faculty recruitment to the man who described the theatre as an "oasis" for transplanted urbanites—each person who stayed voiced enormous respect for the work and testified to its impact.

Peter Carnahan remembers watching Franz Xaver Kroetz's *The Nest* and finding it "hauntingly familiar," only to realize that the actors were speaking in Bloomsburg accents, dressed in Bloomsburg clothes, all carefully observed, all registering "at the periphery of your consciousness." The power of BTE's work on its community become the stuff of legend: the friends who treated themselves to a spree in Manhattan after seeing *A Coupla White Chicks Sitting Around Talking*, the women who found the strength to leave tired marriages after a first encounter with *A Doll's House*. BTE audiences feel the pride of ownership. This theatre belongs to them and they to it. It is a place within a place.

*   *   *

Shelley Remaly grows impassioned talking about BTE. A former president of the theatre's board of trustees, she seems unable to imagine life in Bloomsburg without the theatre. "BTE bit me and kept me bit," she says. A decade-long resident of the area, Remaly has fought for BTE's economic survival and even stepped in to help in the office during a long search for a new administrative director, setting up her two-year-old's toy box next to the theatre's computer. She credits the company for taking her twelve-year-old daughter's appreciation for literature "to a whole new level." Running through Remaly's conversation are references to BTE as a model for the community at large, in the members' "excruciatingly democratic and brutally honest" process and in their devotion to an ideal. "It's great for small-town people to see them struggling and surviving for what they believe," she says.

Remaly's husband Don is a family doctor, who donates his services as company physician. He has delivered ensemble members' babies and cared for guest artists gratis, the kind of generosity BTE often inspires. In 1983, board members Judith Savage and Mary Wright spent more than 200 hours hand-upholstering 382 theatre seats, as part of the Krause Theatre's renovation. With a few occasional helpers, the women removed 22,000 screws, tore off old covers, and—at eleven stitches per seat, stitched on new burlap foundations (cut free by Millco Industries, which manufactures ladies undergarment lines for stores like Sears and J.C. Penny) with heavy-rug needles, all to save the theatre $24,000.

Phyllis Bernatonis, a customer service rep at the United Penn Bank, has regularly given the theatre up to twenty-eight hours of her life each week, volunteering backstage on more than twenty shows—out of respect for what they do. Still, the former Bloomsburg policewoman would agree that BTE gives as good as it gets. "It's like having an extended family; there's always someone here who can come to your rescue."

Millco's owner, the late Marco Mitrani, a philanthropist (read "angel from heaven") of the old school, whom ensemble members credit with saving the theatre from financial ruin on several occasions, gave a different kind of aid to the company to acknowledge what he received from it. Mitrani wrote BTE their first $20,000 check during its early capital campaign, simply because, as he told them, "You're good at what you do, and you're willing to sacrifice for it." A Turkish-born Sephardic Jew, the benefactor refused to allow Laurie McCants to cry when he announced the gift, accepting, instead of tears, a kiss on his septuagenarian cheek. His wife, Louise, whose habit it was to thank BTE for allowing her to donate money, gave (outright) to the company the old shirt factory they now use as shop and rehearsal space, inquiring, according to Dowd, "Can you use another building?" This same Mitrani Building was renovated for BTE at no cost by a construction company with little to gain from its generosity— the business was moving out of town.

Not everyone in Bloomsburg goes to the theatre, even among BTE's closest friends. Restaurateurs Maria and Russell Lewis's busiest hours— evenings and weekends—make seeing shows a rarity. Norman Mael, general manager for Magee's Main Street Inn, is an ardent spokesperson for the theatre, who understands the painful push-pull of small-town life on artists: "*A Christmas Carol* is a good example of how they're damned if they do (some people don't want to see it again) and damned if they don't (some insist on it every year)," he points out. But with three young children at home, Mael's only seen one play in three years. "I've only been to the Capitol movie theatre twice," he adds.

Strangely, this casual attitude toward theatregoing—while it might not pay the rent—makes BTE feel like any other business in town. Like a bar or clothing store, it has its devotees, often-shows, occasional browsers, and hardcore avoiders. The free Saturday morning town preview of the touring children's show *Land of the Rising Sun* brings lots of young moms and dads (who might, like Mael, be stuck at home at night) and winterized bundles of kids. Lacing the audience, looking much like everyone else, are BTE members, BTE spouses, and BTE babies. "They're unique and colorful," Maria Lewis points out, "but you don't really pick them out of the crowd as actors. It's not unusual to see them on the downtown business associate boards and participating in Chamber of Commerce events, so the community has a very positive feeling about them."

Like Bob and Constance Miller, several members of the ensemble have found the local Quaker meetings compatible with their collectivist leanings. The Quaker philosophy of "working through things by consensus" has had spiritual if not practical influence on the group's decision-making process. A carefully articulated "struggle has emerged," in the words of thirteen-year-ensemble veteran Whit MacLaughlin, "to allow individual voices to be heard." Postproduction critiques, in which everyone has a specified amount of time to talk without feedback or interruption, mirror methods used in twelve-step recovery programs. Play selection meetings can resemble impassioned congressional debates, with compromises struck, filibustering (picture Jimmy Stewart in *Mr. Smith Goes to Washington*), members exhausted into agreement—all aimed at unanimity. (All seasons have been selected unanimously, except for one, which passed with a single abstention.) Each decision, from director selection to the confirmation of membership, is reached through group vote by what administrative director Steve Coppick fondly dubs "the eight-headed monster."

Like an open learning exchange, three-hour-long weekly labs expose the artists to outside teachers and specialists (T'ai Chi or dialect or Alexander method) and give them the chance to teach each other (stand-up comedy or "what I learned in Japan at the Suzuki workshop"). End-of-year actor slips, confidential evaluations written from each member to each member, seem like a diplomatic form of Maoist group criticism. "Keystone" projects, like last season's *King Lear* or next season's *The Women of Bacchus*, orient the actors toward the future, engaging the entire membership in developmental work on a monumental production over a two-year stretch. MacLaughlin often thinks about 19th-century utopian experiments when considering the company's structure. "We are an experiment in community in front of a community," he says.

It was in 1984 that Leigh Strimbeck became the first actor welcomed into the ensemble after Krause's death; she currently serves as ensemble director, a rotating position. In this role—which all see as a kind of "powerless leader"—Strimbeck "listens to the collective and then speaks in its voice." The ensemble director functions partly as producer (with the technical staff reporting to her, for example), partly as spokesperson in the community and press, partly as administrator (overseeing the nightmarish logistics of scheduling in advance every member's year hour-by-hour), and partly as chief liaison to the board. All this for an extra fifteen dollars a week and the distinction of being the only one on payroll exempt from striking the scenery at the close of a show.

The leadership structure has evolved over the years and was for a time shared between two or more members. Now the job is voted on yearly and usually held for a few seasons running. Despite the support of an associate ensemble director (a post now filled by original company member James Goode), it's a job that many resist and others burn out on. The past three directors have been women—McCants, Dowd, and Strimbeck---a fact that most attribute to its listener/mediator demands and a more palpable competitiveness between the company's men. There may even be some inbred comfort in matriarchy for this group that Miss Krause built. Currently, Strimbeck thrives in the spot, takes pride in speaking for the whole, and competently handling producing responsibilities. The stretch helps her "stay scared," she explains, which lets her know she's growing, even as she stays in one place.

For much of the ensemble, the play-selection process ensures they can stay scared—challenged—as artists. The troupe spends dozens of hours each fall reading plays, as a large group or in smaller "pods," and writing reports on them. In the winter the company hammers out a five-play main stage season through relentless talk and argument, chaired by one of the actors and observed by members of the board. Those wanting to direct in the upcoming year submit project proposals or push for certain plays, but directors are only chosen—by vote (even on those hired from outside)—after the season's picked. Then auditions begin. Actors submit their role requests to the ensemble director, but since the director's choices are, in the end, more strongly weighed, every role is auditioned for. The auditioning seems to go on forever, as ensemble members try to surprise the directors most familiar with their work. Finally, guided by the ensemble director, director choices and actor choices are merged into what Strimbeck calls "the individual's artistic path through the next year," and then supplemented by guest artists from New York and elsewhere.

Play selection is the center of the company's collective process; it is the place where democratic structure joins with aesthetic identity. The moment of choice is the moment when ensemble begins to speak to audience, when community feedback (whether from regular board questionnaires evaluating the work, comments in the drugstore, or "Saw the show, not your best!" shouted from a car window) intersects with artistic choice. This process guarantees eclecticism in every season. The actors' input and the director's fight for the personal project guarantees passion. While the ensemble director's responsibilities expand and the core company threatens to shrink, this is the sacrosanct task of the group. "If play selection is ever handed over to one person," Strimbeck prophesies, "that will be the end of the company."

Any American community is both fueled and endangered by tension between the individual and the group. Certainly, the nation's theatre's historic pull between ensemble and individual recognition prove the point. BTE has lost numerous members over the years: those who tired of small-town existence, who tired of theatre, who doubted life after Miss Krause was possible, and who wanted more widespread attention. This year BTE may be losing a mainstay, actor/director Martin Shell, who bought into "Miss Krause's tremendous, out-of-reach goal" shortly after the group's founding. His departure for graduate school would diminish the ensemble to seven, a loss of two in as many years. Highly regarded among audiences for his versatility and ability to transform from role to role, Shell is going through a psychological separation, a search for creative identity he fears he submerged in the group's own. Shell, the father of a three-year-old son, worries that devotion to the company has left him with few practical outlets and "too many eggs in one basket." Still, he imagines working with these people the rest of his life. They share, he says, "a common heart."

If BTE does, in fact, live off a common heart, it resides in the community at large. The town gave the theatre its start and, according to James Goode, "our future" as well. "Our creative ambition was given the go-ahead," he continues. "I'm not sure that the townspeople knew for sure that was what they were doing and what it would involve. We didn't either. But we were never told—as could well have happened here—to get out, nobody wants you. From the beginning, people here said, 'Go on.' "

Elizabeth Fuller finds an appropriate metaphor for BTE's development. "You turn carbon into diamonds by putting it under intense pressure and a lot of heat. If you took the ensemble of college-based actors that they started as and didn't apply the pressure and the heat, you wouldn't have what you have. To survive in these circumstances, to keep pushing for economic dignity as well as for excellent work has resulted in something more than just growing older." Goode, like so many of his colleagues, cries when he talks about Bloomsburg, when he realizes, "We've been given the gift of growing up."

This article was originally published in *American Theatre*, July/August, 1991.

Chicago Impromptu

1. Building a Where

In the beginning, Viola Spolin wrote the word, "improvisation" and the darkness that was upon the face of Chicago theatre filled up with light. And the light revealed imaginary space and real people—children first, then college students, then grown-up actors—playing within the imaginary space, passing it between themselves, shaping it into objects, transforming it. And the make-believe space grew solid. It changed into neighborhood bars with small stages and storefront theatres and large institutions, and more people came to inhibit them. Too often, when players departed the space, it seemed that darkness fell again upon the face of the city. Other times there was dazzling light.

And also in the beginning, Spolin asked the first question: "Where are you?" And though it was a simple question that took simple answers—"I am in the kitchen by the toaster and the pantry is on my right and the yard beyond the windows on my left"—it also provoked a different kind of speculation: "Chicago.... Where is that? What does it mean to be in Chicago in 1953 or 1968 or 1990? Who are we when we stay in Chicago and who are we when we leave? What is community?"

And from the questioning began the begetting, which, too, started with Spolin. Her real life son, Paul Sills, begat (with the help of others) the Playwrights Theatre Club which begat the Compass Players which begat Second City which begat too many famous people to list, though these included David Mamet, who became the first Chicago playwright and begat St. Nicholas Theatre. And Second City also begat Stuart Gordon, who begat the Organic Theatre Company, which gave many others the courage to begin begetting on their own. Spolin and Sills begat a community and taught it to improvise. And so it improvised itself an identity: it created a Where.

The "Where," Spolin tells us in her groundbreaking 1963 *Improvisation for the Theatre,* referred to by many in her native Chicago as "the bible," is the environment, the "field" upon which the student-actor plays. Within the Where things happen; people come and go. And every change influences the actor. Some changes may even transform the Where.

Torn between two media-rich coasts, Chicago is a Where that has been transformed several times over during the past three decades. As a theatre town, it has emerged, struggled to survive, defined itself, and called the attentions of the world upon its own head. Pieces of it have threatened to come apart with every worldly success.

Naturally, a place so varied can't be pinned down by a single descriptive phrase. Even Mark Twain noted the city's evanescence, calling it "a city where they are always rubbing the lamp and fetching up the genii, and contriving and achieving new impossibilities…She outgrows [the visitor's] prophesies faster than he can make them." Still, Spolin's simple "where are you?" invites speculation; it beckons us to look at Chicago, to try to divine something of its spirit.

As I write, the Chicago theatre community (which includes the audience) is engaged in its own process of self-celebration and self-definition. The native-born Steppenwolf Theatre Company basks in the glow of Broadway success for its production of *The Grapes of Wrath,* adapted from the John Steinbeck novel and directed by Chicagoan Frank Galati. Meanwhile, with the help of the Special Collections division of the Chicago Public Library, the citizens of what homeboy Mamet calls, "Windville" can see their recent history flash before their eyes. "Resetting the Stage: Theatre Beyond the Loop, 1960-1990" exhibits scripts, posters, programs, correspondence, costumes, set renderings and models and photographs from these boom years. At the heart of this archivist's dream is a single question: "Is there a Chicago style of theatre, and, if so, what is it?"

The answer to this question falls somewhere between yes or no, according to Scott Fosdick, guest curator of this special exhibit. It would be ridiculous to ascribe a singular quality to so diverse a scene. On the other hand, Fosdick writes in the exhibit's catalogues, "Anyone who has followed Chicago theatre knows that when an out-of-town visitor asks, 'What's it like?' you don't answer, 'Just like where you come from,'" What that style might be is even harder to say. "Sometimes that aesthetic… seems an empowering, energizing thing, as when David Mamet speaks of the lessons he learned as a busboy at Second City or carrying a spear for [director] Bob Sickinger at Hull-House in the 1960s," Fosdick continues. "Other times, it seems rather silly: [Remains Theatre co-artistic director] William Petersen once bragged to an interviewer that when a Chicago actor spits on himself, he doesn't wipe it off."

In another catalogue essay, actor, director, and critic Gary Houston chooses a Midwestern metaphor to describe the scene, one planted firmly in the earth. "Put Paul Sills and the fifties and sixties groups or movements he sired… in the center of a tree trunk. Give it two branches—on one side, The Reality Makers; on the other, The Story Tellers.

"For the tree's roots," Houston goes on, "put Paul Sills' mother, Viola Spolin, and her still-in-print book, *Improvisation for the Theatre.* "

Spolin's own roots are sunk deep in the soil of community. A first-generation American Jew and a natural athlete, the woman who has been called "the great space mother" grew up on the northwest side of the city,

142

possessed by a superhuman passion for street games. At eighteen she began training under Christian Scientist Neva Boyd, a Northwestern University-based sociologist who taught a life-course in "play," including sports, folk-dancing and games of every stamp. Boyd's Recreational Training School operated out of Hull-House, a community center founded in 1889 by another pioneer, Jane Addams, for the settlement of a local immigrant population so huge that one early-century observer speculated that "all the millions of human beings disembarking year upon year upon the shores of the United States were unconsciously drawn to make [Chicago] their headquarters." (In fact, the U.S. Census from the year Hull-House was founded reveals that 855,000 out of the 1.1 million citizens of Chicago were "white foreign stock—either foreign-born or American-born children of immigrants.) Spolin's games were born at Hull-House, beginning in 1938, when she taught and supervised creative dramatics for children, while working with adults under Franklin Roosevelt's WPA. Throughout our century this kind of partnership—Hull-House providing the space for artists to fill—would usher forth more than Spolin's games; it would produce America's first little theatre, house the company that began the flowering of Chicago theatre in the sixties, and provide an upstart suburban troupe named Steppenwolf with their entrée into the big city.

"Paul brought my work into the world," Spolin told Janet Coleman, author of *The Compass,* a just-published history of Chicago's first improvisational theatre. Certainly, Sills, born a week before Thanksgiving in 1927, went into what he calls "the family business" and introduced that business into the professional theatre. The business was play, and the work was a series of games or, as Coleman tells us they are known in Brazil, "Violas."

Each game centers on one aspect of imaginative reality: transforming space, fashioning objects out of air, creating a "where." The rules provide the player with a clear focus or "point of concentration." By keeping their "eyes on the ball" and staying within the rules, the players free themselves to act spontaneously and creatively in the imaginary world. Moreover, they learn to share space, to take impulses for action off of others, to give and take. Spolin's work provides an alternative to American versions of Stanislavsky's writings on actor training. In the Russian's methods, the actor is motivated by internal needs and desires; the character is the actor's creation. The games, on the other hand, allow character—an extension of the player's self—to emerge spontaneously, as the performer plays with others. The motivation is built in; action is generated not from psychology but from contact with others in space. Moreover, the improvisational nature of the games roots the actor in what Spolin calls "time present." According to Sheldon Patinkin, artistic director of the National Jewish Theatre in suburban Skokie and artistic consultant to Second City, the games "give the actors a sense of what it means to behave publicly as opposed to acting. And all you have to do is follow the rules."

Patinkin began working with Sills in 1953 as part of the Playwrights Theatre Club at the University of Chicago, the first stab at blending Spolin's training with theatre practice. Over the course of Playwrights' two-year-and-twenty-five-play life, Sills used the games to move away from psychological acting and to build a sense of ensemble among such actors as Edward Asner, Mike Nichols, Elaine May, Zohra Lampert, Anthony Holland, and the woman who would be his second wife, Barbara Harris. At a time when theatre in Chicago meant touring productions of last year's Broadway hits, the precocious company—many of whom had graduated from the progressive U. of C. while still in their teens, a feat made possible by the school's policy of admitting anyone who passed its entrance exam, with or without a high school diploma—dared its community away from the Republican complacence of the fifties with productions of plays by Brecht, Büchner, Schnitzler, and the Jacobeans. Through it all, Sills taught the games. When he could, he brought their originator in from Los Angeles—where she was beginning to write her "bible"—to do the same.

Ultimately, the leftist leanings of the young company brought the theatre down. Involvement with artists blacklisted by the House Un-American Activities Committee and Joseph McCarthy's Senate inquest, and the announcement of a reading of a screenplay about a New Mexican zinc mine strike by Hebert Biberman of the Hollywood Ten (a project abandoned after a vote by Playwrights company members), incited political pressure to close the theatre. Prodded by the office of newly elected Mayor Richard J. Daley, the fire department did the deed. A 1903 fire at the Iroquoi Theatre had provoked new laws making only proscenium stages legal and requiring hydraulic fire curtains fed by 26-inch water pipes. These were now invoked.

The laws, which made it impossible for small theatres to exist, would be amended in 1973, thanks in part to *Chicago Sun Times* theatre critic Glenna Syse's persuasive editorials, thus clearing the way for the Off-Loop theatre boom.

Between the death of Playwrights and the rewritten codes, theatre artists had to be canny. As Sills explains, they had to adapt to the absurdities of political life in the land of the robber barons. "You'd start a bar and that way you were immune from prosecution. You didn't have to worry about codes or anything. Money talks and drinks are money. Bars in those days didn't need more than one exit; theatres had to have three exits. You could smoke in the bar and you couldn't in the theatre. That's why Compass Players and Second City started with liquor licenses." Booze has always mixed with blood in Chicago's veins. Even the original Hull-House was wedged between a saloon and funeral home or, as it was then described, "Twixt Drink and Death."

Fire laws notwithstanding, the spark provided by Spolin's work—spread mainly through Sills' regular Saturday morning workshops—ignited the dreams of David Shepherd, a transplanted New Yorker with a small inheritance in his pocket. An idealist like Sills, Shepherd envisioned a political cabaret that would bring theatre to the working classes, confronting them with the issues of the day. Also like Sills, he would see the brainchildren of his idealism grow increasingly adulterated.

The Compass's form—improvised plays based on scenarios worked out in advance—was grounded in the tradition of commedia dell'arte and in the games Shepherd had played with Spolin and son as part of Playwrights. This became the nation's first improvisational theatre; it would spawn numerous heirs, including Shepherd's own St. Louis Compass and Chicago's influential Second City. But it would never become the theatre Shepherd and co-founder Sills hoped for. Designed for the working classes, the Compass drew its burgeoning audience from the university's intelligentsia. With success, the amateur company grew increasingly professionalized. Material ceased being improvised: success led the performers to "freeze" whatever worked. More and more, the ensemble gave over to the will of individuals. "Compass became a vehicle for soloists," Coleman observes, "individuals concerned and fearful for their own approval and success,"

Throughout the three-and-a-half decades following the Compass's 1955 debut, what David Mamet calls "a community of groups" has been challenged by outside acclaim for its members. As early as the Compass, the "second city" (as *New Yorker* writer A.J. Leibling condescendingly dubbed it) was becoming a place to leave, as players Nichols and May and Shelley Berman "graduated" to a national audience in New York. Companies that arguably did their best work when nobody (outside of this secondary Midwest burg) had heard of them became star factories. More than anything else, as the Organic Theatre and Steppenwolf would later prove, success has plagued Chicago theatre.

Though Chicago's Compass soon folded, it is impossible to overstate the imaginative influence the group had. Epitomized by wildcards like Severn Darden, Del Close, and Elaine May, the early Compass and Second City companies behaved like erudite lunatics unleashed at a cocktail party in the suburbs. (A fellow Chicagoan, the comic Lenny Bruce, known and admired by many of Sills' crowd, might have been found at the same soiree, shoving sticks of dynamite into crawlspaces and setting the rec room on fire.) Jack Viertel, writing in the *Los Angeles Herald Examiner* about *Sills and Company*, a 1985 reunion production with many of Sills' early players, captures the excitement of the best Sillsian improv: "You can practically feel their brain waves screaming helter-skelter toward one another, hoping for that mystical collision that will produce a miracle: a laugh that's true. A humanistic laugh."

Gregory Mosher, who headed Chicago's Goodman Theatre in the late seventies and early eighties before becoming director of Lincoln Center Theatre in New York, thought the Compass people were "amazing people, a bunch of yahoos and madmen." Like their offspring at Second City, they understood, he says, "the power of four bentwood chairs and a voice saying: 'We now take you to a doctor's waiting room.'" This no-props-only-chairs attitude has inspired Mosher's work, most notably his bare-bones staging—a foodless, plateless, silverless booth in a Chinese restaurant—of the first act of Mamet's most successful play, *Glengarry Glen Ross*. *Chicago Tribune* entertainment editor Richard Christiansen agrees that Sills, under whose direction many actors did the best work of their careers, has proved to be Chicago theatre's most influential father figure. Even two decades after Sills moved on, Christiansen says, "the idea of finding a way through improvisation" persists.

All along, Sills' greatest talent, and his legacy to Chicago, has been for gathering and inspiring such groups. After the Compass moved to St. Louis, Sills—whose touch was better suited to short improvisational sketches than to the evening-long-improvisation plays Shepherd envisaged—and partners Bernard Sahlins and (ex-Compass Player) Howard Alk opened up a nightclub revue in a former Chinese laundry. The format called for short scenes created largely from rehearsed improvisation and partly from audience suggestion. Second City (whose name ironically spit back Leibling's condescending label) became a staple of Chicago and spread its web of influence wide, most notably into television and film via many originators of NBC's *Saturday Night Live*. It became—and still is—an eccentric international family, a brood that playwright Jeffrey Sweet once pegged as a cross between the Waltons and the Corleones. But as the show's format grew set and once-improvised work was passed down in fixed form from company to company in Windville and elsewhere—and as the idea of company degenerated, with early performers like Alan Arkin and Barbara Harris "discovered" by New York and succeeding ensembles less interested in the foundation the games provided—Sills grew restless. When he walked out of rehearsal and onto a plane for New York, he left a startled Patinkin at the rudder, where he remained until likewise leaving for points east in the late '60s.

For Sills the idea of community supersedes the urge to make theatre. He considers his work "para-theatrical." "It runs alongside the theatre," he explains, when I meet him at New York's New Actors Workshop, a school he started recently with Nichols and George Morrison, at which he teaches—what else?—the games. In fact, community—in a spiritual, even mystical sense—underlies the theory of games for which Sills serves as spokesman. In Sweet's chock-full oral history of the Compass and Second City, *Something Wonderful Right Away,* Sills quotes his favorite philosopher, Martin Buber, to explain: "The heavenly bread of self-being is passed between man and man." This interaction is possible in the "free space" created by the games. Former Sills-protégé Patinkin puts it another way: "When you drop all the life problems and just invest yourself in solving problems within the rules of the game—and since the rules are always about getting what happens next off the person that you're responding to—it creates a sense of community."

Sills returned to Chicago in 1963 with some vague "communitarian" notions. He launched a series of ventures, all based on Spolin's work. Mother and son's Games Theatre, in which audience members joined rather unsuccessfully with performers in playing the games, evolved into Story Theatre, which presented evenings of theatre built from fairy tales developed through improvisation. Robert Falls, artistic director of the Goodman Theatre and, as a suburban high school student and downstate under-grad, a card-carrying "Second City fanatic," was not alone in being "blown away by the simplicity and wonder and magic" of Sills' later creation. The success of this enterprise carried Sills to Yale Repertory Theatre in New Haven, the Mark Taper Forum in L.A., onto television and, as Sills marvels, "all the way to Broadway with a few fairy tales."

Always politically motivated, Sills maintains that Story Theatre was "a reaction to '68," a time "in which chaos seemed to loom." Nineteen-sixty-eight was The Year That Was in Chicago, as "Boss" Daley called on police to overrun Yippie protestors occupying Grant Park during the Democratic National Convention. It was the year Abbie Hoffman and Jerry Rubin, members of "the Chicago Seven," led their theatrical romp through Judge Julius Hoffman's courtroom, where they had been brought up on conspiracy changes and where the trial's eighth (and only black) defendant, a future Oakland, Calif. Mayor named Bobby Seale, was tied up and gagged in the halls of justice. This same Yippie band that brought street theatre to American politics held regular town meetings in Sills' theatre—in the original Second City space and next to its new one. Sills testified at their trial. Meanwhile, on the billboard outside Story Theatre could be read the words, "Coming, *The American Revolution,*" an announcement for the project Sills would develop and produce for two years "of high exaltation."

Sills seems to have regularly created communities in order to leave them, a tendency that underscores contradictions in his character. The same director who inspired lifelong loyalty from performers has been known, in frequent moments of frustration, to throw chairs at them. While most acknowledge that his volatility and impatience have calmed over the years (I found him both kind and eloquent outside the classroom and just a bit less so inside), past colleagues have seen Sills alternate between gentleness and anger like a spiritual giant with a raging itch. (His difficult nature, many friends say, is magnified in his mother.) "What Paul was then was a really inspirational, though basically inarticulate, genius and a real artist," explains Patinkin. "You had to interpret what he was saying because a lot of it was body language and grunts and groans. When he wasn't communicating with his body language, he'd get very angry." In *Something Wonderful Right Away*, which reads equally well as a *Rashomon*-like character sketch of Sills and as a history of his first companies, Alan Arkin describes Sills' genius for "putting a group of people together who somehow set each other on fire." Former Second Cityzen Avery Schreiber calls him "a great technician of the human spirit." Others portray him as "brilliant," "charismatic," "democratic," "impatient" and "juvenile"—all handles that could as easily be affixed to the city itself.

In Sills' own eyes, his mother, not he, is the genius. "I'm a guy with an ordinary head. She's a great sage. She measures her words. She has written one of the very few books that will outlive everybody." In one interview, Jeffrey Sweet theorizes that "one of the reasons why Paul and Viola are so into the games is that they find it difficult to make contact with people in unstructured environments. So they created games to create a structure in which they feel secure to communicate." Everyone agrees, finally, that Sills is the man who never "sold out."

Whatever psychological or mystical motivations drove mother and child, they simultaneously unearthed and invented an art form indigenous to their "where": improvisation. Improvising is what Chicago does. It's the way the city's pulse expresses itself, whether through the native blues music or the meanderings of day baseball in Wrigley Field (where expectations of Cubs' wins have long been beaten down) or through the surge and sprawl of the "big shouldered" city's architecture. Chicago builds with any tools it has on whatever's there. Two weeks after the "toddling town" was leveled by fire in 1871, people began rebuilding it on the mud. The home of the renaissance of American architecture and famous designs by Louis Sullivan, Frank Lloyd Wright and, more recently, Mies van der Rohe feels improvised, with grand 100-story skyrises pressing up against scrappy projects and coherent prewar neighborhoods spilling into the postwar 'burbs. "Chicago doesn't think," says Sweet. "It just does." And you can almost hear the pounded rhythm of its doing, even as Carl Sandburg heard it in his famous *Chicago Poems:* "Bareheaded,/Shovelling,/Wrecking,/Planning,/ Building, breaking, rebuilding…"

*   *   *

2. The Legacy

If Sills was an inarticulate seer, Robert ("Bob") Sickinger was a self-proclaimed "doer." A pioneer of Philadelphia community theatre, Sickinger came west to run the theatre arm of Hull-House, that original garden of Middle America's urban culture. Sickinger's purpose was clear: "We are creating an audience, a climate," he told the critic Glenna Syse after his appointment in 1963. "That must come before the theatre in Chicago can prosper. We must build into the fabric of neighborhood life a place for theatre to flourish close to the grass roots of American democratic culture."

Hull-House had never lost touch with those roots, a connection often kept alive by theatrical production. From the earliest days of the settlement center, Jane Addams had used the arts as a means of forwarding native and immigrant culture, through concerts, readings, craft classes, and exhibitions, a project that eventually earned her the Nobel Peace Prize. In 1900 Addams handed stewardship of the house's dramatic program over to Laura Dainty Pelham, who, up until her death in 1924, developed and championed the first Little Theatre in America, with productions of work by the likes of Shaw, Ibsen, Pinero, and Hauptmann, as well as international classics performed by immigrants in their native tongues (the first was Homer's *The Odyssey* in Greek).

Sickinger shared Pelham's mission, except that in place of Shaw and Ibsen he presented gutsy Chicago premieres of works by Beckett, Jack Gelber, Albert Camus, Harold Pinter, Edward Albee, Leroi Jones, and Athol Fugard. From the 1963 opening of the 110-seat Hattie Callner Memorial Memorial Theatre in the Jane Addams Center with Frank D. Gilroy's *Who'll Save the Plowboy*—Christiansen of the *Trib* called it "the most exciting, significant, and promising Chicago theatrical event in years"—to his resignation six years later, he made good that mission. Sickinger not only presented daring productions in a handful of Hull-House centers, but he made professionals out of community theatre people, including Jim Jacobs and Warren Casey, who would go on to write *Grease*, actor Mike Nussbaum (who was working for an exterminator company when Sickinger got his hands on him) and a young high school student named Mamet. "From the streets, and from the actors who lived here," Sickinger showed theatre hopefuls what the city could be.

*   *   *

Sickinger's torch for making Chicago possible for theatre was passed via Sills to a wild eyed student from the University of Wisconsin-Madison, whose production of *Peter Pan*, featuring nude dances from Neverland, had pricked the wrath of local authorities. Stuart Gordon was born in Chicago and forged at the Second City smithy. He had seen his first revue there at thirteen, started his own high school comedy group called the Human Race, and spent summers with Second City's touring company. After the Madison Buildings Department, fueled by cries of "Obscenity!", closed his Broom Street Theatre, Gordon came home and introduced himself to the man who had and would continue to have the strongest influence on his work, Paul Sills.

Sills convinced Gordon that Chicago would leave him alone to work and helped the company find space in the sanctuary of the Holy Covenant Church. The space was free; the censors were gone. The only thing lacking was air conditioning. So, when Sills took Story Theatre out of town, he offered Gordon's Organic Theatre Company his cooler venue in the newly organized Body Politic, a three theatre building found in 1969 by Jim Shiflett, the head of the Community Arts Foundation and ex-student of none other than mother Spolin. (Shiflett ran his own Grotowski-style Dream Theatre in one of the spaces there.) Gordon leapt at Sill's offer of a summer home and, when Sills didn't return, stayed at Body Politic for three-and-a-half-years.

Armed with Spolin's "bible," Sill's heir apparent and his tribe proceeded to create some of the most exciting, unexpected theatre Chicago has ever seen. The Organic could only have sprung from the head of the sixties: anarchic in spirit, improvisational in method, colorful, electric, populist, and completely zonked out. With a wildly talented gaggle of actors that included Dennis Franz, Meshach Taylor, Cordis and John Heard, Andre DeShields, Carolyn Purdy-Gordon (Stuart's wife), and Joe Mantegna (who, coming from the Organic, fit easily into the role of ultra-hippie Berger in the Chicago cast of *Hair*), the company presented an eclectic array of works, from a fifteen-word *Odyssey* to a commedia version of Voltaire's *Candide*, from a two-part *Huck Finn* to *Bloody Bess*, featuring a vengeful woman pirate, to what they billed as "the world's first science fiction epic adventure play in serial form," *Warp*. If the now-famous Steppenwolf pack are brawling, working class toughs, chugging Old Style and trashing neighborhood bars to the sounds of Springsteen, the Organics were gonzo commedia troupers, acid tripping across the speckled moons of Procyon. In terms of physical energy, Gregory Mosher observes, "They made the Steppenwolf company look like a ladies' tea party. They were completely wild," he goes on, "carefully rehearsed but totally daring. You need someone to dive off this 20-foot platform? No problem.'"

Underneath the comic-book energy and the anything-is-possible aesthetic was Gordon's fierce devotion to the concept of company, an ethic he claims to have inherited from Sills. In Gordon's words, Chicago provided "an environment where companies could stay together." Everybody who knew the work of the Organic under Gordon—who left in 1985 to write and direct movies in Los Angeles because under the pressures of institutionalization "I could no longer do company"—recalls the commitment to "the group." For Robert Falls, "the model theatre has always been Stuart's company with all those actors. That defined for me what a company was." Mosher recalls that "they were always working for the company; you know, dividing the money out of the cigar box at the end of the week." Perhaps the highest compliment comes from Sills himself: "Nobody's done what Stuart Gordon has done. He has done thirty-some shows, all unique and strange, growing out of company, with other people sharing well—a sense of loyalty."

A corollary to the two men's company commitment is their shared dedication to the community at large: the audience. "Stuart and Paul were really *popular* entertainers, popular theatre artists," says Falls. Gordon agrees. "Sills taught me that separating the commercial from the art is stupid. The first duty of a theatre is to get an audience." In fact, Gordon credits audiences for Chicago's theatre boom: they were daring and hungry; they supported artistic risks. "The audiences really made it happen," he explains. Moreover, he argues, echoing the sentiment of many Chicago artists who applaud local newspaper reviewers for compassionately supporting fledgling theatres and theatrical experiment, "The critics—in particular Richard Christiansen—did a great deal to discover and let the audience know about the companies."

In Chicago Gordon found out that all art, like all politics, is local. The city has "a to-hell-with-the-rest-of-the-world attitude," he says, pointing to journalism by way of example. "The latest story about the latest City Council hustle is on page one, and then on page three or four you read 'Nuclear war declared.'" Plays about the town itself go over big at home, but, Gordon claims, only if they tell the truth: "Chicago has a very low bullshit tolerance." When the Organic developed *Cops*, for instance, based on a script by Terry Curtis Fox, they talked to a great many police officers but never showed these "technical advisors" the finished script, which "ended with police gunning down unarmed suspects." The moment of reckoning finally came when the cops saw the full show. "We didn't know if we were going to get arrested or what," Gordon recalls. "I came up to a technical advisor and he said, 'They should have kicked the guy.' And I said, 'But he's already dead.' And he said 'So what? That's what we'd do. Kick the shit out of him, and then show the neighborhood what happens to somebody who tries to shoot a cop.'" Police officers became the biggest segment of the audience. "They loved the play," Gordon says, "because it was truthful. The idea that someone would do a play about their lives was flattering." Once, during the run, Gordon avoided getting a speeding ticket when the arresting officer learned he ran the theatre doing *Cops*.

If the student inherited the teacher's ethics, he likewise adopted the master's tools: Gordon and company brought improvisation to playwriting. Several of the theatre's most successful shows, including *E/R (Emergency Room)*, which ran for three years and became the basis of a TV series, were built by the company playing Spolin's games and improvising in front of a tape recorder. The process was a matter of survival as well as preference, asserts Richard Fire, the Organic's current artistic director who joined as an actor in 1971. "We learned that when we tried to adapt other people's work we didn't have complete control," he says. "We adapted Roald Dahl's *Switch Bitch* and Dahl came out and raved about it and brought a producer from London. We signed a letter of intent—they were going to take us to London. A few weeks later we got Dahl's version of the script in the mail. It was terrible." As a result of the author's intervention, the company could never perform its version of the piece again.

Out of this experience, and a similar one with Kurt Vonnegut's *Sirens of Titan*, the troupe redirected its improvisational energies to its own source material. The funniest moment in *Switch Bitch* had come out of an improvised "Spill the beans" scene. In it, a group of men, planning to swap wives in the middle of the night without giving their identities away to the women, had to tell each other how they made love, so that their wives wouldn't be surprised by a different style. The success of this exercise (and the demise of the project as a whole) made it "clear that we had to use this approach to write our own thing from scratch," Fire remembers. "Then nobody could take it away from us." In this mindset, the company took Mantegna's idea—to make a play about a group of Cub fans he'd met in the centerfield bleachers at Wrigley Field—and began. Each actor followed one of these people around; back at the theatre they improvised from the characters, taped the improvs, structured the story and boiled it down into the script that became *Bleacher Bums*.

When *Bleacher Bums* played in New York, most of the actors got hired to do other things. After *E/R*'s success, Gordon contends, the theatre's board of trustees expected every show to run three years. "The biggest problems we ever had at the Organic were problems with success," he says.

Still, the greater success was the one that built on Sickinger's: Gordon and his colleagues proved that it was possible to make theatre in Chicago and to make some kind of living doing it. They proved that limited money needn't limit the imagination, and that onstage anything is possible. The company Mosher and Falls call "the best of Chicago" stirred a generation of young imaginations to conceive dozens of young theatres that would be the city's "Off-Loop" theatre movement. One of these groups was Fall's own Wisdom Bridge Theatre, where, under his 10-year artistic directorship, he pointed the city toward the kind of director-centered aesthetic he currently explores at the Goodman, in concert with associate directors Frank Galati and Michael Maggio. "Directors have taken the point in Chicago," says Maggio, and Falls' ascendancy proves it. Labeled a grown-up Stuart Gordon with a literary bent, Falls brings Organic-style zest and no-holds-barred theatricality to Shakespeare, Brecht, and other "adult" classics.

But it was a theatre that broke out of the Gordon mold that introduced a new kind of polish and professionalism into the arena, inspired by its teacher and founder, a local playwright named Mamet.

*   *   *

It's hard to imagine Chicago as it would have been if David Mamet had never taken up teaching. It was teaching that pushed him to the typewriter—where he wrote scenes to illustrate his lessons. It was teaching at Vermont's Goddard College that allowed a cluster of students to form around him, the same college-age students who, when he called them to Chicago in 1974, would come and establish the St. Nicholas Theatre Company.

Mamet's own teachings provided the foundation for St. Nicholas, as that theatre built up a sizable training program to supplement its production work. Striving for simplicity, the Mamet way grafted the moment-to-moment truth seeking of his New York acting coach, Sanford Meisner, with the stripped down reliance on language he'd witnessed while bussing tables at Second City. As a high schooler in Chicago, Mamet had worked with Sickinger and taken workshops from both Spolin and Patinkin. By the time he returned in the seventies, though, it was clear from the way his young colleagues at St. Nick revered him that he was the pupil no longer.

"Mamet cast himself in the role of the romantic, Chicago tough guy," says Falls, invoking the names of other Windville journalist-writers: Ben Hecht, Charles MacArthur, Nelson Algren. Ever ready to play the hack, Mamet more than once claimed to write plays so his theatre wouldn't have to pay royalties. Indeed, he sometimes seemed like a character out of Hecht and MacArthur's *The Front Page*, the cigar-chomping ace with one ear to the ground and one to the poker table. And good ears they were. Mamet's dialogue crackled with the rhythms of city talk, as if he'd worn a wire every day of his life. *Sexual Perversity in Chicago*, the play that began to make his name in Chicago, even though (or because) many found it offensive and vulgar, grew out of conversations he'd overheard at Second

City, or so the story goes. It premiered in 1974, oddly enough, at the Organic, under the direction of Stuart Gordon.

This auspicious coupling of Mamet and Gordon appears strange in retrospect because the pair—as evidenced by the theatres they founded— were as different as Hemingway and Pynchon. In Gary Houston's version of Chicago theatre's family tree, Mamet's work belongs to the "Reality Makers" and Gordon's to the "Story Tellers," along with Northwestern's Robert Breen and Frank Galati. Steven Schachter, former artistic director of the now-defunct St. Nicholas, confirms that St. Nick's goals were not the Organic's. "All the other young theatres [read Organic] were very hippie-esque in the way they worked. We tried to bring a corporate—in the best sense of the word—aesthetic into a garage theatre. It was a unique way of working." This "corporate" approach insisted on a kind of professional perfectionism, which Schacter says "filtered down from David." It meant that everything, from the graphics to the lobby to the playing of scene five, had to be perfect, reflective of the theatre's serious intent.

Having gotten the theatre going, Mamet moved on to see his plays performed at the Goodman and across the country, and finally resigned from the St. Nicholas's board when Schachter scheduled a play he found anti-Semitic. His theatre, which had grown in a burst and upped the city's ante of artistic discipline for all time, folded shortly into the new decade, after Schachter and managing director Peter Schneider both lit out for a new territory.

By the time St. Nick had packed it in, Mamet's work, under Mosher's sure-handed direction, had breathed new life into Chicago's flagship Goodman Theatre, which until the late sixties housed the Goodman School of Drama shows with guest professionals. First as head of the Goodman's Stage 2 and later as artistic director, Mosher premiered Mamet's *American Buffalo, Edmond,* and *Glengarry Glen Ross,* among others. In the process he helped to cement the native playwright's career and turn the long-drowsy theatre around.

Mamet's own stay in Chicago was brief—a total of only eighteen consecutive months, according to Mosher—but his imprint remains. He introduced a new level of professionalism to the developing theatre scene; he reinvented Midwestern machismo and opened the way for the second generation of Chicago playwrights that is emerging today (including James Sherman, John Logan, Rick Cleveland, Keith Huff, James Yoshimura, Lonnie Carter, Steve Carter, Claudia Allen, Alan Gross, Sally Nemeth, Sherry Narens, Dean Corrin, Jeffrey Sweet, and others). Finally, by lending the community his ear, he gave it its voice. "Mamet wrote the gospels as far as Chicago theatre is concerned," Patinkin observes. Mosher agrees heartily, attributing to Mamet much of the credit for elevating the scene "from footnote to paragraph to chapter" in American theatre history.

"David is the lynchpin between generations," Mosher suggests. "He is the apex of it all."

*　*　*

Mamet helped the Chicago theatre grow up; the Steppenwolfs kept it young, as if the banner over their theatre proclaimed "Adolescence is more." Mamet seemed to some a culmination of all Chicago theatre before him; the Steppenwolf youngsters from Illinois State by way of the North Shore appeared out of nowhere, like a Mack truck in the kitchen—a great, noisy, racing, smelly fluke.

Steppenwolf admitted no indigenous influences, except for rock-and-roll music, a couple of college teachers, some early movies by Martin Scorsese, Mike Nichols, and John Cassavetes, and their moms in the suburbs. They were incubated and hatched in a church basement in Highland Park four years before they moved to Hull-House. "That's how we grew up together," says Jeff Perry. "Totally dependent on each other for all society."

The wolf gang enjoyed a healthy supply of what Houston calls "vital arrogance," the belief that "before-we-got-here-there-was-nothing" that propelled many Chicago companies into being. They've even been known to ruthlessly parody actors from more established ensembles (e.g., Mantegna). Perry, who founded the company in 1976 with Gary Sinise, Terry Kinney, and others, agrees that he and his pals were naïve and arrogant. "It was like an adolescence, which we purposefully arrested for years," he explains. "Adolescence is when you say, 'This is my personality and I'm not going to get sucked into yours.' Only in later years did we see what others could teach us."

For a creature so adamantly of its own making, Steppenwolf displayed genetic similarities to its Chicago ancestry. Like Sills, these ensemble members were basically inarticulate, committed to the present and driven to work within a company. They shared a physical dynamism and lack of manners with the Organic crew. They were as macho—women included—as any Mamet characters. And, in the tradition of the Compass, the early Second City, and the Organic, they represented a miraculous mass of talent. (In addition to those mentioned above, John Malkovich, Laurie Metcalf, Joan Allen, Moira Harris, and Glenne Headly were all founding or early members.) Working along the Sills line, where character is basically a modification of the actor's self, Steppenwolf took the Chicago knack for company acting—bouncing off the other performers, as if improvising—and pushed it deeper, until the most tightly orchestrated moments felt like emotionally charged jam sessions.

After Steppenwolf ventured downtown in 1980 (something they had done briefly in '78 for a St. Nicholas production of Lanford Wilson's *Fifth of July*, directed by Schachter), it wasn't long before they ventured even farther. "*True West* was like the opening of a door," says Rondi Reed, who joined the ensemble of her college-mates at the time of its Hull-House move. As she tells it, the company was having trouble getting rights to plays controlled by New York agents who have never heard of Steppenwolf. Reed remembers Sinise, artistic director at the time, selling them on the idea of taking *True West* to New York, "saying, 'We need to get out of Chicago. We need to get our foot in New York to be able to get first crack at some of these scripts.'" She also recalls being justifiably terrified at the prospect. "We knew how good Gary and John Malkovich were," she says; the thought that the world might find out too was life threatening to the troupe. Perry, who relinquished his role in the Sam Shepard play to Sinise, in order to hold down the fort as artistic director, agrees that this first New York move swung "the double-headed sword of success" at Steppenwolf. "The life and ideals of the company were hanging in the balance," he explains, and yet, the national acclaim for the show "filled our [Chicago] theatre for the first time in our history." This national recognition had a lasting impact at home, too. It set off a chain reaction that is still felt there: dozens of tough-talking, bushy-tailed new companies a year create themselves in Steppenwolf's image.

The *True West* episode caused deep and lasting rifts in the company and, by kicking off a series of similar New York moves, began a new phase in its development: the nonresident company or, as Perry puts it, "trying to figure out how to create ensemble work with people spread all over the place." He assesses the progress: "It's a losing battle that we win sometimes." Reed sees this as the challenge of growing up, "to keep the flame going." They both concur that starting in Chicago enabled the theatre to mature at its own pace. "If we had been in New York or L.A.," Reed hypothesizes, "it would have torn us apart much earlier, before the formative stuff got set."

For Steppenwolf, growing up now equals growing up bigger— expanding the ensemble and building a new five million dollar space (they currently inhabit the old St. Nicholas theatre). The company will move out of what Schachter calls "a cozy, warm and welcoming" arena theatre and into a whole new relationship with an audience used to dodging the actors' spit. The graduation will allow these artists to make theatre on a larger scale, a process begun with *Grapes of Wrath* in a rented house. A new kind of space means a changing aesthetic for a theatre renowned for big explosions in tight surroundings.

That's where Frank Galati comes in. Expansive, generous, and articulate, Galati couldn't be more different from the Steppenwolf spit-on-the-face, punch-all-the-pronouns stereotype. An already mythic figure in Chicago, Galati seems to begin where the city's theatre history leaves off. Before becoming a professor of performance studies at Northwestern, Goodman associate director, and a Steppenwolf ensemble member, he studied with Sickinger at Hull-House, with Steppenwolf mentor Ralph Lane in high school, and at N.U. with the legendary Alvina Krause and chamber theatre pioneer Robert Breen. Breen had written the major textbook on readers' theatre, which brought non-dramatic literature to the stage by framing enacted scenes with narration, a technique that left an indelible mark on Galati's work, as well as exciting a young Paul Sills. In Story Theatre, Sills "absorbed Breen's narrator," cut him out, so that the actor would move between narration and character; in *Grapes of Wrath* and earlier work, Galati preserves the narrator's presence. In addition to directing, adapting, and writing (and writing for the screen, e.g., *The Accidental Tourist*), Galati acts and acts big—"He's Zero Mostel out there," says Remains Theatre's Larry Sloan—and thinks big, ready to realize epic novels, abstract painting or grand opera on the boards. His knowledge of all kinds of literature is, likewise, enormous.

All past roads in this community lead to Galati; similarly, many paths to the future appear to rise from him, including Steppenwolf's own. Reed anticipates that the grandeur of Galati's vision will open up the scope of Steppenwolf's work, as it has in *Grapes*. "Frank has been an infusion of maturity," she says, "personal and artistic. He's been inspirational. I maintain that he was sent to us for a reason. He's a teacher, and I think we need that. We're only now ready to embrace someone like Galati." Indeed, it's a strange marriage: Galati's literary sensitivity and grand theatricality paired with the feral down-and-dirtiness of Steppenwolf. It's a marriage that could only be made in Chicago, a city named, depending on who you ask, after a fortress, a polecat or the wild onions that once grew there. Whatever the source, the meaning of this Native American phrase is apt: great and powerful.

Reunions, John Steinbeck tells us, can't last. When the Joad family is reunited at the beginning of *The Grapes of Wrath*, they're enjoying a temporary reprieve from the dust storms of life. Before long the Okie clan will be blown apart, their kin buried in ditches along the westward road and—despite Ma's fiercest efforts to keep family together—scattered every which way to the winds of change. Reunions can't last.

Or can they? Onstage at Broadway's Cort Theatre, the dispersed can come together again night after night; the broken can be mended whole. For Steppenwolf—one of a line of Chicago groups that struggle between the family ethic of the ensemble and the individual destinies of its members—the production is a metaphor-in-process, a parable of heritage and continuity, an allegory about the effects of geography and economic reality.

In the plentiful folklore of Chicago theatre, one old saw recurs. It goes: when actors arrive in New York, they look for an agent; when they come to Chicago, they look for a company. The adage could be extended to say: when Chicago came to theatre, it was looking for a community. From Jane Addams and Viola Spolin to Paul Sills and David Shepherd to Bob Sickinger, Stuart Gordon and David Mamet—and on to all the I.S.U. students who became Steppenwolf, and all the others who became one of the hundred-plus other companies in town and to the still rising heirs of Mosher, Galati, and Falls—the pioneers and descendants of the city's theatre community have sought what might be called the holiness of the Where. It's a concept that Steinbeck's ex-preacher Jim Casy understands: "I got to thinkin' how we was holy when we was one thing and mankind was holy when it was one thing. And it on'y got unholy when one miserable little fella got the bit in his teeth and run off his own way, kickin' and draggin' and fightin.' Fella like that bust the holiness. But when they're all workin' together, kind of harnessed to the whole shebang, that's right. That's holy."

This article was originally published in *American Theatre*, July/August, 1990.

What We Talk About When We Talk about Good

What We Talk About When We Talk About Good

> What people read and like is good: that is what good means.
> —Randall Jarrell, *The Age of Criticism*

If theatre critics didn't exist, would we invent them? If we did, if they sprang full-blown from the collective head of the artists of the American stage, what shape would they assume? What questions would they ask, what qualities possess? How would they talk about art?

Sony Pictures invented a critic over a year ago, David Manning of the (real) *Ridgefield Press*, a Connecticut weekly; his job was to praise Sony films for quote ads, at least until he got fired for being non-existent. I give theatre people more credit. We would invent critics, I imagine, not merely to praise us—nor, certainly, to bury us. But we would invent them sure enough, and our new critics would look a lot like the old ones. They'd be better informed, maybe, more sensitive to intention, more invested in description and evocation than judgment (of the thumbs up, thumbs down variety). They'd understand context for work, perhaps, and even demonstrate their love of the theatre, maybe, but essentially they'd be the same guys or, newly diversified, the same women.

I've been writing and worrying about critics and criticism since the mid-'80s. The words and worries keep returning to an interdependent tangle of people who make theatre and people who write about it. More specifically, they return, self-reflexively, to those of us engaged in developing and producing for the stage. What is our complicity in the system of American criticism? What is our responsibility for changing it? What is our power? In short, how can we expect critics to change their tune when—in the realm of critical response—we sound so much like them? Theatre people may not be responsible for the moribund state of criticism, but we must be responsible for imagining it back to life.

Two personal experiences bracket my thinking about this responsibility to recast criticism. The first began in February 1990 when *American Theatre* published my essay, "The Critical Knot," which through analysis and polemic explored the dependency of theatre people on criticism—for approval and marketing—even when that criticism resembles abuse. The essay, written at the height of congressional attacks on the arts, drew on the language of those attacks—anti-theatrical, violent, and infantilizing—and on then-current psychological writing, especially that of Swiss psychologist Alice Miller, about child abuse and society's institutionalized hatred of children. It paralleled the relationship between critics (journalistic, professional, familial, and interior) and artists, as perceived stand-ins for willful, unruly children in the America of Bush *père*.

The essay encouraged theatre people to rethink their ambivalent, even compulsive relationship to criticism: that is, the way we fight for freedom the superego—the internalized, symbolic "father"—while at the same time craving Dad's (the critic's) approval at every step. I suggested specific, if extreme, pie-in-the-sky ways to end this dependency, including stopping the use of quote ads for publicity (if we don' believe 'em when they pan us, why should we quote 'em when they rave?) and searching for alternative methods of audience development, limiting free tickets for critics, lobbying media for more in-depth features, giving up on reading reviews (as a community), and asserting the moral rights of artists, in accordance with the international Berne Convention, which gives writers and fine artists in some countries "The Right to Protection from Excessive Criticism." Moreover, I called for "new sources for and forms of supportive, constructive criticism from within the theatre community."

While I felt sickened by the attack-letters *American Theatre* received from critics—even 11 years later I can't bring myself to quote them—I was troubled more lastingly by the outpouring of affirmation and praise from friends and colleagues in the theatre. I expected critics to miss the point— no one likes to be compared to a child abuser, even metaphorically and for the sake of argument. But I've never been able to shake the thought that many of the theatre people who felt the essay spoke for them were avoiding its central premise: that as a profession we help foster a system we loathe.

Over the next ten years, I searched for ways to link up theatre artists and critics by casting them as parts of a single community of people who share a love of theatre and investment in its future. I wrote and spoke about it. I profiled critics, evaluated their journalistic work and book-length collections in print—reviewed the reviewers—trying to make sense of both the system and the people working in it. At New Dramatists, where playwrights' works-in-progress are never reviewed, we brought in critics (as dramaturgs, readers, and panelists) and co-hosted annual playwright/critic lunches with Columbia University's National Arts Journalism Program's fellows.

Last year at a day-long gathering of five critics/arts journalists and five New Dramatists playwrights, organized with freelance critic and biographer Alexis Greene, I had an epiphany that, like the "Critical Knot" letters, changed the direction of my thinking. In the morning all ten participants took part in a playwriting workshop; in the afternoon, led by former *L.A. Times* critic Daniel Sullivan, they wrote a pair of reviews of a short play, authored anonymously by a leading American playwright and performed staged reading-style. Again, it was the artists who surprised me most. I was less shocked that the critics' playwriting exercises *sounded* more like plays than the playwrights'. (Working with uniquely talented playwrights, I'm awash in plays that defy convention and strive for new, often unfamiliar dramatic forms.) The jolt came when the playwrights wrote reviews. Not only did they sound like criticism (think Algonquin Roundtable), but in a couple of cases, they sounded like savage criticism (think Dorothy Parker). Perhaps it's unfair to generalize from so small a sample, but I became convinced—a conviction that had been growing for years—that we carry a kind of categorical criticism in our heads, a shared idea of what critical response sounds like. And the category is "the pan."

*   *   *

I went to see a play – *The Stone* by Abromowitz. I must say, I really loved it – and Lars Helbig especially, in the role of the doctor. That whole day I thought about the play. And then the next night, I had dinner with Joan. She'd seen the play the week before and had found it sentimental, and Helbig's acting she'd found very broad. When she said those things, the performance that was sitting in my memory was poisoned. It died. Every moment of it died on contact with her words—every moment's hopeful little face turned purple and died. In the days that followed, it was painful to revisit what had become of the memory I'd had. Finally I emptied the whole evening out of my mind like trash.

—Wallace Shawn, *The Designated Mourner*

We all know Joan. We've all been Joan. The negative response— sought or unsought—seeps through most conversations about plays and production unnoticed, a usual poison. I've often wondered if, at least in the world of new play development and production, negativity—in the guise of identifying a play's problems—isn't mistaken for intelligence and insight. Playwright Bridget Carpenter (*Fall*) once theorized to me that Americans resort to negative criticism because they see being positive as proof of stupidity, ignorance, shallowness. I think she's right. Have you ever seen people at post-play discussions champing at the bit to share their MOST IMPORTANT insights? Have you ever heard a MOST IMPORTANT insight that didn't say what was WRONG, what needed fixing? In this way, critical response from within the theatre resembles the criticism we complain of from outside. Despite the love of theatre that brings someone to the audience (as spectator, colleague, or critic), despite the best intentions toward the work itself, the critical coup is achieved in the act of pointing out the problem. Diagnosing the malady makes us wise. The force of this coup, the energy with which the negative assessment is delivered, always tips the tonal balance until—out goes the good air—"every moment's hopeful little face" turns purple and dies. The critics? They are us.

How different this is from our natural responses to works of art. While as humans we bring critical capability to all we survey—assessing what we like and don't like, what we find good and less good—our basic human responses to music, say, or a painting include a complex mixture of emotion and intellect, identification and rejection, boredom and wonder, memory and longing. Our interest ebbs and flows. We turn back to our own thoughts. We grow aroused or sleepy. We think about people we've known. We feel smaller than the genius that animates the symphony, maybe, or superior to the guy who assembles a collage from objects found in alleys. In other words, we respond to art with an intense and intricate subjectivity comprised of body, mind, spirit, and heart. Our critical responses, meanwhile, are usually centered in the logical mind and, to the extent we engage feeling, in the generalized realm of what we like or don't.

In "A Few Maxims for the Instruction of the Over-Educated," Oscar Wilde observes, "The only thing that the artist cannot see is the obvious. The only thing the public can see is the obvious. The result is the Criticism of the Journalist." Here, typically, Wilde uses epigrammatic overstatement to seize on a truth: art is mostly concerned with the invisible. Whether attuned to spiritual mystery, sexual energy, glancing, mutable truth, or the subtle dynamics of human interaction, the aim of art is nearly always the elusive invisibilities that underscore our lives—that which cannot be *reported*. People turn to art with a desire, hope, or instinct for that unreportable something. The journalist, by leaning and training, reports, and the language of that reportage—because it lacks the vocabularies of body, emotion, and soul—has, at its disposal, only the analytical, inquiring mind with which to seek the unseen. That language can only be partial. The journalistic critic, therefore, can unearth a play's structure, for instance, as a way past more obvious narrative facts, but he or she hasn't the language to evoke the physical sensations that run through the body when the orchestra stops playing and the ensemble continues its soaring fugue *a cappella*. The critic can describe the moment as a joy or a thrill, but to suggest more than that, that the moment is one of spiritual connection, for example, or to recount a personal memory triggered by the flight of song might appear, well, uncritical, not to mention silly.

This discrepancy between critical language and natural human response has come home to me in the most personal way over the past couple of months. I carry in my date book a sheaf of emails and letters, written mostly by friends and colleagues, in response to my first novel, recently published. As journalistic reviews of the book trickle in and as I hear directly from readers I know, I'm struck by how different in kind published responses are from private ones. Many of the letters and emails contain personal information about the reader—memories brought to mind by the novel. Many of them speak about the way they read it—fast or slow, in the middle of the night or on a train. They talk about the writing, sure, but they also ask questions of the writer as a person. Where did this or that come from? Did I know that such and such had happened to them, too? And they ask questions about the book's setting and period. It's a novel about identity within the family and, among other things, mental illness, and many have talked movingly about their own families.

Is there any reason to think that feedback like this wouldn't have been helpful during the dozen years it took to write the book? Certainly, it would have made the process less lonely and countered the erosive fear that nobody would be interested in a story like this. It would have helped me "hear" the work, having it read back to me in these ways, and provided new insights, details, meat for the story's bones.

It's a dead end, I've come to believe, to expect a fuller, more human and invested response from critics, especially when papers and their editors are pushing them to be consumer guides, cutting pages and column inches, treating theatre as a lesser child of the entertainment industry and devaluing cultural criticism in general (when we reinvent critics we'll have to do the same with editors and publishers). On the other hand, there's no good reason for the supporters and makers of theatre to rely on the partial, journalistic language we've adopted. In fact, we have every reason to expand it, mess with it, and make it multidimensional, precise, physical, spirited, and full of feeling. We just haven't figured out how to do it.

Formal and informal discussions of new work almost always center on two questions: "Did you like it?" and "Was it any good?" The first of these leads mostly to limited, irrelevant answers. The second—because the theatre community has no common definition, vocabulary, or agreement about artistic quality (nor, probably, should it) – leads straight to hell. I polled close to 50 playwrights – members of New Dramatists and graduate playwriting students at Yale School of Drama—to find out what they mean when they say a play is good. Of dozens of fascinating answers, there was only one they all agreed on: a good play does what it sets out to do. One writer added, with Matthew Arnold, that what it sets out to do should be worth doing. (Who, I wonder, will decide?) Judging a play on its own terms frees us to consider a play good even when we don't like it, many of the writers explained. It would help if more people made that distinction instead of conflating matters of taste with those of quality, and analysis with opinion. There's no end to the possible ways of talking about plays and production. It's just that we've settled into, essentially, one way. And there's no end to the possible, productive questions we might ask of a play or a production. How does the play use the theatre? How does it live in time and space? How does it fit in a body of work? What does it say about the world? How does it say what it says? How does it work? (As opposed to, "Does it work?") How does our personal experience of it change as it unfolds? What's strange about it? What's familiar? What's the relationship between the strangeness and familiarity? And my favorite: what is it?

Partly, I suspect, building a new critical vocabulary from within the art will come from redefining the aims and questions of our own conversation. Just as a different "super-objective" can change a performance or a different "spine" can alter a production, so different intentions can transform critical discourse. As long as we see the goal of new play development, for instance, as fixing plays or making them better, we'll have to begin with what's wrong with them. What if the goal of dramaturgy were stated differently. If, instead, we strove "to sustain the writer through the difficult work of writing the play," responses might be more about identifying successes and articulating the specifics that challenge and excite. Or if the aim were "to help writers evaluate a play's effectiveness on their own terms," we might be called upon simply to describe the work back to them without feeling or judgment, in order for them to hear exactly *what it is* they've written and to determine *in the privacy of their own artistic consciences* how that stacks up against what they wanted to write.

I'm excited to see many theatres experimenting with the process for critical response pioneered in the early '90s by D.C.-based choreographer Liz Lerman. Lerman's system gives the artist a fundamental power: the option to invite criticism. This model for peer response to work-in-progress begins with affirmation of each work's specific accomplishments, what respondents find "surprising, challenging, evocative, compelling, delightful, unique, touching, poignant, different for you, interesting," in Lerman's words. The second step is guided by the creator's questions – attempts to get feedback on specific aspects of the work he or she is exploring. Then the respondents form their own opinions into neutral questions, again with the assumption that questions lead more naturally to illumination than does telling the artist what's wrong or how to fix the piece. The fourth step provides for "opinion time," with the creator(s) retaining the prerogative to invite the opinions or to refuse them. Two additional steps allow for discussion of the work's subject matter—and possibly related responses, such as personal stories—and for continuing to work on the work in the context of the feedback session.

In my experience, Lerman's system helps create a safe environment for exploration and constructive exchange. It works best when the generating artists have specific questions they want addressed. It can feel a bit formal or rigid, especially with artists who know each other's work and ways of talking, but it allows for a surprising amount of ground to be covered in a short time and provides a structure for restraining grandstanders. It's aimed at fixing the problems, but grounded in celebrating the accomplishments. I wish there were more such models out there.

Specifically, I'm interested in pursuing a more constructive, examined subjectivity in critical feedback within the theatre, a process whereby the thing we do best—getting people literally and figuratively in a room together—is reflected in our discussions. Theatre is unabashedly inter-personal, unquestionably live, but we can easily distance ourselves in conversation. It's a distance familiar from journalistic criticism, where critics for the most part rely on opinion (subjective response) stated as reportage (objective stance). Critics admit there's no such thing as objectivity and even scoff at the suggestion that they see themselves as objective, yet their language and tone comes from a journalistic tradition in which the author is depersonalized. The critics who have risen above this tradition (for good or evil) have done it through the force of their personalities (Shaw good, Simon evil), their incisive clowning (think Algonquin Round Table again), or the passionate clarity of their aesthetic values (e.g., Clurman or Brustein).

The current crisis in criticism inside and outside of the theatre may be related to a culture-wide transition. As we transform from a culture of homogeneous authority (where people could talk about good with relative comfort) to one of jangling diversity, the vocabulary of critical distance and journalistic objectivity has lost ground to that of personal essay, confession, memoir, and the performance art of punditry. Whether we respond to art in print or conversation, we face the challenge of constructing an "I" that reveals and questions itself as it goes—monitoring the place of perception in the formation of judgment—while remaining humble. In other words, the responder's "I," written or spoken, must never mistake itself for the subject, that is, the work of art being examined.

It's a tricky business. There are alternative critics who explore point of view in this way and always seem to be talking about themselves. Others use the "I" almost as a replacement for phrases like "this reporter," without self-consciousness. The one theatre critic I've read who seems sensitively engaged in exploring the role of the subjective in her responses is *New York Times* culture critic and, now, Sunday reviewer Margo Jefferson. Jefferson comes across as smart, enthusiastic, widely read, and personally probing, as though in addition to evaluating productions, she's determined to understand the role of identity and cultural influence in one's approach to art. Sometimes haltingly and sometimes vivaciously, Jefferson switches between observation, opinion, and self-reflection in her essays, and by doing so investigates not only the "I" of a review, but the "we." In her review of Pamela Gien's *The Syringa Tree*, for instance, she begins with her own response:

What moved me most was that I could feel so many things, full-out sometimes, at odds or in conflict at other times. And I could keep switching my attention from life to life and story to story, even those that were fragmented or partly submerged, then supply what was left unsaid.

From that revelation, she can hypothesize about a more communal response: "The play of the small against the large, the individual and the group, personal actions and political or social consequences: this is what we crave from the theatre." While Jefferson can seem to be struggling in this middle ground, I believe that struggle is worth it and worth taking a cue from in our own conversations about art.

"No artist needs criticism, he only needs appreciation," Gertrude Stein writes in the voice of Alice B. Toklas. "If he needs criticism he is no artist." If it's true that theatre people have internalized the voice of negative criticism, then Stein may be right. If we are the critics, then we are also the self-critics; if we've learned to accentuate the negative within, we may have even more need for appreciation from others. However much we need criticism, it's clear we need it in a different voice, unveiled, expressive, more nuanced, precise, and wholly human. If we would reinvent criticism, we have to start with ourselves.

This essay was originally published in *American Theatre*, September, 2001.

Stage Door Johnny: John Lahr's *Light Fantastic*

For the better part of four years, in the pages of *The New Yorker*, John Lahr has been waging a lover's rebellion mounted, largely, against criticism itself, against the practice of edged objectivity and pithy judgment, against vitriol and, most especially, against opinion. Now the documents of his quiet assault have been collected as *Light Fantastic: Adventures in Theatre*, making it possible to see the contours—the aims and limits—of this rebellion.

Lahr hasn't exactly banished opinion from its place in reviews, but he's unseated it, revoked its privileged position as the equal partner of "description." Where it reigned, he installs extensive historical and dramaturgical research, interviews with artists, copious quoting from the plays themselves, and shifts of focus from what he personally dislikes (a Steppenwolf production of Odet's *Awake and Sing*, for example) to what's of lasting importance ("the depth of [Odet's] perceptions about character, language, and the punishing waste of spirit in democracy's obsession with success…"). In effect, he's all but left reviewing behind in favor of the interpretative essay. "At the end of an essay," he explains in his introduction, "I want the reader to know more about the event than just what I think about it…I want the makers to be part of the production's story. The essay becomes, to my way of thinking, a more colorful and accurate record of events—a kind of criticism that conjures the life of theatre as well as the life of the play."

Whenever possible, Lahr gives up his aisle seat for a dressing room armchair or a place just offstage. It's a perspective he relishes, that of insider-outsider, silent admirer. His ardor speaks through his process and his prose. Playwrights Joe Orton, Harold Pinter, Tennessee Williams, Tony Kushner, Neil Simon, and Brian Friel receive his loving, detailed attentions; performers Fiona Shaw and Anna Deveare Smith inspire his rapture; director Ingmar Bergman, an almost religious devotion. His valentine to "Tap Messenger" Savion Glover is, I think, the best single piece in the book—the one that most thoroughly transforms the reading of criticism into the *seeing* of live performance.

Lahr even allows himself to get carried away. His description of Liam Neeson's entrance in *Anna Christie* steams off the page:

> He towers above the rest of the cast like a kind of sequoia of sex. His amalgam of sensuality and sensibility sends an electrifying charge through an audience. When he washes up on Christopherson's coal barge after surviving five days at sea, the audience sits where Anna

stands: eyeball to eyeball with a force of nature. He compels immediate attention and belief. He is a stoker. He is catnip to women.

At least once, Lahr doesn't wait to get to his typewriter to voice his excitement: Watching the final rehearsal (from the wings, he confides in a discreet parenthetical) of British comedian Barry Humphries' triumphant one man/woman show as the unflappably gorgeous Dame Edna Everage in 1989, Lahr, "obsessed like everyone else with getting Dame Edna tuned up for the challenge of opening night," shouts a helpful word to the star.

Affection sparks Lahr's will to write, as his pursuit of Dame Edna makes clear. At her 1981 show *An Evening's Intercourse with Barry Humphries*, Lahr tells us, "I was blindsided by one of her startling observations and fell off my seat laughing. I can't account for the next two minutes of the show. I was on the floor. Afterward, I determined to write about Humphries from the wings." And so the tickled critic becomes the enamored chronicler, and not just for a one-night stand. Lahr's laughter translated itself into a book: *Dame Edna Everage and the Rise of Western Civilization: Backstage with Barry Humphries*, a chapter of which can be read here in an earlier incarnation. Once bitten, he's forever bitten. You can see how he sustains the biographer's fascination, the dogged devotion necessary to spend years following in the footsteps of his father (the comedian Bert Lahr) to write *Notes on a Cowardly Lion* (1969) or dredging the mad, murky farce of Joe Orton's short life for *Prick Up Your Ears* (1978).

*   *   *

It's hard to escape the feeling that Lahr's life's work is, in part, a son's work fueled by a son's love for his father, a marvelous clown who could (and sometimes did) forget his offspring's name. "To his children," Lahr writes in *Notes*, "[Bert] Lahr is a friendly absence, a man who, induced to reveal himself, is at once humble and childishly stubborn, concerned and curiously aloof." At the outset of his career, the son traveled thousands of miles over several years' time to piece together his father's life, and, then, through his writing, labored to resurrect him. "'Was it different in the early days, Pop?'" he asks, standing in his dad's dressing room, with the puppy dog attentiveness of Happy Loman. "That's another story, kid," his father explains. "Some other time, OK?" Now, all these years later, he spends this same devotion on clowns and comedians of all stripes, ensuring their place in our cultural memory.

Lahr rarely theorizes; he wastes no words to undo distinctions between high and low culture, art and popular entertainment. He jumps right into the job of enshrining comics alongside serious writers, generation-defining actors, and innovative directors. His portraits of comics sprang to life for me, even when I didn't know the subject (as with the following description of the English music hall "monkey king of comedy," Max Wall):

> In the pauses, Wall pulled a face. He had a broad forehead and a large chin and those teeth. He wasn't exactly a picture postcard, but you couldn't take your eyes off him. Wall's game was to relax the audience with sight gags and silliness, and then goose it with honesty. He referred to himself as a boy and then cringed at the word: 'How much imagination can one man have!'

Always the romantic, Lahr is drawn to the sad-sack underlives of these same clowns and comic writers, the way he was when digging up the frigid brutality of his father's childhood. He describes the "atmosphere of loss" that fed the "frantic energy" of Oscar Wilde's household and the drunken solitude at the end of *Beyond the Fringe* comedian Peter Cook's life.

> He lived quietly, by his own defiant standards, lobbing his little jolts of joy and fury into the community when the voices came to him. Like all great comedians, he understood his gift well enough to know that he couldn't reliably control it. When you're hot, you're hot, as they say, and when you're not, you're not. His life made a spectacle of both sides of that equation: the glorious transformation and the punishing demoralization. He was resigned to doomed contentment.

The desire to unearth the roots of the creative act goes hand in hand with Lahr's gift for research. When he's not sipping tea with a director or ale with an actor, he's hunkered down in the library, poking through journals and early drafts of masterworks. Last year he discovered an early Arthur Miller short story that contained the seed for the character of Willy Loman in *Death of a Salesman*. Earlier, he edited Orton's diaries and selected correspondence.

I've come to think of Lahr as less of a critic than a benevolent, long-distance dramaturg with a trust fund: someone with the budget to cover world theatre by traveling from England, where he lives, to America, where he was born, and, on special occasions, to the continent; someone with the stick-to-it-iveness to keep tabs on a Pinter or Stoppard for decades without letting his interest flag; a very educated someone, who writes the smartest, most spirited program notes you could want. (Earlier in his career, Lahr served as dramaturg for both the Lincoln Center Theatre in New York and the Guthrie in Minneapolis.) His close readings—of Kushner's *Perestroika* and Edward Albee's *Three Tall Women*, for instance— illuminate and untangle the knottiest texts. On the other hand, because he loves textual analysis, and because he goes out of his way to avoid stating negative opinions (except of Stephen Sondheim, whose "perverse brilliance" he repeatedly blames for the death of the American musical), he's also capable of bogging down in a dramatic lit-crit land, until you can't see performance for the plays.

*   *   *

I don't mean to suggest that Lahr's accentuation of the positive and blend of journalism, scholarship, and review is entirely new or even new to him. The late Kenneth Tynan, Britain's start critic/dramaturg/producer, stands as a clear model for Lahr. Their game is much the same, though Tynan had none of Lahr's humility, and Lahr has little of his mentor's opinionated dazzle. For Lahr, the "light fantastic" is something other people trip; for the brilliant Tynan, by contrast, ever at play in the fields of the lauded, it was something to catch. Lahr's current brand of compassionate criticism is also continuous with his earlier writings for *Evergreen Review* and the *Village Voice*. From its subtitle to its final ode to Muhammed Ali, Lahr's 1973 collection of essays and profiles, *Astonish Me: Adventures in Contemporary Theatre*, reads like a somewhat overheated *Light Fantastic*. Lahr has mellowed since then, and the theatre has, too.

Lahr's rebellion isn't for everybody. I've heard him complained of as "the village explainer," which, at times in his lengthy "Playwrights" section, feels apt. He's also raised hackles by making his jaunty passages from the journalistic world to the artistic one, spending the night at a producer's home, for example, and then praising his host's production record in print. I personally believe this intimacy with artists makes one *better* able to write about them, so I wasn't particularly troubled by this practice. Then I saw Lahr's book jacket, on which three of five gushy blurbs are written by artists he praises inside. The faces of two of these also adorn the book's cover, among a gallery of drawings by Paul Davis. Lahr is a thoughtful, trustworthy critic, but the selling of his book looks a bit like the selling of his book.

I've also heard Lahr dismissed for, essentially, dismissing American theatre (with intermittent and high-profile exceptions) in favor of Hollywood and an Anglo-American straddler's existence. The truth of this situation is particularly painful, since (with the very different exceptions of Robert Brustein, whose critical opportunities in the *New Republic* have dwindled to an average of once-a-month, and Margo Jefferson at the *New York Times*) there is no theatre critic in mainstream American journalism with the advantages of space, think-time, and readership that Lahr has. At present, he turns those advantages mostly toward performances that either can't be seen in America or (if they can) outside of New York. Does he therefore have a responsibility to cover more native ground? Probably not, but I, for one, wish he would.

In the process of restyling the *New Yorker* into an art-and-culture "fanzine" by slimming it down and chirping it up, editor Tina Brown has done at least one noble thing. She has given an important critic the unique luxury of following his theatrical bliss. I wish more editors would follow her example and more critics would follow Lahr's. While we can savor the fruits of one essayist's passion, they, alone, can't satisfy. American theatre still has empty seats reserved and waiting for critics with his intelligence, compassion and clout. It also has standing room in the wings.

This article was originally published in *American Theatre*, May/June, 1996.

Isn't It Rich? New York Theatre According to the Man the *Times* Made

My favorite Frank Rich lead is two words long. It kicks off his review of Robert Schenkkan's Pulitzer Prize-winning epic *The Kentucky Cycle* and sums up the style and substance of the six-hour saga, as well as Rich's dismissive attitude towards it. "Remember plot?" the critic asks. Of course we do. It's a classic Rich move—smart, assured, incisive, and entertaining. It's the "Jesus wept" of his oeuvre, two words that say it all.

Remember Rich? Of course we do. For nearly 15 seasons as chief drama critic for "The Paper," he held sway over the New York (and by extension, the national) theatre. He's back now, with *Hot Seat: Theatre Criticism for* The New York Times, *1980-1993*, a 1050-page compilation of his reviews and essays, and his words have lost none of their force. But reading *Hot Seat* with a kind of dawning alarm of non-recognition, I'm tempted to respond with a more famous quip: "I knew Frank Rich, and you're no Frank Rich."

This hefty collection—not even a quarter of his total output—raises so many questions. Was the "butcher of Broadway" a pussycat? Did the myth of Rich's reign obscure the reality? Did he not occasionally mutate into some kind of demon barber of the Great White Way, pen red with the gore of gratuitous critical slayings? Did the theatre community overstate the power of the *Times* or did Rich, by denying its absoluteness, understate that power? Here he is, smiling out from his author's photo, looking less like Sweeney Todd than the Commish. And here he is, speaking from page after page in a voice of reasoned clarity, a confident no-nonsense man, still brimming with a boy's love of the theatre. What's wrong with this picture? What's missing? Rich is everywhere and nowhere in this book, just as he was omniscient and absent in his reviews.

Reexamination can't dim his significant talents—formidable intelligence, wit, persuasive power, and sheer writing verve. Rich does nearly everything well. Probably his second greatest talent is for explication, for magnifying details to reveal the worlds contained within. "It's not until late in Act 2 that the audience hears the noise of breaking glass in David Hare's *Plenty*," he writes in 1982, "but long before then, we've become terribly familiar with the harrowing sound of things going smash. A partial list of the evening's casualties would include at least three lives, one empire (the British), the egalitarian ideals of a generation, and many of the conventions of the traditional narrative play." As he animates a play's particulars, he almost always does it on the playwright's terms. (Notice, even, the way, Zelig-like, Rich allows Hare's British cadences to creep in: "things going smash.") I'm thinking of the way he defends Stephen Sondheim and James Lapine's *Sunday in the Park with George* against accusations that their characters are less than human. "[The authors], too, regard their 'characters' only as forms to be manipulated into a theatrical composition whose content is more visual and musical than dramatic. As a result, when Seurat finishes *La Grande Jatte* at the end of Act I, we're moved not because a plot has been resolved but because a harmonic work of art has been born."

I'd rank Rich's ability to capture the complexities of an actor's portrayal up there with his gift for exegesis. He's good at making us see and hear the actor at work and even better in illuminating the interpretive power of a single performance. When Christopher Plummer's Iago "vows to turn Desdemona's 'virtue into pitch,' his eyes burn and his arm whips through empty space as if to stir a witch's cauldron. Weaving 'the net that shall enmesh them all,' he turns the word *enmesh* into a shudder that seems to envelop the audience like a web. Yet he doesn't stop there. The scariest aspect of this villain is that his malignancy really does seem motiveless." Rich just as vividly charts Ian McKellen's exhilarating transformation as Salieri in Peter Schaffer's *Amadeus*, from "a sophisticated, if sadly servile, figure" to a "hideous, eerie devil who can't separate his own fearful nightmares from those he is trying to bring to his prey. As he disintegrates in defeat, we see the birth of the aged, cackling Salieri, slack-jawed and stooped, who is the evening's narrator."

Rich especially loves leading ladies, and this collection contains a sheaf of valentines to Katherine Hepburn, Claudette Colbert, Elizabeth Taylor, Jessica Tandy, Billie Whitelaw, and Lauren Bacall, to name a few, testimonials so fervid that even mixed reviews read like raves. His paeans to Stockard Channing compose a leitmotif of critical affection that, apparently, began when, as a Harvard student, he first glimpsed her in local productions. Like a stage door Johnny leaving increasingly impassioned notes with the doorman, he follows her from *A Day in the Death of Joe Egg* to *House of Blue Leaves*, *Woman in Mind*, *Six Degrees of Separation*, and, ultimately, *Four Baboons Adoring the Sun*: "Only those who hate emotions could be untouched by the sight of this woman rising from the ashes of unspeakable suffering to face a blinding new day's sun with eyes ablaze in joy."

His eye for design is also keen, and also keyed to the play text. Watch how his description conjures the set of *Plenty*, for instance, and you know what he means when he refers to the play's "hallucinatory, nightmarish quality that makes it feel...like a disorienting Nicolas Roeg film."

John Gunter's sets float like haunted Magritte rooms within the stage's walls, which are papered with a ghostly black-and-gray mural of a bygone romantic England. Jane Greenwood's costumes, meanwhile, anchor the characters in vivid social reality. The lighting designer, Arden Fingerhut, gives the gloom of contemporary London a remarkable variety of dreamlike textures even as she creates the dangerous, pulse-quickening glow of a nocturnal war-torn France where parachutes plummet from the stars.

Rich's only other book, co-authored, was an appreciation of the great Broadway designer Boris Aronson, and you can tell that appreciation as part of a more general design ardor.

No, you can't fault a reviewer who writes like this, all vivid prose (hardly ever showy) and critical acumen. And there's more. Surpassing every one of these significant strengths is his true genius. Rich never fails to shape gem-perfect persuasive essays; his reviews are models of the form. And he does it on a daily deadline, usually within 16 hours between curtain down and copy due.

Let's pick one at random: *Fool for Love*, Circle Repertory Company, May 27, 1983, Rich's fourth season. Here's the lead: "No one knows better than Sam Shepard that the true American West is gone forever, but there may be no writer alive more gifted at reinventing it out of pure literary air. Like so many Shepard plays, *Fool for Love*...is a western for our time. We watch a pair of figurative gunslingers fight to the finish—not with bullets, but with piercing words that give ballast to the weight of a nation's buried dreams." Notice how he goes right for the play's literary or thematic heart. Right out of the gate he's making sense of the play, and nearly every detail is lashed to his thesis. The theatrical event he calls "an indoor rodeo." The leading man is "some sort of rancher" with no range to ride. Character reveries are "as big as all outdoors." Finally, and characteristically for Rich, he ties his essay together, summarizing the play's achievement and the reviewer's main argument at once. "Like the visionary pioneers who once ruled the open geography of the West, Mr. Shepard rules his vast imaginative frontier by making his own, ironclad laws." Again and again, Rich proves himself the best (and fastest) short essayist in the East.

He's equally good in the long form, and this volume contains at least three of his major essays for the Sunday *Times*: one a scholarly history of the American musical, culminating in Sondheim's *Sunday in the Park*; one a pre-death eulogy of Joseph Papp (and of significant producers in general); and one his valedictory piece, "Exit the Critic." Rich was ambitious enough as a writer to keep topping himself. He was also ambitious enough as a taste-maker to use his longer essays to hammer home the points he made in his reviews. His essay on Sondheim's *Into the Woods* is a good example, as is his Papp salute. Not content to classify Sondheim's fairytale musical as a lesser work—"the convoluted story has a strangulating effect on the musical's two essential sources of emotional power, its people and its score"—he feels compelled to re-review it in a weekend piece, in case we missed the point. "[Sondheim's] new placid musical leaves the unmistakable impression that his art is spoiling for a fresh fight."

When he notes Papp's retirement, he makes sure to anticipate Papp's successor's forced retirement as well, cautioning everyone, most of all Papp's appointed heir, Joanne Akalaitis, that she's a questionable replacement. "But are her instincts those of a producer? The answer will have little or nothing to do with her talents as a director"—Rich has already called these "uneven." "If she's doing her job to the fullest, she probably will be directing infrequently anyway. Nor will her producing prowess have much to do with her abilities as an administrator, or her nose for possible Broadway transfers, or her public positions about the Palestinians." Here's vintage Rich. His will to persuade is so strong that he'll make his case as often as he wants. It's a short step from kicking a play he's already pronounced dead to pronouncing artistic directors successful (Andre Bishop) or failed (Akalaitis) before they've begun their tenure.

Unfortunately, Rich's reiterations are mostly excised from this collection, for obvious reasons. He's determined to give us the best of the era and, in the tradition of hilarious critical pans, the woolly worst (e.g., *Moose Murders*, a visit to which "will separate the connoisseurs for many moons to come").

However much he leaves out, he can't hide his compulsion to win arguments. There are many verbs that apply to the critic's work. To consider, to question, to wonder, to examine, to evoke, to judge, to explain—any of these might describe the action of reviewing. But Rich is driven to persuade. He wears his smarts on his sleeve and writes as one who knows. It's why he seems so at home now on the Op Ed page. He's a born opinion shaper, best and brightest in his class, top form at logic and rhetoric. This stance or critical persona makes it hard for him to admit uncertainty or awe.

It also makes his violent rejections of brainy artists suspect. He wrote of Tony Kushner's *A Bright Room Called Day* (he conveniently leaves out that review), slamming Kushner's erudition and political ambitions so globally that he failed to notice the writer's talent. It's not surprising that the overreaching experimental directors he abhors—especially Lee Breuer and Peter Sellars—are assaulted on intellectual terms. Calling their work "intellectually unsynthesized," "pretentious," or "over intellectualized," he's eager to lay the avant-garde finally to rest. Am I the only one who detects a strain of fierce intellectual competitiveness in Rich?

Rich likes what he likes, and he's entitled to his tastes. He takes dangerous leaps, though, by basing his definition of theatre on personal preferences. For instance, he dislikes didacticism and, so, defines it out of theatre. As a result, he fails to feel the raw power of Larry Kramer's polemical *The Normal Heart*. He values the well-wrought over the ambitious, so he praises technically proficient directors and writes unforgivingly—even meanly—about the excesses of American "auteurs."

He's obviously drawn to smart, urbane plays in the tradition of Philip Barry, especially those that marry sentiment and wit, so he not only inflates the achievement of many smallish contemporary comedies, but contributes to an unconscious "taming" of American playwrights. He praises Tina Howe's "perceptive," "graceful" writing in *Coastal Disturbances*, "distinctly the creation of a female sensibility," without encouraging the wild, fantastic theatricality of her earlier work.

Time and again, Rich, a liberal thinker, reveals himself a theatrical conservative. He loves work that is about contemporary life, but which feels like the plays or musicals of his youth. Rich tips his own hand when he talks about *Six Degrees of Separation*, John Guare's foray into the Barry tradition and, to Rich, his "masterwork." Though I share the critic's enthusiasm for Guare, I find his reasoning as odd as it is revealing. "Though Guare quotes Donald Barthelme's observation that 'collage is the art form of the 20th century,' his play does not feel like a collage....This work aspires to the classical aesthetics and commensurate unity of spirit that are missing in the pasted-together, fragmented 20th-century lives it illuminates." Rich delivers his aesthetic in a nutshell: write about the century, but avoid writing like the century.

Hot Seat feels like Rich's attempt to correct his impersonal critical stance. He adds an introduction and epilogue and glosses his reviews with current commentary, both updating the history and anecdotally placing himself within it. Suddenly, we catch sight of Rich as a character in this history (we always knew he was), attacked in print by David Hare and Andrew Lloyd Webber, besieged by crafty producers and press agents, even sexually molested in his aisle seat by the Living Theatre's Julian Beck. These annoying notes provide too little revelation too late and come to seem like additional evidence for old arguments. Rich even offers a prickly pair of lists of failed plays he praised and long-running productions he reviewed negatively, fuel for his contention that rumors of his power were greatly exaggerated. "Where is this power of the *Times*?" he asks rhetorically when a romantic comedy he finds sublime fails on Broadway.

Although I believe throughout that Rich loves the theatre—no one who didn't could write as vivaciously about it (see his inspired testament to the record-breaking 3,389th performance of *A Chorus Line*, if you need convincing)—late in his reign he invests himself in his reviews in new ways. Who cares if he overrates *Marvin's Room*? At least he was present at it, body, mind, and heart. In his final review—of *Angels in America*—he's so eager to write himself into the picture that he elides his farewell with that of the central character: "His indelible gesture feels less like a goodbye than a benediction, less like a final curtain than a kiss that blesses everyone in the theatre with the promise of more life."

His increased vulnerability in his final seasons begins to mitigate what W.H. Auden called "the lie of Authority." For most of his career, though, Rich capitalized on this authority by denying it, by leaving himself out. Even retrospectively, Rich literalizes that power, arguing as if it's merely a financial fact, success or failure at the box-office. I wish I could persuade him otherwise. If you want proof of the power of opinion—the true power of the *Times*—you needn't tally the performances of *Cats* after Rich panned it. Instead, hold this book in your hands. Check out the Random House imprint. Then look for another book of such length about the theatre published by a major house in the past three decades. You won't find it. Rich has written the theatrical history of his time, and it will certainly be *the* history. Frank Rich, who in his time was the first work on the New York theatre, will, now and forever, have the last word.

This article was originally published in *American Theatre*, September, 1999.

From Butcher to Bambi: Ben Brantley Takes the Page

In the year's most famous musical math application, *Rent* creator Jonathan Larson wondered, "Five hundred twenty-five thousand/six hundred minutes/How can you measure the life/of a woman or man?" Now Larson's posthumously blockbusting-pop-rock opera has moved uptown and with it one of its most vivacious champions, *New York Times* theatre critic Ben Brantley. The 41-year-old Brantley's rapid rise from neophyte second-stringer to chief critic in hardly more than three years keeps the meter running on a different kind of calculation—how can you measure an era of critical influence, the weight of a single critical voice?

Of course, the reviewer whose influence remains to be quantified isn't Brantley himself. It's the "Now am I fled, Now am I dead" presence of Frank Rich, whose intonings, like those of Shakespeare's rude mechanicals, seem to resound even from the critical grave. When Brantley took over as main man on the theatre pages last month, Rich had been gone for two and two-thirds years. Still, assessing Brantley's appointment can't happen in pure light. Rich's shadow—the legacy of his 13-year season—is too long.

Brantley's appointment plays like the latest of a series of efforts by *Times* editors to mitigate the effect of Rich's power, to make *Times* theatre coverage less talked about, less influential than anyone imagined. First, they tagged former *Washington Post* and then-Sunday *Times* Arts & Leisure critic David Richards to succeed him. Richards was, after many years of solid work, a watered-down or, more accurately, burnt-out version of Rich himself, a kind of Bush to his Reagan. When Richards fizzled, the eternally energetic Vincent Canby was shuffled in from the film beat. With nearly 45 years of experience, a chipper prose style, and unflagging generosity, Canby proved almost unassailable, while his presence turned down the intellectual heat that, radiating ambition, Rich had brought to the job. More, his heart-on-sleeve enthusiasm has positioned him as good angel to *New York* critic John Simon's bad one; like Simon, the consistency of this role has rendered Canby's commentary dismissible and mostly useless.

Brantley came on board from staff writing positions at *The New Yorker* and *Vanity Fair*, both under Tina Brown, and, simultaneously, four years of writing short movie reviews for *Elle*. He replaced the doggedly devoted Mel Gussow, covering mostly Off- and Off-Off-Broadway and regional theatre. Rich was instrumental in picking Brantley—his wife and colleague, Alex Witchell, had been Brantley's first editor at *Elle*. She suggested him to Rich, who sponsored Brantley for the job. In spite of that influence, Brantley has proven himself not-Frank in important ways, ways that further diminish the sway of "The Paper" over the American theatre. His ascension carries the subtext—"We have listened and heard. No more Butchers of Broadway. Just fair, readable reviews."

As a result, Brantley's promotion has been greeted with remarkably widespread goodwill from people in most walks of theatrical life, including producers and other critics. This potential era of good feeling stands in contrast to his initial hiring, which many, led by *Variety*'s Jeremy Gerard, derided on the basis of his inexperience. The derision was aimed less at the new boy than at the grand old *Times* itself. "They didn't really have anything to beat me with at that point," Brantley told me recently over iced tea at the Waverly Coffee Shop, "because they didn't have any evidence." Several hundred reviews later, Brantley seems to have assuaged much of the doubt that greeted him and helped create the once-unthinkable possibility that the theatre and critical communities won't have the *Times* to kick around anymore.

Brantley displays many of the virtues that make a good critic, and, in stark contrast to the sometimes brilliant and overreaching Rich, few of the ambitions that make a great one. He's a smart, entertaining writer, refreshingly free of that congenital tic that makes too many critics appear to prefer the sounds of their own opinions over the productions they witness. His most fervently positive and negative reviews share a quality of feeling respectfully mixed. He neither sneers nor goes blind with love. Sustaining visions matter to him; so do revelatory details.

His review of Britain's Cheek by Jowl's production of *The Duchess of Malfi* at the Brooklyn Academy of Music is a good example. Brantley later praised the production as a highlight of last season, yet his review, clearly positive, is warts-and-all clear-eyed. "And in spite of dry patches of tedium and wet ones of psychosexual excess, the troupe ultimately achieves something very rare: the rethinking of a well-known classic in a manner that will never let you look at it in the same way again."

By contrast, Brantley found the Royal Shakespeare Company's visiting *A Midsummer Night's Dream* mostly slick and soulless, but a moment in the play-within-a-play had, for him, a brief and astonishing reality. "There is a profound generosity in this moment: a benevolent, Jovian nod to actors of all levels and stripes."

Whereas Rich had the tendency to get swept away in the persuasiveness of his own terrific prose, Brantley usually maintains his lively balance, looking for the best while seeing whatever's there. Playwright Nicky Silver, for instance, "creates a web of pervasive, often startling images of appetite and decay" in *The Food Chain*, but also "seems torn between the urges to shock and to ingratiate in sometimes uneasy ways."

Rich's move to Op-Ed has been so natural that it confirms the central complaint about his tenure (the one he always denied)—Rich didn't write to report on what he saw; he wrote to shape opinion by expressing opinion. Whether exalting or insulting, the cultivated authority of his voice made it easy to feel his responses were objective truths. His objective stance was, hypocritically, fired up by the intense personalness of his reactions. If you didn't please him, you offended him. For instance, Rich, who would, in his critical swan song, use the triumphant *Angels in America* as a metaphor for his own departure, nastily slammed author Tony Kushner for the earlier *Bright Room Called Day*, accusing Kushner of "opportunism" and his play of being "juvenile" and "fatuous," the "product of a reading list." Rich, by implication, was incisive, politically savvy, and above self-aggrandizement.

Brantley, by contrast, comes across as just another guy in the audience. Even when he's ecstatic, there's something disarming about the way he positions himself. Although *Bring in 'da Noise, Bring in 'da Funk* makes him "Sing hallelujah!"—an exclamation that much more convincing because it is so goofily out of sync with his usual voice—he does so as one of the crowd. "You actually feel that you've somehow joined the dance."

The theatre world might feel residual anxiety over Rich's influence, but Brantley doesn't. He's grateful for Rich's "very, very generous spirit in the time we worked together," thinks he's "a terrific guy," and still heeds one of the few pieces of advice Rich gave him—to avoid lengthy plot description. He also enjoys reading him. "When I go through Nexis, looking up earlier reviews of a production or of an actor, and Frank pops up on the computer screen, the energy still just spurts out at you. I admire that tremendously. There must have been a period of viciousness that I wasn't aware of for him to have earned this 'Butcher of Broadway' epithet. Personally, I think he was really easy on certain things."

The men's differences, though, go beyond taste. Rich was born to punditry. He has a critic's disposition, a writer's gift, and little of the reporter's humility. Brantley accurately portrays himself "as a journalist first," before writer, before critic. Both of his parents and his late brother were newspaper people, as is his sister Robin, who also works at the *Times*. He describes them as "a family of artisans, with a craft that was passed down." Indeed, Rich's worldly perceptions nearly burst the seams of the review form, a valuable if dangerous straining. Brantley's intelligent, well-made, and rounded little essays usually feel containable by the space they fill. I can't quite imagine him following Rich to Op-Ed or writing book-length works of criticism or history, like longtime *Times* men Walter Kerr and Brooks Atkinson. Nor is he a natural for the extended think pieces required (and rarely delivered, despite talented but oddly constrained attempts by the outgoing Margo Jefferson) of the Sunday critic. "I love daily journalism. I like the energy of it. It curbs my tendency as a wanker. I have a high metabolism."

Brantley's aesthetic ambitions remain similarly understated. While nothing reveals a critic's aesthetic leanings like time, Rich helped time along by, from review to review, reiterating his opinions about each artist's body of work. Brantley has yet to reveal too much beyond a desire to take his theatre case by case. "First of all, you try to figure out what they're trying to do on their own terms. Then you can step back and say, okay, do I even like the genre or whatever? But it's so rare that things even have their own internal logic that I'm admiring of anything that sustains it."

By his own estimation, Brantley's aesthetics are founded more on core emotion than on theatrical form. Ranging over examples as divergent as Brian Friel and *Rent*, August Wilson and Karin Coonrod's production of *Victor*, he elaborates. "If I have any agenda, I guess—it's not even an agenda. I'm heartened by a return to feeling, a trying to identify feelings after this long, cold age of irony. It's easier to deal just with surfaces. Nicky Silver's *Raised in Captivity* seemed to me to be about just that. About a generation—if you can talk in such general terms—or a specific person who had willed himself into a position of distance. It's about the kind of emotional anesthesia that occurs and then trying to break out of that. When does the wall come down? Something like that has to be there for me. I'm not talking about darkness, but there has to be some kind of emotional magnet in the play."

As the first example of a *Times* downtown critic booted uptown, it's hard to discern whether Brantley, who was raised in North Carolina and divides his time between an apartment in the East Village and a house he shares with a friend upstate, has tastes running in either direction. He has disparaged, in conversation and print, both the hit Broadway musicals that fill his new province—on *Victor/Victoria*: "I was really offended by that"—and the clunky technology of commercial spectacle. "I love musicals....And I don't like seeing them turned into theme-park rides. I love Pirates of the Caribbean, but it's not what I want to see on a Broadway stage." Still, a single musical moment can make him kvell. "Sometimes something will break through the machinery. *State Fair* was just an incredibly surreal experience for me. I mean, to see Kathryn Crosby on stage and then to turn around and see, sitting several rows behind me, the Phantom of the Opera—i.e., David Merrick with the coat and the hat and the gloves—looming from his seat. It was just this weird little world of retreads up there. There was so much show-business history coming from so many directions. Then you had this moment when Scott Wise dances, and it's bliss."

Brantley has also made public his lack of enthusiasm for some leading experimental lights, especially directors Anne Bogart and JoAnne Akalaitis. "There're always stunning effects in Akalaitis's work, but sometimes they're trying so hard, and they always have these signature flourishes they bring to it. The first time you see it, you think, 'How does that relate to the play? This must say something profound about it.' Then you realize it's just their signature. It's like Fred Astaire and Ginger Rogers, a certain dip that's always going to be in the number. And that I don't really think is fair to the plays. I liked *The Medium*; it's probably what I've liked best of what I've seen of Bogart's. Obviously, there's a whole movement in theatre where it's all from the outside. There are certain examples of that I respect, but I don't have a natural affinity for it."

Though not drawn to these two artists' work— and he's careful to insist on an open, play-by-play approach—he can gush over their peers. "I love Richard Foreman. There's vitality in Richard Foreman. And in the Wooster Group, too. [Wooster group director Elizabeth LeCompte] is fabulous. I've only been able to write about them once, because they're not open for review. I can go see it, but I can't write about it. I would have loved to have written about their *Emperor Jones*. It was so smart. I'm a real fan. Mel wasn't. Nor was Frank, particularly. I try not to say, 'This wacky deconstructionist stuff. Who cares?'"

Post-Rich, the subjects of critical taste and power are difficult to distinguish. His dog-with-a-bone determination to inhale or deflate the careers of artists he admired or deprecated—culminating at the end of his reign with the simultaneous unseating of Akalaitis and anointment of George C. Wolfe at the New York Shakespeare Festival—made him a lasting force. He may have been unable to stop a pre-fab hit musical or keep a play he loved running, but he could close plays, dictate commercial moves, and blow up—in both senses—reputations. The defining gesture of Rich's animus was his return from Op-Ed for the New Year's critical summary of his final season. He created a "comeback of the year" award for the Public Theatre under Wolfe mere months (and no significant productions) after Akalaitis's replacement. It was a nasty, know-it-all, nail-in-the-coffin move that prematurely trumpeted Wolfe's fulfillment of Rich's own prophecies. Brantley, it appears, wants none of that, with the possible exception of playing champion to individual works. "You want to get people to go. There is this cheerleading aspect."

If, beyond this, Brantley sees himself as a shaper of public taste, he hides it well. The *Times* has often been accused of going soft on Broadway, the street where its biggest advertisers live. While Brantley denies ever being guided to go gently, he's more suited to reasoned reform than fiery revolution. In person and on the page, he comes across as open, sporadically exuberant, thoughtful, and slightly self-conscious — a happily conscientious theatre fan with excellent journalistic skills and an underweening ambition. He lights up talking about specific writers, actors, and productions, but he amiably shrugs off big-picture questions on the state of anything--criticism, theatre, or the form's connection to current cultural life. "Of course I think about it. It's very dangerous to make pronouncements, though. To a certain extent, I do have to keep blinkers on. If you start thinking about the big picture, you get dizzy. I don't allow myself to think, 'Holy cow! I'm the chief critic of *The New York Times*.' You start thinking about the lessons of Greek tragedy and answered prayers. You are in a powerful position, and you have to handle it responsibly, but you can't think about that on a daily basis or else you gag. And that's really dangerous. You try to keep your response open and approach it again, play by play."

This modesty is probably good for the individual productions he writes about—it may also help him avoid the abuse or, rather, consolidation of power Rich was regularly accused of. It could, contrarily, be bad for a theatre floating its way out of America's cultural concerns. The strength of Rich's voice created debate, both inside and outside the theatre community. Too often, this debate was about Rich himself, but at least it was heated. Brantley's reticence on broad matters feels like an abdication of responsibility. While it's too early to judge him, it's not too soon to hope that as the American newspaper critic with the widest exposure, he'll take the lead and do the more risky work of thinking out loud about theatre—its place in our lives, its development, its necessary changes. I doubt Brantley will remake himself into a crusader, but he can do more than he's done this far to make connections between works and across the space where the stage ends and the audience begins. When Brantley wrote his second review of *Rent*, after its installation on Broadway, he tallied the production's gains and losses in its new, oversize digs. A little more than a month before his relocation, he discussed his own. "This interview is an example of what I'm losing. I don't really like being public. And it's much easier not to be public when you're second-string. Also, you're a more obvious target. It's a fine tradition—hating the chief *Times* critic. It's easy to like someone who seems to have less power. Otherwise, no. It'll give me a greater freedom of choice, although I've been pretty happy with my slate. I like doing it. That's the main thing."

Computing the theatre's gains and losses will take time. For better or worse, Brantley may never light a fire in the belly of Broadway, may never achieve the mythic, make-or-break stature that Rich did. But if he keeps going the way he began, his critical math will always be clear—"One play at a time."

This article was originally published in *The Village Voice,* October 15, 1996 and is reprinted with the paper's permission.

Richard Gilman's *Chekhov's Plays*:

The Music That Hasn't Yet Been Heard

The chemistry that attracts critics and scholars to their subjects is an impure science. Affection mixes with ambition. Personal enthusiasm reacts with professional determinism—the need to publish where none has gone before. When things click, calculation meets dumb luck. There's nothing, however, dumb about the luck that drew Richard Gilman to Anton Chekhov.

Gilman claims to have begun his full-length study of Chekhov's dramatic works "for the same reason people write seriously on any subject—that they perceive a space waiting to be filled." This restrained (coy?) explanation ignores attraction, Gilman's infatuation with the man he dubs "Chekhov the sane, lyricist of the prosaic." It says nothing about how right or inevitable, even necessary, their pairing seems. Personally, I've looked forward to reading *Chekhov's Plays: An Opening into Eternity* since I first heard Gilman was working on it more than six years ago. It was, I believed, an excitement waiting to happen.

There will always be space to fill in American Chekhov criticism. By virtue of his universally acknowledged humanity, his wit and kindly detachment, the self-effacing Chekhov has emerged as modern drama's most admired, most enigmatic saint—the he nobody knows. He always seems to know us, though. Chekhov died only four years into this century, but even at its end his plays keep revealing themselves—and ourselves—anew. Many smart books have been written by the likes of Maurice Valency, J.L. Styan, Harvey Pitcher, and Laurence Senelick, but the Russian writer is too slippery for singular analyses. Studies that zero in on his plays' themes or structure, emotionalism or historical context end up feeling partial. The best American writing on Chekhov comes in isolated chapters, found in wide-ranging surveys by Eric Bentley, Robert Brustein, Francis Fergusson, and, yes, Richard Gilman.

With an eloquent essay in the still-remarkable *The Making of Modern Drama* (1974), Gilman announced himself as a critical kindred spirit, as sympathetically attuned to Chekhov as anyone writing in English. *Chekhov's Plays* affords Gilman, a professor of playwriting and dramatic literature at Yale, the world and time to revel in the "amorous interchange" Chekhov inspires. It lets him do what he does best: wonder over detail.

This book is, throughout, a meeting of minds or, more precisely, of consciousnesses. Consciousness, the way it moves and changes across time or within a body of work, has, for the past two decades, occupied Gilman's most fervent attentions. Sometimes, as in *Faith, Sex, Mystery*, a 1986 memoir of Gilman's conversion to and, five years later, departure from Catholicism (he was born and raised Jewish), that consciousness is his own. In his more usual role as theatre critic and thinker, as in *The Making of Modern Drama*, he trains his sights on dramatic literature "as a source of consciousness."

*   *   *

More than any 20th-century playwright, Chekhov's consciousness—his point of view or ideas about things—remains elusive, supple, shifting. "Everything in this world is changing, mutable, approximate, and relative," he wrote to a fellow writer in 1886, a dozen years before his major plays would prove it so. That's the way Gilman likes it. "We live in a succession of such temporary fulfillments, such temporariness in general," he once argued, that "we borrow [language's] seeming permanence in order to escape the anguish that a full recognition of the provisional nature of existence would induce in us." Gilman didn't write these words about Chekhov's work. He wrote them about the "strange life" of the word "decadence, " whose eponymous biography he published in 1979, in an attempt to chart the chameleon-like definition of that cultural concept through history. Here the chameleon is Chekhov. The landscape within which he conceals himself is the plays.

So Gilman wanders through Chekhov's plays, on the trail of their changeable creator, and he wonders as he wanders. He notices things with the keenest eye. He'll zoom in on a word—Chekhov's choice use of "surmises" in his definition of what an artist does. Or he'll distinguish a playable fact—how in *Vanya*, Sonia, after learning that the doctor she loves doesn't love her back, says nothing on the subject for the last quarter of the play. When Tuzenbach in *The Three Sisters*, before going off to a duel in which he will almost certainly die, says to his future wife, Irina, "I didn't have any coffee this morning. Ask them to fix me some, will you?" Gilman rhapsodizes. "Where has emotion been rendered with more painful astringency than that? A displacement, an inspired shifting of feeling onto innocuous words that impregnated with grievous fatality, will remain in our memory more securely than any direct rhetoric of loss." Then he shifts gear to remark: "Had this been a scene between two lovers on the eve of their wedding, the risks of sentimentality would have been overwhelming. As it is, that Irina intends to marry the baron out of affection and esteem instead of passion radically undercuts the potential reign of the melodramatic."

Gilman investigates everything he finds in a prose that, while occasionally puffed up, is more often as elegant as any being written about plays. Savor, for example, what he says about the "grief of the actual" in *Uncle Vanya*:

Lyricism doesn't transform or redeem the weight of sorrow; it doesn't even physically lighten it. What it does is place it, environ it, bring it into intimacy with the soul which, tested by grief, learns about itself. At the same time lyricism makes visible the hidden and speaks of how grief makes us human; the beauty that inheres in sorrow is our recognition of mortality, which happiness obscures.

When he writes of the "condition…of living within time" in *Three Sisters*, he elaborates in a voluptuous sentence too long to quote entirely here:

> I mean being caught in [time], resident in it, experiencing it as chronology or duration only in its most superficial or apprehensible manifestations but more deeply as a place, a habitation; being rocked in it as the cradle of all we do; knowing it as a wholeness, indivisibility, but more often in fragments; trafficking with it as myth; projecting everything ahead to await its presumably transforming arrival as future….

The path Gilman cuts is, broadly, chronological. After a preface, in which Gilman haunts Chekhov's Russia and begins to hatch the idea of this book, and a chapter on Chekhov the man, Gilman tracks his way through the five major plays in order: *Ivanov, The Seagull, Uncle Vanya, The Three Sisters*, and *The Cherry Orchard*, stopping to discuss the youthful mess known as *Platonov* and the failed *The Wood Demon*, later re-imagined into *Vanya*. For the most part, his readings gravitate around a central issue or set of ideas: love and art in *The Seagull*, for example, or the possibility of renewal in *Cherry Orchard*, but he treats these ideas rather idiosyncratically. Refusing to separate them from the action, characters, relationships, he treats them as what he calls "ideas attached to bodies…notional presences."

* * *

His method then consists of mapping these embodied notions as Chekhov sets them spinning. Chekhov's revolutionary dramaturgy, Gilman argues, turned away from linear action towards the portrayal of a "condition" (a word Gilman borrows from Henry James) and the creation of a "dramatic field." Through "a continual deflection of absolutes," the playwright refused to allow "linear progressions of theme or character-ization to coerce us toward fixed conclusions." As Chekhov's eye moves freely, as he deviates "from an expected narrative line" or as his writing "suggests so much more than it directly says," so Gilman digresses, in his words, hunting implications as he goes. Gilman follows Chekhov's

> 'glance,' as it falls, with unparalleled clarity, on the most minute particulars, on the extreme momentariness of our experience. It's this approach toward the humble, the casual and fragmentary, the scorned—the very basis of the revolution Chekhov brought about in the theatre—which sets free the previously unknown, what we might call the music that hasn't yet been heard.

Gilman's approach—he calls it "digressive," "straying and hopping," but sometimes it feels more associative or, in stretches, desultory—counters what he sees as criticism's

> violent act[s] of excision, in which we pluck out a subject like an entrail before stuffing it back into the body, [so] that we can talk about it in isolation….What criticism so often does to drama…is to speak of the ideas within a work, its motifs and themes, without their sensuousness, the intricacies of their relationships to physicality—to speak of them, really, as if they can be contemplated in isolation, detached from bodies and the meshings of character, detached, indeed, from each other.

Guilty as charged are: 1) Marxist and otherwise social critics who treat Chekhov as a prophetic voice of either Russia's revolutionary history or the fall of the leisure class; 2) close readers who lift themes—"gaseous abstractions, inert thought"—out of physical context; and 3) those who seek Chekhov in one or another character's words . Chekhov distinguished himself, Gilman rightly asserts, by his "exquisite neutrality."

For all Gilman's rightness, both about Chekhov and as the man for the job of explicating him, I found this book vaguely disappointing. I loved the sentences and marveled at many of the sights along the way, but found it hard to keep Gilman's train of thought in focus. Often I found myself searching for a cogent thesis statement to keep me keyed in—searching in vain. He wears his process on his sleeve, and that creates a couple of problems. First, his own central ideas dissipate and lose their pull. Second, Gilman's process never reads as satisfyingly as his more direct textual insights. (A couple of particularly annoying passages are the preliminary notes he includes at the start of his *Seagull* chapter and an imaginary dialogue between Chekhov and a friend on the subject of time in *Three Sisters*.)

In *Faith, Sex, Mystery*, Gilman's fascinating self-honesty competed, at times, with a cloying solipsism. This tension seemed allowable in a memoir. Here, on the other hand, a much smaller degree of self-interest does considerably more damage; it intermittently obscures Chekhov's plays and muddies Gilman's larger points. Too frequently Gilman, not Chekhov, seems to be the subject.

These disappointments are, I suspect, mostly personal. The book has been widely and positively reviewed, and critics seem to have found Gilman's exit-ramps only irksome. I suspect, too, that my discontents stem, in part, from my overblown expectations and from the moronic hope that someone, sometime, will catch Chekhov definitively and forever.

Thumbing back through the pages of Gilman's early (1961-70) collection of theatre writings, *Common and Uncommon Masks*, I found my head shaking involuntarily. The voice of these pieces—mostly reviews from *Commonweal* and *Newsweek* with a smattering from *The New Republic*—is, in its harsh certainty, so resoundingly different from this later Gilman that I can only assume that someone killed off the younger critic and stole his name.

I like him better now. He's more inquiring, less know-it-all. Still, I kept wishing the two could meet and fuse: the edgy, rational critic and the wise and eloquent old philosopher. Then, maybe, Chekhov would have met his match.

This essay was originally published in *American Theatre*, September, 1996.

The First 100 Days: Life After Frank Rich

"He's gone," we said, spent and relieved, like the characters left behind at the end of a Chekov play. "He's gone."

Who would have thought it possible? A hundred days have passed, and about half that many plays have opened: *Abe Lincoln in Illinois, The Red Shoes, No Man's Land, Three Tall Women, Damn Yankees, The America Play*. The world of New York theatre criticism, which for thirteen years was synonymous with Frank Rich, is trying to move on without him.

Post-Rich, the *New York Times* repositioned two veteran critics and kept its latest draft choice, Ben Brantley, on the second string. The *Daily News* nudged Douglas Watt out after fifty-plus years covering theatre. Edith Oliver, likewise, appears to have retired, following more than three decades at *The New Yorker*. A recent addition to the same magazine, John Lahr, has begun breaking the rules. What was until recently an eerily static critical landscape is finally changing. Only Rich himself doesn't seem to notice. Like a ham actor, intent on showing us how well he dies, he refuses to leave the stage.

David Richards, Rich's heir, is an altogether different man. Rich became chief drama critic at age thirty-one with less than a decade of, primarily, film criticism under his belt. Richards brings to the post a long history of related experience—ten years reviewing theatre for *The Washington Star*, followed by nine at *The Washington Post*, capped off by three as Sunday critic at the *Times*. No one can accuse the paper of hiring a writer unfamiliar with the theatre beat. If Richards was ever passionate about the theatre, though—and I suspect he was earlier in his career—it rarely shows now.

Rich exhibited no scruples against loving loudly and crying salty tears. At its worst, his emotionalism seemed sentimental and awkward, the proud trumpeting of a white bread brother from another planet who'd just discovered his first feeling. At best, he was the kind of celebrant who, singing praises, could make statues weep. By contrast, Richard's most salient quality as a writer is his lack of ardor. Possibly, years of reviewing theatre for the only major paper in what was then a largely wannabe-professional town burned out his capacity for deep interest. That's an occupational hazard. Maybe, as some suggest, he avoids hyped-up responses in order to temper the persuasive power of his job.

Richards positions himself in with an imagined audience that shares his perceptions. To that end, he leans on phrases like "few would doubt…" or "you are apt to find…" This detachment affords him equanimity. He won't spare praise when he feels it's earned, as he did with Eric Bogosian's new show, and he's comfortable giving points for trying. He credits *First*

193

Lady Suite writer-composer Michael LaChuisa with ambitions "more bracing than the musical itself" and pats *The America Play*'s Suzan-Lori Parks on the back for her "dense yet haunting personal vision."

Although he rarely comes to life, Richards is confident and readable. He has none of Rich's swift-arrow writing grace, but his prose never plods like erstwhile Off-Off Broadway *Times* critic Mel Gussow. Gussow, no great wit, was devotion itself. Richards, by contrast, is a theatre-*liker*, a thorough journalist, and a competent observer. But a clear critical vision never crystallizes. (A performing arts librarian told me he kept trying to form a mental image of Richards for his reviews. He couldn't do it.)

If anything, Richards is a playwriting critic first and foremost. He casts one eye on writerly promise: "The dialogue is gritty, but antic and sassy too," he says of Cheryl L. West's *Holiday Heart*. "Ms. West has an ear." His other eye is trained on the dramaturgical flaw: "The farther the play strays from the odd couple at its center, however, the more it sacrifices its originality," he qualifies dully in the same review. He faults Timberlake Wertenbaker's *Three Birds Alighting on a Field* for keeping the central character's transformation offstage. "That's short-changing an audience," he says, adopting his most didactic tone.

His responses to writing he doesn't like run from nasty to vaguely pissy—*Unfinished Stories* "ultimately boils down to a small, whining play about some disagreeable people who can't get along." He's at his most heated when offended by a playwright's failure. *Those the River Keeps*, David Rabe's short-lived latest, "comes perilously close to self-parody. And that's at its best moments. The rest of the time it just seems a shameless self-indulgence. The speeches are overwritten. The emotions are bloated. The misery, of which there is an unending supply, is sodden and shapeless." Other reviewers made similar points, but didn't hammer them home so club-fistedly.

Unlike his predecessor, who wasn't afraid to write about himself, Richards refuses to personalize, with the notable exception of a *Post* piece on his own sleeping disorders and a *Times* throwaway about his addiction to tennis. Likewise, whereas Rich made his heterosexuality seem integral to his support of gay writers and AIDS plays—taking his sons to *Falsettos*, for example—Richard's sexuality never enters the work. In other ways, too, his reviews, while demonstrating knowledge of theatre, come vacuum packed, rarely opening out to the world at large. His kudos for Tony Kushner's *Perestroika*, for example, niftily avoids mention of the play's politics. Rich, by comparison, was boy-*Times*, eager to prove he'd be just as wise at the world desk, constantly linking theatre events to global issues. (Rich could be blinded by his own political pretensions, though. He failed to see any sign of talent in Kushner's earlier play, *A Bright New Room Called Day*, dissing it as "fatuous," "a product of a reading list." Richards, with less to prove, saw instead an "ambitious, disturbing mess," a work of talented excess.) Richard's mind stops short of revelation, somewhere on the outskirts of insight.

Richards is less flashy and ambitious than Rich, and his aggression can be more quietly dispiriting for being subtextual. Rich reveled—and excelled—in the trenchant. Not for nothing did David Mamet dub him, along with *New York* magazine's diabolic attack dog John Simon, "the syphilis and gonorrhea of the theatre." Richards's hostility runs more between the lines, taking the air out of a work and any potential for audience interest. His bloodletting of Anne Bogart's production of *The Women* relied on snide digs and quiet innuendo—"[interpolated songs] turn *The Women* into one of those vaudeville shows that Ms. Bogart admires"—more than on direct disapproval. As a result of this irked undercurrent, Richard's jokes can fall flat, and his vaguely negative lead and closing paragraphs can go clunk. When it rears its head, as in the Rabe pan or his trouncing of *Damn Yankees* (about which he was nearly alone), Richards's hostility is neither witty nor provocative.

If the *Times'* "new" principal critic reads like old hat, its fairly new second-stringer is a find. Ben Brantley, an under-forty who came to the paper last July by way of staff positions at *The New Yorker* and *Elle*, possesses that rare quality that can sustain a critical career: intellectual curiosity. Richards evaluates a work's surface. Brantley—at least equally skilled at evoking a production's appeal—tries also to get inside its ideas. He's well versed in the writing of dramatists he reviews and sure-handed in describing performers and performances. Solo artist John O'Keefe, for instance, doesn't merely speak his lines, "he seems to exude them, as if they were sweat or tears." Spalding Gray seesaws "between satiric clarity and paranoic murkiness... wry detachment and truly retrospective despair."

Occasionally, someone suggested to me, Brantley tries too hard, labors too long over his thesaurus. Nevertheless, he writes as a critic at the excited beginning of a career, unlike some of our long-run, beaten-down regulars. No wise-acre upstart, he's a clear thinker, lively stylist, and reviewer of integrity, interested in works on their own terms, even if they're bad.

Brantley's also no Pollyanna. He has found flaws in diverse shows, from the Living Theatre's *Anarchia* to Irene Worth's *Portrait of Edith Wharton*, from Peter Parnell's *An Imaginary Life* to *Smiling Through*, a British music-hall entertainment. He never gets prickly and doesn't take artistic failures as personal affronts as Richards sometimes does.

Richards and Brantley share an asset Rich lacked: the ability to write in what *Newsday* critic Linda Winer has called "the middle voice." This is the land between rave and pan, north of thumbs down and south of thumbs up. As the dailies cut theatre coverage to a bare minimum, description and critical inquiry ground to "like it or not." The *Times* regulars are still allowed sufficient space—with a bit of restraint they may be able to expand this middle territory and avoid the hard-sell/hard-kill techniques Rich used to enhance his clout.

What to say about the "new" *Times* Sunday critic, Vincent Canby? After twenty-five years as that paper's chief film critic, he's still a dandy writer, avuncular and chipper, who comes across as primarily a consumer advocate. He'll do just fine for people trying to pick a play to plop down sixty bucks on; those who want to learn or think about the theatre may need to look elsewhere.

Despite some early-career theatre reporting and a couple of playwriting credits, Canby is a film critic. His appointment in what should be the slot for a major theatre essayist reaffirms the *Times* editorial indifference toward the art. You needn't know too much, care too much, or keep up too much to qualify. (Plus, I wonder about long-term plans. At 69, Canby may choose to retire soon. Was the assignment intended as a pre-retirement plum?)

The only lengthy theatre essays to appear since Rich left prove the case. In the first, Canby compared the use of special effects in the theatre and film (with emphasis on fog). In the second, Richards catalogued nicknames given by theatre insiders to famous flops. Finally, Canby broke loose with an anecdotal tour of ticket prices and available seating for Broadway's big four. How will we keep up?

The most important addition to the New York critical scene is one the *Times* magazine failed to mention in its hotly debated profile of *New Yorker* editor Tina Brown. Brown brought back to New York a real theatre critic, and she gave him real space to write. Not only is John Lahr the best critic going—a knowledgeable, passionate thinker and splendid writer—but he's doing something new. Lahr blends criticism with journalism, history and dramaturgical insight with reportage, review with interview. He identifies "a frontier patch of eastern Kentucky" as *The Kentucky Cycle*'s protagonist and examines the effect of property and ownership on the American character. He cuts to the "panic about a point of view" at the heart of Howard Davies's *My Fair Lady* revival. Whereas the set's "Magritte images are models of estrangement," the Shaw-inspired musical is "rooted in the reality of place and a problem...where the English class system is writ large in the transformation of Eliza from street urchin to society belle."

Like his apparent model, Kenneth Tynan, Lahr effectively combines the intellectual rigor of criticism with a fascination for entertainment and celebrity: the *show* of the biz. He speaks Neil Simon-ese as fluently as he speaks Kushner. He isn't afraid to talk to the artists themselves, to ask them what they're aiming for, unlike Rich, who seemed to fear that contact with the people he reviewed would damn his eternal soul to journalist hell.

Fourteen years ago, in the *Village Voice*, Erika Munk wrote a response to Frank Rich's appointment as chief *Times* critic, decrying his "lack of expertise, commitment, and passion," a lack, she concluded, that was "exactly what the *Times* wants." While he confirmed many of her fears, he proved her wrong on these. A reader might despise Rich's taste, question his motives, and resent his power over the American theatre, but it was, ultimately, hard to disparage his writing skill or doubt his devotion to an idea of the theatre. His reviews of Tony Kushner's *Angels in America* exemplified both. The theatre gods had arranged *Angels* part two, *Perestroika*, for Rich's swan song. In the radiant farewell salute of the play's hero, Prior Walter, wanting "more life" after a five-year battle with AIDS, Rich saw his own goodbye. As the critic later told *Times* magazine readers, he wept over his review, tearfully revising the closing sentence to heighten this identification: "'Bye now!' cries a smiling Mr. [Stephen] Spinella as this great epic draws to a close, raising his long arm and throwing it back in an ecstatic wave. His indelible gesture feels less like a goodbye than a benediction, less like a final curtain than a kiss that blesses everyone in the theatre with the promise of more life."

And so, he blessed us and exited to the op-ed page of the *Times*. But whose name has remained on everyone's lips, as if it were an expletive tic shared by a community with Tourette's syndrome? Frank Frank Frank. *Theatre Week* ran a cover story on his legacy. His *Times* magazine ode to himself, "Exit the Critic" (surely he titled it ironically), has fueled a firestorm of response from *The Daily News*, the *Voice* (in two separate pieces), *The New Republic*'s Robert Brustein, and Dramatists Guild president Peter Stone. The most recent eruption hit newsstands three weeks ago, when former *New Yorker* critic Mimi Kramer analyzed Rich's critical style for *New York*, tracing his twin love of power and self through to the tips of his subordinate clauses. Kramer also dished: Rich had "mentored" and romanced her (and others like her) when his first marriage was breaking up, and she dumped him. You can almost hear the offstage voices calling, "Die again, Frank! Die again!"

Time tells on critics in strange ways. Some last—Clive Barnes and John Simon have racked up more than thirty years, Michael Feingold nearly twenty-five, Howard Kissel almost twenty—some don't. Some see their tastes mellow or alter. Some sustain themselves by their love of theatre. Some, by love of power. Others, like Lahr and (potentially) Brantley, have an intellectual curiosity that keeps them vital. Still others— Simon, for example—seem driven, for better or worse, by belief in their own opinions and superior smarts.

Finally, there are those who don't know where to bow out gracefully. There may be a remedy: let's give him our benediction and wave ecstatically goodbye.

This article was originally published in *The Village Voice,* April 12, 1994 and is reprinted with the journal's permission.

Double Vision: *Comic Agony:*

Mixed Impressions in the Modern Theatre by Albert Bermel

The finest critics evoke, by the tone of their unspoken voices and the passion of their recurring concerns, a setting. Picture Eric Bentley, for example, arguing fine points of political and dramatic theory over dark beers in a raucous German café. (Brecht's fat cigar jabs the air from across the table.) Or imagine him in the reading room of the British museum, sitting where Shaw used to sit, poring over stacks of books, whose range of subjects boggle the less capacious mind. He is writing *The Life of the Drama.*

Robert Brustein's moral-critical fervor suggests a courtroom, better yet a judge's chambers, charges with purpose, as if in time of war. Maybe he's hammering out *The Theatre of Revolt* in a private library, like some wise Talmudic scholar, surrounded by young rabbis, who dream of surpassing him but fear they never will.

Richard Gilman, on the other hand, might appear at one of those Socratic after dinner affairs Plato writes about, where worldly banter turns spiritual. He speaks last—the topic, theatre—but he veers into the unknown: faith, hope, humanity's fragile dance. His lovely sentences will be transcribed into *The Making of Modern Drama.*

In *Comic Agony: Mixed Impressions in the Modern Theatre,* Albert Bermel conjures up his own perfect setting: the theatre itself. It's where he comes from and where he belongs. A longtime playwright, translator and scholar of Moliere and chronicler of the farcical, Bermel's criticism revels in dramatic contradictions that, entering at separate doors, make their swift way towards head-on collision center stage.

Equally at home discussing Woody Allen or Henrik Ibsen, the Marx Brothers or Samuel Beckett, Bermel is both critic and playwright, with one eye on dramatic structure and the other on the hero's frozen smile. He tackles the anguish of the modern theatre with the zest of a French farceur or Attic wit. Bermel doesn't have the reach of such dramatic critical heavyweights as Bentley, Brustein, and Gilman, but he may be the next best thing: the ideal dramaturg—the smartest guy on the theatre staff *and* the most fun at parties.

Bermel shares a kinship with another critic, George Bernard Shaw, in this blending of *joie de theatre* and modern complaint. If, for Shaw, the modern drama arises from "the conflict of unsettled ideas," for Bermel it seems to spring from the interplay of simultaneous opposites. Sometimes, as he argues in his fine 1973 collection of readings, *Contradictory Characters: An Interpretation of the Modern Theatre,* these opposites dwell in the body of a single character creating internal conflicts that spark external ones. In

Comic Agony, his latest work, he locates counterforces in genre: comedy interwoven with tragedy, delight with dole.

"Comic agony" is not, however, according to Bermel, just another word for tragicomedy. Nor is it "a movement, and not quite a genre..." What it is, he argues, is an internationally inspired, almost-genre of modern drama, "an off-shoot of tragicomedy." If tragicomedy alternates between tragic and comic strains, comic agony delivers them up concurrently, allowing the opposites to heighten each other, to create a third thing. "They are threads of contrasting colors in a fabric that is iridescent, neither of the colors and yet derived from both." This double vision is at once playful and intense, offering the delicate thrill of anguished work that refuses to take itself seriously, and the depth of amusement that digs into human pain.

According to Bermel, this contradictory enterprise accounts for some of the chanciest work of the 100-plus years since Ibsen turned to prose. Among the daring whose comic agonizing he anatomizes are such disparate beings as Wedekind, Chekhov, Strindberg, O'Neill, Apollinaire, Ayckbourn, and Churchill. These and others he groups by the relative balance of pain and pleasantry in their work. Do they emphasize trouble over smiles, as Ibsen does in *The Wild Duck,* or do they take "the joke seriously," like Shaw in *Man and Superman?* Or do they, Ionesco-style, "howl at farce"?

These particular critical distinctions allow Bermel to unite his twin fascinations: genre—especially comic (see his *Farce,* an up-to-date race through the history of that form)—and modern character. Along the way, he indulges his pleasure in the playful. He loves the jest, the paradox, the irony, and, mostly, the theatrical detail, all of which he parses in jaunty prose with a storyteller's skill.

His technique, which he describes in *Contradictory Characters,* is to "review forward", as it projecting towards future productions. Sometimes he scratches for the mythic foundations of modern work. In *The Wild Duck:*

> The wild duck in her attic evokes vestigial memories in these figures of a beckoning green past. That past is wild. The spirit of animal abandon and the Dionysian urges, buried in them, gone to the bottom, have grown domesticated. They no longer understand the ancient signals...

Other times, a single word comes life, as when Uncle Vanya, in Chekhov's play by the same name, twice fires his pistol unsuccessfully at his nemesis the Professor, "so impatient for the bullet to fly that he must hope to speed it on its way, to force it to do more damage, by exploding himself into the word 'Bang!'" Always, he keeps his eye on the stage. Bermel makes simple plot description visual:

> The man in general's full-dress uniform lies suspended between two chairs. In front of the chair supporting his feet, a beautiful young woman with red hair whinnies and, without leaving the spot, begins to trot like a horse. The General is a client at a brothel, pretending to be a dead hero. The Girl is a whore with equine and narrative capabilities.

Thus begins a particularly strong chapter on the magnified social satire of Genet's *The Balcony*. Likewise, his evocation of Churchill's play suggests design possibilities:

> In both acts of *Cloud Nine* [one set in colonial Africa, the other in contemporary England] the comic pastoral has gone to seed—first, during what some patriots considered a golden age of empire, now seen as leaden, and a century later, back at home, in the 'motherland.' In what serves townspeople as a pitiable contraction of the vanished open forest and grassland, the realms of green, where miracles might have happened.

In stretching for the contradictory interpretation, Bermel occasionally stretches his point. For example, he overstates the case that Shaw "debunks the ideal of the Superman" in *Man and Superman*. Shaw always inflates with one hand and deflates with the other; he paradoxically debunks and endorses the Nietszchean hero. Similarly, Bermel wants to counter conventional wisdom on O'Neill's light-touched *Ah, Wilderness!* by showing the play as less an "idyll of small-town America" than a portrait of its constrictions. Both readings are intriguing; neither is completely convincing.

Personally, I find the book's scheme much less compelling than its parts. As a work of genre criticism, *Comic Agony* feels cobbled together, with connecting phrases and perfunctory section summaries tacked on. Except for chapters on the so-called absurdists—Adamov, Ionesco and Beckett—in which farce and nightmare are provocatively shown smushed together, Bermel's analyses don't benefit much from placement in this quasi-genre. They're just fine on their own.

Taken individually, these 14 essays offer some new paths through well-trod critical terrain. They help Bermel fulfill his mission: freeing great plays from the stranglehold of stiff critical attitudes and squarely placing these works where they belong—in the theatre.

This review was originally published in *American Theatre*, March, 1994.

The Yes-Work of Criticism

The golden rule of improvisational theatre holds that the improviser must always say yes. No matter how off base or lunatic or cliché your partner's impulse, you must accept it and you must use it. "No" stops the scene. It interrupts the flow of active ideas and kills the trust on stage.

For instance, if another actor hands you an imaginary flower, you must take it and make something of it, however much you dislike the sentimentality of the gesture. If you pretend that you haven't seen the flower or respond to the offering as if it were a toilet plunger, since toilet plungers are funnier than flowers, you've betrayed the truth of the moment and nipped the scene in the proverbial bud.

Like it or not, critics are seen by the majority of people working in this country as the folks who say no. You don't understand the work, they think. You don't care about it. You are abusive in your cleverness and inappropriate in your personal remarks, especially in matters of sexuality, appearance, and race. Moreover, this thinking goes, you're maddeningly defensive. You refuse to 'fess up to your own faults.

From the critic's point of view, of course, this is ludicrous. No one who hates the theatre becomes a critic. At least no one who initially hates the theatre.

When you do say no, it's as a goad to creativity. It's not as an assault on it. Besides, theatre people take things too personally. They're so melodramatic and anti-intellectual. And theatre people are hypocritical, too. They damn criticism but they're horribly dependent on it, both to sell their work through ads and lobby displayed reviews, etc. and to determine their own personal sense of success or failure.

The artistic and critical communities in America are deeply and undeniably divided. They don't think the same. They don't speak the same language. They don't value the same feelings at all and, looking at the same image, they don't see the same thing.

Apparently the only thing these two groups share is a responsibility for and a reliance on the theatre's survival. Artists and critics alike are involved in an uphill struggle to create better art by creating a better environment for that art in a culture that seems determined to negate all such efforts.

Maybe in the context of this struggle, the two communities can find some common ground.

The American institutional theatre is a community in progress. It improvised itself into middle age and now it needs to improvise itself out again.

At its inception the institutional theatre set out to revise the insane gambler's rhythm of American commercial theatre production. This revolutionary revision emphasized three goals foreign to the commercial theatre—the development of a unique body of work, the nurture of a family of artists, and the establishment of deep roots in a community over time.

During its three-decades' struggle to validate itself to the folks at home, the national press, and the theatre world at large, the institutional theatre has too often undermined its own intended goals. It has imitated its commercial counterpart by hard-selling successes with a two-faced dependence on quotes from critics it disdains. It has replaced the mission of creating homes for artists with the practice of type- and star- casting and it has sought national identity in place of local identification, a fact evident in the widespread preference of the resident theatre rubric over the more valuable one, regional.

The next necessary phase of the regional theatre movement demands, I think, that artists and producers, especially those running the theatres, reconnect with their initial goals. It demands that they reconnect with the same sense of radical purpose, the same revolutionary audacity that fueled this theatre's founding, and it demands that they bring to this reconnection the business savvy and political agility that the Reagan/Bush era has forced them to acquire.

The difficulty for critics and editors is to find the story in all of this. Journalists write about small perceptual changes in government. But in the theatre almost all stories revolve around the product, around opening night, the pre-show preview, the review, and the profile of the person most responsible for a hit show.

So, here's my question. Is it possible to envision for the institutional theatre a kind of criticism that doesn't even include reviews? What if you had to tell the story of the theatre day after day without the use of reviews? How would you do it?

Eve Harrington's star-making triumph is only one kind of story. A Wooster Group piece two years in the making calls for another, maybe a more interesting one. The story of actors who work together year after year to make their theatre an integral part of Whitesburg, Kentucky or Douglas, Alaska requires yet another sort of telling altogether.

Amid the negative feelings about most criticism shared by theatre people, I've heard occasional choruses of gratitude about specific critics. This gratitude has absolutely nothing to do with prose style or even how positive or glowing the reviews are. Instead there are theatre communities that feel a certain critic has helped them grow and survive by looking clearly at where they are as a community that's distinct from, say, Broadway, and dealing with them in those terms.

Chicago theatre people cite Richard Christiansen as a major force for growth in that theatre community. Christiansen saw what they were trying to do, where they were in the process, and he told that story to the *Tribune*'s readers. Similarly, for all the bitching about Frank Rich, the Off- and Off-Off-Broadway community expresses regular gratitude towards Mel Gussow for seeing even the smallest theatre's work and for caring about the development of new playwriting talent.

What I'm suggesting is that we theatre artists need to re-think the place of theatre, in light of our own failure to make contact with concerns of the culture. At the same time, the critical journalistic community needs to re-think its approach to theatre, asking even the most basic, naive questions.

Critics and editors can use their considerable influence creatively to encourage readers to re-think the story of a theatre that is no longer all about Eve. To do this, they must, in their own corners of the country, re-imagine what that story is and how best to tell it with—or maybe even without—reviews, which I don't mean to mean without critical opinion.

This requires thinking outside the conventions of theatre reviewing and working harder to attune yourselves to the ideas, spirit, and feelings of the American stage in your specific community. You, the critics, are responsible for telling the story of that theatre on its own terms.

You are members of a community that includes everyone who reads what you write and all the people whose work you see. Isolating yourselves from either part of that community is artistically and politically negligent. It means saying no to a continuing improvisation that is painfully struggling to go forward.

This originated as remarks presented at Critics & Criticism, a symposium at Harvard, organized by Robert Brustein, then-Artistic Director of the American Repertory Theatre, and Bill Kovach, Curator of the Nieman Foundation. Later published in *Nieman Reports*, Vol. XLVI No. 3 Fall 1992.

The Critical Knot

The *San Francisco Chronicle*'s mini-reviews feature drawings of a little white man (presumably a critic) in a theatre seat. The better the review, the more excited he gets, until—if the show is a solid hit—he climbs up on his chair and applauds heatedly, his hands in the air over his head. Forgetting for a minute that even some friendly critics don't clap at a performance, the game is clear. If you can get the clapping man out of his seat, you win. If you can get him to jump up and down or to crawl over the rest of the audience and hand you an award, you win big. If the little man is your father, you win for all time.

In the theatre, the relationship between art and approval is immediate and profound. Unlike any other artistic endeavor, a performance lives or dies by the audience's response. A stage is the perfect place to go to soothe the need for attention—laughter, silence—and to feed the hunger for approval—applause, bravos. Actors, directors, designers, and playwrights sustain themselves through tedious periods of unemployment, poverty, and self-doubt in anticipation of the thrill of the ovation, the high of taking the audience with them when they go. What fires this need for instantaneous—and intense—approval?

And why, in their search for approval, do theatre artists allow themselves to suffer the abuse of the critical community? Moreover, why do theatre people invite this abuse, woo the abusers (critics) into their homes—let them enter at no personal cost, no matter how high ticket prices go, give them free rein there, cuddle up to them, and read their writings over and over, publicly (sometimes even at parties) and privately? Why do we foster dependence on critics: using their words in advertising, blowing up reviews for our lobbies, equating success with "critical success," forgetting the pains of the past with each positive word? Why does the possibility of the little man applauding wildly on top of his chair make us endure the more usual scenario: that same fellow sitting in a heap of indifference, hands plopped in his lap deader than a couple of skinned fish?

Everybody admits that criticism in America is in crisis, that its practitioners neither see themselves on the side of the art nor have enough understanding of the work to provide insight and context. ("I'm a journalist," claims Frank Rich of the *New York Times*, the most powerful critic in the English-speaking world, with dull regularity.) Mostly, critics describe work superficially and pass personal judgment. The fundamental tenet of criticism, granting the work of art what Henry James called its "donnée" or givens—taking it on its own terms, examining what it's attempting to be, is all but forgotten. In its place is "taste," the personal likes and dislikes of the "reviewer" or, in other words, whether the little man in the drawing claps hard or thrusts his thumb down.

We tend to think that the attitudes of critics are distinct, personal things or that, at most, they reflect the tastes of a certain critical establishment. In fact, these attitudes are rich with the biases and ambivalence of a society torn between disdain and fascination: disdain for the chaotic, communal mess of the theatrical imagination and fascination for the games and Eros of the duplicitous stage. The critic has become the mouthpiece for the culture's confused feelings toward theatre. The danger, then, is not that critics will tear the theatre down; they can't do it by themselves. The real peril is that the artistic establishment, eager to please the critical world, will incorporate that world's ambivalence, its distrust of acting, its embarrassment at the rawness of theatrical passion, its fear of experimentation with the unknown and irrational, and its shame about the whole beautiful endeavor. The theatre artist runs the risk of becoming the critic, bringing a kind of negativity or self-hate (defensiveness at best) to everything, she or he does.

"A play is play," Peter Brook reminded us more than 20 years ago. In the eyes of the grown-up world, the players, like all who play, are children. Literally speaking, artists aren't children, nor are critics as important to their development and survival as parents are to children. Still, to break the pattern of dependency on abusive criticism, it's useful to see the activity the way the rest of society sees it: associated with the child, with play-acting, with frivolity, with fantasy and make-believe, with dress-up, with games, with economic naivety, with the reckless—and therefore meaningless—passions of childhood.

If artists are seen as children (and they are certainly treated as such), perhaps their mistreatment—"the anti-theatrical prejudice"—is tied to a cultural attitude towards children. Alice Miller, the Swiss psychoanalyst turned best-selling author of books that include *The Drama of the Gifted Child* and *For Your Own Good: Hidden Cruelty in Child-rearing and the Roots of Violence*, makes a formidable case that psychoanalysis, childrearing and much of contemporary culture reflects a deep hatred of children. Taken together, Brook's reminder of the child-like at the root of theatre and Miller's expose of society's pedagogic brutality (she refers to common childrearing techniques as "poisonous pedagogy") point to a complex and violent relationship between those who stand outside the theatre and those who work and play within it.

The lie of criticism is the lie of parenthood: the critic/parent knows what's best for the artist/child. He sees the artists/children more clearly than they see themselves. This clarity springs from the critic/parent's special gift—objectivity. A century of thinking in psychology, history, and literary theory has crushed the notion that such objectivity is possible or even desirable; the arguments don't need any more rehearsal. What theatre people might consider instead is: how harmful is the idea of objectivity?

The "objective" critic—the outsider with "perspective"— is considered best able to "judge" work because he comes to it fresh, without personal investment. (With few exceptions, the influential American theatre critic has always been a he—a white he.) Critics, though, have a very strong personal investment, whether conscious or not: their work earns them power. They gain power by setting the terms on which work is judged, by dictating standards of taste. They hold sway over artists' livelihoods and self-images; they can say almost anything they want to say about the bodies, faces, talents, brains, or sensibilities of the people they review, and they can say it with impunity. Critics can also bestow media attention or manufacture celebrity, both powers carrying the sexual cachet of dominance over attractive performers. The stereotype of critic-as-Svengali to the helpless or ambitious actress is always with us. Moreover, they have a kind of immortality at their fingertips—the powers to live on in their writing long after performances have died. Most important, they often hold the power to make and break shows.

The little man in the chair can sustain a production's life or, like a god, take that life away. (Frank Rich argues that critics don't close shows, producers close shows. He is right, of course. But he is also being disingenuous. In the commercial theatre at least, the producer, unwilling to risk gargantuan losses after a critical slam, merely does the critic's grunt work: the producer buries the production the critic has already killed.) Non-performed art is different. A critical response may keep viewers out of a gallery or exhibit, but it won't erase the pictures. In the relatively civilized literary world where colleagues—e.g., fellow writers—function as critics, a negative review of a book may limit future printings, but it doesn't burn the copies already in the world. A performance panned, on the other hand, goes away and can't come back, even if the text survives as literature. The critic's version of that work, however, endures. The critic's authority is antithetical to the artist's investment. It corrupts objectivity.

In contrast to the critic's myth of objectivity, the artist never pretends to have anything but a deeply personal investment. The theatre artist's needs are often written, if not all over his or her face, then at least all over the work.

Of course, there are critics who bring a clear political or theoretical agenda to their work, eschewing the rhetoric of objective journalism. This style of criticism, though, whether it falls under the rubric of Marxism, feminism, or any other political or aesthetic framework, while enormously important to readers concerned with social good or harm in a piece of art, provides yet another club to wag over the artist's head. In place of objective truth and discipline, the social critic wields "responsibility." The social responsibility of art, an important and inexhaustible topic for debate and study, is of little help to the creative imagination. Its assertion reinforces the position of critic as grown-up (usually left-leaning grown-up) and artist as adolescent, in need of socialization and moral training. The hand holding the club has the best intentions, making it even harder for the conscientious artist to refuse its mandate.

What, then, is the advantage of having so unequal an investment in the work: one partner coming with passionate need and one with passionless authority and a kind of generalized "love of the theatre"? And what advantage can there be in a relationship as unequal in power as it is in passion? The answers are simple: there are no concrete advantages. The current relationship between theatre artist and critic is unhealthy and unhelpful. In place of constructive partnership, we've worked ourselves into a rut of destructive dependency. It might be fruitful to ask, who are these critics speaking for? Where do their standards come from? And, more important, how can we get out of the rut we've dug?

> Clearly, the whole complex of theatre, dance, music, gorgeous attire, luxurious diet, cosmetics, feminine seductiveness, feminine sexuality, transvestism, etc., aroused a painful anxiety in the [Puritan] foes of the stage, perhaps not only because it symbolized irrational forces threatening chaos, but because it represented a deeply disturbing temptation, which could only be dealt with by being disowned and converted into a passionate moral outrage.
> —Jonas Barish, *The Anti-Theatrical Prejudice*

The daily abuse of the theatre by critics stands side-by-side with centuries of antitheatrical attacks from other quarters: clergy, philosophers, governors, the parents of artists, and even theatre people themselves. In our time these attacks have traumatized theatre as they have traumatized those of us in it. In an extensively researched 1981 book, historian Jonas Barish provides an eloquent and complete account of assaults mounted against the stage from ancient Greece to the present. *The Anti-Theatrical Prejudice* enumerates and analyzes the very abuses—in a historical context—that everyone working in the theatre has experienced. From society's distrust of the changeability of the actor—of the duplicity involved in telling a lie to tell the truth—to its condemnation of the players' lifestyle, from its repugnance for sexual content in spectacle to its fear of the strong cathartic emotion that is theatre's métier—the ancient prejudices against theatre still hold. Though theatre artists are no longer consigned to the burial grounds beyond the city's gates, they are usually condemned to the waste heap of the undervalued and paupered while alive. We still encounter profound cultural neglect (theatre isn't necessary) and amnesia (whatever happened to… ?), not to mention downright virulence spit at the larger arts community from the religious and "moral" right.

Barish ends his analysis in the present, after the theatrical has gained some measure of respect. In 1981, the year he publishes, a movie star becomes president; last year Lord Olivier earned a resting place with poets in Westminster Abbey. And yet, as Barish notes, the bias against theatre has taken root in the theatre itself— turned the theatre against itself, or at least against what has long been seen as theatricality. With reference to groundbreaking artists of the past few decades—Poland's Jerzy Grotowski, Germany's Peter Handke, and our own Open Theatre, Living Theatre, and Robert Wilson—Barish observes the attempts of these insiders to dismantle the stuff of theatricality. They banish impersonation and artifice and shun bourgeois pleasure. In their place, Barish observes, these experimenters make "a science-fiction-like attempt to reinvent the human." The historian takes a dim view of the effects of this recent attack from within: "The rage for authenticity on which the prejudice in its most enlightened version is founded has all but annihilated its object [the theatre], to the point where if, in future, the theatre is to exist at all, it must either return in shame to its bad old ways, imitating, impersonating, storytelling, dealing in illusions and pretenses, or else painfully and grimly carve out for itself some form of antitheatrical self-transcendence in the deepest cavern of its own being."

Indeed, almost a decade after Barish writes, the theatre has more often than not gone back to its old ways, for better and for worse. No transcendent, holy actor has emerged from the cavern of experiment. The guru of the holy, Grotowski, stopped his theatrical inspiration long ago. Among the working avant-garde, the deconstructionists have thoroughly undermined the '60s' noble quest for "authenticity," choosing instead to see all life as performance.

Moreover, recent events have proven Barish's optimism about theatre's renewed respectability premature. With politicians taking role of critic, attacks have been made on not only the sexual and political content of all arts, but specifically on the theatre. It is hardly surprising that one of the first arts groups Senator Jesse Helms chose to research for possible obscenity was the Ridiculous Theatrical Company. Clearly, Helms focused on the group's sexuality—Charles Ludlam's legacy of low transvestite camp as high art. But even without its "gay sensibility," Helms or his cronies have plenty of ammunition. That company is both "ridiculous"— that is, not serious or adult—and "theatrically"—morally—loose. The congressional critic needn't look past the theatre's name to know these wild New Yorkers are the enemy.

Newspaper critics, on the other hand, have of late led vicious attacks on "pretend" by resisting attempts to allow actors to transcend the limits of race by playing roles outside of their color-types, even in non-naturalistic

211

classics. The backlash against color-blind casting represents an attack by rigid, adult, socioeconomic thinking against the world of play-acting, where anyone can be anything simply because we imagine them to be. While Barish may have been overly hopeful about the end of the "anti-theatrical prejudice" outside the theatre, he prophesied the fury of attack we're now seeing in both Washington and the press. "There is no inconsistency," Barish warned, "to which the standard-bearers of prejudice will not resort in order to disguise passion as sober judgment, or any logical rebuttal of their inconsistencies that will abate the intensity of their passion.

This passionate prejudice, he explains, comes from a deep "wish for men to be what they seem...." The enemies of the theatre want stability, clarity, and unity of style and personality because they "cling to a belief in [themselves] as distinct beings, with stable identities." Modern thought and art has long chipped away at this concept of fixed identity. Since Pirandello (at least) we've embraced the concept of life as performance, admitting that character changes from relationship to relationship, that we cast ourselves in roles, act our lives. Modern character is protean and the changeable has always fueled the fear of theatre.

And there is plenty to fear. In this century, identity has grown first self-conscious and then increasingly fragmented. The more roles we play, the harder it is to know who we are, the lonelier we become and the more we threaten the boundaries of accepted behavior—the need for authenticity, upfrontness. Barish quotes psychoanalyst Robert Jay Lifton, who writes about a patient (not an actor) lost in the performance of his life. "Which is the real person, so far as the actor is concerned? Is he more real when performing on the stage or when he is at home? I tend to think," Lifton writes, "that for people who have these many, many masks, there is no home." In Freudian terms, Lifton tells us that the "superego" has disappeared in modern life, and with it the internal structure through which our parents transmit culture's sense of right and wrong.

In the theatre, critics have cast themselves in the role of superego, keeping standards of art—the dos and the don'ts—alive. (Congress, now, is playing critic playing superego—a triple role-play.) But artists—in fact, anyone who would change or push beyond the strictures of conventional behavior—need a way out of the Freudian model. We don't want anyone around to teach us the rights and wrongs of creativity or the no-nos of art. As Lifton puts it, "Protean man requires freedom from precisely that kind of superego—he requires a symbolic form of *fatherlessness*— in order to carry out his explorations." (Italics mine.)

But theatre artists are trapped. They need this "fatherlessness" in order to explore, and yet they desire approval. What's more natural than to go in search of the very father, the voice of the superego, we want to be free

212

from? And so we seem stuck with our father-critics—struggling for freedom to let loose our imaginations and deeper feelings, and frightened by our freedom, frightened back to begging of daddy his applause.

*   *   *

> The arts community is being very childish. And what do you do with children when they misbehave is discipline them. [Sic]
> —Congressman Dick Armey (R- Tex.)

What if father's voice has been, all along, trying to suppress us? What if the moral teachings that make up Freud's superego are not moral after all? What if these teachings are founded on lies and denial? What if the superego is designed to oppress and punish children, to rid the world of imagination, passion, and libido? What if our teachers and guides are abusing us with their "truths"?

The shock "liberal" thinkers expressed when Congressman Armey made the above statement while seeking to cut funding to arts agencies supporting work he didn't like—Andres Serrano's now-famous "Piss Christ" picture and an exhibition of Robert Mapplethorpe's photography—demonstrates a kind of denial that permeates even the most well-meaning artistic circles. That Armey—functioning here in the role of the critic—would suggest a connection between artists and children, and that he would use discipline as a threat of power over either seemed cruel and outrageous. Yet critics regularly try to impose discipline (read "unity") on things they don't feel comfortable with and, in the theatre, penalize the undisciplined with critical death notices. Elinor Fuchs and James Leverett observed this intent in the widespread critical attack on JoAnne Akalaitis's production of *Cymbeline*. (See the Dec. '89 *American Theatre*.) The only difference between the aptly named Armey and battalions of critics disciplining unruly artists everywhere is that he made explicit the equation between parental authority, power (in this case, money—threatening to cut the artist's allowance), and criticism.

To one way of thinking, the critic's role resembles a parent's. The parent, who loves the child, teaches, guides, and socializes that child. Cleansed of all the horrifying passions of childhood and ruled by compassion, the parent's job is to enable the child to likewise overcome unruly emotion and fit in the world. Parents inculcate responsibility, judgment, discipline. They also encourage repression of the tempestuous emotions and wild imaginings that make it hard to get along in the civilized world—the very emotions and imaginings the theatre demands. Naturally, this socialization process cuts two ways. It helps the budding member of society gain some of the skills necessary to survive and fit in the world, while at the same time encouraging denial of a range of feeling (for instance anger) and uniquenesses— a sort of survival by self-negation.

Effective and loving childrearing is possible, of course, when parents, having worked through their own childhood traumas and rediscovered the childhood spontaneity and emotion buried under layers of repression and socialization, are able to follow their children as much as lead. The healthy parents (or in the transference of therapy, the healthy analyst) can listen to the child's language and allow the child's experience full validity, accepting that childhood passions are powerful things. They needn't see their son or daughter's pain, joy, anger, or apathy as a reflection of their own success or failure as a parent, but as a part of the child's own unique and very real experience of life. Healthy parents allow children to be, rather than attempting to "break them" of childishness, prepare them for the "realities" of adulthood or foist on them any rigid version of reality. There is no advantage to a parent who abides by a myth of his own objectivity—knowing what's best for the child—anymore than to a critic who thinks he knows what works on stage or what's best for an artist's career. The best of both recognizes the fierce conviction and intense needs accompanying the child's or artist's work and listens with special care to their unique language, which may seem distorted, naive, unsure, or even ridiculous, but which in fact is attempting to describe personal reality in a way most adults have long given up on.

Too often, though, the parent/critic sees himself as culture's cop, who, like Congressman Armey, thinks it's his responsibility to break willful artists of their unruly ways, to "discipline" them. Another congressman/critic, California's William Dannemeyer, who wants to eliminate all federal funding to the arts, put himself in the dual role of supercop (ready to wipe out obscenity in a single budget cut) and one-man-deprogramming bureau (publishing a book recommending that homosexuals be trained out of their aberrant propensities). There is little difference between Dannemeyer's agenda and that of a critic like *New York* magazine's John Simon, who frequently comments on the relative beauty or sex appeal of actors. Critical obsession with artist sexuality represents a kind of incest—in other words, abuse of power and authority that oversteps the boundaries of decency and respect for someone else's body. On one hand, such comments reflect a fascination with the sexual presence of artists; on the other, a perverse desire to subjugate the one who fascinates. The artist's maxim might be: explore the things you fear. The critic's version: beat the thing you fear into submission; kill it if need be. When critics attack the children of the arts, attempts to dominate them sexually are never far behind.

*   *   *

Only when we realize how powerless a child is in the face of parental expectations (that he control his drives, suppress his feelings, respect their defenses, and tolerate their outbursts) will we grasp the cruelty of parents' threats to withdraw their love if the child fails to meet these impossible demands. And this cruelty is perpetuated in the child....As a result, children really tell lies; that they, not their parents, are the only ones who have to struggle against feelings of hatred.

  —Alice Miller, *Thou Shalt Not Be Aware*

Psychologist Alice Miller's line of thought amplifies Barish's history in interesting ways: it isn't just the theatrical exercise that stimulates prejudice and triggers abuse, but any behavior reminiscent of childhood. Indeed, society's institutions mask a deep-seated hatred of children, and the artist is our culture's most prominent child. Like abused and neglected children, theatre artists are stuck with two unsatisfactory alternatives: to withdraw from the world into one of their own or to keep screaming for attention until they get it. These paths are not mutually exclusive; on the stage we vie for attention by creating a world apart.

In *Thou Shalt Not Be Aware: Society's Betrayal of the Child*, Miller explores another kind of dependent relationship through the story of an activist colleague named Gisella, who worked to organize support groups of prostitutes to defend them from societal discrimination as well as humiliation and violence at the hands of their pimps. "Yet scarcely one of these women," Gisella found, "who had openly expressed their boundless hatred for their oppressors at the group meetings, was able to take advantage of the opportunity she now had to break free....All it took was for the hated procurer, whose death his victim had so passionately desired and whom she had more than once wanted to murder so that she could finally draw a free breath, to be helpless—for example, to cry or to be sent to prison—and his victim would then go to every conceivable length to help her persecutor, would visit him in prison, and the like."

Gisella was baffled by the "repetition compulsion" of the prostitutes' behavior, a pattern she only began to understand when she started treating Anita, a 15-year veteran of the profession. Anita's case demonstrated the hold of early childhood trauma over present-day behavior. Anita had grown up at the mercy of an "alternatively cruel and affectionate" stepfather. Prostitution gave her a sense of control over her clients, a control that allowed her to beat back feelings of powerlessness still active from her youth. Anita's fantasies kept her locked in an abusive relationship with her latest pimp. She envisioned an idealized man—her real father— who would protect her from all the abuse. Memories of her actual father

215

coming back from the war, playing with her and then dying became part of this fantasy, Miller explains. These memories turned out to be false, idealized versions of what had really happened. In fact, as Anita found out in analysis, the father had come home, struck an arrangement with the stepfather and often expressed his "affection" for his daughter sexually, masturbating with her in his lap. Anita's remembrance of her real father's behavior (which trauma had let her erase by idealizing him), and her ensuing grief, released her from her compulsive behavior and allowed her to get free from her (idealized father)/pimp.

There is a "repetition compulsion" at the heart of the artist-critic relationship also. Theatre artists foster the illusion that they can control the audience, win over their feelings, and thus undo the powerlessness they as society's outsiders feel. How like Anita we are, hating the critic who abuses or misunderstands us and still forgiving and putting ourselves in the same position again and again. The dream of the ideal critic persists through it all: he will understand, he will be moved in spite of his professional code, which won't let him clap and frees him to rush out of the theatre even as we bow. The ideal critic will stay long after the curtain falls; he will praise us; he will come back to the show with his friends; he will salve our feelings of alienation. The ideal critic will pander for and defend us— drumming up business and fending off misunderstanding by explaining the work so that audiences can enjoy it. Because this ideal critic promises one day to arrive, we continue to forgive the less-than-ideal. We continue to take the stage and brace ourselves against sarcasm and dismissal and inappropriate sexual comment. We wait for the good daddy, no matter how many abusive stepfathers sit in for him. We behave like the "characters" in Pirandello's *Six Characters in Search of an Author*, locked in family dramas of incest and neglect, in search of some author to right (and write) our wrongs. These characters, Barish explains, "are locked in an endless repetition-compulsion. They revert over and over, in speech, in imagination, to the traumatic events of their past."

As in the example of the prostitute Anita, the power struggle between the adult world and the artist is largely sexual in nature. The critic plays the part of the superego, while the theatre artist—in the person of the actor—seems to the world to be a kind of living libido—instinctual, dark, seductive, trying to win over the thoughtful man in the audience, trying to attract him to the fantasy world of the evening. But as long as the critic defines the terms of the relationship, the story we get is the story Freud told our century: The guilt is in the child. Sexuality is the child's fantasy; propriety is the father's imperative.

The Freudian model blames the victim. The child, Freud imagines, has the first unclean thought: to marry one parent and kill off the other. This formulation, however, breaks down when actual guilt is with the parent, when there is real abuse, sexual or otherwise. And real abuse happens everywhere people wield power over others.

Freud knew this and it scared him. In his first major paper, *The Aetiology of Hysteria* (1896), Freud concluded, on the basis of an overwhelming number of reports by his patients of being sexually abused as children, that sexual experiences during childhood were the principal cause of neurotic behavior in adults. The news wasn't well received. The messenger—Freud—got the brunt of his colleagues' resistance to this theory. Over a pressurized next two years, Freud began to doubt his findings, until finally the "truth" dawned on him that the abuses reported hadn't happened at all; they had been fantasized by his patients. They had been the wishes of children.

Time and statistics have proven differently, confirming Freud's earlier findings. The prevalence of child abuse in Western culture is now old, though terrifying, news. As a result, Freud's repression of his "seduction theory" is the point where contemporary psychologists, like Miller, depart from his teachings. They accept the reality of parental abuse. Miller takes it the further step: Society's institutions, including parenthood, are rife with prejudice, even hate, against the child, a fact the world hastens to deny. But the theatre is one world where the "children" can feel the prejudice every time they open up the paper on the morning after press night. And though these children may scramble to find the fault in themselves, they know they are the target, not the cause.

Nevertheless, it's hard to let go of the need to be approved of in the press, just as it's hard for the grown children of dysfunctional families to give up the struggle for love and support from their kin. The solution—the therapy—lies with every individual who would make theatre. To release repetitive and unhealthy behavior now, it is necessary to discover and grieve the traumas of the past. Our reasons for doing this maltreated and misunderstood and occasionally celebrated work are various and unique. Likewise, our solutions to the traumas of the lifestyle will be unique. They may be found in the questions we ask ourselves: how did criticism function in my own family? Who supplied it? How did I react? What kind of feelings did it bring up? What kind of repeating behavior did it provoke? Who am I trying to please?

Solutions also exist in group action and support. Recently, in Washington, D.C., a group of actors assembled a panel of other actors, artistic directors, and one critic to take steps to overcome the damage criticism has done to the actors' work. The title of the one-day symposium was their goal: "Freedom from the Press." This was one kind of step for one kind of artist—not much more than a half-day support group. But support groups can do a lot, and in theatre they need to.

On the other hand, in communities across the country, theatre people have tried for years to strike bargains with local newspapers for more reviewers (to water down individual power), more understanding, and more preview time before critics insist on attending. It hasn't worked. Journalists and editors have their own agendas, their own schedules. Last fall, California's Oakland Ensemble Theatre sent a letter to the publisher of the local *Mercury News* disinviting a critic with a history of racist remarks from future shows. The letter was reprinted by the San Francisco service organization Theatre Bay Area in hopes that other theatres would follow OET's lead. Theatre Communications Group and others canceled subscriptions to *New York* magazine in protest over the latest John Simon incivilities. Unfortunately, like the "children" of any kind of abusive parents, it's up to the abused to change the behavior, to buy out of the system or change it.

Perhaps the first step is to give up on it. Let's change the way we publicize our work. What if the whole theatre community just stopped using "quote" ads and blowing up good reviews in the lobbies? What if we worked together to find alternative methods of audience development, ways of redirecting the dollars we throw at press relations? Theatre Bay Area recently got an in-kind donation worth about $350,000 in the form of advertising for the whole theatre community from one of the nation's largest ad agencies. What if we all stopped letting critics in free, while at the same time, supported all media attempts to do in-depth, feature-type reporting on the work, and put the energy of our press representatives into only the latter? What if we announced community bans on the relentlessly abusive critics? We all know who they are. What if, God forbid, all theatre people stopped reading reviews, cold turkey, and met among themselves instead in a systematic way (maybe with outside colleagues) to evaluate the work, honestly, with an eye to better future work?

Also, we need to know that, like other victims of abuse and prejudice, we have rights. The Berne Convention, which establishes international copyright treaties and laws, in addition to protecting works of art, legislates the moral rights of artists. While these laws apply more clearly to written works and fine art and are harder to apply to performing arts, it might be worth a try. According to an article by Jody A. Van Den Heuvel in this fall's *Journal of Arts Management and Law*, the U.S., although a member of the Berne Convention, lacks the protection for artists' moral rights found in such nations as France. Meetings in 1989 by the U.S. Senate's copyright panel gave little hope for adoption of the Convention's notion of these rights. But Van Den Heuvel's proposal for the development of a federal policy for artist protection needn't be abandoned. Theatre artists should join with writers and painters and film-makers to advocate for the establishment of the internationally defined moral rights.

Two of the five moral rights developed at Berne are particularly appropriate for the theatre: "The Right to Create and The Right of Disclosure" and "The Right to Protection from Excessive Criticism." The first might be of special interest to New York Shakespeare Festival's producer Joseph Papp, who last year was prevented by the *New York Times* from establishing his own schedule for the opening of David Hare's *The Secret Rapture*. It declares that "it is the artist's moral right to determine when [the work) is complete and when and if it should be made public." The second is of interest to all theatre people and may provide a forum for rebuttal in the very media where attacks against theatre occur: "Any unwarranted or abusive attack on the artist or on his work is considered to be a violation of the artist's right to protection from excessive criticism." France, Van Den Heuvel tells us, "provides legal protection for excessive criticism by giving the artist the right to reply to the criticism in the same medium of expression as the offender's remark"! These moral rights suggest that there may be legal or legislative ways of fighting back.

Finally, theatre people have to take some responsibility for training writers who are invested in the theatre and who understand it. There is currently only one major writer/thinker—*The New Republic*'s Robert Brustein—who works both sides of the auditorium, and he is our best. His example, when placed beside those of George Bernard Shaw and Eric Bentley, provides more than enough proof that working in the theatre actually enhances critical perception. Essayists (I hesitate to use the word "critic," because I hope for a new kind of theatre writer altogether) who work in the theatre bring a more personal investment to their work, the kind of passion that burns out for the daily "objective" reviewer. Conflict of interest issues are minor and, as these men have shown, fairly easily disposed of. The real conflict comes when the artist has all the interest and the critic has none.

We have to think imaginatively about a new kind of criticism and a new relationship to it, including developing new sources for and forms of supportive, constructive criticism from within the theatre community. We can't fight critical abuses with one hand and plead for approval with the other. We have to train ourselves to remember what is important about the work and whose opinions matter. We have to let go of the critics our fathers, stop leaning on them, quoting them, looking to them for advice. We have to stop parroting them and, simultaneously, defending ourselves from them. We have to free ourselves of them before we become them.

This essay was originally published in *American Theatre*, February, 1990.

What a Difference a Play Makes

Cino Nights: An Introduction

I miss Joe Cino. I miss his theatre, which was a café. I miss the moment of Caffé Cino, a moment when Judson Church welcomed playwrights under the wide communitarian wings of Reverend Al Carmines, when writers sought to begin a cultural revolution at Theatre Genesis, when Ellen "Mama" Stewart first rang her little bell, signaling curtain time at the global art pushcart called La Mama Experimental Theatre Club. I miss the sound of that bell, the tinkle-tinkle-tink that rang on East 4th Street in lower Manhattan and reverberated around the world. Yeah, I miss what I never had.

I caught the originating bells and ur-tumult in after-shock. Caffé Cino started serving coffee and food on Carmine Street in 1958, with sides of poetry, and added plays to the menu in '61. I entered high school ten years later to find teenaged longhairs rocking Megan Terry's *Viet Rock*, N.R. Davidson's Malcolm X play *El Hajj Malik*, and one acts by John Guare and other children of Cino. Among the first lines I spoke as a freshman actor was "Blah blah blah blah blah blah hostile. Blah blah blah blah blah blah penis" from Jean-Claude van Itallie's *America Hurrah*. My first semester in college—middle of Iowa—I discovered that preeminent Cino writer Lanford Wilson by getting cast in *Rimers of Eldritch*. These crazies had been blowing minds in downtown Manhattan since the sixties were still the fifties. They blew my mind after the fact and gradually, but it stayed blown. And so the explosion that began in Joe Cino's bohemian coffeehouse—walls plastered with posters, torn photos, glitter stars, balls of foil, and a motley of memorabilia almost a foot thick—and changed the shape of our theatre, changed the course of my one Midwestern life as well. It led me, a millennium later, to sit down and write this to you, introducing a collection of plays by another bunch of retroactively blown minds, from yet another generation, plays produced by the Rising Phoenix Theatre, in a series called Cino Nights.

Just to be precise: I miss what I missed, but I'm not nostalgic for that other time. Our nation's theatre is warm and fuzzy enough, and I wouldn't wish for more of its soft senseless familiarity. Who wants familiar? Familiar is a tribute band, opening the graveyards of our imagined youths, so the dead can walk the earth in Peter Max clothes. They were beautiful and painful times, those first days of Off Off Broadway, but the pain was as real as Joe Cino's suicide in '67. Who wants the madness that went with that particular moment of searching? No, I'm not nostalgic for the rats and roaches, not for the poverty, the raw street and drug life, for the hallucination, the bacchananihilation that was the underbelly of so much beautiful dreaming.

I'm nostalgic for an urgency of impulse, a driving drive to make theatre for some pressing, if still indiscernible reason, the reason you have to discover by doing. I'm nostalgic for art that tastes like freedom. I'm nostalgic for theatre that smells like fun.

I can't remember who said that theatre is either easy or impossible. Whoever it was was right. The easy is what we know; it confirms what we know. I want the impossible kind, exploration without end, the challenge to make the beautiful in minutes with a figurative gun to your head. This isn't to suggest that great theatre can only happen when it's thrown together under duress. Astonishing theatre (who wants any other kind?) can be, in the making, fast or slow.

Slow is Peter Brook, The Wooster Group, Andre Gregory—all diamond, impact and edge, the brilliant earthen density, made of pressure over time. Fast means propulsive, the burst and flood of energy that drags the unconscious with it, meaning made on purpose and by happy accident. Overnight play festivals are fast. Weekend intensives are fast. Plays improvised before your eyes are fast fast fast. Fast can be a way to the vital and communal, a way to pack the intensity of years together into mere evenings. Theatre fails in the middle ground between fast and slow—the three-four-week rehearsal, for example, which gives you time to learn lines, get your moves down, and run cue to cue. It's hard, in the middle, to release bursts of the unconscious that happen under pressure, or to drill down the way you can over time.

Cino Nights are fast: a week's rehearsals starting on Monday and culminating with a throw-it-up tech on Sunday afternoon with a single performance that same night. Now you see it, now it's gone. Theatre in the blink of an eye. And the blink of it confirms—no, celebrates—the theatre's ephemerality, its now-ness.

Caffé Cino was an amateur enterprise with professionals. Joe Cino chose artists by instinct or, famously, by astrological sign. His Caffé was part playground and part destination for the devoted. This, I think I believe, is the best way to make theatre: with professionals engaged in amateur activities. In the first Greenwich Village experimental age, in the nineteen-teens, theatre folk were fond of reminding everyone that the Latin root of the word amateur is love. In other words, amateur theatre is love sport. Amateur theatre with professional artists is a double blessing, because it re-connects with the *amour* that gives us our first reasons to create—the love of self at play, the love of imagining, the love of singing/dancing/pretending with others. And it draws on the finest attuned sensitivities of the dedicated artist—the expressive body, the resilient voice, the emotional/creative intelligence and human insight that expands with practice. We say professional theatre artists have "chops," a term that comes from jazz. You need chops to hit the high notes on the horn. To play in the *best* way, though, you need to want to hit those notes *in the worst way*. You want magic? You want astonishment? You want theatre? You want music that hasn't been heard before? Try mixing professional virtuosity with amateur hunger.

God, I love that Daniel Talbot and the Rising Phoenix gang came up with Cino Nights. Yes, it's homage and nostalgia, but out of the longing for what you missed altogether comes something else again. They aren't re-creating Caffé Cino. To do that you'd need to resurrect Joe Cino, give him a broom and a coffee machine, dial the Village back to 1961, bring back the young Ellen Stewart, Al Carmines, and all of them, including Lanford Wilson, Doric Wilson, H.M. Koutoukas, and Leonard Melfi and Tom Eyen. We'd need to make John Guare, Robert Patrick, Terrence McNally, Maria Irene Fornes, and Sam Shepard kids again (which has its appeal but isn't possible even in the impossible theatre). But no, Cino nights are after that elusive grail of the theatre: something else again. The new thing that reminds us. The new energy that re-ignites us. The speed that unearths that which might take a lifetime to investigate and fully express. Something else again and again and again.

Something else again is the backroom of the East Village restaurant Jimmy's No. 43, which gets tricked out anew for every show, becoming, for example, the underground headquarters of a cult dedicated to the Russian poet Anna Akhmatova in Kristen Palmer's *The Stray Dog*. Something else again is Gary Sunshine's *The Best Sex Ever*, in which an ambitious soldier sets out to marry his prematurely old kindergarten teacher on a cruise ship, only to encounter his "butt-boy" from ROTC, the pharmaceuticalized nebbish with whom he had, yup, the best sex ever. Something else again is Adam Szymkowicz's *Clown Bar*, a noir play with a bar full of gangster clowns in full red-nose regalia and an ex-clown cop trying to get to the bottom of his junkie brother's murder. Courtney Baron's *Now I Lie* is something else again, too, a pas-de-deux of loneliness, illness and, finally, death, which appears to be the only perfect thing in life. As is Lucy Thurber's *Named*, where the unspoken and spoken each define love's desire in their own way, and Mando Alvarado's *(O)n the 5:31*, which folds what happened, what might have happened, and what's remembered, into a fluid 10-year love triangle. Jessica Dickey dresses a New York woman in a "farbing" (you gotta look that one up) Civil War uniform, so she can mingle with Gettysburg re-enactors, and, so, makes something else again out of the past. Emily DeVoti tracks down Hitler's Irish sister-in-law and finds her living out on Long Island, and Brigid Hitler's story becomes a twisted lifeline for a struggling writer and an aging actress at the end of her hope. Each of these plays—eight of the seventeen Cino Nights plays to date—is its own kind of new, its own kind of something else again. Some were written fast, some slow, some for all time, some for the blink of an eye. They may recall another moment, but they all live in the theatre present or, as Szymkowicz says of the clown play, "Right fucking now."

You didn't see them? Read them then. Stage them in your own theatre, in the middle of your own café. Mount a marathon—all these plays and all the ones you can find from the original Caffé Cino. You may just hear the tinkle-tinkle-tink of a bell you thought had fallen silent long ago.

This essay was originally written for *Cino Nights*, published *by* The New York Theatre Experience, New York, 2012.

The States of American Playwriting

State One: The Great American Playwright is Dead; Long Live the Great American Playwrights

The Great American Playwright—or the idea of one—is a thing of the past. And though I doubt many of our critics or other makers of reputations will agree with me, I believe the decline of this idea of greatness has been a long time in the making.

Eugene O'Neill, the "father" of American playwriting, is also its haunted son and restless ghost. If O'Neill gave birth to our nation's theatre and died for it, as Tennessee Williams eulogized, he also defined the experimental possibilities of that theatre more broadly than anyone before or since. On the way to his realistic, confessional, autobiographical masterworks, he wrestled with myth, masks, Greek tragedy, expressionism, boulevard romantic comedy, the seafarers' ballad, psychoanalysis, and his own murderous furies, among many other adversaries. For us, O'Neill grew as Strindberg might have had he, in middle age, become Ibsen, in the period of his major prose plays.

But O'Neill was pure American, born in the dressing room of a barnstorming actor-manager, ever the immigrant's son, pen loosed by drink, coming of age with the radicals on the coast of Massachusetts and then, avant-garde, in Greenwich Village. O'Neill stands as the troubled Johnny Appleseed of the American Theatre, ripping up more earth and sowing more seeds than appears humanly possible, moistening the soil with his own blood.

After him a couple of others were admitted into our native pantheon, notably Tennessee Williams, who walked the edge of poetry and pathology O'Neill had cut, and Arthur Miller, who further integrated the classically tragic and the contemporaneously American, and dramatized individual conscience at the place it meets social consciousness.

And then something changed. Simultaneous with the anti-authoritarian sixties, with the liberation-seeking, experimental ethos of the times, something began to change in the relationship of artists to the idea of greatness in the theatre. I think about Edward Albee's career. Albee the Broadway master, was, arguably, the last great American playwright; Albee the experimental playwright and pioneer of Off Off Broadway, on the other hand, seemed to disavow the mantel of his own greatness by refusing to stay in one place, by giving free rein to his own restless experimentalism. Even relatively early in his career, he did the opposite of what O'Neill did, by moving from the domestic, argumentative absurdism of, say, *The Zoo Story* or *Who's Afraid of Virginia Woolf*, towards the stranger terrors of *Tiny Alice* or *Seascape*—leaving the trappings of naturalism farther behind. Albee's artistic rebellion proved many things, among them the limitations of the Broadway theatre, the arrival at which had previously been requisite for greatness. Now the Great White Way, ever in decline, seemed an eternally pale thing, unable to make room for anything but the most naturalistic drama. Even Albee's more recent triumphal return—twenty odd years later—started Off Broadway.

Around the same time, the decentralization of our theatre was picking up speed. From the total dominance of the Broadway commercial theatre in New York—with an extensive national network of theatres to house Broadway tours—the centers of activity began to shift—to a woollier, more adventurous Off Broadway and a collectively energized, impoverished Off Off Broadway, as well as to a burgeoning constellation of regional, nonprofit companies, many originally envisioned in the image of subsidized European rep companies with resident companies and a rotating repertoire of classic and new plays. I don't know what was cause and what effect. Maybe changing dramatic forms followed the diversification of venues or maybe politics, catalyzed by the struggle for American Civil Rights, led at that moment of explosion and flux. Maybe the art came first and places to stage it followed.

Whatever the cause, a new era in playwriting began here: an age not of authority or hierarchy, so much as an era of influence, of democratic spread. This shift—and I believe we're somewhere in the second generation of it—is still being felt. For the first time, many of the most significant voices in the American theatre were voices that would never be heard on Broadway. Some would rarely if ever find a hearing in New York. Others—no less singular or artistically significant—would live for decades in the land of hundred-seat houses with black walls and xeroxed playbills. Now, forty years after Lorraine Hansberry's *Raisin in the Sun* and Albee's *Virginia Woolf* changed the look and feel of Broadway, we still have canonized—or, at least, highly anthologized-playwrights. (I'm thinking of David Mamet, Sam Shepard, August Wilson, and most recently, Tony Kushner, who are, without question, world-class playwrights with the capability of reaching mainstream audiences and with one or more plays vying for a place on everybody's lists of must-reads.) Surrounding them, though, is a whole world of writers whose power, influence, and theatrical vitality make them every bit as deserving of enthusiasm and attention.

State Two: America is Many Americas

Contrary to the impression that America exports its culture, blockbuster-style, I believe that even the American mainstream is unaware of the writers shaping its theatrical culture from the trenches. Furthermore, the culture-shapers, though choosing to work in unusual places and ways, have every right to stand beside our equally talented, international successes. Mostly, I'm dying to introduce you to as many playwrights as I can, even knowing that the litany of their names and qualities will be a barrage and that for everyone I name, there'll be scores I leave out.

You will notice that many of the influences and names I cite, while I talk about influence and democratic spread, have a racial or ethnic component. I'll refer to the vibrant community of Latino/Latina writers working in our theatre, the lineage of contemporary African-American writers revising our history, or the growing influence of Asian-American writers. This is not, I believe, the result of any conscientious inclusion on my part. The world of American playwriting I live in does not operate by quotas, though I fear our producing theatres do. (I'm creeping up on my biases.) I'm merely describing what I see. And I see a profession of playwriting whose unprecedented vigor has come, over the past 15 years or so, from the sound of voices that had previously been exceptions. The generative moment, I believe, happened in the sixties and early seventies, with the wild proliferation of Off Off Broadway playwriting—in clubs, cafes, garages, found spaces. Though its energy has changed, we still feel the repercussions of this explosion, this turning point when all at once writers of skin tones and nationalities and sexual persuasions who had never been acknowledged or supported by the monochromatic Broadway theatre started to throw work on the stage with a vengeance.

The aftershocks have included a slow-motion blowing apart of the myth of a singular, homogeneous America. It would be difficult to single out plays from the past two decades that exacted the damage. Still, I believe our writers have been on the front lines. They've changed the sound and subject matter of the American theatre in part by dedication, mutual support, and numbers. While a quarter century ago, you would have been hard pressed to locate the work or a Cuban- or Mexican- or Chinese-American on an American stage, we now have two generations of each, arguing, elaborating, advancing—even completing—each other. When I began teaching in 1982, I had to hunt to find plays by women in anthologies; now bookshelves lining my office are chockful of them, as are the lists I have tacked to my bulletin board—indispensable playwrights, playwrights whose work I love. In maybe fifteen years' time, Black playwrights have not only transformed the theatre, but radically revised our nation's history. The notable example of this is August Wilson's monumental play cycle, charting the lives of African-Americans in each decade of the twentieth century in a blues-inspired choral idiom—an achievement whose scope and brilliance rivals any in the annals of our theatre. Meanwhile, in other idioms altogether—poetic, formalist, expressionist, confessional, satirical, naturalistic—a generation of African-

American writers is moving through the doors Wilson blew open. In a recent *New Yorker*, Wilson's current director, Marion McClinton, himself a gifted playwright, named nearly a dozen writers who've benefited from Wilson's flying wedge.

Given the demographic givens, few of these plays will translate to Scandinavian stages. I wish to impress on you, though, how important and expanding they've become to our theatre—both in terms of subject and form—challenging our ideas about what makes experience universal and about what makes a play dramatic. Moreover, they've proven absolutely that America is, in fact, many Americas, that the American Dream—a subject of our national obsession for at least a century—is many dreams and nightmares. The spread of artistic influence, through the African-American playwriting community, for instance, is about more than opportunity; it's about the writing itself.

I think of some of my personal favorite playwrights and can't envision them emerging full-blown without the example of the ones who came before. The brilliant Suzan-Lori Parks reconstructs American history by probing the absence of African-American history—what she called in *The America Play*, "the great hole of history" (that play featured a black man dressed as Abraham Lincoln and known as "the foundling father"). Parks and the politically passionate, linguistically vivacious Kia Corthron are two important contemporary playwrights who couldn't exist—artistically speaking—without the precedents of Amiri Baraka's politics and jazz poetry or the intense subjectivity of Adrienne Kennedy's theatrical hallucinations.

In every realm of dramatic writing here, you can see the chains of influence between writers barely separated by time. Comedic writers like Nicky Silver, Charles Busch, Amy Freed, and David Lindsay-Abaire seem to have drunk of the spirits of such slightly older writers as the ever-imaginative raconteur John Guare, the anarchic Christopher Durang, the manic Harry Kondoleon, who died in 1994, and the late Charles Ludlam, our own gender-bending Moliere. There is no Arthur Miller school of playwriting, but it's hard to imagine serious playwright-thinkers like Jon Robin Baitz, Marsha Norman, Emily Mann, or Donald Margulies without him, just as it's hard to imagine such dark satirists of macho capitalism as Keith Reddin or Howard Korder without Mamet. And so it goes: David Henry Hwang, by bringing Chinese-American life to our stages, begets Chay Yew, who is even more violently contemporary and sexual, and Diana Son, who takes the ethnic mix of America for granted and, over time, leaves her Korean heritage out all together.

You can see the influence, too, of playwrights teaching playwrights. Perhaps the most influential American playwriting teacher of the past quarter century is Maria Irene Fornes, a Cuban-born New Yorker whose spare, essentialist, ever-shifting body of work, begun and sustained almost entirely Off Off Broadway, is one of the unsung treasures of the late twentieth-century American stage. As a teacher, Fornes's emphasis on body-centered, subconscious writing has changed the lives of dozens of our finest playwrights, including nearly every Latino/Latina playwright working. From the Chekhovian family comic-dramas of Cuban-American Eduardo Machado to the violent macho border plays of Chicano writer Octavio Solis to the improbable love stories of Puerto Rican-born Edwin Sanchez to Nilo Cruz's art-object-like imaginings of loss and longing, and Caridad Svich's mash-ups of classical myth, blues-rock balladeering, and the ecstatic incantation of desire. Fornes hasn't put her stamp on the plays, so much as provided inspiration to their authors. Two other playwright-teachers have, like Fornes, set this generation of playwriting minds on fire, rather than inducting disciples into a theatrical style: Paula Vogel, whose formally playful work—including *How I Learned to Drive* and *The Baltimore Waltz*—has lured audiences into the dark waters of incest, AIDS death, and domestic violence, and Mac Wellman, one of our most frankly experimental writers, whose satires of American culture—featuring giant pandas and intergalactic furballs—revel in language, language as landscape, language as event.

State Three: Dramatic Form as the Search for Form

I'm struck by how unruly they are, our playwrights. They refuse to swim in schools, even as they show their influences. Maybe the passage from a theatre of Broadway greats to this dramaturgical motley is typically American—the breakaway nation always in rebellion against mother country and father time. Maybe the difficulty of summarizing the current playwriting scene stems from the deep-seated individualism of the American enterprise. In playwright after playwright I've found evidence of an aversion to writing in established forms that I haven't noticed in other countries. Treplev's youthful cry in *The Seagull* for "New Forms" seems to have taken root in the American artistic heart.

I formed one impression during five years of overseeing a playwright exchange with London's Royal National Theatre. It's this: British playwrights tend to write out of and against tradition or convention and have lately succeeded on the world stage because of it. Recent efforts by Martin McDonagh, Mark Ravenhill, and Jez Butterworth, for instance, rely on dramatic structures recognizable from, say Hitchcock or Tarantino films, or linguistic ones from Mamet or Scorcese. They wreak changes on their models and on their models' morality, certainly, but they still work within categories that audiences and critics recognize as "dramatic"—that is, conflictual, confrontational, repetitive, and violent.

For many of their contemporaries in America, I suspect, form equals the search for form. It's something a writer discovers in the process of writing. It is immanent. Think, for example of *Angels in America*. The "fantasia" structure is a kind of non-binding structure, allowing Kushner's imagination to go where it wants, to digress, to elaborate, to move forward and back, like progress itself, one of the play's main themes. The play dreams itself into being. And then the second part, *Perestroika*, dreams itself another way.

This a-traditionalism or setting-out-to-points-unknown feels distinctly American to me. It's the way the country has grown, by brash, intuitive, violent improvisation, inventing itself and discovering itself simultaneously. It's little wonder, then, that improvisational comedy has established itself as a boom industry in the U.S. It's little wonder, either, that American audiences, fed on the dramatic conventions of the old Broadway and the everlasting Hollywood, would find new American writing somewhat alien and hard to recognize or that our reviewers and our producers would dismiss as lacking in drama or quality that which is merely new to them.

State Four: Theatre Theatre Everywhere and Not a Lot of Ink

I've arrived then, at my bias, my complaint: America has not yet created theatres worthy of its artists.

Our community is, I believe, in the midst of a long and wide-spread transition, from the centralized, commercialized, conventional world of mid-20th-century Broadway to who knows what. But because we're a young work-in-progress in a savagely under-subsidized field, the progress has been led by people with a talent for fundraising and outreach. Institution builders have been our pioneers, as opposed to artistic visionaries or champions of the difficult or new. Specifically, I believe that the American theatre—commercial and institutional, in New York and across the country—has not yet developed theatres that can make sense of American playwriting. As a result, we are in the painful state of living amidst a profusion of talent and a scarcity of homes for that talent. The theatres are there—the buildings—but the singularity of vision that gifted writers cultivate by instinct and the diversity of vision that this community of writers has grown to—these accomplishments are betrayed by a theatre that has created itself in the very homogenous image it set out to overthrow. Moreover, with the exception of small experimental ensembles and a few Shakespeare Festivals, we have no acting companies large or long-lived enough to develop the collective vernacular that serves a company playwright. When New York lost the Circle Repertory Theatre a decade ago, which had nurtured Lanford Wilson and, later, Craig Lucas, among others, we lost, perhaps the last mature company to marry acting style to playwriting vision.

Harold Clurman, a founder of the influential Group Theatre in the 1930s and one of America's most important directors, critics, thinkers and, especially, inspirers in the middle of century gone by, describes in his memoir a conversation with the novelist Andre Gide. "The problem with the theatre," Gide remarks, "is finding great plays." "The problem with the theatre," Clurman counters, "is creating a theatre." Clurman's diagnosis has proved prescient.

And so we await and hope for the theatres to come. And the playwrights' fates are tied to those of smaller theatres and newer ones and local ones—the idiosyncratic and passionate, the possible and impossible theatres.

State Five: Might America be a Figment of America's Imagination?

One final thing. I've charted a jump-around, loosely historical path through the playwriting profession today. What I haven't done is locate thematic threads, a way of talking about the "aboutness" of contemporary writing. I'm aware that such attempts to sum up or essentialize our cultures for each other are like those conversations you have when you travel, over beers with tourists from other countries—"the thing about America is... ." In our attempts to overcome cultural distinctions we earnestly engage in drawing them.

Still, every time I think I've put my finger on what seems like a distinctive thread of American playwriting—the fluidity of identity, for example—it slips out of my grasp. This month, for instance, I've read dozens of plays—satires of corporate behavior in California; painful hyper-real portraits of Generation X-ers as lost in themselves as they are in America; a slippery, thoroughly bent sex farce based on Molnar's *The Guardsman*; a Pinteresque interrogation play centered around an ailing, bed-ridden Proust character; a play featuring a serial killer who finds Jesus on death row; and more.

The framework I keep returning to, my personal attempt to make the strongest connection between the largest number of plays, is that of the making of America itself. America, it constantly occurs to me in light of the plays I read and see, is a made-up thing, a figment of its own imagination. It's always been so, a place as an idea of a place, refuge, home, wilderness, possibility, and prison, a nation proclaimed to be indivisible but, we now know, as easily divided as can be. And so I return to the thought that our writers—maybe like the writers of every country—are continually rediscovering, remaking, constructing, and deconstructing, dreaming of and waking to their homeland. Maybe this self- and national-definition that occurs everywhere is at the heart of the American project and its theatrical expression. Maybe our playwrights are always in the process of discovering America and of making it up as they go along. Where they'll land, nobody knows.

This text originated as a speech to the Scandinavian-American Theatre Conference, revised and published in *@nd...*, New Dramatists, 2001.

Gum & *The Mother of Modern Censorship*: Introduction

We are in a faraway country, a "fictitious faraway" country. Two girls, veiled head to toe, stand in a garden bounded by a high wall. They share a piece of gum.

This image—the opening moment of Karen's Hartman's dazzling *Gum*—is a detail writ large, like the ones you find in art books, where a background scene played out in the shadow of a doorway is blown up for inspection. In close-up, the girls' faces become visible. They are smiling with anticipation. This isn't a book of pictures, though; it's a play, blueprint for a living, breathing event. Nor are we studying the background; the hidden has moved center stage. The eye notices the wall that keeps the world out, the clothing that keeps bodies in, the excitement over the gum. Then in a concentrated burst, one of the sisters says, "I have Gum."

I dwell on this opening moment as a way of introducing Karen and her plays to you. It contains so much of what I love about her work: its unexpectedness, the striking yet believable oddity of its setting, the charged vibrancy of its lyricism, its fusion of metaphor and reality, and, most important, the sheer physicality of its expression. Here gum is a tangible—chewable—fact. It is also a metaphor that spreads right through the bodies of the sisters who share it—a metaphor for pleasure, release, desire, transgression, America, the forbidden, the secret sexual act. Overhear these descriptions of the juicy contraband, and note how the actual and metaphorical infuse each other, how the words live in the body and express the body:

> Ordinary. And extraordinary. Hard at first, then sweet. I expected that break but there was none, only yielding. Easy to find a pulse. Everything went wet. And as I chewed I began to feel peculiar.

> [...]

> The juice of the gum became fire inside me.

> [...]

> The spirit of the gum was conquering me. I moved in a new rhythm, as if my body chewed.

And we are in another fictitious country (maybe it's the same one) at the start of *The Mother of Modern Censorship*, *Gum's* companion piece (written first). Again there are two women onstage, middle-aged this time and presumably middle-Eastern, one in a long skirt, one in robes, headscarf, and gloves. Each wears headphones plugged into a boombox on her desk. They listen to cassette tapes, stop the tapes, and throw them in the trash. They are the Chief Music Censor and her assistant. This easy mix of traditional and contemporary, East and West, is no less strange for its familiarity.

If *Gum* has the vivacity of a breakthrough play (and it does—you can feel the playwright's concerns and talents coming together in a leap), *The Mother of Modern Censorship* has the energy of the irrepressible, of a wild improvisation, a sly political goof. In *Gum*, the repression of sexual hunger, of the body—as if desire might be excised from the female body or desiring women severed from the body politic—takes a brutal, tragic turn. In *The Mother of Modern Censorship*, repression takes a turn toward the absurd, as tape after tape goes in the can. The chief censor swears like a trucker. The novice censor sounds like Miss California ("I am very excited about a career in music censorship....I would like very much to be the conscience of society for a long time to come"). And the women responsible for judging music and lyrics (even "deep breathing is a deep offense") have no access to or knowledge of the things they're hired to purge.

Both of these plays began from a single *New York Times* article Karen brought to a workshop led by British playwright David Edgar at Yale School of Drama in the mid-'90s. She had recently returned from a year in Jerusalem and traveling the Middle East, experiences that informed both the choice of clipping and the plays that emerged. Accompanying the article was a picture of three veiled women, listening to American music on headphones, searching for smut.

And so we are in faraway countries that fuse the fictitious and the real, the fabled and the factual. Time, though—and a publication date that coincides with the first anniversary of the World Trade Center and Pentagon attacks, and the subsequent war on Afghanistan's Taliban regime—has tilted them back toward their newspaper roots. When I read *Gum* now, I can't help thinking of stadium executions of women in Afghanistan and the fatal penalties imposed on rape victims in Pakistan. The image of veiled women with headphones now seems less like a humorous invention than an ironic discovery. Plays that two years ago had an air of exoticism about them now feel almost journalistic. These examples of vibrant creative imagination have the added urgency of acts of cross-cultural empathy, conjured in a time of crisis. Fictitious or not, these countries are no longer faraway.

Karen Hartman's plays sing with life. Their remarkable vitality will be apparent to everyone who reads them, as will the unique spirit and intelligence of the artist who bodied them forth. Savor them. Revisit them. See how they grow.

From *Gum & The Mother of Modern Censorship* by Karen Hartman, New York: Theatre Communications Group, 2003. Reprinted with permission.

Shakespeare In A Strange Land

When, in 1964, the Polish critic Jan Kott dubbed Shakespeare "our contemporary," the label stuck. Shakespeare's relevance was nearly tautological; he'd never been of any moment but the present one. And if times changed, then, in the words of the cultural historian Gary Taylor, we'd "reinvent" him. Over four centuries of relevance and reinvention, Romanticism saw *Lear* as a "gothic fairy tale," and postmodernism made a collage of *Cymbeline*. Miranda seemed the ideal Victorian virgin to the 19th century; Gertrude, the object of Oedipal desire to the 20th. Kott showed us the great Elizabethan playwright through the eyes of Soviet-dominated Eastern Europe; there it all was: the grinding machinery of history and the tragic absurdity of the post-Holocaust, Cold War world. Generation after generation has looked to the Bard of Avon to mirror their lives and found him ready to oblige.

But is Shakespeare always our contemporary? Does he need to be our immediate mirror to be important, or might his distance move us as much his familiarity? What thirst in us does he slake that he remains the most-produced playwright in millennial America, and what hunger? This winter, after a year of gorging myself on new American plays, I went looking for a contemporary Shakespeare in a series of New York productions and a few films, and was surprised by what I didn't find: a time like now.

There's no theatrical law that says classics have to apply to us directly to feel alive. Mozart's Clarinet Concerto sounds like nothing else I know, but it compels me from my everyday world, and I love it for that. The same might be said for medieval religious painting or a Dickens novel. Sure, they stir recognizable emotions and cast light on our common humanity, but they also evoke worlds apart from our world. Their remove shows us who we are as if in relief. There is an unspoken convention in America, though, an expectation of the contemporary in classics, even when they aren't literally updated. In this way, most American theatre favors the strange made familiar over the familiar made strange.

We take our classics cozy. If we don't tame them into submission with tradition-period dress, literal readings, hands-off staging—we domesticate them, by making them knowable and insisting that we relate. The impulse to modernize has always been a response to museum Shakespeare. Orson Welles did it at the Mercury Theatre in the 1930s; John Houseman did it at the American Shakespeare Festival Theatre in the '50s. Everybody did it in the '60s and '70s. Now we have two dominant strains of Shakespeare production in the U.S.: the respectful—Anglo-imitating, text-worshipping—and the relevant. At heart these approaches want the same thing, to make us feel at home with William.

Would we expect such sympathy from Ben Jonson, Shakespeare's contemporary? Do we find ourselves mirrored everywhere in Homer or Dante, Lope de Vega or Gertrude Stein? Does the presumption of pertinence hold for Kabuki, Restoration comedy, and bedroom farce? Some kind of "Bardolatry," as George Bernard Shaw called it, makes us show our stripes. Specifically, American theatre is marked by belief in realism (and so we look to Shakespeare for a picture of our world) and universalism (a mixture of faith in art's ability to cross every boundary and the desire to make everyone over in our own image).

Al Pacino's idiosyncratic documentary, *Looking for Richard*, plays out Pacino's career-long obsession with Shakespeare's Richard III. (I hesitate to italicize that name, because it's never clear whether the actor is obsessed with the play or the part, which he's played several times.) The documentary flips back and forth between rehearsals, location scoutings, full-dress performance, interviews with scholars, solo rants on the Shakespearean mysteries, and heated debates between Pacino and his documentarian buddies. All told, the movie compounds like a Talmudic text of *Richard*: interpretation piles on interpretation, scenes break off for commentary, meanings get teased from words, story gets disassembled and structure anatomized. Pacino gives us *Richard* and the acting of *Richard*, academic anecdote and actorly investigation. Finally, the film's prismatic method confirms the play's imperviousness. We need to interpret and comment, to illustrate and explicate, it seems to be saying, because this world of century-old civil war, heroic evil and emblematic deformity is so damn foreign.

The actors are recognizable, though, especially movie stars Winona Ryder, Alec Baldwin, Kevin Spacey, and Pacino himself, the implied seeker of the film's title. The camera, too, can take us places we've been before: the streets of New York City, for instance, on which Pacino and chums solicit passersby for thoughts on the Bard of Avon. Nearly everyone thinks he's great, of course, and many of them can quote something or other, though hardly anyone, including the filmmakers, can get the story of *Richard III* straight.

And no wonder. They don't get much knottier than this one. A "bottled spider" of a Duke (Gloucester) ascends to the throne of England through seduction (of a lady whose father and husband he's killed), political murder (including his brothers', nephews', and wife's), and intrigue (among barely distinguishable nobles with shifting alliances and multiple names). Having risen by means of terror and deceit, he's left alone with the crown he snatched and with his ungodly deformities—withered arm, humped back, gimp leg—a superhuman monster of power. His famous final gambit—hawking the kingdom he stole for a horse to get away on—demonstrates that no one can escape becoming the mincemeat Fortune makes of us all, great and small (except perhaps Shakespeare).

America had its up-to-the-minute *Richard* when, two decades ago, the king was reimagined as president, a different, but likewise tricky, Dick. But now, with the Cold War ended, Shakespeare's grand theme of the tragic inevitability of history seems to have been momentarily contradicted by events. Might America's naive belief in the possibility of change and progress prove true? Directing the play in repertory with *Richard II* at Manhattan's Theatre for a New Audience, Ron Daniels eschews any kind of direct analogy, even as he seeks connection to the play through its politics. In Daniels's production, these are the politics of a morally ruined land, in which Richard of Gloucester, played with zippy relish by Christopher McCann, capers toward his end, unfettered by conscience or moral restraint. Equally nimble of mind, tongue, and affect, he rollicks about, tugging his leather-braced knee with a chain on his withered arm, and loving up the audience with piping voice and the seductive glint of a sweet, nihilistic fool. He delights in other people's deaths, including his brothers', whose absences "will leave the world for me to bustle in!"

This comic nihilism suits our century, and in this way Daniels's interpretation bears the stamp of Kott. But Daniels, a Brazilian-born artist who's enjoyed long residencies with the Royal Shakespeare Company, Yale Repertory Theatre, and the American Repertory Theatre, avoids specific references. Constance Hoffman's costumes, for example—including trench coats, aviator scarves and Eton fashions for the young princes—point toward World War I. But the cast also wears armor and travels through a set, designed by Neil Patel, that alludes to the Renaissance, early industrial modernism, and today. Hoffman and Patel flirt with, but ultimately resist, both Pomo motley and period realism.

Like many of our better directors, Daniels struggles to blend the respectful with the relevant, walking the line between conventionality on one side and reductionism on the other. The creative energy in his production is directed toward the text and, almost, averted from the world in which we encounter it. It's as if the question "Why do this play now?" were answered with, "Because it's endlessly fascinating!" On one hand, this makes for a production both graceful and humble, a carefully orchestrated telling of the story. When there's juice, it comes from the performers, especially the electric Pamela Payton-Wright as the prophetic Queen Margaret, and, in a mostly comic vein, McCann. By staying trained on the play in this way, Daniels runs counter to the kind of reference-translating that American directors often exercise with Shakespeare. What he gains is a loving, if slightly aloof, appreciation of the play's workings, and what he loses are the sparks that fly when worlds—the world of the play and the world of the audience—collide. Change the audience—replace the Friday-night middle-aged theatregoers and young professionals with urban high-schoolers—and the production might make a bigger noise. What for me reads as political history could for a 17-year-old spell power play, ruthlessness, and a kind of life-and-death jockeying for control that hits home. Nevertheless, Daniels's deepest attentions are literary, as is evident in his pairing of *Richard II* with its historical antecedent (though later-written), *Richard III*. This duet is not as natural as it sounds. Four kings and nearly a century stand between them.

Together they celebrate the possibilities of repertory: bounce two related works off each other, night after night, and see what you find. And these productions find a lot. Notably, they uncover an arc of movement from the ceremonial clarity of Richard II's reign to the wasteland bestiality of the later Richard's England, which will, fortunately for England, mark the end of decades-long national civil strife. *Richard II* and *Richard III* are mirror opposites: the former begins civil war, the latter ends it. *Richard II* graphs a fall from power that is simultaneously—for Richard himself—a moral ascent, as the uncrowned king grows in perception and spirit, even as his "gross flesh sinks downward"; Richard III's rise is, by contrast, moral decline, for which he pays with paranoia, isolation, and death.

Richard II begins in a time of monarchical order and ends in a world of usurpation and ambivalence. Daniels establishes this order with great ceremony, beneath a monumental stained glass window that—until it's torn out for *Richard III*—appears to be a part of St. Clement's Church, where Theatre for a New Audience performs. The music is stately, majestic, religious in tone. Candles glow from alcoves in the upstage walls. The court, dressed in ties, ascots, vests and long overcoats recalling Edwardian England, knows its place, and, so, everyone awaits the king, endures his pronouncements, speaks when spoken to. This Richard, the king, was born into the royal, commanding "We, "as in, "We will descend and fold him in our arms." Before us parades the strange pageant of royalty.

But backstage, the king is a lost boy, simpering and prone to flattery, whiny and dissolute. (Oddly, we hear of Richard's moral bankruptcy but hardly ever see it acted out.) Having known kingship from an early age, he has yet to learn about manhood, and so, his private behavior ruins his public reputation. Metaphorically at least, he deposes himself. Literally, he is overthrown by a cousin he wronged, Bolingbroke, who, forcing the crown from Richard, becomes Henry IV.

Now there's an issue for our time: how does a nation deal with a dissolute leader? It's a question that, asked at a moment when all the president's women are on daily exhibition, could hardly be more provocative. So why doesn't it provoke? Here we are, too, at a time of generational shift in leadership, with 40-year-olds as heads of state; here, too, we have a commander in chief who weakens and cheapens his public office with his backstage antics. Yet Shakespeare's unmajestic Richard remains as distant from our shrunken Bill Clinton as Hamlet is from a City College post-doc. Or this: history's most famous princess dies with her lover in a car. The world's eyes follow the faces of her young sons—one a future king—to discern the stamp of her humanity on them. So why doesn't the question of what makes a good king resonate?

In this *Richard II*, oddly, it's McCann in the role of Henry Bolingbroke that strikes the contemporary chord for me. His portrayal is distinctly chilly, almost flat. By contrast to Steven Skybell's variable Richard, Bolingbroke seems to exist only in his actions, entirely in the public sphere. Ultimately this blankness obscures his motivations and inner life, wraps this riddle of a man in enigma, until he embodies politics. If Richard is an outsized Clinton—public persona split off from his private drives—then Bolingbroke emerges as a coup-leading Reagan, merely public, no there there. Interestingly, it's this character, not the king, that anticipates the "cacodemon" Richard III. The characterless man, moved only by the dictates of ambition and political necessity, clears the path for the more ambitious, more politically expedient character of no conscience whatever.

I'm beginning to believe that Shakespeare's distance from us has partly to do with size, specifically the capacity for human suffering, desire, and self-knowledge. Harold Bloom, the great proponent of influence (and the anxiety it provokes) as a prime force in literary evolution, places Shakespeare at the center of "the Western canon" largely because of his unmatched ability to create characters who appear to be self-conscious—as if able to "overhear" themselves—and, so, capable of change. "Shakespeare surpasses all others in evincing a psychology of mutability....He not only betters all rivals but originates the depiction of self-change on the basis of self-overhearing....Shakespeare so opens his characters to multiple perspectives that they become analytical instruments for judging you." And what does Shakespeare make of us? Can there be any doubt he finds us lacking?

There's no comparison between the global reach of an American president's powers and the parochial rule of a 15th-century English king. By contrast, it's hard to imagine any recent president rising to the philosophical majesty that Richard finds in his own downfall. Usurped and imprisoned, death imminent, he enters the looking glass and compares the king he was with his beggared self. "But what e'er I be/Nor I, nor any man that but man is/With nothing shall be pleas'd, till he can be eas'd/With being nothing."

The scale of awareness, suffering, and thought are not the only matters that separate us from these Shakespearean histories; the characters of our lives pale next to the magnitude of character we're confronted with.

Skybell, who plays Richard II in Daniels's production, has the rare ability to project subtle human emotion on a classical scale. He can be every inch a king and a sniveling, fatherless boy, a ruthless self-server and naked soul, even simultaneously. Skybell's Richard is so thoroughly narcissistic that even his soaring insight carries the taint of self-indulgence. His royal presence is, likewise, so deeply embedded that you almost forgive his behind-the-scenes whining. The actor rises to a Shakespearean fullness that makes our public leaders look like mannequins. If an actor of this scope played the president, we might expect greatness. When modern presidents play themselves, we don't.

This underscores the obvious: Shakespeare's theatrical tradition is heroic, our times are not. Oddly, though, the size of Shakespeare's characters' passions, their complexity and that impression of mutability they give off, all these feel foreign, not just to certain public figures but to contemporary humanity in general, as if the gulf between an England at war with itself and an America in the full-flush of self-contentment has, in fact, altered the very makeup of a human being. Are any of us Richards and Lady Macbeths and Juliets? Are we drawn to them because they show us to ourselves, or do they inspire us by the strange, rich magnitude of their creation? Is it even sensible to expect our actors to approximate this richness?

It's easy to find fault with American film actors who, hoping to challenge themselves and venture into the most demanding waters possible, assay the great Shakespearean roles. Of course, there are, in every generation, actors able to cross these rivers, but when I think of the great Shakespearean performers (specifically the tragedians), I always think about actors I've heard tell of but never seen. Pacino's obsession with Richard is almost forgivable because his strengths as an actor— weightiness, violent power, brooding self-sufficiency—make him a candidate for the dark king. It's harder to identify supporting actors who match his size. Winona Ryder, for example, has a small emotional range and thin, contemporary sound that, in scenes where extremes of passion overthrow lives and a nation, seem merely suburban.

Film stars Alec Baldwin and Angela Bassett ventured into the "Scottish play" this winter at the New York Shakespeare Festival and received a critical trouncing for the attempt. Here, in George C. Wolfe's stripped-down production, the demand was on the actors to tap the play's naked, murderous ambitions, its nightmare guilt and fantastic retributions. But in both cases they seemed better able to connect with the physical muscularity of Macbeth and Lady Macbeth than with the roiling fury that killing unleashes within them. These two talented actors were clearly out of their depth, groping for connection. The very prose of their portrayals heightened my sense, at least, of the play's intense otherness. Macbeth is the ur-weird play, where destiny and sorcery, prophecy, and madness impregnate one another, and everything born of their couplings dies, until bodies and babies and words pile together in a bizarre imagistic bloodbath. Certainly the Macbeths would be at home in Sarajevo or Rwanda, but, reduced to the kind of psychological solipsism associated with American Method acting, it was never apparent where this particular duo was meant to live.

The most celebrated Shakespearean production of the New York season happens on the smallest scale. Its downsizing is reflected even in its title, *R & J*, instead of the fuller *Romeo and Juliet*. Beginning at the tiny Expanded Arts on the Lower East Side and then moving to a commercial Off-Broadway production in a studio space at the John Houseman Theatre on 42nd Street, *R & J* reinvents Shakespeare's tragic love story. The adaptation, by Joe Calarco, who also directs, treats *Romeo and Juliet* as a forbidden text, uncovered by four boys at a prep school where geometric principles, Bible verses and Latin conjugations (of "love") are recited in decidedly martial tones. The young men march through their lessons on a barebones, black-box set, before digging Shakespeare's play out of a box. They begin to read the play, trying on the roles, tentatively, suggestively, giddily. Soon they're plummeting headlong into the story of two households "alike in dignity," alike in hatred and repression, whose youngest children are destined to fall in love and die for it. "My love is as a fever," written across a wall, becomes the production's motto. Indeed, the play takes these lads over like a love-inspired fever dream, spiraling towards its crushing end.

Bracketed by verses from *A Midsummer Night's Dream*, *Romeo and Juliet*'s comic twin, the enactment of Shakespeare's play works like drops from Puck's "love-in-idleness" flower, setting off a collective erotic hallucination. The actors breathe together, tumble into place, move in and out of the action. Character is suggested rather than realistically portrayed—a slight stoop for the nurse, a tilt at femininity. The only scenic devices are those that can be manipulated by the actors in full view of the audience: some charcoal gray cubes and a long piece of silky red fabric that, used in stylized ways to represent blood, a ring, swords, bedsheets, and the distance to a balcony, excites like a fetish.

Shakespeare's play provides the story while the main event—or subtextual event—is the secret, shared discovery of erotic feeling through enacting Shakespeare's play. The prep-school uniforms are always within reach; the boys are always boys. This realistic surround releases the production from the demands of realism in the acting out of Romeo and Juliet, by whose story they get increasingly consumed. Calarco and his energetic company bring out the taboo, first-time feel of the relationship between Romeo (Greg Shamie) and Juliet (Daniel J. Shore), the hurried thrill of the forbidden. Finally, the tale they tell goes something like this: four waspish, preppy men-in-training awaken sexually (homoerotically) through their discovery of the power of words (Shakespeare's) and play.

It's been observed that *Romeo and Juliet*'s frenetic eroticism masks a death wish, but here death seems almost beside the point. Dying isn't the worst possible ending; waking up is. Soon the school bells ring again, bodies assume their usual armor, and the synchronized induction of young men into the sexual, religious and intellectual values of the West kicks back into gear. Only one of the men—the actor playing Romeo—resists, cloaking himself in the red fabric, cradling the forbidden book, incanting to himself, "I dreamt a dream tonight."

This reading of *Romeo and Juliet* feels undeniably fresh, even as it blends older approaches to classics—'70s-style psychophysical improvisation, conceptual direction so prevalent in the '80s, and an up-to-the-minute emphasis on sexual and gender identity. But for all its vitality, it's more modernized than contemporary, more reinvigorated than relevant.

Baz Luhrmann's astonishing 1996 movie, *William Shakespeare's Romeo & Juliet*, creates a much hipper, more contemporary gangland analogy: a kind of hybrid of MTV, *The Godfather* and *Mad Max* movies, set in a violent, racially divided, slightly futuristic Los Angeles-like "Verona Beach." Luhrmann's film is a head-on crash of Shakespeare with popular youth culture. It confirms *Romeo* as a play that never loses its contact with our eternally adolescent, death-driven culture. The movie's images of guns, TV, souped-up cars, and graffiti-adorned city-scapes draw on every cliche of teen violence, and Luhrmann's precision about one-to-one correspondence between everything in Shakespeare's world and something in ours is sometimes inspired, always fun. *R & J*, though, neither transports us to Verona nor turns us back on ourselves; we surface in an anglo-inflected, repressive, all-boys school, reminiscent of something from an earlier time in our century. In other words, it ushers us from one distant land into a slightly less distant one. Still, the pulse can quicken in many ways and, while Luhrmann knows how to set hearts racing, *R & J* may prove the richer discovery.

Because we're steeped in Shakespeare, his work will always be familiar, recognizable. Increasingly, however, his plays seem to me like someone else's dreams, dreams about which I can be eternally curious and only momentarily connected. They may be the most extravagant, beautiful dreams ever committed to paper or placed on the stage, but, for this year at least, they remain remote. After a season of reading and seeing roughly 300 new plays, I came to these Shakespeare productions with what I felt as thirst. Maybe this yearning was spiritual, or maybe I hoped for some density of experience I was missing elsewhere. Or possibly I wanted more of what I valued in the best of these new plays—a strangeness born of unique theatrical vision—the shattering defamiliarization of things I think I know. I didn't find it, nor did I find recognition. I found in Shakespeare what everyone finds: worlds impossibly full. Seeing the plays had its satisfactions, but only reading them slaked my thirst. Confronting Shakespeare in the theatre I was left with a different kind of appetite, the almost physical hunger for stories that light into my own and release them, and another, contrary hunger for something that will batter my world and make it new.

This essay was originally published in *American Theatre*, July/August, 1998.

The Singular Hallucination of Alfred Jarry

The famous first word of Alfred Jarry's *Ubu Roi*—the French *'Merdre!'* (Shite!)—erupted naturally from the fat lips of Jarry's compelling repulsive antihero, Pa Ubu, as did all the obscene, scatological perversities that followed. This 'shite!' heard round the world was fired from the pen of a 19th-century playwright who, in the absurd violence of his dramatic creation, seemed to anticipate the century to come. Grotesque, gluttonous, amoral, and ridiculous in the extreme, Ubu has been variously described as a walking Id, the Santa Claus of the atomic age, and, as Jarry's hallucinated 'Other' made flesh. First night audiences, whether they loved or hated this fin-de-siécle Falstaff, knew they were in the presence of something shatteringly new. The poet William Butler Yeats voiced spirited support at the premiere, but afterwards found himself sad and confused. The world appeared to be plunging towards the end of creative possibilities and the beginning of only destructive ones. "What more is possible?" he asked that night in his hotel. "After us the Savage God."

Ubu Roi started life as a schoolboy lampoon, a caricature of one of Jarry's teachers, Felix Hébert. Hébert withstood generations of classroom abuse—verbal and projectile—for a range of crimes: he was boring, bourgeois, pompous, and hopelessly know-nothing about the physics he called "my science." Face to the chalkboard he looked like a grotesque insect; face out he was pig-ugly, his gut a gargantuan mound. Here was the perfect target for a *potache,* the kind of brilliant, smart-ass schoolboy that Jarry typified. Hébert had already inspired a literature of his own, rewritten in evolving student epics as Pere Hébert, PH, Pere Heb, Eb, Ebe, Ebouille, and Ebou, before Jarry arrived at the Rennes lycée in 1888 to give the world a final incarnation: Ubu.

At a time when less than three percent of France's eleven- to seventeen-year-old boys attended secondary school, Jarry's presence at the lycée was a testament to his mother's ambitions. Born to a family whose ancestry included both nobility and insanity (Alfred's grandmother and uncle had been both institutionalized), Caroline Jarry (née Quernest) abandoned her alcoholic, wool-merchant husband to his floundering business fortunes before Alfred was six. In time, she spirited her daughter and pampered son off to Rennes to enroll the boy in school. Jarry described his mother as "short and sturdy, willful and full of whimsy," and, in truth, she was highly eccentric. She valued music and books in a way that seemed improper to her pious Catholic neighbours and regularly made a public spectacle of herself, badgering her beleaguered husband in the street or going out in what Alfred later remembered as Spanish toreador clothes.

As Roger Shattuck concludes in *The Banquet Years*, the 1955 classic responsible for reviving interest in Jarry in America, Alfred inherited the best and worst of both parents, despite his contention that his "worthless joke," "good ol' boy" father had had no impact on him. From his mother, he learned about art, instability, and the spectacle of self. From his father, he inherited a predilection for hard work, dire poverty, and the drink that would help kill him.

Monsieur Hébert's new nemesis cut a figure as bizarre as the bulbous professor himself. Barely five feet tall, Jarry was thought of as a midget, a fact later accentuated by means of outlandish dress. He had, in the words of one classmate, "a forehead like a rock," a chronic hacking cough that contorted his face, and bowlegs that made him look like a "fat bird walking." In school they called him "Quasimodo."

More than a match for Hébert in eccentric appearance, Jarry was brilliant in a way that terrified his teacher (and others) and made a name for himself among uneasy parents and townspeople. According to Shattuck, Jarry and his friend Henri Morin walked the streets disguised as monks and, imitating courtiers, chased townspeople with sabers. In *Alfred Jarry: The Man with an Axe*, Nigey Lennon uses the French word *farouche* to capture Jarry's combination of "wildness, fierceness, sullenness, and shyness." Another classmate described his strange behaviour:

> When he opened the valve of his wit…it was no longer a person speaking but a machine driven by a demon. His jerky voice, metallic and nasal, his abrupt puppet-like gestures, his fixed expression, his torrential and incoherent flow of language, his grotesque or brilliant images…all astonished me, amused me, irritated me, and ended by upsetting me.

In the kind of contradiction he loved, as Jarry's badboy antics became legendary; he was honoured with scholastic prizes in French, Latin, English, German, Greek, and—Hébert's own field—physics.

Ubu became Jarry's obsession. Beginning with *Les Polonais (The Poles)*, his 1888 extracurricular collaboration with Morin, and continuing until his death in 1907 at the age of thirty-four, this incarnation of the bloated Hébert possessed him, not just as a character but as an alternative self. Jarry and Morin restaged *The Poles*, the ur-Ubu, as a marionette play several times. After entering the Paris literary world in 1891 "like a wild animal entering the ring," according to novelist Madame Rachilde, who would become his devoted friend, Jarry published a story entitled "Guignol"—after the slapstick, Punch and Judy puppet shows—featuring a vile, murderous Ubu. Early versions of *Ubu Roi* and *Ubu Cocu* were written and read among friends in the years that followed, culminating in '96 at

Aurélien Lugne-Poe's Theatre d'Art in two history-making performances of *Ubu Roi*. The years leading up to Jarry's death saw the third Ubu play, *Ubu Unchained*, published, as well as two issues of a chronicle, *Almanach Illustre du Pere Ubu*, illustrated by his friend and sometime-marionette-maker, Pierre Bonnard. A two-act version of *Ubu Roi*—with songs—designed for marionettes, under the name *Ubu sur la Butte*, appeared in print in 1906, the same year that Jarry suffered a stroke and nearly died of malnutrition exacerbated by a deterioration caused by excessive drinking, ether-inhaling, and, some say, opium use.

In Ubu himself, the object of Jarry's ongoing inventions, appetite and aggression run unchecked. This bestial, anarchic heap of a man steals, kills, and plunders when he feels like it, runs and hides when he's threatened, and stuffs his piggy face with food and drink through it all. His polymorphous perversity served Jarry's purposes in various ways. Ubu's greed, ambition, tyrannical behavior, and sheer stupidity allowed Jarry to satirize the bourgeois life he abhorred. Ubu's freedom from the restraints of good and evil was, in Jarry's hands, the artistic equivalent of an anarchist's bomb. The sick glee with which the "king" experiences his own baseness was the eternally juvenile Jarry's glee: the joy of the deranged child both hoaxing and wreaking havoc in the adult world.

Moreover, Ubu's clipped speech and robotic manner, derived from the puppets that fascinated his creator, furthered Jarry's attack on theatrical realism, what he called "the stupid concern of our modern theatre with verisimilitude." In fact, claiming that his intention was "to write a puppet play," Jarry requested that Ubu be played masked and that "a cardboard horse's head . . . would hang round his neck . . . for the only two equestrian scenes." Similarly, he asked that descriptive placards replace illusionistic scenery, "the notoriously hideous and incomprehensible objects [that] clutter up the stage." A single actor would stand in for a parade of soldiers, and forty lifesize, wicker mannequins would represent the nobles arrayed against Ubu. This frontal assault on theatrical convention, on all forms of stage representation current at the time, was also intended to bludgeon a blockhead public: "It is because the public are a mass—inert, obtuse, and passive—that they need to be shaken up from time to time so that we can tell from their bear-like grunts where they are—and also where they stand."

As intended, this theatricality proved almost as shocking as the play's opening (and ongoing) vulgarities. Firmin Gémier, the actor playing Ubu, recalled one moment of staging-inspired fury:

You remember that Pa Ubu goes to see Captain Manure, whom he is keeping prisoner. In place of the prison door, an actor stood on stage and held out his left arm. I put the key in his hand as if into a lock. I made the noise of the bolt turning, "creeeeak," and turned my arm as if I was opening the door. At that moment, the audience, doubtless finding the joke had gone on long enough, began to shout and storm: shouts broke out on every side, together with insults and volleys of booing. It surpassed everything in my experience.

Gémier wasn't alone. This aggressive theatricality, founded in confrontation, set a new standard for experiment and provocation, and, so, influenced nearly every anti-realist 20th-century artistic movement. The Dadaists were inspired by Jarry's colorful chaos; the Symbolists by Jarry's emphasis on image over action and by the rough, contradictory beauty of these images. Think, for example, of Jarry's description of the Ubu set:

> You will see doors open on fields of snow under blue skies, fireplaces furnished with clocks and swinging wide to serve as doors, and palm trees growing at the foot of a bed so that little elephants standing on bookshelves can browse on them.

The Surrealists admired Jarry's unwillingness to distinguish art from life, especially as he came more and more to embody his creation—Pa Ubu—in society. As Andre Breton explained, "Beginning with Jarry . . . the differentiation long considered necessary between art and life has been challenged, to wind up annihilated as a principle."

Similarly, Pablo Picasso imitated Jarry's gun-toting (the playwright regularly packed sidearm pistols and sometimes wore a carbine slung over his shoulder) and acknowledged Jarry's influence on Cubism. Antonin Artaud's vision of a "Theatre of Cruelty" stemmed from Jarry's work, an ancestry made concrete in 1926 when he co-founded the Theatre Alfred Jarry. By dramatizing the unutterable horror existing outside and under the life of everyday, Jarry presaged the work of so-called "Absurdists" of the mid-20th-century, especially Samuel Beckett and Eugene Ionesco, who, until his death, held the exalted title of Grand Satrap in the College de `Pataphysique, established in 1949 in honor of Jarry. Pataphysics, a pseudo-science invented by Jarry, is "the science of imaginary solutions," which examines "the laws governing exceptions, and will explain the universe supplementary to this one. . . . " Postmodern art also owes a debt to Jarry, as it fuses art and theater and—in work as diverse as the autobiographical monologues of Spalding Gray, the costumed self-portraits of Cindy Sherman, and the chameleon-like self-promotions of Madonna—explores the idea that what we call the "self" is, in fact, a performance or series of performances.

This performance of self may be Jarry's most haunting legacy, especially given the circumstances of his own life and death. More than just

writing the continuing adventures of Ubu, Jarry began to live them, until
the man himself was obscured by the character he'd created. First, he
costumed himself: he alternated his usual get-up, a bicycle racer's outfit
with a long hooded cape and tall silk hat. He often wore women's blouses
and, on one occasion, attended the opera in a canvas suit and paper shirt
illustrated, in ink, with a tie. His surroundings, most notably the
archetypically bohemian garret where he lived, likewise became stage sets.
"Our Grand Chasublerie," as he called his half-story-high apartment,
affecting Ubu's royal "We," was best described by surrealist playwright
Guillaume Apollinaire:

"Monsieur Alfred Jarry?"

"Second floor and a half."

I was somewhat puzzled by that answer from the concierge. I
climbed up to where Alfred Jarry lived—second and a half turned
out to be correct. The stories of the house had seemed too high-
ceilinged to the owner, so he had cut each of them into two. In this
way the house, which still exists, has fifteen stories, but since it is
actually no higher than the houses around it, it is but a reduction of a
skyscraper. For that matter, reductions abounded in Alfred Jarry's
abode. His second and a half was but a reduction of a story: Jarry was
quite comfortable standing up but I was taller than he, and had to
bend. The bed was but a reduction of a bed—a pallet: low beds were
the fashion, Jarry told me. The writing table was but the reduction of
a table: Jarry wrote on the floor, stretched out on his stomach. The
furnishing was but the reduction of furnishing, consisting solely of
the bed. On the wall hung the reduction of a picture. It was a portrait
of Jarry, most of which he had burned, leaving only the head, which
made him look like a certain lithograph of Balzac that I know. The
library was but the reduction of a library, to put it mildly. It consisted
of a cheap edition of Rabelais and two or three volumes of the
Bibliotheque Rose. On the mantelpiece stood a large stone phallus,
made in Japan, a gift to Jarry from Felicien Rops. This virile member,
larger than life, Jarry had kept covered with a purple velvet sheath
ever since the day when the exotic monolith had frightened a literary
lady. She had arrived breathless from climbing up to his second floor
and a half, and bewildered at finding herself in this furnitureless
'Grand Chaumìere'.

"Is it a cast?" she inquired.

"No," answered Jarry. "It's a reduction."

Jarry's behaviour, always odd, became more extreme. He fished for his neighbour's chickens from a tree and tyrannized waiters in restaurants by gorging on meals ordered, and eaten backwards, dessert first. His speech was Ubu's. He referred to himself as "we" and to the world around him by description; for example, the wind was "that which blows," his bicycle "that which rolls." Novelist André Gide writes that the fascinating Jarry showed no human characteristics, especially in "his bizarre implacable accent—no inflection or nuance and equal stress on every syllable, even the silent ones. A nutcracker, if it could talk, would do no differently. He asserted himself with the least reticence and in perfect disdain of good manners."

Creating Ubu, Jarry progressively became Ubu, until the life and the work of art became continuous. In time, the writer was known to both friends and strangers as Pa Ubu. Shattuck regards this living creation as Jarry's attempt to abandon himself totally to "the hallucinatory world of dreams," an end he abused alcohol to achieve. His intake was almost superhuman: two liters of white wine upon waking, three shots of absinthe before noon, wine and absinthe at lunch, brandy with coffee before dinner, and aperitifs and more bottles of wine during dinner. Alcohol was his "holy water," "my sacred herb." Water, on the other hand, he considered "poison, so solvent and corrosive that out of all substances it has been chosen for washing and scourings." "So it was that through drink and hallucination," Shattuck argues, "Jarry converted himself into a new person physically and mentally devoted to an artistic goal—a person in whom Jarry, the man, spent the rest of his days dying. . . . Thereafter it was as if, like Jonah, he could communicate only from inside the whale. He had found his Other, the flesh of his hallucination."

On his deathbed Jarry/Ubu made a last request. He asked for a toothpick. It was a final gesture—small, absurd, and fastidious, in stark contrast to the unruly tuberculosis that wracked him—from a man who'd made an art of the contradictory gesture. Diminutive, sensitive, and loyal by nature, Jarry had created out of himself a monstrous giant, without sensitivities or loyalties, for whom the only creative acts were acts of destruction. This low creature, Ubu, as the poet Stephane Mallarmé wrote to Jarry, "enters the repertoire of high taste and haunts me; thank you." Likewise, Pa Ubu has haunted the century he ushered in.

"Was Jarry serious?" his friend Félicien Fagus asked and answered:

Absolutely so. As serious as a child or an academic can be serious, who similarly live with absolute values. He carried logic to its natural consequence: the absurd . . . Was he serious? Not at all, since he was

254

as indifferent to the world as . . . the policeman who, witnessing a particularly atrocious butchery, concludes calmly, "That's what I call a beautiful crime."

This essay was originally published in *Ubu: +101*, ed. William Kentridge, Robert Hodgins, Deborah Bell, Johannesburg: The French Institute of South America, 1997. Adapted from program notes for the Anerican Repertory Theatre, spring 1995.

Mamet vs. Mamet

David Mamet possesses something rare and dangerous for a playwright: a voice. Shaw was proof of the dangers; he had a voice, and critics complained (still do) that, as a result, his characters had none of their own. They sounded like "rows of Shaws." Other influential playwrights have taken the opposite path: working for the kind of voicelessness the poet Keats described in Shakespeare as "negative capability." "A Poet," he wrote, "is the most unpoetical of any thing in existence; because he has no Identity—he is continually infor[ming] and filling some other Body." But Mamet has a voice so distinctive that almost anyone who has seen a single play of his can parody it or, at least, get the joke, whether it's the *New Yorker* cartoon that depicts the monosyllabic conversation on "Late Night With David Mamet" or the one about the Times Square beggar, who chastised by a Bard-spouting passerby to be "neither a borrower nor a lender," quotes Mamet back at him, in just two words, second word "you."

At his best, Mamet sets up, via this voice, a crammed-full linguistic world, sealed off from everything but the jagged rhythms of its own fricative riffs. Within this world, Mamet's characters appear neither as puppets nor quite like individuals, but more as creatures feeding at the same language pool. At his worst, Mamet does Mamet, slipping into the kind of self-parody usually reserved for much more limited artists, spent and past their prime. When this occurs, in *Speed-the-Plow*, for instance, it becomes tempting to think of his famous voice as a pose and Mamet himself as a poseur. It's only too easy, then, to see the unexamined misogyny of his characters and their inflated macho cock-surety in the poker-playing, cigar-sucking, con-loving, Chicago-boy-turned-Vermont-woodsman of the Mamet legend. If he's posing, then maybe this playwright of voice is merely a technician, a wannabe Hemingway endowed with a good ear and a flair for simulating power play on stage.

The better Mamet, on the other hand, can be said to have ushered our theatre's naturalistic post-WWII critique of capitalism into the age of Pinter. His rigor and clarity of creation also marked an end of an era of experimental (sometimes sloppy, sometimes exciting) playwriting in America and reinvigorated American stage dialogue with a fresh new idiom. Even his characters seemed new. Whereas many playwrights of the '60s and early '70s experimented with fluid characters who transformed before our eyes, Mamet's creations have always been essentially fixed beings, defined by their actions, limited by their native tongue.

Mamet's recent efforts—*Oleanna, The Cryptogram* and his adaptation/staging of J. B. Priestley's *Dangerous Corners*—show his play-writing talents reconfirming themselves, not exactly stretching, but honing, doing more with less. Unfortunately, Mamet the playwright seems lately to be in the grip of Mamet the director and Mamet the theorist, whose reductive thinking has the opposite effect: that of making less out of more, until it appears that he has turned against himself. The plays are getting the worst of it.

Mamet the playwright knows things that Mamet the director doesn't. Specifically, he understands what may well be one true fact about the theatre: All meaningful plays are mystery plays. Whether it's a mystery of event, existence or self, whether the riddle has us looking to gods, fortune, natural selection, or human psychology for answers, theatre works when it points to something just out of grasp, some ineffable something that, however everyday our actions, guides or makes sense of us. The stage can never do more than allude to this something. It can only offer painted-up suggestions of true beauty, sideshow sleights-of-hand suggestive of actual magic.

For all the prose of his settings—Merchant Marine lakeboat, junkshop, real estate office, living room—gritty reality has never been Mamet's aim. Even his famous guttertalk, tough as gristle, is always elliptical, always grasping. In fact, a guiding problem of his whole body of work may well be to say the unsayable in such a way that it gets heard. His voice emanates from this attempt. So does his impulse to bridge mystery (the unsayable) and social reality (getting heard). Even the violence in his plays, particularly troubling when it happens between men and women, erupts out of frustration with this struggle to describe the things of this world that can't be described.

Such a struggle drives his recent writings, *Oleanna* and *The Cryptogram*, as much as the plays before them. Now, though, even as he displays a greater mastery of his craft, his mind seems more closed, his thinking more fixed. In *Oleanna* the master playwright dukes it out with his lesser self (who, at premiere time, happened also to be in the director's chair). In *Cryptogram*, the clubfisted director (Mamet again) showed little interest in those mysteries his own play reached for. The flailings of language are still the same, only the diction has evolved—from working-class vernacular to educated, middle-class groping. John, the college professor in *Oleanna* whose private conferences with a potentially failing student lead to the destruction of his career, shares the same obsessive need to define and redefine for understanding's sake as, for example, the petty hoodlum Teach in *American Buffalo* from 1975. Even as you read, you can imagine the actors' rhythms—the tic of rephrasing to make clear the incommunicable:

TEACH: What are we saying here? Loyalty. (Pause.) You know how I am on this. This is great. This is admirable…This is swell…All I mean, a guy can be too loyal, Don. Don't be dense on this. What are we saying here? Business.

Or:

JOHN: I'm not a…"exploiter," and you're not a…"deranged," what? Revolutionary…, that we may, that we may, that we may have…positions, and that we may have…desires, which are in conflict, but that we're just human. (Pause) That means that sometimes we're imperfect. (Pause) Often we're in conflict… (Pause) Much of what we do, you're right, in the name of "principles" is self-serving…much of what we do is conventional.

His latest full-length play, *The Cryptogram*, marks Mamet's most sustained exploration of mystery within the realm of family and childhood. It opens on a woman and her insomniac 10-year-old son waiting with an old friend for her husband, the boy's father, to come home. When he doesn't show, and it becomes clear that the friend knew and lied about events leading up to this abandonment, the mother and son's confusion intensifies into a kind of waking dream of dislocation and lost meaning.

Throughout the play, even the most quotidian objects—a photograph, a blanket, a tea kettle—contain mysteries; severed from their significance and history, they become puzzles within the puzzle of the title. Who took this picture, if we're all in it? When did the blanket tear? Does the misfortune of a broken teapot portend greater misfortune? There's no sum of the parts. Each piece must be added on to another before any whole can be glimpsed. "So I'll ask my Dad," the boy John says, anticipating a game he hopes to play on a camping trip with his father, scheduled for the next day. "First thing, you tell me the name of an *object*. Or a *collection* of things…you know what I mean. *A view…*"

Similarly, the first section of *Oleanna* makes language as the inadequate conveyer of meaning—an idea that has always driven Mamet's works—the subject. By play's end, though, that idea has given way to another, smaller one. The result, coming as it did on the heels of *Speed-the-Plow*, Mamet's most predictably mannered full-length play, signaled a developing tendency towards self-sabotage. In the two-person *Oleanna*, John, a committed if abstracted pedant, about to celebrate his imminent tenure by buying a new house, finds himself holding an unscheduled conference with a (to all appearances) quite troubled student. Carol is a strange bird of a young woman, intense and intent on learning but so grounded by her own inadequacies that she is rendered nearly inarticulate. She requires definitions of much of what John says, claims to have read his book without understanding, and displays copious notes from class, none of which make sense to her. It is, I think, a brilliant scene, probably one of Mamet's best, an encounter by two limited, inexplicably damaged people trapped in mutually exclusive languages.

But in the next scene, Mamet trades the existential situation he has established for a polemical one and so begins a process of dramatic self-destruction. John and Carol meet a second time. Some weeks have passed and his tenure (and the domestic security that comes with it) is now threatened by a report she has filed (with the encouragement of an unspecified "group") accusing him of sexism, elitism, and, essentially, harassment (with the suggestion of racism thrown in). He wants to talk through her accusations—maybe talk her out of them. She responds, not as the paranoid, shrinking creature of the first encounter, but as something of a powerhouse, confrontative, debate ready.

> CAROL: You confess. You love the Power. To deviate. To invent, to transgress...to transgress whatever norms have been established for us. And you think it's charming to "question" in yourself this taste to mock and destroy. But you should question it. Professor. And you pick those things which you feel advance you: publication, tenure, and the steps to get them you call "harmless rituals." And you perform those steps. Although you say it is hypocrisy. But to the aspirations of your students. Of hardworking students, who come here, who slave to come here—you have no idea what it cost me to come to this school—you mock us. [...] But I tell you. I tell you. That you are vile. And that you are exploitative. And if you possess one ounce of that inner honesty you describe in your book, you can look in yourself and see those things that I see. And you can find revulsion equal to my own.

Miraculously, she has found her tongue and, in the process, revealed herself as a shrill, feminist harpy from hell, out to unseat John's cushy white ass. Mamet would have us believe that all this haltering twenty-year-old needed was a few weeks initiation with a feminist consciousness-raising group to become CAROLITH: She-Who-Swallows-Smart-Middle-Aged-Men.

What starts as a play about inadequate language becomes one about politically correct language. By their improbable third encounter, he's all but out of a job and she, having charged him with attempted rape (he tries to hold her in his office at the end of scene two), shows up with the motive of blackmailing him into pursuing her group's political agenda on campus, which means banning certain books, including his own, from the classroom. Now we're out of the realm of language at all, into the realm of political oppression. *Oleanna* is Mamet's *The Crucible*; only, unlike Arthur Miller, he believes in actual witches (with a capital B).

The problem isn't Mamet's choice of subject. It's his agenda. He holds his superior creation in thrall to his idea about such things. He conjures an interesting character, and then takes her hostage. He gives her simplistic political motives and makes her an evil puppet. Worse, he deflates the power of his own situation by turning it into a politicized game of cat-and-mouse to make his point about the wall people like her force people like him up against. In a sense, Mamet destroys this play by loading the dice, by replacing mystery with intrigue.

Thrall to a fixed idea plagues Mamet as a director, too, especially of actors. He's articulated this idea as an acting teacher and essayist and, apparently, relies on it in rehearsal. Simply stated the idea is this: actors serve the playwright's story. Story in production boils down to throughline—the action of the play and, from moment to moment, the actions of the characters (in other words, what they try to do to or get from each other). Action equals meaning, he insists, and, since who we are is determined entirely by what we do, action equals character. Everything else—feelings, particular or characteristic behavior, sociopolitical context—is either mere idiosyncrasy, implicit in the text, or unplayable. He plucks his notion of character from Aristotle and his concept of throughline from Stanislavsky, and then boils away their surrounding observations. In his essay "Realism," as elsewhere, he gets quite prescriptive: "The acting, the design, the direction should all consist only of that bare minimum necessary to put forward the action." Though he's engaged in a necessary struggle against Actor's Studio indulgence and introspection, this "only" reveals Mamet's passion and dogmatism.

The bare minimum has served Mamet the playwright. He reduces dialogue to dense stock and strips settings and stage directions to essence. Clearly, his minimalist ideas of acting and directing are integral to his writing aesthetic. In fact, they seem designed to deemphasize the actor's contribution. As a stage director, though, he's either too limiting or not good enough to carry out his own theories. His productions sound like writing—sheer words exploding in air. The crackle of dialogue is the main event. Beyond that, he shuns inner life, subtextual thought, or psychological individualism and offers little in their place. There's rarely anything suggestive or ambiguous about a Mamet staging. The mysteries he reaches for as a writer are swept aside by the "practical" certainty of his system.

In his direction of *Oleanna*, this rigid approach to production reinforced the play's reductivism. Other directors have worked to explore and heighten Carol's unspoken motives or even the dynamics of attraction and repulsion between teacher and student. Mamet ruthlessly refused to consider anything but words (as spoken) and verbs (as enacted). It wasn't until I read the play that I saw how exceptional the first scene is. In Mamet's Off Broadway production it played like a hyped-up lecture-demonstration, emphatic and clipped as an army drill.

The damage done to *The Cryptogram* seemed greater to me, because it's a finer, more elusive play. I'd read it in advance of seeing the premiere at the American Repertory Theatre in Cambridge, and had been more excited by it than any earlier Mamet play. The production took place on a horizontal strip of stage beneath a staircase up to unseen bed- and attic rooms. The flatness of area restricted the actors and emphasized an emotional flatness throughout. As the mother, Felicity Huffman, the most compelling of Mamet's regular actresses, and her director seemed hell-bent on a reading that emphasized the frigidity of the character. The confused, angry, intelligent, trapped woman of the script lost the stage to the cold, narcissistic mother and unfeeling friend. Mamet has sometimes been accused of woman-hate, and these readings of his own character (along with his portrait of Carol in *Oleanna*) support the claim.

The boy was played by a young actor named Shelton Dane who, in spite of obvious talent and discipline, delivered his lines with a coached automation. Here was a strangely personal work rendered monotonal, like painful memories recalled without affect. It might have made an arresting radio play: language heightened, intensity telegraphed, ambiguity extracted, as if anything uncontrolled might prompt listeners (which is essentially what audience members became) to pop the radio off.

Priestley's *Dangerous Corners* is essentially an upper-crust British whodunit, played out among a chic clique of friends of the dead man. The evening builds through a series of maniacally intricate revelations about stolen money, motives for the man's suicide (or murder?!?), and who loves whom. These "intricacies of the human heart" stand in opposition to the hollowness of the lives involved. "Nothing happens here inside," one character explains. "That's the cruel thing. Nothing happens." Mamet, characteristically, showed more interest in the nothing than the heart. Whereas *The Cryptogram* had been scenically flattened—shut in—the Atlantic Theatre Company's stage in the Chelsea section of Manhattan had been opened to the theatre walls to create a latticed summer veranda, a tiered platform for chilling, late-night revelation.

The scenic openness and attention to the public nature of these revelations among friends, who turn out to know very little about each other's private doings, spotlight Mamet's interests and his deficiencies. The production was a fun spin, light and speedy. It stayed fervently away from questions of class and custom, psychology, and even given circumstances (for example, the characters drank all night without noticeable effect on behavior or mood). Private doings were noted, private selves ignored. In fact, each new discovery provoked a group stare outward, as if giving spectators a moment to digest while the characters marked time. Further, the public event never included that invisible group dynamic so fascinating in ensemble situations: the movement of human beings to and from each other. The only invisible thing was information, which soon would come out. The spectre of Stephen Daldrey's chaotic, atmospheric, almost apocalyptic production of Priestley's *An Inspector Calls* the previous season made Mamet's approach feel even spindlier.

Like others before him, notably Brecht, Mamet has never seemed content to be merely a playwright, but has set up shop as a "man of the theatre." But Brecht was, by all accounts, an exceptional director and, most agree, an important theorist. Mamet's writing about the theatre comprises the fuzziest of his essays, but also his most passionate and heartfelt. Beyond his writing, he's an artist who attracts other artists to him. In this way, he functions as a kind of Woody Allen or, more precisely, John Cassavettes of our theatre. He keeps, within his gravitational pull, a coherent orbit of actors, directors, and designers, many of whom have moved with him since the '70s, from Chicago's St. Nicholas and Goodman theatres to Lincoln Center and Broadway. At present, Mamet and his fellow travelers occupy a unique niche of the art that straddles the regional theatre—specifically, the A.R.T.—commercial Off Broadway, nonprofit Off Off Broadway—especially, the Atlantic—and now Hollywood. The persistent loyalty of this cadre of artists is nothing short of miraculous in a theatre that often seems founded on disposability and forgetfulness; moreover, it affirms the loyalty that is the ethical center of Mamet's plays.

On the flip side, though, there has always been something about Mamet's followers (especially his students and former students) that borders on the insular and cultish, a sort of "David speaks the truth; David is the truth" adoration that has tailed him from Chicago. Add to this the unquestioning Great American Playwright status the critical establishment has bestowed on him and you have the unfortunate makings of an artistic prophet. In the end, the prophecy contains equal parts of metaphysical longing and bullheaded dogma—a mixture at odds with itself.

At the opening night party for *The Cryptogram*, I spoke to no fewer than three established directors about their desire to direct the play we'd just seen. Of course, this is the director's party game, but that night they were right. Mamet had missed his own play, as he had with *Oleanna*. They murmured their criticisms as if making final, whispery plans before a coup d'état. So they hovered on the fringes, munching hors d'oeuvres and drinking wine, waiting to descend on the carcass of a new play. Unlike vultures, however, and unlike Mamet himself, their descent would demand that flesh be added to these fine-fitting bones.

This essay was originally published in *American Theatre*, July/August, 1996.

Stealing Beauty: The Plays of Charles L. Mee

Writers find their voices, one theory goes, by discovering in themselves a secret outlaw. Released, this rebel, bandit, renegade rips across a terrain sealed off to the civilized self, plundering as it goes, behaving with the most extraordinary, unruly freedom. Playwright-historian Charles L. Mee's secret outlaw must be some kind of Robin Hood, stealing cultural riches from just about everywhere, and then giving away the spoils to whichever poor artistic souls want them.

Consider the acts of appropriation Mee has performed in recent months: in March, Dance Theatre Workshop audiences saw a Butoh dance/theatre piece created in collaboration with performer Dawn Saito and jazz composer Myra Melford based on *The Pillow Book of Sei Shonagon*, written by a 10th-century Japanese courtesan. "I've stolen stuff from this book for years," Mee says of these "journals filled with exquisite observations about life, court, nature, tea, style, clothing—everything." To these loving details of everyday life, he added texts from Hiroshima survivors and from Saito's own dreams, which is where he got the title, *My House Was Collapsing Toward One Side*. For *Chiang Kai Chek*, which premiered this spring at Arizona's Institute for Advanced Studies in the Arts, Mee lifted texts from ancient Chinese poets and philosophers, biologists and zoologists, and from CIA manuals on advanced torture techniques. Opening June 16, *The Trojan Women: A Love Story*, the third Mee creation mounted by New York's site-specific En Garde Arts, is really two pirated, disassembled plays; "a diptych" is how Mee describes it/them. The first is rooted from Euripides's rubble of postwar-Troy tragedy and the second from *Les Troyens*, Berlioz's operatic version of the Dido and Aeneas myth. Mee not only pilfers the plays; he sacks them, so *Trojan Women*—like Mee's earlier *Oreste*—becomes a dramatic ruin played out in the ruins of classical drama.

The resulting wreckage is being staged by Tina Landau in the burned-out East River Park Amphitheatre, the original home of the New York Shakespeare Festival when Joseph Papp founded it in 1956, and now a stunning example of urban decay. Situated in the middle of one of the city's beautiful neighboring parks, the graffiti-scrawled amphitheater will provide two separate settings, as if to emphasize the split versions of the acts. For Act I, the audience will view the spoils of war in a cavernous backstage room, where girders and pieces of ceiling hang from fire-scarred shell. Behind the destruction through a pair of open doors, Dido's second-act utopia can be glimpsed. When the audience moves to the amphitheater seats for part two, they'll find a pristine, whitewashed world, outfitted with fashion runways, Stairmasters, and a Jacuzzi.

Then there's the Robin Hood part: Mee's giving his plays away—free. Rarely one to demand a percentage, the advent of the internet has made unencumbered access to his work personal policy. Any potential readers, producers, directors, and actors can punch up http://panix.com/meejr, download some of all of the nine scripts there, stage them however they will, and pocket the proceeds. If they want to pay the playwright, that's fine; if not, that's all right too.

Mee assumes that others will rework the scripts, but in case they feel shy about treating him like a dead playwright, he's setting up an internet home page, where his recent Greek plays will appear chopped up and reconfigured, encouraging vandalism by example. This "copyright is wrong" stance might seem like posturing in an artist less engaged in dissolving borders between public and private property, cultural and individual creation. For Mee, however, politics, economics, and art, process, product, and distribution can't be easily separated. "Royalty" is out of place in democratic Sherwood Forest.

"I'd like to do my small part for subverting capitalism and property," Mee explains, pausing midsentence to laugh at his rhetorical humility. "I'm attracted to the idea of things being owned in common," he continues. "The culture and individuals together author a work. So there's something inherently wrong for an individual to rip off the culture and declare ownership." Mee's passion remains understated, tempered by an adamant refusal to lay down moral standards for others. "I don't know that everyone can or should do this. This is an easy moral position for me to take since I have a job," he says, referring to his position as editor in chief at Rebus, Inc, the publishing house where he's currently collaborating on the creation of an encyclopedic medical site on the Internet. "I'm not trying to prescribe. But to me it feels true: the culture is where stuff comes from. I believe in giving it back."

Watching Mee from across the table, there's little to suggest the outlaw. In fact, with his thin, well-carved face and taut upper body, he looks like a runner. You can still see the Midwest of his suburban Chicago youth in his straightforward good looks, and you can hear Harvard, not in his dialect, but in the self-possession of his words, in his learning and quiet confidence. He appears to be at least a decade younger than his 57 years.

When he stands, though, the runner image crumbles. He thrusts one hand through the cuff of a red-painted metal crutch, while the other hand grabs a cane. The damage left by childhood polio makes walking beside him feel like being in the presence of two men with diametrical histories: one strong, privileged, and secure; the other wracked.

Reading and seeing his body of work has the same effect. There is the helpful accessibility of his dozen or so books of political history—which include *Playing God, Rembrandt's Portrait,* or *Meeting at Potsdam*—as if they were written to nudge Book-of-the-Month-Club readers into an unaccustomed density of ideas. Then there are the plays: hallucinatory collages—styled after Max Ernst's Fatagaga collages—assembled from civilization's leftovers, the scraps remaining after cataclysm. Mee's dramatic works are wrecks-in-progress: midair collisions of already exploited ideas, codes of behavior, historical and mythical characters, sexual practices, political dogma, acts of violence, media clichés, and, inevitably, other plays.

"There was this architectural critic at Yale—Vincent Scully—who said that architects basically basically design buildings as a reflection of the structure of their own bodies. I write plays that way. What feels good to me is a play that's broken, awkward, raw, unfinished, fucked-up, because I had polio when I was 15 and this is how it feels inside my skin. That's how the world feels to me."

The lyricism of Mee's language and the clarity of his mind war with the sick shit of his obsessions—torture, violent sexuality, domination, and destruction. Personally I find sections of Mee's plays thrillingly beautiful, and others—his listlike descriptions of sexual violence and torture, for example—more disgusting than any theater work I know. These provoke in me a kind of gut-jerk Puritanism. Mee, of course, is happy to hear it. He even shares the feeling. "If it doesn't make me uncomfortable or sick, then I feel it's a failure of character, that I couldn't bear it, that I couldn't go there."

By pushing himself, he believes he can force the threshold of an American innocence, whose preservation Mee considers "a remarkable historical feat." "In certain very small and limited ways, my life has been horrific," he explains. Moving fluidly from the private realm to the public, he adds, "Certainly, the life of our times for many people has been horrific—most of us are unable to go there. Part of the function of my work is to go there. You can't get civilized until you get there."

Getting civilized is at the heart of Mee's historic/theatrical vision. It's the goal that gives his plays the innuendo of a third act, in which our humanity is clearer, more hopeful—there's work to be done. Partly this aim means bringing the unseen complexities of life to light, as he did in the arresting *Vienna/Lusthaus*, created with Martha Clarke, which illuminated an unconscious landscape of sexuality, death, and destruction in fin-de-siècle Austria. It also means contributing to what art historian H.W. Janson describes as the increasing inclusiveness of human history. *Another Person Is a Foreign Country*, Mee's 1991 collaboration with Anne Bogart for En Garde Arts, might be the American theater's most radical attempt at such inclusiveness. The cast—from whom Mee culled personal stories—included people with Down's Syndrome, dwarves, blind singers, a deaf actor, musicians recently released from a mental hospital, and a transvestite. In contrast to the intricate intimacies or *Vienna/Lusthaus*, this sweeping outdoor pageant, performed in the courtyard of an abandoned nursing home with a history of abuses, made public spectacle of the forgotten and ignored, establishing society's marginalized people—among whom Mee feels a sense of belonging—center stage.

Getting civilized also entails bearing witness to the gaping destructiveness of the Western world. This may be what attracts him to figures like Hecuba, the last standing matriarch of Troy, or to Electra and Orestes, those shattered inheritors of the cursed House of Atreus. Certainly, it explains his attraction to Euripides, the unflinching realist with whom he has kept company for the past few years. Mee has set himself the task—which, with *Orestes* and *Trojan Women: A Love Story*, is two thirds finished—of rewriting the *Orestia*, not as Aeschylus wrote it, but according to Euripides. The final piece of this trilogy, based on *Iphigenia in Aulis*, will not, in Mee's words, "return the world to a secure patriarchal civilization," as it does in Aeschylus, but rather leave "the ruins of the old civilization open to a remaking in a new way."

Remake may be the operative verb in Mee's lexicon, both in his writing and in the hands-off, live-playwright-as-a-dead-one attitude that Mee hopes will let directors be as "free in their work as I was in mine." Little wonder, then, that America's most inventive directors—Clarke, Bogart, Robert Woodruff—have chosen his words to build their own worlds upon. As a citizen and activist, he's likewise bent on remaking the culture. He sits on the board of the pioneering Urban Institution in Washington and recently returned from the Aspen Institutes center in Berlin, where he presented the opening address to distinguished representatives of the European community, who were gathered to consider the 50-year lessons of Europe's post-war union on the verge of its new unification.

Mee has also remade himself as a writer, for at least the second time. In the early sixties, he threw over playwriting for twenty years, during which he wrote his history books. Now, having reentered the theater in the mid eighties, he's reversing the past. "I think I've stopped writing the political history. Over the years I've felt increasingly constrained by the rules of the game, by the sense of objectivity that's required, of marshaling evidence, applying reason, and assessing outcomes in a way that doesn't feel true to me." In his Dada-inspired theatrics, by contrast, "I can make up my own rules. By appropriating and throwing chunks of stuff into a frame, you declare instantly that a new set of rules will be required to create relationships between things."

What the new rules might be, he's not sure. He's clear, though, about his goal: "A broader sense of what it is to be human." This clarity of purpose running through his life and art gives Mee, I find, a compelling

268

integrity. Of course, *integrity* is a strange word for someone with such disparate selves: civilized thinker and outlaw, nineteenth-century mechanist historian and post-World War I radical artiste, healthy man in a hobbled body. Strange, too, for a man so devoted to destruction.

This article was originally published in The Village Voice, June 25, 1996, and is reprinted with the paper's permission.

Epic-Cure: History That Heals

> They've all gone to look for America.
> —Paul Simon

History is back. Playwrights are bringing it back, urging the theatre from its obsession with the self and family to an investigation of the nation and its legacy. Even the names ring out with a sense of moment and place, regional or national rooting: *The America Play; The Kentucky Cycle; Twilight: Los Angeles, 1992; Angels in America.* The "Me" decades are skidding to a halt before the approaching millennium, while such playwrights as Suzan-Lori Parks, Robert Schenkkan, Anna Deavere Smith, and Tony Kushner begin reexploring the "We," that odd congregation of "others" called America.

Each of these recent works paints our time as diseased, uncertain. Each probes the racial, ethnic, and sexual gulfs so visible from the precipice of century's end. Each offers a tentative, suggestive, inconclusive vision of healing and redemption—new ways of seeing a land that, "although battered and bruised," as Schenkkan says of the Appalachian hills where his *Kentucky Cycle* is set, "still remembers." Kushner's *Angels* takes place primarily in the near-present and *Twilight,* Smith's one-woman choral epic, lodges us firmly in the after-burn of the 1992 L.A. riots; still, all these plays shuttle us, at least by allusion, through generations of struggle: slaveries, deaths, civil war, civil rights, immigration, new frontiers.

These plays make theatrical history, too. They remove us from a recent time when the mainstream American stage was said to have no politics, no memory, and no scope. The small-cast, one-set, cheap-to-produce, American domestic drama that's been our staple for the past decade or more looks even punier next to the new epic: the great, groping, revisionist, American history play.

Out with the living room. In with what Parks dubs the "Great Hole of History" and its pun-implied twin, the Great Whole. An African American in her early thirties, Parks has the linguistic audacity to entitle her work *The America Play,* a mockingly exclusive moniker, calling attention to itself as the single work of its kind, the single history as told by the marginalized—the *other* as the *only.* Kushner has his own kind of post-domestic-naturalism audacity: for seven hours, his "fantasia" spans our country and the heavens above, Angelic principalities to America—gay America, straight America, Jewish, Mormon, African, you-name-it America. Unrelated lives interpenetrate; Brooklyn becomes Antarctica; the souls of the dead link up to repair the ozone. The freedom of his imagination makes anything seem possible, even hope.

The Kentucky Cycle sweeps away the kitchen-sink unities, too, taking one plot of land and telling the seven generation, marathon-length tale of its rape, pillage, plunder, and resale. Then there's the inspired Anna Deavere Smith, theatrical America's roving reporter, speaking in the tongues of South Central L.A., giving communities their own voices, one person at a time.

These epic impulses aren't new, and that's part of their power. They're as American as Melville and apple pie. They connect the theatre of the '90s with sources as diverse as the waning "American Century." Smith's testimonial drama—one stop along a series of pieces called *On the Road: A Search for American Character*—recalls the Federal Theatre Project's Living Newspapers and documentary film; her vocal/gestural mimicry blends Brecht's epic acting with comic impersonation. *The Kentucky Cycle* plays like something out of the '30s: part Group Theatre social drama, part Paul Green-style outdoor historical pageant, and part WPA mural. Gertrude Stein's literary experiments on Americans and their making and Adrienne Kennedy's lyrical hallucinations influence *The America Play*'s verbal *jeu d'esprit* and racial phantasmagoria. Kushner, meanwhile, who feels to me more European than his contemporaries, mix-matches Brechtian stagecraft and ideology with gay camp, Caryl Churchill-like splicing of fantasy and gritty reality with Shavian excess of wit and of words. (Even *Angels*'s subtitle evokes Shaw's similarly apocalyptic *Heartbreak House*. "A Fantasia in the Russian Manner on English Themes" becomes "A Gay Fantasia on National Themes.")

Like most American theatre, such epic ambitions derive in part from Eugene O'Neill. Like him, these artists possess one thing that lends their attempts power even where they fail: reach. Prior to writing his famous autobiographical masterworks (*Long Day's Journey Into Night* and *Moon for the Misbegotten*), O'Neill embarked on (and abandoned incomplete) a vast, nine-play, historical cycle: *A Tale of Possessors, Self-Dispossessed*, a name that equally suits Schenkkan's own nine-play saga. (You might turn this around to describe August Wilson's decade-by-decade, African-American history cycle-in-the-making. Call it: *The Dispossessed, Self-repossessed*.) Unlike contemporary epicists, however, O'Neill's obsessions remained firmly planted within the four walls of the family manse. "I'm not giving a damn whether the dramatic event of each play has any significance in the growth of the country or not," he wrote a friend. "The Cycle is...the history of a family....I don't want anyone to get the idea that this Cycle is much concerned with what is usually understood by American history, for it isn't."

If, as Tennessee Williams said, O'Neill "gave birth to the American theatre and died for it," his legacy, dominant since the '40s, was this preoccupation with family. Eighties theatre shared this fixation, zooming in on family dysfunction. The epics of the '90s, by contrast, view the world wide-angle. These are shifting landscapes, roiling stews to the nouvelle theatrical cuisine of the past decade. Like Shakespeare's histories (also written at the close of a century, the 1590s), these works focus on an ailing body politic, civil blood; like the epics of Bertolt Brecht, they turn history into parable, tale telling into political dialectic. Often, as with *The America Play* and *Twilight,* they are defiantly a-psychological. Moreover, they aren't content to paint the problems; they dream of solutions, healing cures.

Parks, for instance, ends her play with a young black man, Brazil, climbing out of a huge pit, at least the size of the stage. His mother, meanwhile, paces the hole's periphery, listening for history's echoes through an ear trumpet. The image of his father—the man who dug the hole—dead and dressed like Abraham Lincoln, glares out from a TV screen. Brazil's father spends his life reenacting Lincoln's assassination in a theme park, as if all black history stems from the man who "freed the slaves"; until his final exit, Brazil spends his life digging for relics of his father's confused life.

By replaying the death of Lincoln, Parks brings American history into collision with the absence of African-American history. She broaches a new national narrative by means of puns, all self-contradictory. The Hole is the Whole; the forefather is the "faux-father," which means false and sounds like enemy; the digging is—even a generation after emancipation—"spadework" done by a family of "diggers," both of which echo racial epithets; and the black man who imitates and resembles the president is not the progenitor of the nation but its orphan or "Foundling Father." By trying to excavate a history for himself where there is none, Brazil digs his own grave—as his father had— out of which he must eventually climb.

Schenkkan's cycle is more conservative to begin with, and more narrative. He follows Shakespeare's lead by reconstructing a conflict-laden, multigenerational history of a land. As he traces a single spot in the hills from homestead to sharecropper's cabin to coal-company-owned slum to United Mine Workers headquarters to wasteland awaiting strip mining, he concurrently charts the fates of three families, two white and one black.

Horror piles upon horror; every ounce of vengeance has to be had. Having started the cycle, Schenkkan condemns himself to finish it. He conjures an act of reconciliation with the land and its ghosts: Joshua Rowen, scion of the land's original settlers, turns a shotgun on his companions to protect the recently unearthed corpse of a baby girl, 200 years old, preserved in a bunting of beaded buckskin. A recovering alcoholic, Rowen buries the child (who, unbeknownst to him, was his great-great-great aunt) and, by doing so, unites the ghosts of his ancestors in a tableau of harmony. Recovery of the land gets equated with recovery from alcoholism; the proper burial of a once-rejected half-Indian baby spells delivery from our violent heritage.

Smith, on the other hand, starts simple and lets life's complications accrue. She never manipulates, but instead lets our sympathies go where they will. She remains aloof from her characters, even as she captures them incisively. She refuses historian-speak—the surety of the single voice—opting instead for inclusive oral history. She serves up the knotty contradictions of racial and ethnic unrest and leaves us to untangle the knot. If she delivers any remedy at all, it's a talking-cure.

Her ending exemplifies a mindful, hands-off attitude. As Twilight Bey, one of the architects of the Crip/Blood gang truce, (echoing earlier words of cultural critic Homi Bhabha) she/he reminds us that the limbo-light of dusk is a valuable time, a time when, paradoxically, we can see things we miss in the light.

> I see darkness as myself.
> I see the light as knowledge and the wisdom of the
> world and
> understanding others,
> and in order for me to be a, to be a true human being
> I can't forever dwell in darkness,
> I can't forever dwell in the idea
> of just identifying with people like me...

Now is such a time, she suggests, standing against the twilight sky in Dashiki tunic and Kente cloth hat; it's an opportunity to identify with difference, to see, in the ethnic tensions of our nation, truths about the American character that more usual light obscures.

In *Angels,* difference is more ideological than ethnic, and the battle is fought, not in the streets, but in the body, mind and heart. Stasis versus progress—these are Kushner's dueling ideologies. The former is embodied by conservative Republicans, specifically in the compelling evil of Roy Cohn, and by the Angels, who want mankind to "hobble" itself, to grow roots and stand still. Progress means liberation—racial, sexual and individual liberation—and the mysterious work of building a better world. Even on a personal level, *Angels* concerns staying still or moving on, as one partner in each of the two central couples leaves, one abandoning his sick lover, the other his agoraphobic, valium-popping wife.

Kushner precisely locates the play in contemporary history, 1985-1990, the height of the Bush/Reagan era and the beginning of the restructuring of Eastern Europe. This also covers the five years "prophet" Prior Walter has lived with AIDS. Kushner scours this premillenniul moment for the real sources of disease. He keeps his perspective (and ours) flipping. His sweeping vision closes beneath the statue of an Angel, commemorating the Civil War dead. The emaciated Walter stands before it, surrounded by friends, waving at us and reminding us that the "Great Work" of life is always just beginning.

If history will guide us in this great work, though, it won't be exact. Kushner's prescription is necessarily as murky and difficult as Smith's, if more pleasantly upbeat. He combines images of disease (AIDS) and death (Civil War) with those of spiritual awakening (the Angel) and healing (her cleansing fountain). He adds a blessing for "More Life." Kushner leaves us with "a kind of painful progress. Longing for what we've left behind, and dreaming ahead." This painful progress is our hope in the time of transition, twilight, restructuring, and revision. One century dies, and a version of America dies with it. Another stands waiting to be born. We dream restlessly forward.

This essay was originally published in *American Theatre*, July/August, 1994.

I Have Often Walked…

> Enough, no more. 'Tis not so sweet now as it was before.
> —Shakespeare, *Twelfth Night*

Everything I know, needed or not, I first learned in musicals. Really. That's where I encountered Shaw, Wilder, Aleichem, Bergman, Voltaire, LaGuardia, and, via *Hair*, "Fellini, Antonioni, and Roman Polanski (all rolled into one…Claude Hooper Bukowski)." I first saw *Uncle Tom's Cabin* there, in the original, Siamese version. I built up my vocabulary from musical "libretti": foreign words—*dites-moi, wilkommen, L'Chaim*—and native ones—"sodomy" and "rape" (in a ballet!). I memorized America's original 13 colonies not for school but for the finale of *1776*. I discovered that "You've got to be taught" about prejudice; that might doesn't make right; and that Puerto Ricans and Polacks—farmers and cowboys—should be friends. (If this seems a pathetic introduction to the Western world, imagine what today's young actors and audiences associate with Victor Hugo or T.S. Eliot.) Even now, in spite of waning interest in the Broadway musical theatre, the tunes of Rodgers, Gershwin, Bernstein, Loesser, and Loewe can sound to me like calls from a lost home.

I doubt it's just me. Every night *Oklahoma!* opens somewhere in America. Six hundred times a year every year—tonight and tomorrow night and the next—a curtain goes up on Aunt Eller churning butter to the lone strains of Curley's "There's a bright golden haze on the meadow…" Or try this: In North America, close to 2,700 Rodgers and Hammerstein productions get mounted annually. If you ran them as a festival, one right after another, they'd last from midnight on Jan. 1 through the following New Year's Eve.

American theatre producers understand the power of these siren songs, and so, without a clear course for the future of the American musical, they increasingly turn to the past. Last season, for example, three major musical revivals landed on Broadway—*My Fair Lady*, *Damn Yankees*, and *Carousel*. All banked on the preconscious pull of the postwar musical, even as they struggled to look at the works afresh. Nostalgic feeling makes them resonant; their simplicity marks them as out-of-date. Are these musicals deeply superficial or surprisingly deep? Do they offer escape from reality or popular culture as high insight? Are they a window on America, like inadvertent snap-shots of our national soul?

For all their murkiness, these latest revivals make one thing clear: the classic American musical has come unmoored. It drifts between reminiscence and reinvention with no direction home. If these are theatrical classics, we're still too close to free them from their original context of postwar American celebration. If they're merely the best of a bad lot, they arrive too crammed with associations to be cast off.

The most contemptible of these revivals, *My Fair Lady*, got caught in the crossfire between Tourism and Auteurism, Concept and Greed. The production combined a TV star—Richard Chamberlain—as Professor Henry Higgins with a talented newcomer—Melissa Errico—as his creation/pupil, Eliza Doolittle, who, as everyone knows, turns from a hardworking guttersnipe to an unemployable "lady" in the course of Higgin's sadistic elocution experiment. In this instance, revisionist directorial and design vision shot it out with the producers' ambition to recapture the magic of Lerner and Loewe's long-running 1956 hit. The resulting swiss cheese offered mere hints of the surrealist restaging director Howard Davies had in mind, and only a bit more of a hint of (what everyone claims was) the charm and sparkle of the Rex Harrison/Julie Andrews gem.

Two production credits sum up the revival's schizophrenia. The first identifies Julian Holloway as Alfred P. Doolittle, the roustabout dustman-philosopher, a role originally created by Holloway's father. Holloway *fils* was terrific in the music-hall turn, deftly putting his stamp on the part while conjuring up the ghost of his rubber-faced dad. This is the traditionalist's dream casting: a new spirit that falls no farther than a foot or two from the tree.

The second credit reeks of commercial-theatre intrigue: "Scenic design based on original designs by Ralph Koltai." Koltai, an associate artist at the Royal Shakespeare Company, was responsible for a string of fascinating design ideas that, finally, had nothing to do with the rest of the production. From a looming phrenological skull in Higgin's Frankenstein-lab-like home—with nightmarish, oversized books, test tubes, gears and mega beakers—to the Magritte-esque singers suspended in the air against a blue-sky backdrop during the "Ascot Gavotte," Koltai's dream images pointed the way toward a new *My Fair Lady*—too new, obviously, for the producers, who relegated him to "based on" status. Apparently, Davies suffered the same fate, as he flew back and forth between New York and London, while producers Fran and Barry Weissler brought in doctor Tommy Tune and others to make the production look more like what people remembered.

Whatever Davies had intended to do by strange-ing up the familiar musical was undone, but not completely. As a result, the show was a half-baked thing, like a summer stock mounted by a directing school "whiz" with two weeks' rehearsal, a couple of unexamined ideas, and a choreographer (in this case Donald Saddler) who knows how the thing "should be played" (that is, how they did it in the original). Ultimately, such a revival makes the old days appear golden and reduces the present to an exercise in comparative handicapping, of the sort I overhead at the intermission: "Chamberlain is a three to Harrison's ten; this girl is maybe a five or a six to Julie Andrew's ten." "She's delightful," a woman responded. "She'll be *big*."

Carousel, by contrast, hit New York's Lincoln Center Theater from London accompanied by shouts of wild critical approval. It promised a brand new, well-acted, "dark" vision of Rodgers and Hammerstein's most lyrical masterpiece. Some of what was promised gets delivered. Lincoln Center's *Carousel* is well-acted—for a musical. It at least *looks* brand new, as Bob Crowley's magical designs invest a spare dreamscape of early 20th-century New England beauty with the ominous threat of equally American violence. And, if it never transcends the limits of its genre—the all-singing, all-dancing musical play—it certainly emphasized the dramatic over the musical, to the detriment of Rodger's score, which is often badly sung, and, at first, to the benefit of Hammerstein's book.

What initially brings the libretto to life is director Nicholas Hytner's attack. He treats *Carousel* like a dramatic play, a thing of passion and ideas, and he draws from it a dialectical tension that, revealed, seems both obvious and entirely new. This tension is between *Carousel*'s romantic lyricism and its violent domesticity, between music and prose. You can see it most clearly in Michael Hayden's Billy Bigelow, the barker who trades a footloose life for marriage to the dreamy Julie Jordan. Aware that "there's a helluva lot of stars in the sky," this drifter-turned-husband also knows that "two little people" like them "don't count at all." He's crazy in love with Julie and he beats her for tying him down. America presents Billy with a choice: be a free man and outlaw like his violent homeboy Jigger, or become respectable like Mr. Enoch Snow, the capitalist prig with a fleet of well-oiled offspring. In other words, choose self-rule, sexual abandon, isolation, and death, or community standards, comfort, familial love, and dull life. This conflict makes new sense of Billy's climactic "Soliloquy": he's stuck between speech and song.

This is right where Rodgers-the-lyrical and Hammerstein-the-prosaic are stuck. When Rodgers' melodies soar, Hammerstein keeps their feet on the ground: "If I loved you, time and again I would try to say all I want you to know…." When Hammerstein gets stuck in the mud—"This was a real nice clam bake. We're mighty glad we came"—Rodgers keeps the music stepping lightly. The tension serves them, but it also tears them apart. By the end of Act I, reality has impeded to such an extent that the play stops singing for five consecutive scenes, none of which are particularly effective here, before crashing into intermission via "Soliloquy" (on which Hayden strains badly).

By Act II the depths have been plumbed. Billy's death succumbs to Broadway sentimentality and his return from heaven is just plain goofy. The choral finale, "You'll Never Walk Alone," feels easy, tacked on. Only Sir Kenneth MacMillan's ballet between the white-trash daughter Billy left behind and a leather-vested tough who abuses her re-ignites the battle between lush lyricism and violent waste. MacMillan heightens the dance's sexual violence, brings out the Freudian resemblance between the lover and the dead father, and moves the troubled girl through a chaos or painted horses—the fanciful carousel from the Act I waltz—spent and busted-up by years.

Otherwise, Hytner establishes a structural tension in the first half that the second half can't sustain. The book won't support too much hard-hitting realism, the songs never become a score, the characters are finally too thin, and the nontraditional cast—an integration of nonacting singers and semi-singing actors—make moments either well sung or well acted, rarely both. Hytner's insightful approach shows up the flaws in the genre: It's not opera and it's not drama. It can move one way or the other, making for a fascinating tension, but it can't go as far—towards lyricism or realism—either.

Some of these problems go away when a musical refuses to take itself as seriously as *Carousel* does. That's certainly the case with *Damn Yankees*. Unlike Davies and Hytner, Jack O'Brien cares more about celebrating the conventions of the musical than breaking them. From the ballpark hawkers in the lobby to the swell costumes he saves for the curtain call, O'Brien tries not to show us what we don't know about this 1955 musical, but to epitomize what we *do* know about it.

Even if you've never seen it, you know the story. An old guy, Joe Hardy, tired of seeing his ball team lose to the unbeatable New York Yanks, sells his soul to the devil in exchange for a season as the greatest long-ball hitter ever. Getting his dream, though, means losing his "old girl," the wife he abandons every summer anyway for "the game." In the final inning, of course, Joe'll have to choose between heroism and home. But first he learns a painful, if reversible, lesson (the same lesson, incidentally, that serves as moral for Henry Higgins and Billy Bigelow): "A man doesn't know what he has until he loses it." That's it. Wifey lures hubby to the theatre with tix to a show about sports, and everyone leaves singing "You Gotta Have Heart." Meantime, middle-American values reign supreme: moderation, fidelity, honesty, good-humor, and, in case you missed it the first time, heart. Proof positive of critic John Lahr's observation that "Musicals are America's right-wing political theatre because they reinforce the dreams of the status quo."

Naturally, no one expects us to take this fluff seriously. In fact, the brilliance of musical comedies by the likes of George Abbott, Richard Adler, and Jerry Ross is in the way they create sentiment and comment on it at the same time. O'Brien sees that quality and raises it; he turns the whole evening into a valentine to the '50s, skewering the gray-flannel years and loving them to pieces at the same time. With the help of his designers and the clever choreography of Rob Marshall, the director celebrates Eisenhower's America from green stamps to soap-on-a-rope, from pastel houses made of ticky-tacky to cocktail-napkin innuendoes. Moreover, O'Brien and company celebrate the form of '50s musical comedy itself: strong, belting singers, athletic dancers, and musical numbers staged to parody the style they're written in.

Who cares if Act II almost falls apart? Everything is as it should be: zippy, cocky, flip, and dumb as a post. *Damn Yankees* is like a fun, old buddy who confirms himself by being himself.

The passage of time might sever us from these musicals enough to reveal their true worth. As of now, they feel incomplete, part old, not-quite new. Because they confirm what we know and almost forgot, they feel warm and welcoming—and for that same reason, embarrassing.

This essay was originally published in *American Theatre,* November, 1994.

The Shaw Beneath the Skin:

Bernard Shaw: The Pursuit of Power by Michael Holroyd

> Without my veneer, I am not Bernard Shaw.
> –George Bernard Shaw

"You have wakened the latent tragedy in me," George Bernard Shaw wrote to the actress Mrs. Patrick Campbell, when their love affair aborted in the fall of 1913. "I am as lonely as a God." If latent tragedy and preternatural loneliness exist in Shaw, the biographer must dig through an Everest of words and ideas to unearth them. If there is a man beneath the veneer, the portraitist must preserve the dazzling surface even as he scrapes it away.

Critics have accused Shaw-the-playwright of creating puppets where the characters should be, "rows of Shaws" to make up the cast of the longest-lived pageant of self-promotion in the past two centuries. As his own master press agent—and perhaps forefather of the modern celebrity-artist politico—Shaw even threw his voice into the mouths of his early biographers, overseeing their work, buffing up his image as polymathically perverse social wit, substituting ideas about life for life itself.

But biographer Michael Holroyd will have none of Shaw's ventriloquism. In the first two parts of his three-volume *Bernard Shaw*, Holroyd remains convinced that there is a tragic Shaw beneath the skin and that he's ruled as much by childhood traumas as by ideas. "Shaw's tragedy lay in the need to suppress," Holroyd tells us, and like all buried ghosts, Shaw's came back to haunt.

Neglect in his youth by a narcissistic and otherwise-engaged mother and a drunken cipher of a father, "Sonny," as Shaw was then called, sought refuge in music, art, theatre, and ideas about everything. G.B.S. was a self created to keep Sonny's anguish at bay. Shaw "became the author of himself," according to Holroyd, "though not in a way that might ultimately be in his best interests." From the nettle despair, the young G.B.S plucked the flower workaholism, as if continuous labor and thought could change the brutal world to a shining one. For this analyst the key is compensation—brilliance of mind to fill in the spaces love forgot.

Lovers of what critic Max Beerbohm called the "loud, rhythmic machinery" of Shaw's brain have been praising Holroyd's gargantuan achievement since the 1988 publication of the first book, *The Search for Love*. Many devoted Shavians, however, have taken time out from celebrating to express uneasiness over the psychoanalytic framework Holroyd lays out in part one and continues through the sequel, *The Pursuit of Power*, which covers the Irish-born dramatist's days from 1898-1918. Less ardent admirers—and I suspect this includes most American audiences and theatre people—will better appreciate Holroyd's line of inquiry. Who hasn't wanted *more* of Shaw, despite an already-exhausting body of work from 94-plus years of life? Who hasn't at some time left off his work as if from a vegetarian feast, overstuffed and unsatisfied? The "more" we want from this giant, though, isn't a requirement of further reading—it's something deeper, something human. Holroyd probes for, and finds, the human Shaw in the Superman clothes.

This "enough already / we want more" ambivalence to Shavian out-pouring began with his early readers and audiences and continues to present day. Every fan is a closet detractor. "You are a great force wasted," his old friend and critic William Archer writes him after reading *Man and Superman*. Debating chum G.K. Chesterton read the same play and argued, "[Shaw] has always prided himself on seeing things and men as they are. He has never really done so...." Shaw masked his serious intents in a sexless frivolity so unrelenting he provoked Virginia Woolf to describe the style of his half-dozen early one-acts as that of "a disgustingly precocious child of 2—a sad and improper spectacle to my thinking."

Once he put the 19th century behind him, G.B.S. enjoyed intermittent booms in popularity. Still, in spite of (or perhaps because of) his constant good humor and bottomless prolixity, the public appeared ever-eager to show the difficult man the door. Nowhere is this more evident than in Shaw's first burst of British acclaim, dramatically described in volume two. Renown began with the publication of *Man and Superman* in 1903, hit stride with the 1904 success of *John Bull's Other Island*, peaked with *Major Barbara*'s first performance in 1905 and again with *Pygmalion*'s in 1914 ("the climax of Shaw's career as a writer of comedies," by Holroyd's reckoning). But when the writer confronted England with his objections to World War I in the 1914 pamphlet *Common Sense about the War*, his rising career smashed on the rocks of national jingoism.

Like Sonny's "search for love," the maturing G.B.S's "pursuit of power" never achieves its end, Holroyd explains. His marriage to Charlotte remains "unconsummated," his British theatre revolution stalls, and his reach for political power falls short. In everything, Shaw's impotence grows in almost direct proportion to his fame. The Shaws' marriage is a "conspiracy of denial," and his tortured liaison with Mrs. Pat—likewise unconsummated, as I read it—turns the tide of life toward the tragic. His plays begin to find an audience but attempts to float a true repertory company producing new works fail and others to create a national theatre dissolve.

Even within the plays themselves, Shaw's heightened power lead to spiritual crises. The most pronounced occurs with the writing of *Major Barbara*. Here's Holroyd at his best, applying the novelist's skill and the critic's perception to the researcher's rigor, conjuring a Shaw whose characters get out of hand and turn against his hopes for them. The argument of Andrew Undershaft, munitions mogul, pragmatist, and servant of the war-god Mars, become too persuasive until the playwright, too, succumbs.

Likewise, Shaw's torrent of words redoubled with his increasing political impotence. His distance from the Fabian socialists—his political comrades for decades—grew into a virtual rift. His outspoken "realism" about the horrors of the "Great War"—couched in typically provocative terms, like the advice to both English and German soldiers to "SHOOT THEIR OFFICERS AND GO HOME"—isolated him almost irreparably from his countrymen. Moreover, a frustrating campaign to abolish the Lord Chamberlain's censorship powers backfired, leaving him stranded among colleagues who didn't support his stand. "The typewriter became his heartbeat," Holroyd writes. "But for the first time it seemed as if all the thought and feeling of this work was issuing nowhere. His job of creating the mind of the country had been taken away from him. "

Still, "nothing succeeds like failure," G.B.S. quipped, and his notoriety proved it true. As told by Holroyd, Shaw's life was a struggle to prove the paradox true on all levels: Shavian optimism was fueled by the energy of failure and loss. Holroyd reads the plays as Shaw's "spiritual autobiography," his attempt to reconstruct the traumas of childhood into an exuberant social revolution, to harvest diamonds from the dirt of his impotence. Holroyd makes that autobiography explicit without losing the dazzle of the Shavian veneer, the gush of ideas or the evolution of this singular man's talent and philosophy. The achievement is masterful; it reads like a wide-ranging 19th-century novel. And like a great Victorian serial, it makes us impatient for the final chapters.

This review was originally published in *American Theatre*, May, 1990.

Catching Light

Bernadette Peters

You don't need a George Seurat to know that an artist shows us things we've never seen before. This goes for playwrights or pointillist pioneers, and it goes for performers. This season Bernadette Peters played Sally Durant Plummer in *Follies,* by Stephen Sondheim and the late James Goldman. It was one of those daring, body-, mind-, and soul-committed turns we've come to expect from her.

You know the story: the first and last reunion of Follies girls, thirty years after those spectacles came to an end. Sally's life has never lived up to her glory days. She's still stuck on her first love, Ben, despite the fact that they've both been married to other people for years. Sally's despair, her consuming regret and lovesickness, is everywhere in the book and lyrics. What I'd never seen before is that this despair is a kind of madness. In Bernadette Peters' hands, Sally lived in memory and dream, agitated, sleepless, "not going left, not going right." "Am I losing my mind?" she sings, and as a result of one of the bravest performances I've ever seen in the musical theatre—we think, yes, you are losing your mind. And it's not only heartbreaking; it's new. We see the story we know anew.

Or recall her performance as Rose in *Gypsy.* What drives this quintessential stage mother? Why does she sacrifice her children to a ferocious ambition they clearly don't share? Of course, I've always understood the answer with my brain, but my heart never really got it. Then I saw Bernadette Peters and I glimpsed in light something that had only been shadow: Rose as a girl. Before the mother's ambition came the child's desire. When it's Mama Rose's turn, we see the young star she might have been. She dances. We are her mirror. "What I got in me...If I ever let it out, there wouldn't be signs big enough. There wouldn't be lights bright enough."

That Bernadette Peters would change our way of seeing was apparent from day one. On a postage-stamp stage amidst the homemade, tin-foil, Bohemian glitter of Caffé Cino in 1960s Greenwich Village, young Bernadette Peters entered the wider world as Ruby in *Dames at Sea,* and we never saw the ingénue the same way. "My name is Ruby," she said, "and I'm a dancer. I just got off the bus and I want to be in a Broadway show." Nearly twenty years later she'd wash up on the shores of Manhattan once more, this time as Emma the hat maker from London in *Song and Dance.* Over the course of 20 songs and a solo hour, she went from envying "that drive in the eyes of New York girls" to hating herself for becoming one of them. "Take that look off your face," she tells the hardened realist in the mirror, "you were better naïve."

This is the journey that Bernadette Peters leads us on again and again, in different keys, from openhearted wonder to heartbreaking disillusionment and back. She's the girl inside the woman and the woman revisiting the girl she was. They live side by side. Bernadette Peters understands, as well as any performer I know, the way our own double selves live inside us, our potential curled in wait, the shells that harden around us melted by the early dreams that refuse to die.

In this way her performances carry within them both past and present, as do so many of the roles she plays. Sally Plummer dwells in the lost dreams of young Sally Durant. Mama Rose is the woman she is *and* the girl with a dream. The beautiful young witch of *Into the Woods* bursts out of the ancient crone. In *Sunday in the Park with George*, Seurat's model Dot lives on in her own daughter, Marie, as an old woman almost a century later.

Bernadette Peters will always be our most joyful, sweet, and youthful star, and we never lose sight of that. She may be a vengeful witch or a monstrous mother, the jaded Grande Dame or an aging chorus girl on the verge of madness, but she is also always Ruby with "nothing but tap shoes in her suitcase and a prayer in her heart." Her more recent performances carry echoes of previous ones, the way mature love can be graced by the harmonics of youthful romances.

Again and again, she's served as our hero in the battle between innocence and the harsh realities of what the Witch calls, simply, "the world." "Don't you know what's out there in the world?" she sings. "Someone has to shield you from the world…"

And if these gifts of emotional daring and human insight weren't enough, she brings to the stage something just as rare: a devotion to serving the words and ideas of other artists, the commitment not to self but to character and story. Pick any song you've heard her sing, and you'll know what I mean. Hear in your mind her distinctive diction, the bright youth and vibrancy of her tone, her melodic purity and the precision of thought behind each word. She is indelible and transparent at the same time. We watch and listen to Bernadette Peters—how could we do otherwise?—but someone's always up there with her: Jule Styne, Irving Berlin, Andrew Lloyd Webber, or Sondheim. She is never alone.

The most moving tribute I've ever witnessed was Stephen Sondheim's memorial salute to Michael Bennett when the great director/choreographer died in 1987. Sondheim took the stage of the Shubert theatre and sat at the piano. He briefly described the first time he had played the song "Move On" from *Sunday in the Park* for Bennett. Bennett had listened with his back to the composer, staring out a window. When the song ended, Bennett had turned to him,

Sondheim recalled, and with tears streaming down his face, blessed this extraordinary song.

Then Sondheim sang it, this musical exhortation that has become such a signature for both its creator and for Ms. Peters. I say he sang it, but really he pounded it out. He croaked it, raw with loss, desperate with the need to keep going. Anyone who was there will remember. It was sheer emotion, horrible, beautiful grief. He banged and cried out the song inside the song, its bone and blood and nerve.

I hold this image in mind suspended alongside that of Bernadette Peters singing the same artistic anthem. Only she's singing with startling clarity and incomparable beauty. And as she sings, she is rapturous—a word that elsewhere, she has rhymed with "Isn't it funny how artists can capture us." She captures, rapturously, the same passion and drive, the same cry of the heart that the creator pounded out of his own song. She adds melody to his percussive grief; she adds precision to his naked emotion. She urges George Seurat on and, in doing so, crystallizes the contradiction of every crazy creative endeavor—the gorgeous fulfillment of art and its raw, wounded heart. If you've ever heard her, you can hear her now: "Anything you do, let it come from you—then it will be new. Give us more to see."

Adapted from a speech to New Dramatists' Spring Luncheon, 2012.

David Wheeler: In Memoriam

Life-altering teachers become voices in your head. It's the way they keep teaching you, long after you've left the classroom. They get inside your brain and set up shop, firing off questions that become your questions, etching synaptic pathways that become your trails of thought.

David Wheeler's voice in my head is a mad scientist voice, a Mr. Magoo voice. It murmurs quietly, spinning out ideas, impressions, insights with a psychoanalyst's curious cool and then Blam! "HEDDA! HEDDA GABLER!" he half-shouts, as if he's crying, "EUREKA!" or "Mr. Magoo, you've done it again!" Or he enthuses in the wild Panamanian accent of his mentor, Jose Quintero, to make a point about brother-sister love in O'Neill. That's the way David did it: You'd think you were talking to a literary soul (you were) until he startled you back into the theatre—a land of truth *and* passion, insight *and* surprise. He startled you toward discovery.

David Wheeler was a teacher—mine in the directing MFA program at Boston University in the seventies, before he switched to Harvard, where he taught until almost the end of his eighty-six-year life in January. More and always, though, he was a director. He taught like a director, an indirect director. He whispered into your ear and pushed you into the ring. He paced outside the ropes and watched your every move.

His work wasn't to pass on knowledge or impose his vision but to *unleash* you, the way he famously unleashed a generation of actors, first at the mythic Theatre Company of Boston, which he co-founded in 1963 with another fine teacher, actress/producer Naomi Thornton, and ran until it folded in '75. The actors he let loose there are legendary: Al Pacino, Dustin Hoffman, Robert DeNiro, Stockard Channing, Paul Benedict, Ralph Waite, Jon Voight, Robert Duvall (who, word has it, once punched him over a failed sound cue; David smiled back), Blythe Danner.

"His gift was his ability to move with the actor," wrote Pacino, who was, with Benedict and Waite, was one of David's lifelong floating company members. "To allow the freedom necessary for the actor to express wherever his or her gifts led them." This is how David worked with everyone, student or star: he set your freedom in motion.

Mostly unsung nationally, despite having directed Pacino in *Richard III* and David Rabe's *The Basic Training of Pavlo Hummel* on Broadway, he was a local theatre hero in New England. He directed 17 productions at Trinity Rep in Providence, RI, and his work graced practically every theatre in Boston, including, for 25 years, the

American Repertory Theatre, where he was a resident director. How in today's world can a director make happen all that he did: 80 TCB productions in 12 years? Over his lifetime: at least a dozen Pinters, 10 Becketts (I observed his *Waiting for Godot* at ART in '95 when I came to dramaturg there), three DeLillos, and four Rabes. He ate plays for breakfast. He dreamed them at night. He was never finished.

What a combination he was: trained in psychiatry and comp lit, he was uniquely actor-attentive *and* thoroughly text-attuned. He loved actors and trusted them. Well into his eighties, he'd call me to praise a new find, a brilliant actor or actress. (Recently these paeans were often about his son, Lewis, who's become a light of the Boston stage.) Then he'd ask me to send him new plays. New plays were his life-blood. At TCB he was devoted to Albee, Beckett, and Pinter, Ed Bullins, Adrienne Kennedy, and Sam Shepard when they were new. Nearly 50 years later, his final production was Suzan-Lori Parks' *Book of Grace* at Company One, new now.

Now was everything in David's theatre—the actor's moment, the electricity of relationship, the play's immediacy. He was lost in now. How else could he back into the orchestra pit while studying his actors—another Magoo trait? (He'd bound in the next day wearing a neck brace or on crutches.) How else could his work feel so alive?

David would show up in class with shopping bags full of dog-eared books. He was a lit-crit bag lady. He'd pace in his sneakers and tweeds, hands waggling or finger jabbing the air, pencil moustache adding silent movie dash to his leading man looks. Murmur. Eureka! Murmur. Eureka! Everything was investigation for him, everything was discovery. And the work was never done, even after opening, even, I like to think, after death.

This obituary was originally published in *American Theatre*, March, 2012.

Can a Solo Performer Act Alone? On Agony, Ecstasy, & Daisey…

This is a work of total subjectivity. I want you to know that from the outset. I also want you to know that I'm not tight with Mike Daisey. I mean, I've met him. He sat behind me on a plane and we chatted. I think we met briefly another time, too. Not too sure, and I don't know who could verify something like that. Of course I'm one of his 70,000 Facebook friends. (This figure may be exaggerated. The only fact-checkers I know are busy on my new book, which is a work of non-fiction. I don't want to interrupt them.) I've seen Daisey perform and think he's terrific, comparisons to Spalding Gray aside—that's just a taste thing, very subjective. I missed his recent solo show, *The Agony and the Ecstasy of Steve Jobs*, for reasons that aren't dramatic enough to include here (you know, leave the dull bits out). I wish I had seen it, especially so I'd have some credibility, writing this. Just for the record, though, I have never seen any 13-year-olds outside of the Foxconn factory in Shenzhen. I don't recall ever posing as an American businessman in China. I don't know how to spell Hexanne.

These days, I love not being Mike Daisey. That's the god's honest, subjective truth. Of course, it would have been great to have had a sold-out, extended run at the Public Theater of my one-man show, if I ever had one, and to have had a smash return engagement there. But who would want this public shaming? I mean, wow, the way Woolly's former marketing director wagged her cyber-finger and called for a boycott of the guy's work. I mean she and her staff worked their asses off to get all those "butts in seats." They "got Mike in every major news outlet in DC, and the buzz, hype, and importance of the show only grew along the way." They believed in the guy. "We believed you, Mike!" (I made that quote up.)

And cripes, to be shunned that way by the Public Theater artistic director, once that shit hit the fan with *This American Life*. I mean the artistic director didn't even mention Daisey by name, whereas a month before you'd have thought he'd personally created Daisey out of the rib of Adam. Now it's just: "We would not have called it nonfiction had we known that incidents described in the piece were fabricated. We didn't know, and the result was that our audience was misled." "Our audience was misled." Isn't that what they call the passive voice? That's abandonment. Talk to the hand, Daisey. Man, that must feel bad, third-grade-I-just-peed-myself-in-class bad. And who'd want to be slaving away over all those truth-clarifying edits and carefully worded disclaimers before my (Daisy's) encore run at Woolly Mammoth in D.C. (It's hard enough fact-checking a whole book of historical documents. Did I mention I've got a new book coming out? TCG, summer 2013. Watch for status updates on Facebook. I was going to ask Mike to put a link on his blog, but now no way. I think I should maybe de-friend him.)

I guess Daisey got what was coming to him. I mean by now we all know—I mean this approaches the status of fact—Mike Daisey BETRAYED everyone. He BETRAYED his audiences, his collaborators, the journalists, the activists, the Chinese factory workers. He even betrayed *Ira*. (In case you've been asleep in a dark forest lately, *Ira*'s that nasal radio guy from Chicago. I'm a nasal guy from Chicago, too, but I don't know him and we're not FB friends. Do you think he'd confirm my request if I friended him? Do you think he'd interview me about my book? Probably not after this Daisey mess.) Worse even than *Ira*, Daisey betrayed THE TRUTH.

You have to admit, though, he made some kick-ass radio. (I listened twice in a row fascinated, appalled, morally confused, and made sure my son and wife listened. Awesome!) But was it worth all the betrayals? Daisey betrayed the capital T Theatre for sure, and, at least the first time around, he betrayed the *This American Life* gang (MSNBC, the *Times* Op-Ed, the list goes on). Then it took him so long to apologize. I mean, so long. I raised a family of four during those on-air pauses while Ira was grilling him. (I didn't really raise a family. That was hyperbole.) First he *sort of* apologized. Then, after keeping us waiting for, what, a couple of weeks, he apologized to just about everyone on his blog. His public confession was nicely done, though the guy blogs so much that after a couple hours, you had to wade through a bull-load of posts to get to the *mea culpa* one.

The theatres really rose to the occasion, though. They've decided to check facts next time. I mean, that's heavy. (Thank god, they finally figured out what dramaturgs are good for: fact checking!) Those theatres don't do much 'splaining, as Ricky Ricardo used to say. You usually don't see this kind of out-there contrition when they discover a managing director embezzling or, even, when they caught that pedophile running a children's theatre in the Midwest. They certainly don't waste their time on "sorry" when they ignore their missions (and nonprofit status), taking all that money from commercial producers to do plays and musicals they haven't even read. But you gotta hand it to them for saying sorry this time out. I guess things are on the upswing. At least subjectively. I guess, too, it makes sense that they sort of apologized to their audiences and attacked or shunned the artist, seeing as how the audiences *pay them* and they have to *spend* six or seven percent of what they make at the box office on the artist. What a waste of funds! I hear you can get a good telemarketer for 10% of the cost of a ticket sold; why do they have to give playwrights nearly the same?

Arrggh. This gets me so confused. It's exciting and all, but my mind goes all tweezer-like with the parsing of the meaning of TRUTH and LIE. I haven't had to concentrate so hard since Bill Clinton messed up that girl's pretty dress and called into question the meaning of the word "it."

And I don't think it's over yet. I'm still in suspense. Where's the smoking gun? I keep thinking that someone or something else was BETRAYED and no one has noticed. I know this sounds stupid, but I gotta ask: did Mike Daisey act alone? For such a big betrayal he must have had accomplices, right? I mean people helped him put this piece on. They commissioned him. They encouraged the guy.

Something about this doesn't smell right, as my grandfather the butcher used to say (I made that up; my grandfather was a druggist). Like why in the first place do we think the theatre's a journalistic medium? Hasn't anybody read any plays from the last 2500 years (inexact number, but who has time to Google when you're on a roll)? I mean, what are facts to him or he to Hecuba, right? Personally, I like my theatre subjective. I like that Chekhov fellow, cranky old Albee, and—yes, he was neurotic—Williams. I liked Spalding Gray. They always make a big deal out of things, those theatre characters, because all they've got is their subjectivity. They're stuck with themselves, embedded in their ways of seeing things.

But I guess that kind of thing—the way people are—doesn't cut it anymore. Maybe that's why the people running theatres have wanted playwrights to write *about* stuff, you know, important stuff, like those rock star journalists do. Clearly it pays off. I mean, man, they're awesome, especially those guys on TV, CNN, and MSNBC. Talk about creds. Like *Ira*. Since Bush-Gore, maybe, and certainly after 9/11, everywhere you go you see journalists telling us what's what. 24/7 and even on the Internet. Talk about drama. I mean, news guys are born playwrights—like that guy Lawrence Wright, who wrote about Al-Qaeda and the towers and then took it on the road, right to the Public Theatre. Now that's theatre.

The Brits get it. Like David Hare, writing *Stuff Happens*, just as it was happening! Glad the Public had the sense to snatch him up, too, especially since nothing American playwrights are doing can be called important, at least until Daisey got the message. Arrggh. I'm bummed that he botched it. So bad for American journalists—I mean playwrights.

Wait, that's it! If we want theatre to move to the center of culture, if we want to get out of the margins, we should be like journalists! Awesome. And talk about getting butts in seats! Perfect, what with all the news junkies out there. Journalism solves the marketing problems altogether, 'cause you get *issues*. You can explain everything to ticket buyers, you can actually let them know the play is *about* something, as opposed to all those subjective or poetic or domestic or personal or quirky or whimsical or non-narrative or just plain weird imagination-y things all those MFA graduates are writing these days. And baby, we need butts in seats to pay our marketing departments and to let us know that the theatre is BACK! We are part of the cultural conversation.

Yes! If the imprimatur of these hot theatres can get a guy on Public radio, the sky's the limit: Op-ed pages! Spreads in *New York* magazine! Punditing from here to Punjab. Hell, if theatre can only change the world, we won't have any trouble 'splaining why we have a hundred administrators on staff (and on health insurance) to every one artist. Like when that dude in La Jolla realized that, since he couldn't be a rock star, he could be *like* a rock star by staging all those rock musicals and operas. We can do that too, journalist-style, hot off the press and on to the stage. We don't have to go on *Ira's* show; we can *be Ira*.

Don't get me wrong: personally, subjectively, and in the privacy of my own heart, I love all that political theatre—that Laramie project stuff, and those Culture Project folks who got all those innocent folks out of jail, not to mention the goofy documentarians like the Civilians. I mean political theatre rocks. I'm still a kid, that way: I like **all kinds** of theatre, including activist and documentary (especially Anna Deavere Smith, whom I revere—reavere?—and think of as America's great Brechtian performer) (I'm blushing now). And Kushner, man, his shit is true *and* wild. But this Daisey thing has me thinking that subjectivity and maybe even fiction are retro retro retro. You gotta believe that the people running these theatres know what their audiences want. I guess they just want the facts, ma'am, so playwrights get on board. Journalism is the answer.

I think it was Ezra Pound who said, "Literature is news that stays news." (Who has time to check this stuff? It's pretty much what he said, unless it was *Ira Glass* who said it. No, Pound. I'm 98% sure.) But now I see he had it backwards: News is literature, only faster! Buzzier! Hype-ier! More important!

That's the patho-tragedy of Daisey. He couldn't get out of his own way. He couldn't walk away from himself the way those marketing and artistic director types eventually walked away from him. He was, in the end, Mike Daisey, subjective man. Subjective Daisey made the best theatre of the year—even if it was on the radio—the theatre of his own unraveling. Could his play of (sort of) facts have been as heart-stopping as it was to hear him lying and covering and hemming and hawing and justifying and falsely testifying and (pause) (silence) (way more silence) (Beckett half-smiles approvingly; Pinter smirks)?

Maybe the public agony of Mike Daisey was such great theatre precisely because the contradictions and complications of human character are so darn rich, so compelling. I mean, Daisey's undoing had it all—the private lie, the public cover-up, the rise, the fall, the ambition and hubris and tragic flaw. And like all really good stories, the faults of the protagonist were no less than an extension of the faults in the people—and institutions—around him. I mean push a playwright/performer close enough to the edge and pretty soon he'll jump. Eyes on the prize, baby! Wait, though, whose hubris is it, anyway?

But like I said: Arrggh. It's confusing. But you gotta admit, it was fun while it lasted. And that's entertainment—or, at least, news.

This essay appeared originally in *howlround,* April, 2012.

Roger Berlind

The producer Roger Berlind is, even to the artists he's worked with, something of an enigma. I asked some of them to help me solve the riddle of Roger, the secret of his success. He's "a kind gentleman of literal and spiritual support," according to director Michael Mayer. In the words David Auburn, author of *Proof*, he's "a courtly guy, and a quietly humorous one." John Patrick Shanley, who worked with Roger on *Doubt*, goes further:

> Roger is an elusive, austere, unexpectedly merry, sly little boots. He comes on cat feet. He's in your show before you heard the door open. He turns to iron in adversity, and is mellow as a spring breeze when things are going well. He understates the world around him to its benefit. He is the bridle on the stallion, the handguard on the hero's sword. I like him.

Now we're getting somewhere: "sly little boots," "iron in adversity," "mellow as a spring breeze." It sounds like Roger is the Stealth Producer. "He understates the world around him to its benefit." Is that how he does it? Here we are, in the theatre, where everyone's job is to create drama, where we impassion and conflict and dramatize, and the man at the helm, this kindly, courtly producer, understates the world to keep it real. Is Roger Berlind, who puts his money where his Mona Lisa smile is, the ballast man, and the guy ropes guy who keeps everything from blowing away?

Yes, that's his strategy, but what's under it? What makes him tick? What's his secret secret? For answers I turned to John Guare, and he outed Roger to me. Listen:

> [Roger] had wanted to be a song writer, and while he was a hell of a lot better than the song writer in my play, *House of Blue Leaves*, he knew his limits, got into finance, made a bundle and set up shop on Broadway....
> I remember making a round trip to Williamstown to see a play. We drove back to New York through the summer night singing every song we could think of that had moon in the title. "Blue Moon." "Old Devil Moon." "Moonlight Becomes You." We challenged each other. "Moonlight Savings Time." "Reaching For the Moon." And it dawned on me that Roger was completely moon struck. Roger's secret was he was still that daffy song writer dreaming of Broadway—new plays—old plays.

Who *are* the biggest dreamers in the theatre? That's easy, right? Playwrights are the big dreamers. Playwrights dream the first dreams. They commit them to paper. They hallucinate other people to join the dream—actors, producers, audiences. They dream that a life in the theatre can compensate them, despite all evidence to the contrary. Playwrights lead the way in the hopeful, pie-eyed lunacy that is the theatre.

But playwrights aren't the only ones. They may be the first dreamers, but producers are right there with 'em. Who else so willingly stakes everything on such a losing proposition? Who else loves the theatre so recklessly, so against all reason, that he flies in the face of good judgment, business sense, and experience, investing his life and money and the lives and money of other people in an impossible pursuit in a perpetually dying art form?

Who has the song in his heart and the dopey grin on his face as he dances happily toward the edge of the cliff, if not the Broadway producer? Watch the producers at the Tony Awards. Clutching their statues, pushing and shoving like five-year-olds at the Mister Softee truck. Giddy and success-drunk like Maenads in a wine bath. No self-respecting playwright would ever prance around like that.

Is it possible? Is it possible that Berlind, so elegant and kind, so friendly and apparently at peace with the world, has the jumping bean heart of a child dreaming of double-dip cones? Is it possible that the man—a director of Lehman Brothers, for god's sake—is really a jittery Romeo, staring up at a balcony where Juliet is belting out songs from *Kiss Me Kate*?

It's not only possible; it's true. The secret's out: Roger Berlind is Mr. Dreamer. Mr. Moon in June.

Playwrights and producers live in two separate economies. Playwrights, like all artists, live in what essayist Lewis Hyde calls "the gift economy." We talk about the writer's gifts. Writers often view their own plays as gifts, coming from somewhere both inside and beyond them. Playwrights deliver work into the world as gift and yearn for it to be treated as such. Producers, as we know, live in the market economy. This is especially true of the commercial producer. Their work is quantifiable. It relies on product, demand, return on investment.

They need each other, the playwright and producer, a mutual dependence that makes their relationship so vital and so volatile, fraught and full of promise. The writer who lives only in the gift economy better have a good day job, a deep sense of self-worth, and a lot of friends. The producer who lives only in the marketplace misses the very essence of the human exchange that is the theatre.

The great producer is the one who can move easily between these economies, that of gift and that of market. The great producer fights for the best in both of these worlds without ever confusing them, never mistaking gift for commodity, no matter how hard he has to sell it. The great producer is, in the words of playwright Nilo Cruz, an "emissary" between these realms. From his experience with *Anna in the Tropics* Nilo has this to say:

> Producing in the theatre is literally being able to shed light into darkness, to transfer an unrealized dream to reality....A producer with a vivid imagination can see beyond what is written on the page... Nowadays, one hears horror stories about producers wanting to take control over the execution of a work, but that was never the case with Mr. Berlind. On the contrary, his main concern was in giving his audience inspiring works of art.

"The artist," Joseph Conrad writes, "appeals...to that in us which is a gift and not an acquisition—and, therefore, more permanently enduring." In other words, the poet speaks to the poetry in us. The musician calls out our song. The playwright taps our latent empathies and inspires us to imagine and play. By doing so, they link us, enduringly, to each other.

We hear the artist's appeal—"to that in us which is a gift." Producers like Roger Berlind appear once in a blue moon. A sly little boots with a song in his heart, such a producer hears that appeal and brings exacting, practical passion to making the gift real.

Originally delivered as a speech to New Dramatists' Spring Luncheon, 2011.

Julie Taymor

We have been told of a great fall, a great failure. Here is an American auteur director, the papers announce, making sense of that old phrase, "the daily bugle," who has over-reached, plummeted from the sky, taking untold performers and investors with her. Sixty-five, then seventy-million dollars, how many injuries, how many previews, closings, postponements—a sick fascination with a theatre of hubris, as if failure in the theatre were news, as if the greatest artists in history haven't all produced colossal failures and embarrassments. As if money has never been wasted, artistic effort never misdirected.

I haven't seen *Spiderman* yet. I'm waiting till it opens. But I have seen a lot of bad theatre, a lot of shitty, wasteful, expensive art, even by my favorite artists (of whom Julie Taymor is one). And I, like you, no doubt, have spent a lot of words on the importance of failure. I've demanded for playwrights what Arena Stage founder Zelda Fichandler called "the fifth freedom"—the freedom to fail. I've urged greater ambition, greater reach, bigger dreams. I've protested the lack of opportunities for women to work on the same scale as men, even men of lesser talent. And, personally, I find no pleasure in the lemming-like public spectacle surrounding Taymor's production (which she co-authored with another writer I love, Glen Berger). In fact, I wish the newspapers and their reviewers (I can't honor them with the term "critics," even spit from the tongue) would look to themselves and watch their own comic book demise.

Anyway, I can't and won't forget that Julie Taymor is one of my contemporaries who have most inspired and delighted me. I can't forget the challenge of her imagination, the categorical dare of her "authorship" as a director (which is why I consider her a playwright). Now, it seems to me, is exactly the moment to celebrate her, to marvel (forgive the pun, O please) at her vision and body of work.

The challenge of her imagination: You can't imagine Julie Taymor's production. You can't even pretend to get inside her head. There is no inevitable Julie Taymor staging. The script isn't fully authored until she's done with it. There are only possibilities, and they lie beyond our ability to imagine. Nobody can imagine the way she does.

How could you? You'd have to think in every dimension. You'd have to think words, painting, sculpture, space. You'd have to think music. You'd have to think bodies and wood, clay and silk, leather, shadow, light. You'd have to think the face masked. You'd have to think opera. You'd have to think cinema at its edges where film and theatre meet. And you'd have to think dance, because everything in Taymorland dances: Roman soldiers in armor, Comedia clowns, hospital beds and men of bones. The world turns and we dance—across deserts and battlefields, under water, through gardens with singing apples rising 20 feet in the air.

You'd have to imagine all this. And then you'd have to make it real. "Anything, everything is possible," a character says in *The Green Bird*. And with Julie Taymor, it is.

More than all this, more even than imagination, you'd have to think deeply, deeply through time, through the cultures of the earth. There's an image I cherish, even though I never saw it. Julie Taymor, maybe 21 or 22 years old, living in a place called Peti Tenget in Bali with a theatre company of her own, dancers, musicians, and actors from Java, Bali, France, and Germany. Hindus, Muslims, Christians. They share a deserted hotel, built on, and haunted by, a graveyard. No electricity or running water. They eat together on grass mats, and day after day for a year, eight or nine hours a day, they train each other—in Javanese dance, in Balinese dance, Lecoq mime, and mask performance. Somehow they know to follow this young woman. Somehow she knows—has known since she went to Sri Lanka at fourteen and Paris at sixteen—that hometown Boston isn't enough, that this country isn't the world.

How did she know that? What was she seeking? We talk about ambition in the context of "career," but what is the ferocious ambition that would lead someone that young to places so unknown, exchanges so profound. What is the passionate world-view that actually encompasses the *world*?

I took a walk with Julie once. We were at a retreat together north of the city sometime in the late '80s. I knew about her work, mostly from photos of her designs for *King Stag* and *The Hagaddah* and from friends at the now-defunct Ark Theatre, where she did some of her earliest New York directing. Somehow she and I wound up driving to the Storm King sculpture park and walking the grounds together.

Soon after our walk I saw one of the most miraculous things I've ever seen in the theatre—*Juan Darien*, the carnival mass she and Elliot Goldenthal wrote. There is no spoken dialogue in *Juan Darien*. The story's told in music and imagery. It unfolds before you, the way dreams do, but the visual vernacular is South American, mural, carvings, myth.

A jaguar becomes a boy. He begins as a rod-and-string puppet, transforms to a doll, becomes a Bunraku puppet, and, then, a flesh and blood boy, the only unmasked actor on stage. An entire village appears, inhabited by shadow puppets. It's so small, so close, you feel you could hold it in your arms. We see a tiny classroom under a minute bell tower; there are hand-puppet students and a teacher nine feet tall, sporting five pairs of spectacles on his nose and hair made from the pages of an open book, which flap like crazy when he gets mad. A globe begins to glow and spin, and inside of it a flower blossoms, sprouting leaves.

In *Juan Darien* we watch transformation. Our cells vibrate. They are little mirrors, emulating what we see. We enter, moving *inside* a transforming world, and, so, we are transformed—by possibility, by endless life in intimate parade, by the reach of the artist's imagining. Our souls vibrate. We reach, too.

I take a walk with Julie Taymor in a sculpture park and then I encounter this. And so for 20 years, every time I've watched a production or movie of hers I've wondered, what did she see, walking that park? How did the landscape look to her? What did she make of the steel statues, or the stone figures, the shaped hills and dips of earth? What does Julie Taymor see?

There's no end of astonishment in what she sees. *Titus:* a general pours sand into the soldier boots of his five dead sons. Sand that could be their ashes. *Transposed Heads:* two young men in love with the same woman lop off their own heads. Their severed heads dance in the air, finally landing, attached to the wrong bodies. *The Lion King:* giraffes lope across the stage—or are they men on stilts? Gazelles leap. The whole natural world, impossibly, fills the stage. *The Green Bird* flies up and descends as a man.

Julie Taymor is watching actors read at music stands and they get to the part where a boy vaults, spider-like, from web to web. A girl falls from the sky. How will they do it? I can't see it. But Julie Taymor can. And if she can see it, she can make it happen.

Her ability to craft what she sees is up to any miracle. Her solutions are never what we'd expect. How do you show boys dying in the marshes of Vietnam? Butoh dancers, women caked in white clay, fall on their backs on the surface of a lake, lifeless masks floating beside them. How do Frida Kahlo and Diego Rivera tour the New York City of the '30s? They stroll through a pop-up metropolis, made of postcards, a paper-doll world. You want the sun to rise on the Serengeti? Cut the sun from silk and raise it, strip by strip from the stage floor till it fills the upstage wall.

For all her gifts, at bottom, Julie Taymor is simply a great storyteller. Moment by moment, startling image by startling image, she never loses sight of the story. Break down her brilliant imagery and you'll see the simplest of choices, all in service of story. One example: Frida Kahlo, stuck in America, is homesick. She looks out a window and what does she see? A painting of a dress on a clothesline, a painting of a dress the colors of Mexico. The painted dress begins to sway in the wind. It comes real. She is home.

Whether it's a tale of the humanity of the animal kingdom or of the bestial in us, Julie never loses sight of the human heart. I saw *The Lion King* over a decade ago with my then five-year-old son. I remember the circles and the wildebeest stampede and the elephant in the audience. I remember the grassland headpieces. But what I remember most was my son turning to me when the King Mufasa died and, seeing the tears on my face, saying, "It's sad when fathers die, isn't it?"

This is what stories do: they reach to us, culture to culture, world to world. We sit in abandoned buildings and show each other what we know. We tell each other tales in dance and song, image and word. Stories are the world's dreams, and Julie shows us those dreams, in images at once deeply familiar and shockingly new, images that, in John Lennon's words, call us "on and on, across the universe." You think you know the Beatles' song "Let It Be"? Watch it sung by a young black boy with his back against the tire of a car, while Detroit riots around him. Hear it sung by mourners at the boy's funeral. We know it *and* we hear it for the first time.

She reaches back centuries into the Japanese Noh Drama, rummages through the masks and lazzi of Commedia, draws on Indonesian shadow puppetry and Greek masked drama, Shamanic ritual and Indian classical dance. She is at once the most contemporary, experimental artist and the most ancient practitioner.

My faith in the theatre is tenuous. It's challenged every day. Sometimes I feel like I spend my life searching for the art and artists who will re-excite that shaky faith. And I've found a few artists of my generation who continue to inspire me. I keep looking for those rare theatre makers who can do what Peter Brook describes, mingling the rough, the holy, and the immediate: who know and use the theatre's rough magic. Who touch the sacred. Who make the art alive, here, now. There's one, Julie Taymor, who, try as she might, never fails. In her *Tempest*, Helen Mirren, as Prospera, speaks the words:

> I have bedimm'd
> The noontide sun, call'd forth the mutinous winds,
> And 'twixt the green sea and the azured vault
> Set roaring war...

The sorceress details the majestic fury of her sorcery:

> ...graves at my command
> Have waked their sleepers, oped, and let 'em forth

By my so potent art.

Julie Taymor. Her so potent art. But in the end of *The Tempest*, Prospera will break her staff and bury it in the earth. She will abjure her "rough magic."

Thankfully Julie is a young magician. A sorceress at the height of her powers with decades ahead and centuries behind her, from which to draw. She takes this globe and sets it spinning. It glows. She stands on the verge of places still uncharted, worlds we can't possibly imagine. What do you see, Julie? Show us.

This text is adapted from a speech to New Dramatists' Spring Luncheon, 2010, later republished in *howlround*.

Horton Foote

You can now Google map the town of Wharton, Texas. You can view Horton Foote's homeland from satellite, zooming in or out at will. If you zoom in, you can see it from street level: low buildings, scrub, and a pickup truck. If you zoom out, you find the towns whose names we know from Horton's plays—El Campo, Glen Flora, and Egypt. Further out, you see those complicated Meccas of Houston and Galveston. Keep pulling back and you can locate the poles of Horton's life—Pasadena, California on the west, where he went as a teenager to study acting—and New York on the east, where, as an actor, he came at age 20 and where, for 73 years, his theatre life was centered. Farther north is a later artistic home, Hartford, and farthest, the family's home in New Hampshire, where he wrote, among other things, the nine plays of his *Orphans' Home Cycle.* including *Lily Dale, The Widow Claire,* and *On Valentine's Day.*

The most extraordinary map of Wharton, though, can be found in the life work of Horton Foote, reimagined as the town of Harrison. For more than 70 years, he charted the place and its people, detailed its culture and customs, and located its personal dramas in history. He traced its changes, and ultimately its passing. Horton Foote's map is a meticulous miracle. "This is always the end of the journey for me," Horton writes. "Wharton is my home."

Listen to how he describes entering that home, his prose as luminous as his dialogue:

> First, there is the quietness, or the lack of sound, and then very faintly I begin to hear the tree frogs, the katydids in the pecan trees around the courthouse square. I hear the waltz of a Mexican dance hall, the blues from a black restaurant, a woman saying good night to a neighbor, a whistle from some mockingbird that mistakes the brightness of the night for daylight. I was born and raised here. I know the people. I have heard a hundred times the tales of the town's beginnings, the events of its life from the time it was established.

There is no body of work in the American theatre to compare with Horton Foote's. No one has written for so long about so few square miles—the concentrated plot of land that is the land of his family. No one has zeroed in so intimately over so many years on his own kin, their neighbors and friends. No one has spent so many decades remembering. Horton Foote is our finest rememberer. "These are my people and my stories, and the plays I want to write," he said. "The only ones I know how to write."

A great rememberer must begin as a great sponge, and this is how I picture young Horton Foote, a bookish boy with those same astute, merciful eyes, seeing everything, listening to everything, soaking everything up. That's how he presents himself, too, in his memoirs and essays, the listener among talkers in a time of stories, when living rooms and sitting rooms, gallery porches and dining tables were the stages of the world. Life was played out there, but more, it was recounted.

In Horton Foote's plays, as on the domestic stages of his childhood, the big scenes often happen elsewhere, offstage. Usually, they've already happened. Fathers drink and die. Women marry men they must marry, not the ones they choose. A mother abandons her son to make a home for her daughter. A son walks into the water to drown. Fortunes are lost, children die, and farms go to seed. Whole towns fall off the map.

Out of memory, Horton gives us life at its most concentrated and full. But even more than life, his gives us *lives*. These lives, especially those of his parents and grandparents and their relations—overheard, pieced together, imagined—are so rich for the rememberer, so *ongoing,* that he must detail them in their entirety—1890, 1911, 1917 and 18, 1924, '53, '87. These lives are as real to him as those of the present, maybe more real. And so he spends his long lifetime making them real to us in turn.

The world won't stop changing, Horton reminds us of that. Memory is a bulwark not against that change but against the loss it brings. You can almost break his plays down along memory lines—those who would remember—who must remember—and those who would forget. I love how in his plays people introduce themselves by talking about their parents, who their people were, what happened to them. It's almost a way of making love, as in this scene from *Courtship* between Horace Robedaux and Elizabeth Vaughn—the characters based on Horton's mother and father.

> ELIZABETH. My mother was born on a plantation on Oyster Creek. Her father was a planter. But he didn't prosper. My father came from East Columbia. His father died when he was twelve.
> HORACE. My father died when I was twelve.
> ELIZABETH. Yes, I know. Your mother lives in Houston.
> HORACE. Yes, I don't like Houston. I like it better here.

On the other side of this push and pull between memory and forgetting are characters with no use for the past. They wish only to move forward, like Horace's sister, Lily Dale, in the play by the same name:

> LILY DALE. I want to think of now. This minute. Why do you always want to talk about the past? What Papa did or didn't do? I don't care what he sang and I don't care what he called me. All I know is that he smoked cigarettes like a fiend and was a drunkard and broke my mother's heart, and he died and left her penniless to go out into the world to work and support two children.

We dwell in the feeling of the past or we deny it. Both have a powerful energy, both carry a mighty freight. This struggle between remembering and forgetting, between forward and back, activates Horton's plays and becomes his true subject.

Don't let the gentleness of his spirit fool you. Horton Foote's cartography is the product of Olympian ambition. Like a tender, merciful God, he sought to possess an entire world by loving it ceaselessly. He tried to stop time by remembering. He dared to bring the dead back to life. He pursued these ambitions with an obsessive singleness of purpose and executed them with almost-perfect humility. Again, in his own words:

> It is a vanishing world, the world of these plays; no, not a vanishing world but a vanished world. Of all the characters in the plays, I am now the only one living, and yet I say to myself isn't it all reappearing, only in a different way?...Here in Harrison (Wharton) I hear the old stories of men and women trying their best to find ways to live and survive in a somewhat less-than-perfect world. Their stories tell of bravery and loss, treachery and strength, and courage. The old stories, as old as time, are retold in the times of this day, of this time. I think sometimes that Randall Jarrell speaks for me in his poem "Thinking of the Lost World":
>
> "All of them are gone
> Except for me; and for me nothing is gone."

Nothing is ever gone, Horton Foote proves, as long as there are people to remember, to write it down. Nothing can be lost, as long as there are artists brave enough and persistent enough, to try and capture the ephemeral grace of our lives.

Adapted from a speech to New Dramatists' Spring Luncheon, 2009, later published in *howlround*.

Andre Gregory Sees the Light

In winter when the fields are white, I sing this song for your delight.
  —Humpty Dumpty, *Through the Looking Glass*, Lewis Carroll

Walk through any museum. There's a retrospective for a major
contemporary artist: life and work spread out before your eyes, wall
after wall, and room after room. You can see the influences in the
early painting, the way the style morphs from cubism to collage. You
can see the moment the artist stumbles onto a subject that will define
her career. You might locate a moment where the influences are
suddenly submerged, where that artist's "voice" becomes his own.
Then come the experiments of mid-life and, just maybe, in late life,
something wholly new.

Where is the museum for theatre artists? How do you display
the ephemera of this art? How do you sum up periods in an artistic
life, in a form where so little of the work remains? If I were the
curator of such a museum, I would reserve, in a central spot, a series
of small rooms for a major—and singularly marginal—director
(sometimes actor, and recent playwright) whose work has defined for
me the possibilities of an ideal theatre, whose commitment to process
sets an unattainable standard for my own, whose productions have
been seen at intervals of many years by only handfuls of people. The
exhibit, celebrating an American master named Andre Gregory,
would be called, after a book Gregory himself has never read, "Great
Reckonings in Little Rooms."

"To describe Andre's contribution gets into something which is
enormously intangible," suggests Wallace Shawn, the playwright and
actor who has for more than 30 years served as Gregory's double, one
half (hard to say which) of their Jekyll-and-Hyde team, their Laurel-
and-Hardy act. "His genius lies in the area of psychological truth,
which is intangible. Robert Wilson is another theatre genius of our
time, for example. If anybody asks you what's so special about
Robert Wilson, you can open a book and show three photographs of
a stage that Bob Wilson has filled with the product of his
imagination. Andre's greatest accomplishments are really in the
realm of human insight and psychological truth—and truth is
notoriously hard to define."

Life and work, a blurry distinction for most artists, is
particularly murky for Gregory, whose spiritual searchings are the
subject of *My Dinner with Andre*, the 1981 film he co-wrote and stars
in with Shawn. He socializes mostly with his longtime collaborators,
including actors Larry Pine and Gerry Bamman, with whom he is
currently working on *Endgame*. Thirty years after they mounted a full

production of this Beckett play, they are at it again; two years into rehearsal—including for audiences last October at Provincetown Repertory Theater in Massachusetts—they have what Gregory calls "a sketch." (They will bring it to the Chinati Foundation next month, a contemporary art museum in Marfa, Tex., founded by sculptor Donald Judd.) Louis Malle's 1994 movie, *Vanya on 42nd Street*, which documents Gregory's production of Chekhov's *Uncle Vanya*, captures the bleeding of life and art from the opening shot. Gregory and the actors walk, singly and together, along Manhattan's 42nd Street toward the theatre; they mill with the invited audience before two of the chatting actors, still in their street clothes, simply begin Scene one, amid the very real ruins of a not-yet-renovated Victory Theatre. This month at Los Angeles's Roy and Edna Disney/CalArts Theater (REDCAT), Gregory will, in addition to screening *Andre* and *Vanya*, read from his play-in-progress, *Bone Songs*, which is, in its bones, a passionate conversation with his late wife, Chiquita, across two worlds: "afterwife" to afterlife.

While Gregory has never comfortably swum in the mainstream, he's witnessed and participated in all but a few of the major theatrical currents of the past half-century, in and just out of the theatre. He's left his mark everywhere he's gone. From his beginnings at the Neighborhood Playhouse and the Actors Studio, he discovered the Berliner Ensemble. He was instrumental in the founding of three of the earliest regional theatres and was fired from all of them quicker than you can say, "board relations." His *Alice in Wonderland*—begun in 1968 with the Manhattan Project, a company he started with a group of students from New York University, and first performed more than two years later—remains one of the seminal works of the era, right up there with Peter Brook's *Marat/Sade* and *A Midsummer Night's Dream*, the Open Theatre's *The Serpent* and the work of Gregory's mentor, Jerzy Grotowski. In the late '70s, around the time Grotowski stopped making productions and began his so-called paratheatrical events, Gregory, too, for a combination of personal, spiritual, and professional reasons, left the theatre and, literally, went into the woods (and desert and numerous spiritual communities). When he returned and made *My Dinner with Andre*, the theatre pioneer became a pioneer of independent film and then, inexplicably, a successful character actor in Hollywood, playing in films by Peter Weir, Woody Allen, Brian de Palma, and Martin Scorsese.

It's harder to place the work he's been doing since returning to the theatre in the early '90s, mounting tiny-scale productions for audiences of 12 or 30 or at most 40. They are meticulously spontaneous, painstakingly intimate things, often and forever in-process. His *Master Builder*, translated by and starring Wallace Shawn as Solness the Master Builder, has been seven years in the making. These creations don't dazzle, the way the daring physical virtuosity of the Manhattan Project's *Alice* did. They don't incite scandals, the way Gregory's early regional productions did. The work is almost filmic, but never seems canned, glossed, or anything but live. What happen in these small spaces are great human reckonings: what happens is simply Chekhov or Ibsen or Shawn, simply life, under a psychic microscope, life at its most complex and, well, simple.

Gregory's childhood is a well of the dramatic, and the unconscious fount of all his theatre work to date. He was born in Paris, 1934, the year Hitler became Führer of Germany. His Russian Jewish parents, a wealthy international businessman and a captivating society hostess—he refers to them as "Macbeth and Lady Macbeth"—were conspicuously absent during his otherwise privileged early childhood. He suspects that they were occupied "trying to set up an escape with a cushion" in order to stay ahead of the horrific events on the march in Europe.

"My father got out of Russia a year before Stalin came to power, went to Berlin," Gregory explains. "Left Berlin the year Hitler came to power, went to Paris. Three weeks before the Germans invaded Poland we left for England. As a little kid I was outfitted for a gas mask. We came over to the States on one of two sister ships. I watched the other ship torpedoed and people drowning. We picked up survivors." He was five at the time.

If Gregory's childhood home was a place to wrestle demons, it also provided a window to a stunning, wide world. "My mother had always been surrounded by people like Horowitz, Rostropovich, Laurel and Hardy, Dietrich, Garbo, Basil Rathbone, Charles Boyer— these were the people that I grew up with. When Horowitz was having his nervous breakdown and couldn't perform, we would go over every week to his home and before dinner there would be gin rummy and after dinner he would play for us for hours. My childhood was quite amazing—like Treplev's," he adds, citing the young artist who shoots himself at the end of Chekhov's *The Seagull*.

A brew of petty tyranny at home and martial tyranny outside instilled in Gregory a twin fascination with evil and power that drives his engagement with work and the world. "In my background power was an extremely malevolent force, so sometimes in my life I've had trouble differentiating between power and strength, the positive aspects of power." His *Master Builder* is all about power; his *Vanya* was about a man embracing powerlessness. In his latest stab at *Endgame*, Beckett's eerie-comic dance of power and dependency between master and servant, Gregory has let evil into their sealed room.

Gregory's new *Endgame*, begun after, and as a result of, the World Trade Center attacks, takes place in a shelter, an environment designed by longtime collaborator Eugene Lee. "It's the kind of place John Ashcroft would like to see us all in," as Gregory (who thinks President Bush is the "anti-Christ, this religious maniac coming with Christ's word") told an audience in Provincetown. And Beckett's end-of-the-world landscape has a bunkered feel, a world of duct tape and homeland insecurity. Each night of these open rehearsals is clearly an improvisation, in which the two actors (the play's other two characters, Nell and Nagg, who live in ash cans, are created, garbage-puppet-like, by Clov, who mimics their voices) try radically new tacks in hopes of finding moments that work. One thing is already clear: in this dark haven, Clov's clowning is far from the rough vaudeville of the first *Endgame* Gregory directed in Philadelphia in 1965 and remounted shortly after to open Robert Brustein's theatre at Yale School of Drama. Today Clov clowns like a guy posing for photos at Abu Ghraib.

Gregory's father hated the thought of him in the theatre and fought with him about it until the end of his life. One night, though, the older Gregory lost quite a bit of money to a regular poker partner, Jean Dalrymple, the prominent New York producer. "He said to her, 'Listen, you cleaned me out. Can't you give my son a job?'" Dalrymple did just that, taking Gregory with her to the Brussels World's Fair in 1958—where she oversaw theatrical production—as her assistant and sometime stage manager. Once there, he met his future wife, Chiquita, who was working as a fair guide, a perfect job for a half-German, half-Argentine woman fluent in six languages. At the encouragement of a teacher he'd had at Harvard, Gregory made the easy passage from Brussels to Berlin.

"I'd never heard of the Berliner Ensemble. I'd never even heard of Brecht. So I went for three days. The poster outside the theatre said: *Das Leben von Galilei*. I knew so little that I thought that was the *Good Fisherman of Galilee*. *Galileo* lasted about four hours with one intermission. It was all talk. I was absolutely staggered, because I could understand almost every single moment on the stage, because every single moment was so clear. So I stayed for a year."

Gregory was one of a couple of hundred people observing each rehearsal run by Brecht's widow, Helene Weigel, in these years immediately after Brecht's death. (Grotowski was another, though he and Gregory didn't meet for another decade.) "It was an amazing experience. I saw *Arturo Ui* rehearse, and then I saw it 20 or 30 times. I saw *Galileo* 20 or 30 times. That was absolutely the defining moment of my creation as a director. People think I'm sort of a disciple of Jerzy's. You couldn't really learn anything from him. Because it was

Michelangelo. With the Berliner Ensemble, you could really learn what the art of directing was. Lee Strasberg once said that a director in the dress rehearsals should be able to put earplugs in and be able to understand what's going on on the stage. But I've never seen that done except with Brecht and Grotowski."

Strasberg, in whose private acting class Gregory studied, was another great, lasting influence, if one embraced less vivaciously. The lesson of Brecht's productions at the Berliner Ensemble was, Gregory says, "clarity, simplicity, and telling the story—Brecht had a sign over his desk saying, 'Simpler, and with more laughter.'" Strasberg, by contrast, taught him the "the value of the actor's contribution, and that as a director you are simply there to give the actor a little courage to go a little further in the direction the actor's already going." Strasberg's other lesson: "Logic logic logic."

Even as he was being inspired and shaped as a director, Gregory couldn't see himself doing anything creative and thought he'd follow the family business line and become a producer. Encouragement came in a hush from Martha Graham, the mother of modern dance, who taught movement at the Neighborhood Playhouse. "I was incredibly awkward and overweight and embarrassed to be in leotards and trying to do these Graham movements. And one day she came and she whispered into my ear, 'You know darling, you have no talent, but you have such a big heart. One day you'll be a great artist.'"

In 1965, Gregory told a *Tulane Drama Review* theatre conference, "I'm scared that the regional theatre, by the time it is mature, will have bored the shit out of millions of people all over the country." This was after he'd been fired from the third regional theatre he'd helped found.

According to his 70-year-old self, this firebrand 31-year-old former artistic director "is arrogant. He's saying there will be no regional theatre. He's an angry son of a bitch. Because he never chooses to be part of the establishment. Even though it's his own choice, he must be angry about this. Because the establishment for him represents those primal people who had power—the parents."

But angry and arrogant or not, by most accounts this young director represented a hope for the new resident theatre movement that few could match. Gregory has always been interested in finding structures for theatre appropriate to the times, and the early regional theatre was just that, with subscription bases and spaces that created a strong foundation for the work. Or so he thought. He turned quickly from pioneer to outcast.

His 1963 production of Max Frisch's *The Firebugs* opened Seattle Repertory Theatre, where he was associate director, with a bang of critical acclaim, though he was fired from a second production by artistic director Stuart Vaughan (some have said because he was too avant-garde; others claim that Vaughan was threatened by Gregory's talent), who was in turn fired shortly thereafter. He then founded Philadelphia's Theatre of the Living Arts and quickly made it one of the most vital, watched, and controversial of the theatres springing up across America.

"I took Alan Schneider to lunch," he recalls, describing an encounter with the early regional theatre's leading director. "And I said, 'Mr. Schneider, I'd like to direct. How do I do that?' And he said, 'Well, if I were you, I'd start your own theatre.' And I said, 'How do I do that?' and he said, 'Oh, I don't know; that's your job.' There were very few theatres then, so I bought a map of America and started putting flags in cities—black flags for cities that already had a theatre, red flags for cities that didn't have a theatre but were kind of shitty cities, and a gold flag was no theatre, interesting city. Philadelphia was one of them. I got a letter of introduction to an interior designer in Philadelphia and asked if he could help me create it. I said, 'If you could get three friends to throw three parties, I would come and talk about my vision. And over two years I talked at, I think, 432 dinners, luncheons, breakfasts, cocktail parties. Out of that, literally one-to-one, I got 10,000 subscribers and I started my theatre. You can only do that when you're young."

Robert Brustein called Gregory's first *Endgame* "profoundly original." The play, he wrote, "has never been funnier or, in my opinion, more powerful." Regional theatre historian Joseph Wesley Zeigler claimed his talent was "too large and too vaulting to be absorbed and served by a theatre just born." Critic Julius Novick, though repulsed by much of Rochelle Owens's *Beclch*, a play of violence and Artaudian cruelty set in an "Africa of the mind," felt that Gregory's wild, overgrown, environmental production had an uncommon sense of urgency, as well as "an authority and amplitude not often encountered in the regional theatre…. It is clear that any theatre [Gregory] runs is going to be an exciting theatre." As the Los Angeles Board of Education found out when they hired him to run the Inner City Cultural Center, bringing classic theatre to urban high schools—he served up a black Gentleman Caller to Laura in *Glass Menagerie* and a naked, bathing Tartuffe, provoking the censure of the Catholic Church—some theatres run by Andre Gregory were the wrong kind of exciting.

"If he were a European," Wallace Shawn says of Gregory, "I think that he would probably have a huge institution at his disposal, money from the state and groveling worshippers at his feet doing his bidding, which is what you see when you go to Germany, for example. Andre is a gigantic talent and artist and innovator. But the reality, which is comical in a way, is that not only does he not have those things, but I feel that 98 percent of the theatre people either don't know of him or consider him an amusing eccentric of some kind. I mean, they're not awestruck by him, which they ought to be."

Then Andre Gregory discovered two small things that changed his life: a theatre in the Caribbean and a book. "A friend who was the head of the Rockefeller Foundation sent me down to Trinidad, either to get me out of the country or because he thought I was having a nervous breakdown after being fired from all these places, to do a report on this unknown writer and director, Derek Walcott. When I got there, I saw amateur actors, who had jobs during the day, working all night for no money and taking rum breaks instead of coffee breaks and creating this wonderful work. And I thought, 'Oh, you don't need a theatre, you don't need a board, you don't need a subscription audience, you don't need a lot of money. All you need is a room with some people from the same planet that you're from.'

"The book was Jerzy Grotowski's *Towards a Poor Theatre*. "The Grotowski question—'What can the theatre do without?'—and its answer—that all it needs is basically one actor and one audience member—was a radical thought, which has changed my theatre life to this day, because the size of my audience is defined by the work itself, the space is defined by the work itself. The question is always to find out what is essential to the theatre."

Small is big. The notion has guided him ever since.

In 1968, Gregory had just directed one of those legendary Broadway failures, a comedy about bestiality called *Leda Had a Little Swan*, whose producer closed it the night before opening. His reputation, as some kind of *enfant terrible* with a string of firings and failings behind him, preceded him. He taught at NYU for six weeks and then assembled a group of five students—a sixth ensemble member would push her way in later—to start a company to do something, but nobody knew what.

The Manhattan Project started by making its way through the psychophysical exercises in Grotowski's book. They noodled around with *'Tis Pity She's a Whore* and kept working, albeit desultorily, when Gregory left for Paris to study with Grotowski in person. Shortly after his return, they bumbled onto *Alice in Wonderland*.

If there ever is an Andre Gregory exhibit in a theatre museum, surely the walls of one room will be covered with the hundred photographs Richard Avedon took of Alice in 12 studio sittings in 1970 and '71. They comprise, inarguably, the finest collection of photos of a single production in the history of the American theatre. They capture everything that exploded through that room of doors

Eugene Lee constructed for the play: the momentum, wildness, joy, acrobatic daring, ensemble verve and edgy emotional volatility—the great delinquent lunacy of it all. Lewis Carroll blows Alice up into a parade balloon. The caterpillar smokes his hookah on the backs of four actors who form a mushroom. Humpty Dumpty, an egg smashed on his face, falls from a tower of chairs. And a crazy-ass tea party happens over, under and all around a ravaged wooden table.

The play was created through months of lengthy open-ended improvisations; Gregory would famously sit silently for hours at a time, while the actors played. "I like to think I'm being so democratic in allowing the actor to do whatever he wants, only very delicately and politely suggesting that this might be better than that," he said during the run of *Alice*. "But it may be the most egotistical way to be a director. I mean, everyone knows that directors like to play god. Well, there are small gods and big gods. The small gods have to show their power so they move people around a lot and lay down the rules. But what could be more egotistical and closer to the image of god than to be completely absent? That to me is the cruelest and most interesting god of all."

The Manhattan Project stayed together for close to ten years, staging an *Endgame*, Shawn's *Our Late Night*—after they'd abandoned the idea of him adapting *Peer Gynt*—and a *Seagull*, full of the tensions of a company pulling apart. When *The Seagull* became his "first big public failure" and the company broke up—following his mother's death—Gregory, rather than imitating Treplev, took the metaphorical route out. He quit the theatre.

Everything Gregory describes to "Wally" in *My Dinner with Andre* is true: the all-night improvisations in the forests of Poland, the trek across the Sahara desert with a Buddhist monk in search of a way to do Antoine de Saint-Exupéry's *The Little Prince*, the ritual burial—naked and alive—the years away from friends, the alienation, the beauty, the wreckage, and the terror. He had fled New York and the theatre, fled his mother's death and that of his company, and started "asking those questions," as "Andre" explains in the movie, "that Stanislavsky said that the actor should constantly ask himself as a character—Who am I? Why am I here? Where do I come from? And Where am I going?—but instead of applying them to a role, you apply them to yourself."

But if the events were real, the "Andre" of film is a character Gregory invented partly out of self-indictment and partly because, once he and Shawn had spent two years writing the screenplay, he couldn't find the way to play it. "I stumbled upon four voices. One is Andre the spoiled rich kid. One is Andre the spiritual used-car salesman. One is Andre the Peter Brook. And the fourth is the voice of sincerity, which starts to appear a little bit at the end of the film."

My Dinner with Andre has the feel of a single conversation, a casual, and for Shawn, dreaded, encounter that keeps descending deeper, into the under-self, into the shaky foundations of that self, as they're challenged by the person across the table. If you aren't watching the cuts, it's easy to think the film's shot by two cameras in a single take. But Gregory and Shawn rehearsed for 14 months before Louis Malle filmed it, so the ease is hard-won. "The acting in *My Dinner with Andre* is as close to great Brechtian acting as you come, because you're given the illusion of utter simplicity and spontaneity," Gregory says. "But underneath is all the depth of the long rehearsal process."

In addition to helping catalyze a new generation of independent filmmaking, *My Dinner with Andre* kicked off a new career for Gregory, one that was all "about the fun of being in the movies and making quite a bit of money. Walking around the Warner Brothers lot, dressed as an Arab with a beard and shooting on the sound stage where they shot *Casablanca*, was just incredibly romantic."

Even in this make-believe world, life and art fused for Gregory, most oddly when he auditioned for and landed the role of John the Baptist in Scorsese's *The Last Temptation of Christ*. "Scorsese didn't know my work, and oddly he'd never seen *My Dinner with Andre*. He said to me, 'Do you know anything about shamans?' And I said, 'You're looking at one, Mr. Scorsese.' He smiled and said, 'Can you show me anything shaman-like?' And I said, 'If you can give me about 45 minutes to get into a trance state, sure.' So they came back 45 minutes later, and I was completely naked, chanting and dancing. I was in a trance, so I didn't see that he went out of the room to get a little movie camera. Afterwards, he said, 'I'm sending this to Hollywood; they've never seen an audition like this one.'"

"I think you're born a shaman," Gregory says. "The shaman goes down into the darkness for the tribe, to bring light and growth to the harvest. The difficulty in our culture is that, unlike the Native American culture and many others, it's not recognized and there's nobody to train you. So you're unconsciously a shaman for a long time, which often means you go down into the darkness and you don't know how to come back up."

When Chiquita became ill in the late 1980s, Gregory devoted himself to her care for three years. Andre the actor was soon forgotten by Hollywood, but, as he began work on *Uncle Vanya*, his first theatre directing in a decade, he felt "like a young man returning with all the enthusiasm and excitement of someone who'd never directed before." The shaman was coming back up.

During this period, first in rented lofts and later in his own living room, Gregory has fashioned something "like my own version of the Actors Studio, but on a much smaller scale. It's kind of a gym for actors, where whenever they're not out making money, they come and work with me." These comings and goings make for great logistical complications, but they allow Gregory to rehearse several projects at once—as with *Vanya*, Shawn's *The Designated Mourner*, and, most recently, Ibsen's *The Master Builder*. "I've been rehearsing *The Master Builder* for seven years, and I've only had all the actors in the same room once," he says.

Gregory views *Master Builder* as a culmination, his finest work, even though no audiences have seen it. He's aiming for something akin to what he found across the table from Shawn in *My Dinner with Andre*—iceberg acting, where you only see the tip but the layered experience of a lifetime comes with it. You feel the depth, but the actor needn't reveal it, needn't play it. Gregory is forging a hybrid style: the intimacy of film acting and the fullness and ambiguity of the living human moment. *Vanya* was theatre recorded on film; *Master Builder*, utilizing many of the same actors, started as a theatre project and became a screenplay and film-ready staging in search of a filmmaker.

"Working with Andre as an actor," Shawn explains, "year one, year two, year three goes by on the same role and you're understanding possibilities and truths in the script that you could never possibly have guessed at at the beginning of the process. But you are also bringing forth things out of yourself that nobody has ever seen before, including you.

"As actors, from the first minute we encounter the text, we are interpreting it through the filter of our own brains, which are mainly a heap of clichés. With Andre you learn to peel those clichés away— crawl out from under them—and let the vast possibilities of a text come out."

When at the end of *Vanya*, Dr. Astrov (Larry Pine) begs a kiss from Yelena (Julianne Moore) before she leaves forever, despite months of buried passion, he simply and respectfully kisses her cheek. When she kisses him goodbye, throwing a life's caution to the winds, she lands on his lips, but only fleetingly, with all the ambivalence and non-commitment she's brought to the rest of her encounters. Similarly, when Astrov says goodbye to a Vanya whom we know to be devastated and at the end of his rope, the doctor's serious farewell provokes only a flippy finger wave from Vanya, determined, one suspects, not to "go there."

It's clear from watching an open rehearsal of *Endgame* that Gregory's process is that of trying everything and keeping only what's profoundly right. It's a process, for Gregory, of discovering the parts that fit the whole: "If you look at a De Kooning painting, you know that if you take out one single line of it the fabric of it will disintegrate. And there are thousands of lines or strokes or gestures in a painting. Where that comes from god only knows, that one particular brushstroke. Why it has to be there, we don't know. But when we look at it we know it's right. So I'm not sure we're talking about truth. Strasberg would find it truthful as long as it was emotional. Brecht would find it truthful as long as it was clear. I guess with me, I just feel that brush stroke in this moment from that actor today is part of the tapestry.

"The best example is Busby Berkeley," he adds gleefully. "Busby Berkeley said that a woman in the chorus line can't just be beautiful. Each one has to fit next to the other like a series of pearls on a necklace. That's it. You're looking for a series of truths that fit together."

Andre Gregory has taken up painting. This may be his new artistic project, as he spends more time in Truro on Cape Cod with his new wife, Cindy, where, like Prospero, he jokes, only every third thought shall be of the grave. He's traveled far from his John the Baptist self: "What I can't love, I attack...God demands anger." His personal god now demands joy.

Gregory's project has always been "a spiritual confrontation with the darkness." He has always surrounded that darkness, cushioned it in light and laughter to make it easier to take in. (When I called his house after the elections, on his answering machine he was singing "Springtime for Hitler.") His heart has always been trained on illumination: his own, the play's, the audience's. "If one person is illuminated, it's a miracle. I'm after that one person. It's lighting a flame of life in someone."

Late last year, he tried to paint a wintry scene—a tree without leaves, the last green grass, stormy clouds, dead leaves. He showed it to Cindy. She was deeply moved. She saw springtime on the canvas, early spring. "Even if I try," Gregory marvels with his dancing eyes and wild, Cheshire Cat grin, "I don't seem to be able to create the dark."

This essay was originally published in *American Theatre*, March, 2005.

August Wilson

Sometimes the world gets it right; sometimes the right people get celebrated for the right reasons. Sometimes artists come along whose talent matches their ambitions. When they do, their example encourages other artists to value their own gifts—their songs, to use August Wilson's word. This example emboldens others to take great risks in the belief that their grasp can match their reach.

Sometimes even the American theatre gets it right—as it did with August Wilson. Sometimes our community, our industry, overcomes its cowardice, its aversion to the new and unknown, its love affair with the one-shot, and—as it did once upon a time with August Wilson—invests in an artist over the long haul, invests in a body of work.

I wish that every playwright I know could share the path August cut through the American theatre, a path that is surely the most extraordinary convergence in our national theatre history. The O'Neill Theatre Center, New Dramatists, the Playwrights Center, Yale Rep, Penumbra, Seattle Rep, The Goodman, The Huntington, and a constant constellation of regional theatres, even Broadway itself—none of these places gave him talent or hunger or ambition, but they joined impossibly together in a collective belief in his gift, anteing up with human, creative, professional, and artistic support. Even our champions need people to champion them; even our groundbreakers need friends to help them pave the new roads.

There's so much to honor, so many staggering accomplishments. I'd like to honor another August Wilson, too—a writer of staggering potential. Another August, another year, another place. It's the early '80s, and he's staying in a room in Seventh Heaven, what we call the third floor of the old church that houses New Dramatists. It's one of the Spartan, monk's-cell dorm rooms we keep for our out-of-town playwrights. And in that room at that time, that August Wilson is writing a play. It's called *Mill Hands Lunch Bucket*, after a Romare Bearden painting. At some point, there or elsewhere, he crosses out the words "Mill Hands Lunch Bucket" and replaces them with "Joe Turner's Come and Gone."

Or maybe he's reading under a tree in summer in Waterford, Connecticut, or smoking out in front of the Playwrights Center in Minneapolis, any of his usual haunts, where the image of solitary writer is belied by the warm, chatty camaraderie of these busy playwright hives.

"What are you working on, August?" someone asks.

"I'm writing a 10-play cycle, one play for each decade of the 20th century. It'll encompass slavery, the African Diaspora, the migration of five million blacks to the north, and the lives of Africans in America against the backdrop of our evolving culture. One character is as old as slavery; she'll die at 287. They're meant to be performed at every theatre in the country and then on Broadway."

"Cool," says the other playwright, who then proceeds to spin an equally improbable, grandiose, world-changing scheme, concluding with, "Can you come to my reading on Monday? It'll be six hours long. We'll read Act II another day."

And August might respond with, "Cool," another way of saying "Yes," the word we prize above all others in the land of playwrights. "yes is a world," writes e.e. cummings, "& in this world of yes live (skillfully curled) all worlds."

By celebrating this earlier August—the one with so many worlds still skillfully curled inside—we celebrate every master playwright *in posse*. By honoring this earlier August, at the typewriter, searching for the "healing song" and the "binding song" that his plays offer for so many of us, we honor every playwright setting out or halfway home, every playwright.

We wish for them what we wished for him: We want them to be seen as they are *and* as they can be: artists with improbably vast worlds inside of them. We want their songs heard and their gift of tongues valued. We want them to define the future and inspire the future's future. And we want the American theatre to do right by them, lovingly, play after play, for the long haul.

Of the many things I love about the late August Wilson's work, I value most how clearly he saw what *is*—the damage our ever-present history does and has done. I value how—while remembering holocaust and horror—he never lost sight of strength, joy, and resilience, what he called "the highest possibility of human life." And I deeply value how every soul and every image lives in the complex web of that humanity—body, mind, heart, and spirit.

And while I can only marvel along with everyone else about the sweep and magnitude of his epic project, I also relish the details—the carvings in the piano—all his beautiful specificities. I think, for instance, about the things August's characters carry, the objects they hold. Levee's horn, Troy's baseball bat, King Hedley's seeds and his determination to grow them in rocky soil, Floyd's guitar, Solly's walking stick with a notch for every slave he conducted to safety. And with these life-giving objects, they hold others—the machete, the gun, the knife, and all the money that changes hands—the necessary and talismanic cash.

For each thing they carry, we glimpse a truth they hold to be self-evident—their right to freedom; their connection to ancestry, its sufferings and its gods; their determination to survive; their possession of a moral law that runs deeper and truer than man's laws.

There is never a good time to lose an artist-leader like August; certainly there is never a good time to lose one so young (he was just sixty). He saw the premiere of *Radio Golf*, the final play of his Century Cycle, at Yale in April of 2005 and died that October. It was a tough and disturbing historical moment, nationally and on the world stage, a time to rage at the violence of power. The cowboys were in charge and they were running roughshod over the sacred lands, including our own.

As Nobel laureate Joseph Brodsky has written, "Cowboys loathe mirrors." It inconveniences them to hear the cry of "the world's future, and to recognize it...as a chasm suddenly gaping in the human heart, to swallow up honesty, compassion, civility, justice..."

In those dark days (maybe the days are always dark) we especially needed artists like Wilson, with his profound ability to be mirror, to hear the cry, and to keep his heart open and your spirit engaged. (Maybe we always especially need artists like him, need mirror, need to hear the cry with open heart and engaged spirit. Now we need him, now and tomorrow and tomorrow.)

I'll never forget the scene in August's penultimate play, *The Gem of the Ocean*, in which the young Citizen Barlow is handed a paper boat, called the Gem of the Ocean. The boat he holds carries him, mythically and magically out to sea, to a city at the bottom of the sea—the City of Bones. It is a beautiful, gleaming city, built from the bones of the dead, the slaves who died in middle passage. This is the way August carries us, magically and mythically, showing us beauty from bone, life from devastation, humanity from the greatest evil. His mysteries are our maps, our way back and our journey forward. We need them and we need him.

I can feel the space where he stood. I can feel the missing connections that we, as a field, forged to make the great network that sustained him through that grand achievement. That achievement is complete, but it's also left an ache for what comes after. I miss his next play, and his next.

This text is adapted from a speech to New Dramatists' Spring Luncheon, 2004, later published in *howlround*.

Meryl Streep

What comes to mind when you hear the name "Meryl Streep?" Which Meryl Streep do you see? Reviewing her work in the past weeks has been like revisiting the education of my own heart. Scenes I didn't know I remembered were, in fact, engraved in my memory: moments, gestures, phrasings, the pass of information behind her eyes.

Here's my Meryl Streep. It's May, 1976. My teacher is taking our class to the Phoenix Theatre for a matinee double bill of Tennessee Williams' *27 Wagons Full of Cotton* and *A Memory of Two Mondays* by Arthur Miller. He's been kvelling about this actress he directed in Brecht's *Happy End* at Yale, and now we're going to meet her, this Vassar grad named Meryl Streep.

In the Williams one act, she plays "Baby Doll," a dopey, giggling girl in a voluptuous woman's body, too lazy to string together a thought, hanging out in the heat like something that needs to be petted. In Miller's elegiac memory play, set in the sales room of an auto parts dealer, she plays a smaller role, Patricia, a smart young secretary, prematurely worldly, the eternal other woman at 23. By the window stands a sleek brunette where, minutes before, a zaftig blonde lolled on a porch swing.

How lucky was I? It was the first time I'd seen actors play in rep and there I was, in the presence of this fabulous chameleon. Everything we celebrate her for today was apparent in those turns: her empathic imagination, her behavioral insight, her inner clown, and the sheer theatrical joy she conveys in the act of acting.

Artists may be born with greatness inside them, but, in the theatre at least, they need each other to grow into that greatness. From Baby Doll then to Mother Pitt, Ethel Rosenberg, and Rabbi Chemelwitz in *Angels in America*, Meryl Streep's dazzling—and still-young—career is a lesson in creative community: the devotion of friends and colleagues from Robert Brustein's Yale—all those uncommon women; the championship of the inimitable, indomitable Joe Papp and the Public Theatre; her ongoing pas de deux with the brilliant Mike Nichols; the unbroken circle of repeat performers and writers, who form her extended repertory family. Time has proven what seemed apparent early on: as luminous as she is, as lit up from inside, she's an ensemble player in her bones.

This is the Meryl Streep I carry, the artist of promise, the actress at the outset, reveling in the company of others.

"No one can ever have made a seriously artistic attempt," Henry James writes, "without becoming conscious of an immense increase—a kind of revelation—of freedom." I love this phrase, "a kind of revelation of freedom," and the challenge it poses—of possibility, awareness, change.

Watch the end of *The Hours*—the movie made from Michael Cunningham's tour de force novel. Meryl Streep plays Clarissa Vaughn, known as Mrs. Dalloway to her best friend Richard, a poet dying an anguishing, isolated death from AIDS. Abandoned in early childhood by his mother, Richard is the truest love of Clarissa's life, her troubled heart. When he jumps to his death on the eve of a literary tribute in his honor, Clarissa is the one abandoned, left to make sense of his life and his place in hers.

Late that night Richard's mother arrives at Clarissa's and, sitting at a large round table, still set for a party that never happened, tells her story. She confesses, really, why she abandoned her children, admits to the cruelty of the act, describes it painfully but simply—without defensiveness—as a choice between her own death—her own suicide—and life.

But her story is not the scene. The scene takes place in Clarissa's eyes—Meryl Streep's eyes. They're a study in contradiction. You sense the struggle to remain courteous, but you can't miss the hard fury, the shaming judgment. This frail, sweet old librarian is the "monster" of Richard's life. But something in the woman's honesty undoes Clarissa. A wall cracks, and curiosity flashes through. Then something stronger than curiosity: a kind of hunger. Clarissa doesn't say a word; Meryl Streep doesn't say a word. She listens ravenously. She's staring a new point of view in the face. Confusion enters in, and I swear I see terror. The narrative she's held so dear is under siege. New truth, new complexity, new awareness wins the day. And change plays through her like electricity passing through the intricate grid of a hidden city.

This moment—this radical act of empathy—is my idea of the artist's freedom, the courage to face down truth, the leap of compassion, a moment admitting change.

At a crossroads in his life, Vaclav Havel confronted what he calls "the challenge of example," which for him meant a world with no emergency exits, no moral off-ramps. At our current crossroads, too, artistic daring is, increasingly, tied to acts of political courage.

Yes, she's simply an actress, but we live with the challenge of her example. May the world share her capacity for transformation and grace; may it proceed, as she does, by means of compassion for and identification with others. May the power of individuals exist in harmony with the spirit of company, ensemble, community. And, from this point forward, may America produce many more images of beauty, play, mystery, and art, and may the world know us by these.

This text is adapted from a speech to New Dramatists' Spring Luncheon, 2004.

Acknowledgements

My list of thank yous is 25 years long. It would never fit in these pages. Some of these thanks, however, can't go without saying.

Most important, my dear friend and longtime editor Jim O'Quinn at *American Theatre* magazine gave me the space and encouragement to discover my voice and what to do with it. Without him none of this would have been written.

I am indebted to many other readers and editors, especially to the late Ross Wetzsteon, Robert Brustein, Lindy Zesch, Emily Morse, Joel Ruark, Juanita Brunk, and Mindy Levine. Had Doris Grumbach not read a review of mine out loud in a class called "The Art of Literary Journalism" at American University in 1983, despite disagreeing with everything I wrote in it, and had a guy whose name I can't remember not hired me to write book and, later, theatre reviews for the now-defunct *Washington Tribune* as a result, it never would have occurred to me to attempt that very literary journalistic art. Thanks to both of them.

Caridad Svich said yes to publishing this collection faster than any writer has reason to hope for (literally between the time I sent a late-night query and when I woke the next morning). I'm amazed by and grateful for her devotion to getting theatre writing into the world.

To the subjects of the stories and profiles included here—thank you for the constant inspiration. And that goes for the writers of New Dramatists and theatre artists everywhere.

In recent months, I had lots of help with this manuscript, notably from my friend, the amazing Liz Duffy Adams, who had my back, as well as from a batallion of assistants I conscripted, led by Julia Anrather. These involuntary volunteers included John Budge, Margot Connolly, Jahna Ferron-Smith, Jenny Morris, Patrick Robinson, Jen Schiller, Courtney Ulrich, and Hannah Yukon. I couldn't have finished the job and dealt with the effects of 25 years of technological change without them.

This long project has mostly been a labor of love, and I feel lucky to have stumbled into it. I feel luckier still to have been a loved laborer, and, so, I'm forever grateful to the home team: Karen, Guthrie, and Grisha.

About the Author

Todd London has served, since 1996, as artistic director of New Dramatists, the nation's longest-lived laboratory for playwrights. In 2009 Todd became the first recipient of Theatre Communications Group's (TCG) Visionary Leadership Award for "an individual who has gone above and beyond the call of duty to advance the theatre field as a whole, nationally and/or internationally." He's the author of *Outrageous Fortune: The Life and Times of the New American Play* (with Ben Pesner), *The Artistic Home*, and *The World's Room*, a novel, among others. Todd's next book, *An Ideal Theatre*, an anthology of founding visions for American theatres, will be published by Theatre Communications Group in 2013. "A Lover's Guide to American Playwrights," his tributes to contemporary playwrights, appears on howlround.com. He has won the prestigious George Jean Nathan Award for Dramatic Criticism for his essays in *American Theatre* and a Milestone Award for his novel. Under his leadership, New Dramatists received a special Tony® Honor and the Obie's Ross Wetzsteon Award. Todd currently serves on the faculty of Yale School of Drama. He has two sons, Guthrie and Grisha, and is married to playwright Karen Hartman.

NoPassport

No Passport is a Pan-American theatre alliance & press devoted to live, virtual and print action, advocacy, and change toward the fostering of cross-cultural diversity in the arts with an emphasis on the embrace of the hemispheric spirit in US Latina/o and Latin-American theatremaking.

NoPassport Press' Theatre & Performance PlayTexts Series and its Dreaming the Americas Series promotes new writing for the stage, texts on theory and practice, and theatrical translations.

Series Editors: Randy Gener, Jorge Huerta, Mead K. Hunter, Otis Ramsey-Zoe, Caridad Svich (founding editor).

Advisory Board: Daniel Banks, Amparo Garcia-Crow, Maria M. Delgado, Randy Gener, Elana Greenfield, Christina Marin, Antonio Ocampo-Guzman, Sarah Cameron Sunde, Saviana Stanescu, Tamara Underiner, Patricia Ybarra.

Website: www.nopassport.org

NoPassport is a sponsored project of Fractured Atlas. For online donations go to www.fracturedatlas.org/donate/2623

More Titles from NoPassport Press include:

Antigone Project: A Play in Five Parts by Tanya Barfield, Karen Hartman, Chiori Miyagawa, Lynn Nottage and Caridad Svich, with Preface by Lisa Schlesinger, Introduction by Marianne McDonald. **ISBN 978-0-578-03150-7**

Migdalia Cruz: El Grito del Bronx & other plays *(Salt, Yellow Eyes, El Grito del Bronx, Da Bronx rocks: a song)* Introduction by Alberto Sandoval-Sanchez, afterword by Priscilla Page. **ISBN: 978-0-578-04992-2**

Envisioning the Americas: Latina/o Theatre & Performance A NoPassport Press Sampler with works by Migdalia Cruz, John Jesurun, Oliver Mayer, Alejandro Morales and Anne Garcia-Romero, Preface by Jose Rivera. Introduction by Caridad Svich. **ISBN: 978-0-578-08274-5**

Rinde Eckert: Orpheus X and Other Plays. Introduction by Jonathan Chambers. **ISBN: 978-1-300-44158-8.**

Catherine Filloux: Dog and Wolf & Killing the Boss Introduction by Cynthia E. Cohen. **ISBN: 978-0-578-07898-4**

David Greenspan: Four Plays and a Monologue (Jack, 2 Samuel Etc, Old Comedy, Only Beauty, A Playwright's Monologue) Preface by Helen Shaw, Introduction by Taylor Mac, **ISBN: 978-0-578-08448-0**

Karen Hartman: Girl Under Grain Introduction by Jean Randich. **ISBN: 978-0-578-04981-6**

Kara Hartzler: No Roosters in the Desert Based on field work by Anna Ochoa O'Leary **ISBN: 978-0-578-07047-6**

John Jesurun: Deep Sleep, White Water, Black Maria – A Media Trilogy Preface by Fiona Templeton. **ISBN: 978-0-578-02602-2**

Carson Kreitzer: SELF DEFENSE and other Plays *(Self Defense, The Love Song of J Robert Oppenheimer, 1:23, Slither)* Preface by Mark Wing-Davey, Introduction by Mead K. Hunter. **ISBN: 978-0-578-08058-1.**

Lorca: Six Major Plays: *(Blood Wedding, Dona Rosita, The House of Bernarda Alba, The Public, The Shoemaker's Prodigious Wife, Yerma)* In new translations by Caridad Svich, Preface by James Leverett, Introduction by Amy Rogoway. **ISBN: 978-0-578-00221-7**

Matthew Maguire: Three Plays: *(The Tower, Luscious Music, The Desert)* with Preface by Naomi Wallace. **ISBN: 978-0-578-00856-1**

Octavio Solis: The River Plays *(El Otro, Dreamlandia, Bethlehem)* Introduction by Douglas Langworthy. **ISBN: 978-0-578-04881-9**

Saviana Stanescu: The New York Plays *(Waxing West, Lenin's Shoe, Aliens with Extraordinary Skills)* Introduction by John Clinton Eisner. **ISBN: 978-0-578-04942-7**

ALL TITLES AVAILABLE on AMAZON.COM, LULU.COM, Drama Book Shop and more.

Made in the USA
Lexington, KY
27 April 2015